The GIrL
and the
Demon

PAULINE GRUBER

DRAGONFLY INK, LTD.

The Girl and the Demon
Copyright © 2020 by Pauline Gruber

Dragonfly Ink, Ltd.
P.O. Box 2042
Palatine, IL 60078

The characters and events portrayed in this book are fictitious. Any similarity to real persons, living or dead, is coincidental and not intended by the author.

ISBN: 978-0-9910774-4-1

Cover Art by Fay Lane Graphic Design and Illustration
Formatting by Author E.M.S.
Author Photo by Sopho Studio

Published in the United States of America

In loving memory of

Katherine ("Katie") Woods,

the inspiration for the character Katie Stevens,
the greatest BFF any girl could ask for.

The world lost one of its most beloved
when your light flickered out.

OTHER BOOKS BY PAULINE GRUBER

The Girl and the Raven

The Girl and the Gargoyle

CHAPTER ONE

– Lucy Walker –

I stop abruptly once inside St. Aquinas High School's cafeteria. It's so different. The makeover had nothing to do with fireballs or gargoyles. The huge space had been repainted over the summer. One wall features a large mural depicting teenagers of every race. Missing from the group are gargoyles, demons, and witches. Another wall features a massive Wildcat, the school mascot, with daggerlike teeth and razor-sharp claws. So much like Marcus's father, Garret, after he morphed that night he tried to kill me.

"Hi junior," Katie Stevens teases as she grabs my arm. Her smile immediately fades. "Hey, what's wrong? You look like you're going to puke."

I swallow the lump of fear in my throat. *Garret is dead. He can't hurt me now.*

"First day jitters." I suppress a shiver and pull my best friend into a tight hug.

Katie's tan skin glows against the white button-down shirt of her uniform after two months in Fort Myers, Florida. Her white-

1

blond hair looks nearly radioactive from days of sunning on the beach.

In a student body of approximately one thousand four hundred students, we arrive for the second of four lunch periods. Throngs of students shove past us, their conversations so loud that I have to yell for Katie to hear me.

"I don't care that we texted and talked all the time, I missed you like crazy," I say, squeezing closer to her to avoid sharp elbows and pushing bodies.

"I missed *you* like crazy," Katie says. "There's no way I'm going to let my dad keep me until the day before school starts next summer."

I feign grumpiness. "I *told* you—"

"I know you did!" Katie exclaims, her deep ocean blue eyes wide. "But—"

"You were too busy spending those couple of weeks after school ended—"

"With Trevor," Katie says with a grin.

"With Trevor," I say at the exact same moment.

My best friend's expression turns serious. "Things seemed pretty intense between you and Marcus. I really didn't think you noticed."

That's an understatement for what happened when Marcus's father showed up in Chicago. Violent chaos is a more accurate description of what went down in St. Aquinas's gymnasium before sophomore year ended. I killed Marcus's father after he tried to kill me, my father, and Marcus. His thugs tried to take out Dylan. When school ended, Marcus, Dylan, and I were still

2

reeling from it all. But Katie is not part of that world. She has no powers. I can't ever tell her monsters are real. For her own safety I need to keep her as far away from my supernatural life as possible.

"Drama with Marcus's family," I say with a heavy sigh. "Were your dad and stepmom sad when you left?"

"For the first time...yes." Katie laughs. "If I knew getting a part-time job during my stay would make them miss me so much, I would've done it last year. They were actually teary-eyed at the airport. That hasn't happened since I was twelve."

"Katie Stevens, an official member of the workforce? It's about time, slacker," Suzy Rodriguez announces, squeezing out of a horde of students entering the lunchroom. "Thanks for waiting for me." She raises her face and takes an exaggerated sniff at the air. "Sweet, tangy barbeque...I bet they're serving pulled pork sandwiches. One of my favorites. Cloe's too."

Katie and I both hug Suzy.

"Not all of us are lucky enough to have a family that owns a chain of super popular resale clothing stores. Talk about guaranteed employment," Katie playfully complains, tugging on Suzy's long dark brown hair.

Suzy's mom and two of her aunts opened their first store ten years ago and the family is in the process of opening a third location before Christmas. Suzy has promised to put in a good word if one of us wants a job, but I love the kids I nanny too much to leave them.

"Between the stores, creating my art, and running my music blog, I've been working for years," Suzy says with an air of authority. "I'm a pro with art and business. You, on the other hand, are an amateur."

Katie laughs. "I'll have a job for the rest of my life. So what if I wanted one more year of freedom?"

"We're seventeen," Suzy says to Katie and me with a glimmer in her eyes, "and upperclassman." She surveys the lunchroom. Tables are filling up fast as more students bustle around us. Lunch trays clatter onto tables. The buzz of conversation is nearly deafening. "Have you seen anyone else yet?"

"No. We just got here," I tell her.

"Ella and Caroline are there, in the upperclassman section. You can't miss Ella's hair. It's like a burst of flames in the sea of people," Suzy says.

I follow the point of her finger, but don't see them through the crowd. Honestly, I don't try too hard. While I have adjusted to the massive size of St. Aquinas College Prep and the overabundance of homework, my stomach hurts at the notion of having to see Ella every day. "Should we place bets on how long it will take before Ella makes fun of my accent?" I ask bitterly.

Since I moved from Lexington, Tennessee to Chicago and joined Katie's circle of friends the summer before our sophomore year, Ella has taken cruel pleasure in trying to tear me down and make sure I understand the hierarchy of our group. According to her, I sit at the lowest rung.

Katie grimaces. "She's just jealous. Look on the bright side. It's a new year and she had a fun summer. I bet she will be nicer to you."

"You're far cooler than she is. Have you seen her music

4

collection?" Suzy asks, mimicking a gag. She squints across the room. "Cloe's there now, too."

Katie nudges me. "Let's go get food. I'm starving."

One of the reasons Katie and I hit it off so well is our mutual love of food. We're both always hungry. Her mom jokes that we each have a tapeworm.

"When are you going to come over so we can make lasagna and enchiladas for my mom and Jerry?" Katie says as we join the line with lunch trays in hand. "It was your idea to start cooking for them. Now they keep asking."

I am determined to learn how to cook two of the dishes my father used to make for me. Once he returns home, I plan to surprise him by cooking for him.

"Weekday evenings. We can knock out homework first. Or maybe Saturday nights after I get home from nannying for Mr. and Mrs. Douglas."

"Why not Sundays?" Katie asks. "I thought that would be the best day since you're off of work."

Katie has no idea about my witch lessons and demon training.

"My dad hasn't come home yet. I'm still checking on his place on Sundays." My voice falters on that last part. I know what's coming next.

"When are you going to invite me to go with you? I've always wanted to see your dad's mansion," Katie asks as she hands her student ID card to the woman at the register to scan and pay for her lunch.

Sure, come over. Don't mind the demon that may or may not be hanging around, eager to kill me. Pass.

"My dad has strict rules about no friends at his house," I tell her.

"Does that rule apply to Marcus, too?" Katie asks with mock innocence.

The truth is that both Marcus and Dylan Douglas join me at Jude's. Dylan for our joint demon training. Marcus for company and protection while I check to see if Jude has returned or if Seamus McAllister, the aforementioned demon who wants to kill me, is lurking.

At the upperclassman table, I sit beside Katie and as far away from Ella as I can get. I'd rather deal with Katie's sulk over the no invite to my dad's house than Ella.

"It's time to schedule our first social event of the year. Who's up for a séance?" Ella asks, less a question and more of a command to us, her less significant underlings. Leave it to Ella to come up with something dangerous on our first day of school.

Caroline Appleberg grins, revealing her perfect, toothpaste commercial worthy teeth. "The night of your slumber party? Sounds spooky and fun!"

"Maybe we can call on Jim Morrison or Kurt Cobain," Ella says to Suzy. She winks one reptilian blue-green eye.

"Cool!" Suzy and Katie say in unison.

"How about modern-day rock stars?" Caroline mocks playfully, smoothing her silky blond hair with her hand.

Cloe Gardner fixes her deep brown eyes on Ella, her fingers still typing away on whatever game she plays on her phone. "My grandmother says messing with spirits is not a good idea. Something about bad juju."

"Old people have no sense of adventure," Ella scoffs. "I've been reading up on it. I know exactly what to do."

Since when did Miss Makeover become a séance expert? More likely she will manage just enough to cause trouble. Losing my father to a summoned demon last year makes me wonder what kind of unfriendly spirits Ella could accidentally conjure up.

I realize too late that I groaned aloud.

Ella narrows her eyes at me. "Wait...Are you *afraid*, Lucy?"

Such a witch!

I meet her gaze head on. "Nope. Cloe's grandmother happens to be right. It's a bad idea."

Katie's gaze moves from Ella to me, her brows scrunched nervously.

Ella grins, narrows her eyes at me. "So, don't come. The rest of us are going to have a great time."

"It's reckless, Ella. Have a sleepover. Watch movies. Have a dance party or group pedicures. Crank call the football team. But skip the séance. *Please*," I say.

Ella arches a sharp eyebrow at me. "I did a lot to prepare for this. My plans are set. When did you turn into a nervous old woman?"

She and Caroline chuckle.

"Her hillbilly accent is as annoying as ever," Ella whispers to Caroline, not trying all that hard to keep her voice down.

At least Caroline doesn't laugh this time.

"Give it a rest, Ella," Katie snaps.

Caroline claps her hands together, grinning like an over-energized cheerleader. "How was everyone's summer? Come on, we've barely seen each other since sophomore year let out. It's time to catch up."

"I spent most of the summer at the beach," Ella says, an edge to her voice. Is she feeling stung that Katie stood up to her for one of the first times ever?

Everyone else takes turns sharing the highlights of their break. Caroline is sort of dating Dylan's football teammate, Chad. Cloe worked as a counselor at a science camp for kids and is still dating Darick. Suzy juggled her job, her art, her music blog, and time with her boyfriend, Shawn. Katie shared the highlights of her summer in Fort Myers.

"What about you, Lucy?" Cloe asks, pulling her eyes from the screen of her phone.

"Worked, mostly, and hung out with Marcus," I say, focusing on my lunch, *and coping with the emotional fallout of murdering his father.*

CHAPTER TWO

– Lucy Walker –

As the final bell rings on my first day of school, I zigzag my way through the halls, rushing as much as I am able to through the packed crowd. My breath catches at the sight of him. Marcus stands a head taller than most of the students at St. Aquinas, not that he attends my school. Marcus is a senior at St. Patrick's, an all-male college preparatory Catholic high school. He has already changed into blue jeans, a white T-shirt, and a gray and green button-down shirt, which is untucked. His messy chestnut-colored hair begs for my fingers to sink into its thick mass. Our eyes lock and my pulse quickens in response. The smile that spreads across my face is immediate. My day just got a whole lot better.

"Hey," he says as I reach my locker. It would be impossible for anyone without proper school identification to get through St. Aquinas's security, but friendship and favors gained Marcus a permanent guest pass. Marcus pulls me to him and our lips meet. We've both gotten over our aversion to PDA.

As Marcus's fingers wind through my long, black hair and his calming protector touch soothes me, I no longer care about Ella's crazy slumber party plans or facing another year of her biting criticism.

"You're the best," I say, breathless, as I pull away.

"Ready for our date?"

A date. It sounds romantic. Touring my father's house to see if he's made it home is the exact opposite. We keep looking for Jude, but his car remains untouched in the garage, his computer sits in the exact spot on the desk in his office, and his refrigerator—which Marcus and I cleaned after the last of the food rotted—is only stocked with cans of soda, juice, and some snacks that Marcus and I brought over. Sure, Lucifer helped us with the battle in the school's gymnasium against the gargoyles, but afterward he took my father. Originally, I wanted Lucifer to take Jude, but with Garret out of the picture there was no need for my father to be taken to the underworld for his protection and mine. When will Lucifer release Jude so he can come home? Will the ruler of hell use this as a way to control me?

"Any chance you'll let me drive today?" I ask Marcus as we exit the school building. I don't know why I bothered to get my license. Arnold, the long-time driver for the Douglas family, still picks me up and drops me off from my nanny job caring for Dylan's younger brother and sister. It's apparently for liability purposes. That doesn't bother me since I'm not a huge fan of driving in the city. What does bother me is that I have finally grown to love my car and my boyfriend refuses to sit in it.

Marcus slings my backpack over his shoulder, squinting into the sunlight. "It's as if Jude possesses it. Sorry, but I'm miserable every time I climb into that thing."

10

Protectors and demons have been enemies since the beginning of time. Whenever Jude was near, it would trigger Marcus to release his wings. The problem was that most of the time Marcus wasn't in any place private and had to fight to suppress the change. It's painful for him to endure.

I take his hand in mine. "Maybe it's psychosomatic."

Marcus twists his mouth thoughtfully. "You think so?"

I give him a wide-eyed look that screams *Duh!* Since the day my demon father gave me the Lexus as a belated sixteenth birthday gift, Marcus has been a giant grump about it. He doesn't understand that if I had refused a gift from Jude, someone in my life would have paid the price. That's how Daddy Demon works.

"You don't have to come with me," I say, hesitantly. "I can move his car and water his plants without you."

"Don't even think about canceling our date," he says. "Besides, it's too risky for you to go alone."

I spot his black Toyota Camry near the end of the aisle, but he steers me toward the side lot where I'm parked.

"Let's take your car," he suggests. "I want to test your theory."

"Seriously?" I ask, shocked. "Who are you and what have you done with my boyfriend?"

Marcus slides inside my dark blue ES 350 with a deep breath and clicks in his seatbelt. "Let's do this," he says with a nod and a shudder.

As we maneuver out of the lot, static blasts from my stereo speakers. I pound the dashboard twice as Marcus switches through all of my radio station presets. The static persists.

"Must be a loose wire or something," he says through gritted teeth as he switches from the radio to a CD. "I'll take a look at it when we're at Jude's."

"Thanks." I steal a glance at him. The reason for our get-together this afternoon is twofold. In addition to checking on Jude's house, he is going to give me an update on his mother. "Any word from Selima?"

Marcus nods stiffly. It's hard to tell if his grim expression is due to the subject of his mother, the suddenly sucky stereo, or being in my car. Maybe all three.

"The council is taking a hard position with my mother." He rakes his fingers through his hair. "They believe she and Garret were equally responsible. They want somebody's head. Since Garret's dead, they are going after her."

A few months ago Marcus's mother, Camille Bergmann, showed up in Chicago—and in his life—for the first time since he was four years old, bringing along the biological father Marcus never knew, Garret Bergmann. Garret was the leader of the protector clan and on a mission to destroy the powerful demon they believed was killing their kind. That powerful demon was, yep, my father. Let's just say I bet you will never have a more awkward first meeting with your boyfriend's parents.

"But your father was under orders, wasn't he? Or at least he wasn't working alone." I shake my head in disgust. "I hated Garret—given that he was trying to kill you and me and my father—"

"Don't forget Dylan," Marcus adds dryly.

"And Dylan—but how convenient that suddenly everyone is surprised and appalled that Garret was creating a team of psycho soldiers. This was several years in the making. Isn't that what Selima and her mother believe?"

"Exactly. While Camille isn't innocent, she shouldn't be the only one held responsible," Marcus says darkly. "There were others involved. Others who are high up in the clan."

Marcus's defense of his mother is passionate. I struggle to sound invested on her behalf. Since Camille's arrival in Chicago, I never got a warm and fuzzy vibe from her. In fact, she struck me as cold and calculating. What kind of woman abandons her young son?

"I would still like to know where they got all the demon blood to dope the protectors," I say once I merge onto highway I-90. I force all judgment and condemnation out of my voice and strive for curiosity. I don't want my boyfriend mad at me for picking on his mother.

Marcus doesn't answer right away. I risk a quick glance at him and find him busy working through something mentally, his brows pulled low as he quirks his lips back and forth. "Me too. Aiden talked to Max, asked him to look into it," Marcus finally says.

Aiden is not a fan of Max which is weird because I think they used to be friends. I don't know what the beef is between Marcus's brother and the red-haired demon. While Max has always struck me as sneaky, he proved helpful both times I needed him. However, my gut tells me there is more on Marcus's mind than demon blood and Max.

"How long will the clan council hold your mother in custody?" I ask, eager to keep him talking. "Selima said it's only house arrest during the investigation, right?"

"Until they finish their *due diligence*," Marcus mocks, his voice sullen. "They haven't disclosed a timeline."

While we sit idle in traffic before exiting onto I-94, I reach over to squeeze his hand. Camille will never win Mother of the Year, but neither would my own mother. Marcus just got Camille back. It's got to be tough on him to lose her again. What happens if she's found guilty? Is there such a thing as protector prison? Silence stretches between us. I glance at Marcus as he clenches and unclenches his jaw. His eyes fix on the passing landscape once we are moving again and I wonder if he registers anything he sees or if he's focused on thoughts about his mother. That's when I notice his free hand curled into a fist on his lap.

"Since we're testing a theory, tell me how you're doing in my car. Any demon vibe?" I ask, trying to lighten the mood.

Marcus continues to focus out the window. "It's okay."

I give it a couple more minutes. He continues to brood. "Is there something you're not telling me?"

At the same time the words leave my lips, a sick feeling settles like lead in my stomach. The feeling that started when Camille and Garret first showed up in Chicago, the one that told me they would convince Marcus to leave with them. After Garret's death and Camille had been ordered back to the protector clan—wherever that top-secret location happens to be—for interrogation, all the external drama from the battle faded away. Things settled down. That's when the internal drama—the gut-wrenching guilt—took over. I never thought I could kill a person. *It was him or us,* the voice in my head reminds me for the hundredth time.

For months I have been haunted by nightmares of the battle, confronted by the vision of Garret's face, watching the life leave his eyes. I can't sleep an entire night without feeling the throbbing pulse of his heart in my hand as I squeezed the life out of him with my magic. I swore I would never, ever execute that kind of magic again. While Garret's death sticks with me like a thick, dark cloud, my fear of Marcus leaving had been quieted.

That ended two weeks ago. Marcus's mother was placed on house arrest with twenty-four-hour security while the council initiated an investigation. Selima left Chicago to return to the clan to talk to her own mother and their friends. The grim look on Marcus's face clues me in that things are not going well.

He narrows his big brown eyes, scrunches his brows fiercely. "I have to go. Soon. The council is questioning everyone who has knowledge about the army, anyone who was at the battle. Those who survived." He mumbles that last part.

My breath sticks in my throat. I can't pull it in and I can't push it out. Marcus will go to Camille, to the protector clan. He has never been around other protectors—*gargoyles* as my father would say. Will he come back after being around his own kind? After he tastes what it's like to feel *normal*? What about Garret's death? Will that become part of the council's inquiry? Will Marcus be blamed for what I did? Could all of this be a ploy by Camille to take him from me? From everyone else who loves him? My lungs burn.

"Accelerate, Lucy!"

Cars honk behind me. A dark red SUV speeds around us, the driver flipping me the bird as he passes.

My lungs fill and the daze clears. I grasp the steering wheel firmly with both hands and press my foot on the gas pedal. My car responds immediately and lunges forward.

"I have knowledge about what happened," I say, an edge of panic in my voice. "Will the council want to speak with me? I should go with you."

Marcus shakes his head. He rests his hand on my thigh. Within seconds the panic diminishes. "So far questioning is limited to protectors. Selima is coming back to Chicago. She and I will go to the clan together once they call for me."

"You don't know when that will be?" I ask. The calm in my voice surprises me.

"Maybe two weeks. I'm really not sure. Selima will fill us in once she gets here," Marcus says. He studies my profile. "Camille needs me. I have to try to help her."

Once Camille has him, she won't want to let him go.

"I know," I say, determined to keep my eyes on the road. The panic is gone, but sadness takes its place. If I can focus hard enough, maybe the tears won't fall.

CHAPTER THREE

– Lucy Walker –

"We've been at this for two Sundays in a row. It doesn't work!"
I drop the shoelace-sized leather string and the crystal attached
to it on the stack of maps covering Persephone's kitchen table.
The gemstone lands with a heavy thud as I scrape my chair
back. With the heels of my hands, I rub my dry, tired eyes.
Persephone's head turns in my direction, her black, wiry curls
bouncing with the movement. She and Gram, together with
Henry Klein, were best friends. They also happened to be witches.
While the gene skipped Momma, I was the lucky one who
inherited Gram's magic.

The tiny yellow and orange wildflowers that decorate the
wallpaper past Persephone's shoulder grow fuzzy in my vision.

*"You're destined to be a great witch, Lucy. Your grandmother
was powerful, more than Henry, more than me. Once you
inherit her powers, we will teach you how to use them."*

I still don't believe Persephone. The demon powers I inherited
from my father continue to develop. My witchy powers, despite
everyone's efforts, have not.

"Be patient, Lucy," Persephone says from across the table where she and Henry study the *Book of Shadows*. "Scrying is the most difficult divination skill to master." She eyes the golf ball-sized crystal, her forehead creased. "You need to relax, open your mind. Some visions are the tiniest of glimpses. Pay close attention."

I shake my head at the same time I pull my hair over my shoulder and twist it roughly around my fingers. A gentle late afternoon breeze moves across my skin, thanks to the open window above the sink. "According to Aiden, we can't locate my father through scrying if he's in another dimension."

Henry uses his finger to mark his spot in the spell book as he peers at me through his wire-rimmed glasses. The deep sea-foam green of his Polo shirt highlights the green of his eyes. "We can't be sure Lucifer took him...home."

I roll my eyes. "Home for demons is hell, Henry, which is absolutely another dimension."

Henry gives me a wink and nods at the crystal, encouraging me to get back to work. "Which herbs did you use to supplement your divination powers?"

"Broom and cherry," I say.

Persephone stiffens, her expression alarmed. "Good grief and goddesses almighty. You didn't make tea with the leaves of the broom plant, did you? It's poisonous."

I shake my head. Standing, I pull a small fabric bag with fancy drawstrings from my pocket and present it to them. "I made a sachet. Dried broom leaves plus cherry pits. Nothing ingested." I stuff the bag back into my pocket and sit down.

"Excellent choices. Those dried leaves are also great for protection," Henry commends.

Persephone utters a sigh of relief and sips her tea.

"Since you mention protection and the only being I currently need protection from is Seamus McAllister, could you provide clarification about demons and immortality," I say as I palm the crystal, absently wondering once again if I will pick up energy from the magical object.

Persephone and Henry both nod, urging me to continue.

"Jude—and demons generally—are immortal. That part I get. But how does one die, get destroyed...or whatever? If I'm going to try to slay Seamus, I need to know. I mean, I get it that my fireballs can disable him, but I want to know how to get rid of him...permanently."

"You never told her?" Henry asks Persephone, surprised. He turns back to me quickly. "Not that you should ever confront him on your own."

I nod. "Of course."

Persephone's mouth puckers in consternation. "I had assumed Jude and Aiden covered that. She would use her demon powers to destroy him, since they are currently more powerful—and more in line with what's needed to get the job done."

Henry pushes his glasses up his nose and eyeballs me gravely. "Beheading and fire."

I wince. *Beheading?* Almost immediately I register the second thing Henry said. *Fire.* The very thing some demons are gifted with—the ability to create and throw fire—can destroy them? Suddenly I recall the night of the homecoming dance when Jude killed Seamus's daughter, Daphne, in a blaze. My shock turns to revulsion as I remember the smell.

"When Jude killed Daphne, he didn't decapitate her," I point out.

Henry frowns as he considers this. "He would've had to separate her ashes, then buried them in different locations."

"No way around that rule," Persephone confirms.

I nod stupidly, unable to shake the memory of Daphne's screams—no matter how brief—and that horrible smell.

I will the nausea down. "Decapitation and fire...why separate the ashes?"

"Because skipping that last step makes the first two pointless," Persephone admonishes me. She huffs mightily as she pushes herself out of her chair. She winces.

"Persephone." I jump out of my chair to help her.

Henry reaches for her at the same time.

Persephone waves us both away. Once standing, she takes several breaths. Her face is red from the effort. "My hip. It's determined to make my life hell on earth." She moves to the stove to fix another cup of tea. "If a demon is burned to ash, he or she can regenerate. It's only if the ashes are separated and kept apart that a demon is truly destroyed," she says on her way back to the table.

What was Garret's plan the night of the battle at St. Aquinas? Was he and his ginormous team going to decapitate the demons that night? Did he have a flame thrower waiting outside the gymnasium with the rest of his morphed soldiers?

"This is the only way to end Seamus. If you and whomever else is helping you don't dispose of his ashes properly, he will come back," Henry says, eyeing me so intently it's like he's trying to burn this information into my brain through my eyeballs.

When Seamus McAllister returns to Chicago—and we all know it's only a matter of time—will I have the opportunity and the skill to destroy him before he kills me? Could I finally have a chance to live my life without someone trying to slaughter me?

Persephone clears her throat. "Time to get back to your lesson." She points to the decorative bowl three-quarters full with rainwater sitting on the counter. "Maybe water scrying is more for you. Put the crystal aside and give it a try. Did you read the book I gave you last week?"

I nod halfheartedly. "There's no point," I mutter to myself as I slump onto the chair and pick up the leather strap. Jude's in hell with Lucifer, against his will. Now that Garret is dead and no longer trying to kill my father, I should be honing some other magical skills to help get Jude back instead of wasting my time with magical GPS. If Jude and I took on Seamus together, we could win. After we separated Seamus's ashes, my father would know the best places to hide them.

During my training session with Aiden earlier today, I once again asked for his help to bring my father home. Of course, he said my suggestion to summon Lucifer was pointless. The door between our worlds never closed after I brought him to Chicago to help save my father and me from Garret and his army. He can go between dimensions any time he wants to.

"He's been aboveground having a grand time while Jude's stuck managing things in the underworld in his absence," Aiden had said.

"Lucifer's here?" I had asked, a squeak in my voice as my heartbeat thudded in terror.

Aiden shook his head, impatiently tossing one of several massive haystacks he had set up around Jude's backyard in order to train me to hurl them using spells and hand gestures. "Not *here* in Chicago, but aboveground, so to speak. It's been a long time since he's been away from his own dimension. No doubt he's traveling the world, living it up like a king. But..."

I had raised my eyebrows at Aiden's tight expression. "But?"

"You're his namesake..."

His words left me unsettled. "I know...I know...a much bigger deal than being a goddaughter."

Aiden's glare was immediate. "Lucifer will be back for you."

Every muscle in my body clenched. His words struck me as a threat. Or a warning. Maybe both. "That's what you keep saying."

"He's not going to tolerate your snotty attitude or your defiance. Jude's a pussycat in comparison."

While Jude is all demon-dad like—short tempered, violent, and absolutely clueless when it comes to parenting, *especially* a teenage girl—he had developed another side. He cooked delicious meals for me—*vegetarian* meals. He rented movies and took the time to watch them with me, sitting in his fancy rose-colored chair while I lounged on the adjacent emerald green couch. He wore a sort of bored or tolerant expression the whole time. When I studied his face, though, I noticed his eyes soaked in every little detail on the TV screen.

My father was also protective in a ruthless sort of way, training me so I could take care of myself against Seamus and

22

Garret and all the other enemies who hate Jude and, by extension, me. Jude is fatherly in a dad-on-steroids kind of way, but he does love me. It's all his good traits that help me to try to move past the bad parts.

My cell vibrates on the table next to the map, pulling me back to the present. My witch mentors glance at me, their gazes heavy with expectation. Marcus and I are supposed to meet up tonight and I still have to figure out what excuse to make to Henry and Persephone. I read my boyfriend's text message.

Any luck scrying?

No. I want 2 bail, but H and P might skin me alive.

I palm the crystal absently. What if Persephone and Henry have been wrong all along? Maybe I'm not destined to be a great witch like Gram. Even with Lola, the family raven and Gram's familiar, passing Gram's powers to me nothing much has happened. The witch powers seem unresponsive. I don't know what to do. What if my great and powerful destiny leans more in the direction of my demon genes?

My phone buzzes again.

I prefer u w-skin intact. Working late at St. Pat's w-Father Bill. Let's meet 2morrow night instead. It's time 2 go flying.

My heart sinks. No Marcus tonight. I raise my gaze to meet Persephone's.

"You're not planning to cut your lesson short are you?" she asks, eyebrows raised.

"I'm not going anywhere," I tell her, feeling deflated.

"We heard about Marcus's plans to attempt to help his mother," Henry says. "How are you holding up?"

Just the mention of Marcus leaving causes a lump to form in my throat. Of course they know. Did Marcus tell them? Or had Aiden filled them in? "Okay." I turn away from their watchful eyes and move to the counter. The delicate cream-colored lace curtains that decorate the window above the sink shift as another breeze blows through, providing relief from the late August heat. Persephone's apartment takes up the third floor of my uncles' three-flat apartment building. They inherited it from Gram after she died. My uncles and I have the largest apartment on the first floor while Marcus and Aiden live on the second floor.

As I pause at the counter I allow myself a moment away from the scrutiny of my witch mentors. Marcus appeared unaffected when he informed me that he would be leaving soon. How is it so easy for him to go? How could he postpone our night together? Suddenly we have so little time left.

That fear of Marcus leaving is nothing new. There is an expiration date on our relationship. The countdown started the day we met and never stopped. I hadn't been sure what would take him from me until the day his mother showed up in Chicago. The fact that she's with the protector clan, under investigation for her part in Marcus's father's crimes should've put me at ease. If she is found guilty and incarcerated, she will go to prison, right? Then she can't manipulate Marcus into leaving with her. Who knows what will happen with the investigation? Meanwhile, the timer keeps counting down. That blasted *tick-tock, tick-tock, tick-tock* echoes around my brain like a cruel joke, threatening to drive me crazy.

What happens when the timer runs out and Marcus leaves? Will the pain of missing him destroy me? I had watched Momma fall apart every time one of her relationships ended. Marcus is a million times better than any of the deadbeats Momma dated. Plus, I am nothing like her. The fact remains that Marcus is going to leave to try to help his mother and he will be around a whole bunch of other protectors for the first time in his life. Marcus will no longer be the freak he considers himself to be. How liberating that will be for him. Why would he want to come back to Chicago?

Darkness fills my mind as my gaze falls to the bowl of rainwater on the counter next to me. With a sigh I hold my hand over the bowl, absently moving my fingers as if to play the keys of a piano. A deep need takes over, a need for relief from the heaviness inside me. If I were in the massive backyard of Jude's Lake Forest house, I could hurl fireballs. That always releases the darkness, the heavy sadness. Inside Persephone's kitchen that isn't an option. Gently, words slip into my thoughts like a poem. The phrases appear in my mind, random at first. I repeat them quietly. The sounds are nothing more than whispered sorrow as they pass through my lips.

Bring on the rain
Allow it to wash away my pain
His leaving preordained
Loss of a loved one, again

Even my dreams know my time with my boyfriend is coming to an end. Two nights in a row I felt the crushing weight as we said goodbye on the roof, a black suitcase at his feet which was covered with decals featuring some of his favorite bands, while his hands cupped my face. His eyes burned as the words he has only ever uttered in my dreams passed through his lips: "if only you hadn't killed my father."

Bring on the rain
Allow it to wash away my pain
His leaving preordained
Loss of a loved one again

My fingers continue tap, tap, tapping the air above the beautiful pale blue glass bowl. All of a sudden drops of rain the size of tears drip from my fingers into the bowl. Startled, I nearly cease the movement of my fingers. I force myself to continue. As I repeat the words the rain continues to fall from my drumming-on-air fingers. A surge bolts through me. *I am performing a spell. This is witchcraft!*

A loud gasp to my left gives me a start. Persephone. Henry flanks my right side, his eyes wide.

How had I slipped so deeply into the spell that I didn't hear Persephone and Henry's chairs scrape as they pushed away from the table? The creaky old floorboards should have given them away as they approached the counter, especially Persephone with her bad hip that makes every other step land more heavily than Henry's.

"When did you learn to do this?" Persephone asks, her voice full of awe as she studies the water droplets.

As I slow the tinkling motion, Henry urges me to continue, fascination in his voice. I continue to make it rain in the bowl and hope neither of them notice the tears brimming in my eyes.

Persephone and Henry are like family to me. I love them both, but there's no way I can share my feelings with them. Even now as they witness my magic—magic caused by fear and heartache—it feels wrong to be in their company. I should be alone right now.

The oppressive weight of my emotions lingers, the sound: *tick-tock, tick-tock, tick-tock*, continues to repeat in my mind.

"Can you shift the spell like we talked about during our last session?" Persephone asks. Her voice is eager, encouraging.

I release the spell and the raindrops cease. With a flick of my wrist, I change the movement of my fingers to a twirl, slow at first and gradually picking up speed. I focus on swirling water.

If only you hadn't killed my father. Marcus's voice from my dream accuses.

A breeze hovers over the bowl, then dives into the water. The liquid laps and waves, animated with the power of the miniature wind, splashing onto the countertop. That's when it hits me. This absorption into the magic...into the spell work...is something I usually feel when performing dark magic. It's a new feeling when executing white magic. A glimmer of optimism and hope edges into my mood.

I move my hand in a gentle, slow rhythm, encouraging the water to sway, back and forth, back and forth. I find the motion of the rainwater hypnotic, soothing.

"Tell me your thought process, from start to finish," Henry urges.

His request causes me to mentally scramble. There is no way I am going to share my emotional turmoil over Marcus, or the never-ending guilt over murdering his father during the battle. Never mind that it was done in self-defense.

As much as possible I erase the emotion from my face, from my voice. I respond as Lucy the student, not the girl who will soon lose the one guy who has ever made her feel special and worthy of love.

"I focused on making it rain," I say.

Henry grabs his notebook from the table and logs my intention together with his own observations. Only after he and Persephone have experimented with a spell and perfected it will they put it in the *Book of Shadows*, the spell book they—and Gram—have kept since the beginning.

"Don't you see?" Henry whispers, his voice filled with excitement.

"See what?" I ask weakly, not sure if he was talking to Persephone or me, but suddenly feeling wrung out. The whole point of today's lesson was to locate Jude. "None of this is going to help bring my father back."

Henry's bright expression falls. Persephone touches my arm.

"I don't know when—or if—Jude will come back. Now Marcus is going to leave." So much for keeping my emotions to myself. There's no stopping the stupid tears. My willpower is gone. I swipe at my cheeks. I gesture to the rainwater, where I had magic-made tears. "I can't get excited about this. Not when it hurts so much."

"I'm sorry, Lucy," Persephone says. She doesn't try to hug me. That's not who she is and I'm grateful.

"Can I go home now?" I ask glumly.

Henry nods. He doesn't hide his disappointment.

Chapter Four

– Lucy Walker –

"Open your eyes," Marcus calls over his shoulder. "I can't be the only one to see this!"

It's Monday night and Marcus and I are at his favorite forest preserve just outside of Chicago. His voice—heck, his entire body—vibrates with excitement. That's how it is since Selima taught him to fly. Like enthusiasm mixed with jet fuel. It pretty much matches the level of terror I feel riding copilot. Before his sister helped him develop his skills, Marcus solely used his wings to descend from the roof at home and land safely and soundlessly onto the ground in the backyard. I'm guessing he did the same when he was at St. Pat's Church, but all of that's nothing compared to actual *flying*.

As I try to open my eyes, the wind against my face forces them closed again. My hair whips every which way, stinging my cheeks. My stomach tumbles in nauseating somersaults. "I can't!"

Marcus pumps his wings, the muscles in his naked back straining with the movement as he maneuvers to keep us airborne. I cry out as we drop several feet. The weightlessness causes my stomach and heart to collide inside of me. Marcus shifts to the left sharply and I tilt hard with the movement. Immediately, I realize I overcompensated. Marcus adjusts quickly and leans in the opposite direction, his wings pumping hard.

"Sorry!" I squeal.

I tighten my legs around his jean-clad waist to avoid falling off of him. By sheer instinct I nearly shift again, but I clutch his shoulders and fight the urge. My heart thunders in my chest. *Why did I let him talk me into this again? It's not getting any easier.*

Marcus reaches for my leg and squeezes. His brief touch does nothing to comfort me. I dig my fingers into his shoulders. He doesn't complain.

It's like riding your own personal pegasus, I tell myself as I force myself to breathe.

"C'mon. This is amazing. You have to see it!" Marcus calls out once we're steady again.

I peek out of one eye. It takes a moment for my vision to adjust to the darkness. So many trees we could collide with. A screech sounds to my right. An owl. The one part of being in the woods that I thoroughly enjoy is the opportunity to see or hear wildlife. If we're lucky, maybe we'll spot opossums. Or maybe we'll hear the rapid flutter of bat wings overhead.

"You were so jealous when I first learned to fly—I mean *really* fly. What happened to that?" he asked the first time he took me flying, after I begged him to immediately return to the ground.

"I'm over it," is all I could say at the time, my voice and legs shaking.

If only I could burrow my face into the warmth of his neck now, stretch along the length of his back. Maybe that would help to make flying less scary. I remind myself to give his wings the room they need to move.

"You know I would never let anything happen to you, right?"

It's hard to believe that I have confronted murderous demons, crazed gargoyles, and Ella. Yet, here I am a total scaredy-cat over flying. I'm pretty sure it all comes down to a lack of control and a fear of splattering all over the ground.

"Next time I will park my butt on the grass and chill out with the nighttime critters while you fly," I suggest.

"Balk...balk!" Marcus teases, mimicking a chicken.

My legs tighten their grip around him as I lean in for just a second—bowing my body forward so I don't crush his wings—and nip his shoulder with my teeth in response.

"Whoa! No biting, fang girl." Marcus's entire body flexes, grows rigid. That's when I remember the scars on his shoulders, scars not visible in the darkness.

I regret the playful move immediately. "I'm sorry."

My eyes scan his back and shoulders. I didn't see anyone bite Marcus during the battle between the demons and gargoyles (those franken-soldiers don't deserve to be called *protectors*) at St. Aquinas back in May, but we discovered them hidden among his many other wounds later at his mother and father's condo. His body was a mess of gashes, burns, and bruises. He was in so much pain. I shudder at the memory.

Just as quickly, I plant a kiss in the exact same spot.

After two more passes over the treetops, occasionally dipping between widespread clusters of box elder, black cherry, and elms, we land in the open field where we originally took off.

I slide off Marcus's back. My legs quiver after clenching his body the entire ride. It feels good to be back on solid ground even if I do wobble a bit. A chorus of crickets rings out, accented with the periodic croaks from bullfrogs. Maybe they're all laughing at me, calling me chicken like Marcus had a little while ago.

Marcus studies me, his grin is gone. "You really don't enjoy it?"

"I really don't."

Marcus frowns, his expression inscrutable. I don't want him to think that I think flying is a bad thing and the free time he has available is limited, so I don't want him to feel he has to choose between flying and me.

"Maybe we could try nighttime picnics? I could eat while you fly," I suggest.

That makes him laugh. He takes hold of my hand, playfully at first. Maybe it's the intimacy of the darkness or Marcus's adrenaline rush. He grows serious all of a sudden. He strokes my palm gently with his thumb and that gesture sends a message to my brain and to my body. My pulse quickens.

I take a step closer and reach up to touch his face with my free hand. As I balance on my tiptoes, I pull his face down to mine. Our lips touch, shifting from tentative to familiar and passionate pretty quickly. Marcus's arms are around me. He holds me tight against him. Sometimes his strength catches me by surprise. It's like he's holding me captive, not that I have any desire to escape. Our bodies press so close it's like we merge into one. His fingers wind through my hair while his other hand keeps me pressed against him. My hands kneed the muscles of his shoulders, his arms, his back, careful around his other scars—the ones that run the length of his back. I don't have access to his body for much longer, so I make sure to get my fill of him.

I never want this to end. The words tiptoe through my thoughts at the same time I release a contented sigh.

Marcus pulls away just enough so that he can study my face in the darkness. "I love you. You know that don't you?"

I nod. "I love you, too." Declaring ourselves like this, in the dark, erases my brief contentment. I pause, nibbling my bottom lip.

"What is it?" Marcus asks, his thumb trailing along my mouth. His exceptional eyesight doesn't miss a thing.

The thoughts I have been keeping at bay most of the night— with monumental effort—return. Marcus's departure. It looms heavily like a parasite trying to suck the joy out of my evening with him.

"I...I can't help worrying about you when you go," I say. Suddenly, I am overcome with a flood of emotion. I am torn between telling him to forget I said anything and bursting into tears.

Marcus's tightens his grip on me. "Worried how? About what?"

I stare off into the night. It would be far easier for me to disappear into the cluster of trees, to share my worries with the croaking frogs or the owl than open up to my boyfriend.

Marcus knows me well enough to know how much I hate this kind of conversation. He pulls me closer. I press my face against

34

his chest. It allows me to open up while avoiding the crippling weight of his scrutiny—even in the darkness—or, better put, my own stupid self-consciousness.

His hands stroke my back and a sense of calm envelops me.

"I don't want to lose you," I whisper.

Marcus pulls back. He ducks so that his eyes—full of shock and surprise—meet mine. "You aren't losing me, Lucy." His hands grip my arms, his calming effect muting my emotions. "I can't stand the idea of being away from you. If it wasn't important, I wouldn't go."

"You say that now," I mutter. I press myself against him again, snuggle back against his chest.

"You think Camille has the power to keep me away from you?" He laughs. "Once we help her work through this whole mess, she can move back to Chicago. My life is here. If she wants to be a part of it, she has to be, too."

The idea of Camille becoming a permanent fixture around Edison Park makes me cringe, but it's better than the alternative. "You promise?"

"I am coming back," he says. His voice rumbles through his chest and against my ear as if to affirm the statement. "Once I meet members of the clan, I hope to go back and visit periodically. With as much fun as I have flying with Selima, it will be a blast to hang out with more of my kind."

My stomach performs another nauseating somersault. The sensation of flight is too fresh. "Yeah, sure...a blast."

Marcus laughs as he hugs me.

CHAPTER FIVE

– Dylan Douglas –

Selima hops up onto my kitchen counter. Her short spikey hair bounces with the movement. I shake my head, grinning at her feline-like grace. All five-feet-six inches of her are solid muscle. She's sexy as hell in a ninja warrior sort of way. What was I doing? Oh, yeah, grabbing two glasses. Lemonade.

The cleaning service came through yesterday, which is a relief. Our house always looks decent, but it's important to me that Selima see it like it is today. Spotless. I try to imagine how she would see it. The honey-colored maple cabinets and black metal fixtures look good against the glossy gray, pink, and cream speckled granite countertops. It smells clean, but not like chemicals or bleach.

I catch myself and chuckle. Since when did I care about the appearance and smell of my house?

"What? Oops," Selima says playfully as she points to her perfectly shaped behind. Her heavily lined dark eyes, probably the most Selima-like thing about her, widen for an instant. She smiles conspiratorially. "Am I going to get in trouble? Is it forbidden to sit up here?"

"Yeah," I say with a stern tone, "so disrespectful."

My cell buzzes on the counter a couple of feet from where Selima sits. The tight black stretchy pants she wears show off her body nicely. I ignore my phone. Probably Nick or Chad whining about football practice earlier today. It's Wednesday, the third day of school, and I smoked them both again during drills before meeting up with Selima. I warned them both for months that they couldn't rely solely on football camp to keep up their skills and fitness. I maintained my training the entire summer in addition to camp. Then again I can't help it that I'm awesome.

Selima takes hold of my hand. The strength of her grip is a freaking turn on.

"I had you airborne during training tonight. Admit it," she taunts.

I flip her hand over, running my thumb over her palm. Gently, I stroke her skin in a circular motion before moving up to her forearm.

"I'm just happy you're back in town. I'll admit anything you want me to," I say softly, flashing her a dazzling smile.

Selima's gaze follows the movement of my hand as it slides up her arm. Her breath catches. The sound is faint, but I hear it. Her eyes close for a moment. When she opens them, I feel a jolt as she boldly looks into my eyes. The moment is hot. I feel the sparks between us. She blinks and a cocky grin spreads across her face.

"For all your worries, you haven't hurt me yet, demon. Not even close," she says.

Selima covers my hand with her own. The skin-on-skin contact makes me shiver.

"Can you get it through your thick skull that I'm a worthy sparring partner? Let go of the fact that I'm a girl and stop holding back."

The idea of getting rough with Selima, possibly hurting her, screams all sorts of wrong in my head. Sure, I get that she's fit, all sinewy muscle and twitch-fast reflexes, but she's so much smaller than me. I held back today. There's no way I can let go with Selima like I do with Aiden.

My cell phone buzzes again on the countertop. Maybe it's Ethan or Brandi? I never ignore messages from my kid brother and sister. Or maybe it's Lucy and something's wrong? She told me about Marcus having to leave in a couple of weeks once the clan is ready to question him. I grimace at the thought. That means Selima will leave again, too. I snatch my phone and read the text.

"Ugh. Why would I have any interest in attending a stupid séance?" I complain, annoyed by the interruption.

Selima eyes me quizzically. "Who's inviting you to a séance?"

"Ella." I slide my phone into the back pocket of my khaki shorts, message unanswered.

"Hmmm..." Selima murmurs. "One of your many fans."

"Are you a fan?" I return my focus to her. "I hope so, because you're the only one I care about."

"Glad to hear it," Selima says, her voice smooth as velvet.

I forget about the lemonade and the text messages as Selima pulls my hand, guiding me so that I stand between her legs. She cups my face. We freeze. Or maybe I freeze while her eyes bore into mine. Lucy has hinted at the power of protectors. Is this what she meant? Hypnotic and seductive, Selima's scent overtakes me. Her strong legs wrap around mine, hold me prisoner. The flutter of her finger tips as she strokes my cheeks, my lips, fills me with insane need.

Breathe, idiot, or you're going to land on your ass.

Sucking in air until my lungs are full, I reach for her. The sweet smell of her hits my senses before our lips touch. Intoxication from any other substance has never felt or tasted this good. The instant our mouths touch, my knees threaten to buckle. Subtly, I lean into her, allow the counter to hold my weight. I pull her to me as carefully as I can while our kiss threatens to overtake me. Her legs tighten their vice-lock around me.

My butt starts to vibrate. It's a phone call this time. I ignore it and it finally stops only to start again.

I pull away from Selima. "If this is Ella again..." I growl as I grab my cell from my pocket.

She raises her eyebrows, looking amused.

"It's Ethan," I say to Selima, pulling away to answer the Facetime call.

"Hey Little Man, what's up?" I ask my eleven-year-old brother. My voice sounds rough, raspy, and I cough in an attempt to clear it. My brain slowly sobers up from hormone overload. I rub Selima's leg as I nod apologetically at my phone.

She waves me off as she takes two glasses and fills them with water from the faucet.

A quick glance at the clock on the wall shows eight o'clock. My step-monster should be home. Ethan never calls me at night when she's home.

"Can you talk?" Ethan whispers. His face is close to the screen and fills it completely. His dark hair is perfectly combed. His hairstyle and preppy clothing tastes didn't come from our father or me. No doubt they were the result of the controlling influence of his mother. My heart thumps uncomfortably in my chest at his overly serious expression.

Brandi, my eight-year-old sister, pushes herself into the frame beside Ethan. Her dark blond hair is pulled away from her face into a severe ponytail. Her eyes are shiny wet with tears.

A lightning bolt of anger rips through me. I shake my head at the glass of water Selima offers and move away from her to the center of the room. "What's wrong, pipsqueak?" It takes effort to keep my voice even.

Selima pokes me in the leg with her foot. When I glance her way, she narrows her eyes and bares her teeth, then points to my face. I look angry? I take a deep breath and attempt to ease my expression.

"Better," she mouths.

What has Alana done now? Is she putting Ethan and Brandi on another crazy diet? Forcing more tutors onto them? Is she stressing them out about grades and future college prospects while they're in elementary school?

"They're fighting again," Brandi chokes out the words. A fresh batch of tears springs to her eyes.

"What about?" I ask. I flex the fingers of my left hand out of a fist.

Why did my father and his second wife bother to have kids? They don't like spending time with them and when they're under the same roof, all my father and Alana do is fight.

"A trip to New York," Ethan whispers, casting a cautious glance away from the phone. Whenever they call it's usually from Ethan's bedroom. Is he afraid his mother will barge into his room and catch them talking to me? She's not much of a fan of mine, so it's a valid worry on his part.

"Why?" I ask. A weekend away for Alana and my father would mean I could spend more time with the rug rats. Lucy would babysit for the whole weekend. "Is Dad refusing to go?"

Brandi's bottom lip trembles.

Ethan swallows hard.

"Mom wants to move us there." His voice shakes with every syllable.

"She what?" I ask, unable to control the ice in my voice.

Selima jumps off of the counter. While standing out of view of the phone's screen, she waves her hands at me, her eyes wide with alarm. She makes the monster face again. I turn away from her.

"Calm down!" she whispers.

"I think she's coming!" Brandi squeaks.

The call ends.

"Unbelievable!" I fling my phone onto the counter at the same time I sidekick a kitchen chair. The chair crashes to the floor, breaking into a dozen pieces.

"Stop it, Dylan." Selima stands across the room from me, her face frozen in alarm. "What's wrong with you?"

"That bitch!" I spit out the words. "She's the worst mother... the worst wife...God, I hate her."

"Right now you're acting like a monster. Get yourself under control."

The room suddenly feels as hot as a furnace. I yank the collar of my St. Aquinas T-shirt away from my sweaty neck. I want to destroy the rest of the chairs. I want to punch someone.

I struggle to get myself under control. Long, slow breath. Repeat. Lucy's lesson from my early demon days comes back to me.

Brave little Ethan fought hard not to cry. Brandi pressed herself tight against his side, scared.

I turn around to face Selima. My anger recedes at the sight of my beautiful, patient girlfriend. Guilt takes its place.

"I'm sorry for being such an out of control jerk. Do you think I freaked them out?" I ask with a sigh.

Selima takes a tentative step toward me. "I don't know. Have they seen you this mad before?"

Have they? I've been ticked off plenty of times around my brother and sister. Usually over something their mother had said or done to further confine them to a life of studies and learning or forced bonding with her society friends' brats.

I nod. "But tonight felt different."

Selima comes close. She slips her hands into mine.

I shake my head, feeling like the worst brother in the world. Ethan and Brandi face their judgy, domineering mother every day. They didn't need me, their rock-solid older brother, to turn into a raging jerk.

"They were scared, Selima. They were scared and I made it worse," I lean forward, dropping my head onto her shoulder. "Lucy and I made a vow to always be there for the kids. I'm a total creep."

Selima strokes the back of my neck. "Send Ethan a message. Let him know you are here for him and Brandi no matter what."

The calming effect of her hands is immediate. She continues to stroke my neck. Her touch is magical.

After several minutes, I pull away from her. "Thank you for that." I press a kiss to her lips. "I need to get rid of the smashed chair before my mom gets home."

I put all the pieces in a pile in the garage next to the garbage bins giving me time to think about my reaction to Ethan's call. Sure, Ethan and Brandi have seen me worked up. I have a little bit of a temper. Tonight was different. My anger has never escalated so fast before. What would've happened if Selima hadn't been here? Would I have flipped out on Ethan and Brandi? Would I have trashed all the chairs?

CHAPTER SIX

– Ella Rosenthal –

"Are you kidding me?" I groan.

This can't be happening during my second week of school. I turn the key in the ignition again. The stupid spinning sound starts again. So much for my new car. Dad's big promotion wasn't so great after all. He said the constant travel was a trade-off for the huge salary increase. I got a new white Honda Accord out of the deal, although it's nowhere near as nice as the Lexus that Lucy's dad gave her. At least I don't have to depend on Caroline for rides anymore.

The problem with a dad who is gone all the time is that he's not here to help when the stupid car breaks down.

I turn the key again. More spinning noises.

Piece of crap!

The clock on the dashboard reminds me that I should be pulling into the school parking lot by now. I overslept. Too much time spent working on content for my new website last night. After ironing my uniform this morning, I decided my hair and makeup needed extra attention. With my new makeup and fashion blog, people need to see me as an expert in my field.

Mrs. Lyerly is going to have my head when I walk into English late. Maybe I should text Lucy and have her relay an excuse for me. A severe case of cramps or something. Better not. Lucy would probably announce it in front of the entire class just to embarrass me. I can't believe she and I have first period together again this year. It's bad enough I'm stuck eating lunch with her every day, but English *and* Civic Law class, too? It sucks.

With a mix of pissed off about my car and irritation about Lucy, I slam the door of my Accord. I am tempted to kick it, but don't want to scuff the paint. It's time to call AAA. Dad stuck the information in the emergency folder before he left for New York. *Again*. I spot an old guy crossing the lawn toward me. He wears a baseball cap featuring a team logo that doesn't belong to the White Sox or Cubs.

This is not the time for a political candidate promoter to spread his propaganda crap. That's when I notice he's not carrying brochures. Halfway across the lawn he lifts his head so his face is out of shadow.

I tense as I recognize Seamus McAllister. The geezer's limp gray hair is a little longer than mine. It actually flows behind him as he walks. He wears blue jeans and a green pullover. I force myself to take in those unimportant details. The old man continues to approach me. We hadn't set another date to meet after he sought me out on the first day of school. I never gave him my address.

"Miss Rosenthal? Do you have a couple of minutes?" Mr. McAllister stops a couple of feet from me.

For a second I worry he will extend his old man cootie hand, which I would refuse.

"Why are you here? We're supposed to meet at my school," I complain. My morning is already the pits. I don't need him adding to it.

The old guy's eyes study me. He takes too long to speak. It's like his brain is two hundred years old and moves at the pace of a slug.

"I am checking in. Have you spoken with Miss Walker? Is she on board with your gathering?"

A chill slithers up my neck when he smiles. I prefer when we met in the back of St. Aquinas's lot, our vehicles parked next to each other. The protective cocoon of my car and being on school premises with lots of people around made me feel safe. I take a few steps back from the old man. "Lucy hasn't agreed to come to the séance yet, but she will. Don't worry." I sounded more defensive than I intended to. Lucy wasn't on board with my plans at all. How was I going to get her to join? I glance at my cell phone to check the time and gasp. "I have to go. I'm seriously late for school."

"It appears your automobile is not working. We have time to finish our conversation," he says, not budging.

Why did I ever agree to help him? I glance at my car, irritated all over again.

"Maybe I'm not the right person to help you," I tell him. "You should go talk to some of her other friends, or her boyfriend, or the guy who was supposed to be *my* boyfriend."

Seamus McAllister smiles again. It creeps slowly across his face. His teeth have a brownish yellow tint to them, which is gross. My grandmother—and my style icon—would never have allowed her teeth to look that way.

"You—not the others in Miss Walker's life—are precisely the person I need to help me. You are the only person who sees her for what she truly is."

"I get it, but…" I look at my phone again and panic ricochets inside of me at the thought of a demerit. "I need to go!"

This was the one condition with my dad—or several conditions within one category: school. No absences, be on time every day, and maintain a B average or better. The front office is going to call my dad to notify him that I'm late to first period. He will flip out over the demerit. On top of that, I want away from this guy. Now.

"What is the consequence if you are tardy to school?" Mr. McAllister asks.

My grandmother fought my dad to make sure I was sent to St. Aquinas College Prep. She even agreed to pay half my tuition every year. All for the sake of a *solid education*. In my grandmother's world, that means finding a suitable husband. The earlier I find a high-quality match, the better, she says. A lot of the good ones are taken by college, apparently. It took my grandmother three marriages to find herself a suitable husband.

The second I screw up one of Dad's rules, that will be the end of it all. I lose what I have built up at St. Aquinas: reputation, popularity, and status.

"My dad is going to kill me."

The old man blinks. "Death is a severe punishment for tardiness."

"You aren't serious are you?" I sputter. "He won't *literally* kill me, but pull me from St. Aquinas. That would be a *disaster*."

Now I'm getting pissed. The old man has to leave. There's no way I'll allow him to ruin my life.

"Perhaps I can assist," the old man says. "Would a telephone call to your school on your behalf help?"

"If you take off, that would help a lot."

Mr. McAllister waves a hand at me.

"Would your father be the one to notify the school?"

"Yes, but..."

Once again he waves a hand at me.

My temper flares. *Who does this guy think he is?*

"Could you play a recording of your father's voice for me?"

A recording?

Mr. McAllister nods at my phone. "My own daughter had a phone similar to yours and she stored recordings on it."

Clearly this guy is one of those anti-technology weirdos who lives without Netflix and YouTube. He probably refers to a paper map when driving places.

I scroll quickly through the voicemail list and reject the last two where he harassed me for overspending at the mall with his credit card. The third on the list should be okay.

"My dad rarely calls St. Aquinas, so if you can sound fatherly that should be good enough."

I play it for Creepy McAllister.

"Hey Ella, it's Dad. Just checking in to see how you're doing. I'm in New York for a few more days working on this deal, then I should be home. You would love it here, honey. I know I've told

you this a dozen times, but I need to bring you here for a visit. The energy and the people are fantastic. You would love the shopping and the food is exquisite. You really should consider college in the Big Apple. I miss you, sweetheart. Be good and study hard."

Sure, Dad, keep pretending like you care.

The old man closes his eyes as he listens to the message. Heat spreads across my cheeks. The fact that a stranger is listening to the call—something private between my dad and me—makes me squirm.

Old Man McAllister nods. "Telephone the appropriate individual at your school."

I bristle at the command. Not many people order me around and this guy—who comes to my house when that's not part of our deal—does it with too much authority. He's taking his brief role as my pretend dad way too seriously.

I search Google for my school's front office number and dial it before handing the phone to him.

He speaks into the phone and a thrill races down my spine.

"Good morning. Who am I speaking with?" he asks.

"Mrs. Jordan, it's Mr. Rosenthal. Ella's father." He pauses. "Ella was not feeling well this morning. No, she's not taking the entire day off. She will make it to school today. She needed extra rest is all."

I watch in utter dismay. This guy is all sorts of annoying, but right now he's a weirdo rock star. He isn't mimicking my father. It's more like he adopts my father's voice *exactly*. "Good day."

The old man focuses on me. His gaze turns cold.

He hands my phone back to me. I pluck it carefully from his fingers, not allowing our skin to touch, and check to make sure the call ended.

"When you give me powers, I definitely want that ability. Well, not just that one. I want *lots* of abilities. Maybe you could run through the list of options sometime," I say, full of exhilaration that I skated past a demerit. "Anyway, I need to take off for school. Just need to order an Uber," I say, pulling up the app on my phone.

"Stop," he says.

Every inch of me freezes. I can't type my school's address into the Uber app. I can't blink. I can't step away. I can't scream. I take a panicked inhale. My lungs actually function and I am relieved. Thank God I can breathe.

"Do you remember what I asked of you?" Mr. McAllister says. His voice is soft and raspy. The combination is bone-chilling.

I try to nod, but can't move my head. More than anything I want to blink. A breeze passes over my face, further drying out my eyes. Tears don't form like they should. A fly buzzes by the left side of my head. I can't twitch or brush the disgusting insect away. It lands on my forehead. Its tiny, filthy legs traipse along my skin. I want to cringe. I want to scream. I remain still as stone.

"You must earn whatever powers I choose to grant you. You will see to it that Miss Walker attends *and* participates at your gathering. Do not disappoint me, Miss Rosenthal." Creepy McAllister studies me.

50

The fly finally launches off of my face, leaving fly gunk on my skin. My contacts are going to be totally ruined. *Please just let me blink!*

McAllister's lips spread into a yellow-toothed smile. "You should give thanks to the others who have sacrificed themselves for us."

Others? What others? Sacrifice? Jesus, I don't care. Just let me blink for hell's sake!

He waves his hand.

My body unfreezes. Off balance, I fall to the ground hard, a loud *oomph* pushing from my lips. I close my eyes as I test out my fingers and toes. Tears stream down my face as I blink again and again. Apart from the burning sensation in my eyes, all of me works again.

"I will visit you again soon," Seamus McAllister says before he turns and walks away.

CHAPTER SEVEN

– Ella Rosenthal –

My car magically started after Mr. Psycho left. Clearly he messed with it. Pulling up to a stop sign a block from my house, I squeeze my eyes shut as I recall the terror of them being stuck open. How long would it take for them to completely dry out? Would they shrink like grapes into raisins? Tears sting my eyes again.

Would the magician have come to the house if my dad were home? The answer comes without hesitation and I feel a surge of anger and bitterness. *No.*

Dad and Grandma's faces appear in my mind, their expressions heavy with disappointment. The psychotic old man made me late for school. If I get in trouble...no more St. Aquinas. Then again, he did call in for me and he sounded convincing.

With my teeth clenched, I finally pull away from the stop sign. *Toughen up, Ella.*

During my drive, I angrily wipe away my tears.

Once in the school parking lot—where all the good spots are long taken—I grab my makeup bag and get to work. I am the most beautiful girl in school. There's no way I'm going to allow a crazy old man to ruin my high school career or allow anyone to see me looking like a mess. I have to think about my image and my followers.

With my makeup and hair finished, I leave my car and cross the parking lot. As I stand before the double doors to the school, I catch sight of my reflection. Seamus McAllister came to town over a grudge against Jude Morgan and Lucy. Once I help him, he will give me powers then leave me alone. After what he did to me today, I can't help but wonder...what does he plan to do to Lucy? I take a stuttering breath, straighten my posture, and walk into school.

CHAPTER EIGHT

– Lucy Walker –

"Earth to Lucy," Sheldon says as he tugs my hair playfully. "Something wrong, kiddo?"

It's Friday evening and dinner with my uncles is consumed with the two of them debating the candidates for the upcoming election, analyzing every decision the Chicago mayor and Illinois governor make, and argue the pros and cons of pending legislation. Their views are basically the same but they choose to debate anyway. Operating on autopilot, I cut apart the stuffed pepper, taking bites of the quinoa, black beans, and onions together with a chunk of the green pepper. I'm startled when Sheldon takes a break from the conversation to check in with me.

One of my new goals is to cut back on the lies I tell my uncles. It doesn't feel right. Besides, trying to remember them all becomes another stressor that I don't need.

"I guess," I say.

"Do you want to share?" Bernard asks. He sets his fork and knife along the edge of his plate and gives me his attention.

Introducing Marcus's departure into a conversation with my

uncles is risky—not so much Bernard, but it could set Sheldon off. Since Marcus and I started dating, he complains about the amount of time I spend with my boyfriend. Then again, Sheldon might celebrate the idea of Marcus leaving for a while. That would tick me off.

"I'm worried about Jude. It's been a while since I've heard from him," I say, opting for the other, safer topic.

"Is he still in China?" Sheldon asks. He slides the pitcher of lemonade across the table and refills his glass.

I focus on the trail of moisture left on the butcher-block table from the condensation pooling around the glass container, not looking at my uncles as I lie. "Last time he called, yes, but he's planning to tour more of Asia and parts of Europe. I'm not sure if he will stop home between trips."

Sheldon whistles low and soft. "That's some trip."

I nod. "He has lots of business to take care of."

If only I could ask my uncles for guidance about my father and Lucifer. I give myself a mental shake. They would lose their minds to know that Lucifer just so happens to be walking among us. No doubt the ruler of hell is attending the opera at the famous La Scala in Milan or the Bolshoi in Moscow. Aiden says that Lucifer is obsessed with the opera and has been attending *forever*. His serious tone led me to believe he meant that literally. The very thought is incomprehensible to me. Like Lucifer, my father is immortal. What must life be like when you will live forever?

Bernard reaches across the table and squeezes my hand. "I'm sorry the trip has taken him away for so long. That has to be hard on you."

"It's harder than I thought it would be," I admit honestly.

"Maybe you could video conference with him periodically? Have you tried that?" Sheldon asks.

The idea of a video conference with my father from hell would make me laugh if I wasn't truly starting to miss him.

I shrug. "He's going to call when his schedule lightens up."

I study my uncles, the only family I have left on earth. Despite everything else going on, I really am lucky to have two of the best men I know as my guardians. Sheldon—Gram's brother—reminds me of her with the same hazel eyes and gray hair. He is wicked smart like her, too. The T-shirt he wears today features the tail of a whale poking out of a body of water while the rest of its body hides from view below the surface. Sheldon collects T-shirts from every vacation spot he and Bernard visit. This one was purchased during their Alaska cruise several years ago.

Bernard, Sheldon's partner for as long as I have been alive, is a great cook, has a calmer disposition than Sheldon, and loves the arts. Unlike Sheldon, Bernard is fashionable. His button-down mint-green shirt is wrinkle-free. His khaki shorts were ironed this morning, the starched fold along the front a dead giveaway. Thanks to Bernard, I have a great wardrobe—far nicer than anything I owned back in Lexington. The most bizarre thought occurs to me just then. Could my uncles handle meeting Lucifer? After all, their meeting with Jude hadn't been so bad. They sat at this very table drinking coffee and eating breakfast together. A night at the opera in Milan or Moscow would be a dream come true for Bernard and Sheldon.

Would Lucifer use my uncles to manipulate me like Jude had

in the past? According to Persephone and Henry, my uncles must be kept in the dark to keep them safe. That has to include any face-to-face with the fallen angel I was named after. He can turn someone to dust with the snap of his fingers. A lightning bolt of fear rips through me at the thought. The smell of dinner causes nausea to twist painfully in my stomach.

"Don't forget we're going to the cemetery on Sunday afternoon," Bernard says, pushing aside the stuffed pepper on his plate to cut a piece of pork chop from the bone. I flinch as his serrated knife screeches against the ceramic plate. In a flash I recall the sound of Marcus's feathers scratching against bone whenever his wings tuck back into the slits in his back. I shudder.

"I'm still planning to go with you," I assure them, although getting the words out and sounding normal takes effort.

The kitchen light bounces off of his knife just then and I gasp. The glint of the blade...just like the knife held against Marcus's throat the night of the battle at St. Aquinas.

As I close my eyes tightly, willing the flashback away, a feeling of overwhelm clutches at me. The table suddenly feels too close, the room too warm. It threatens to smother me.

"Luce? You okay?" Bernard asks.

Silverware clatters against the table and I jump, opening my eyes. Sheldon picks up the fork he dropped, cursing under his breath.

"Headache," I say and press my fingers to my temples in an attempt to relieve the sudden painful ache.

What was it Bernard said? Sunday. Cemetery. Gram's birthday.

After a couple of deep breaths, I raise my head catching both of my uncles watching me intently.

"Do you want some Ibuprofen?" Sheldon asks, his brows furrowed with concern.

I blink. The light in the room is too bright.

"I'll be fine," I lie.

Neither of them looks convinced.

Sheldon finally nods. "If we go Sunday morning, you can still make it to Jude's to check on his house and water his plants. Then we will have a nice dinner once you get home. Just the three of us. We can make one of your grandmother's favorite dishes."

"Sounds great," I tell him, trying to add some oomph to my voice. My head is throbbing. On top of that, there's no missing the way he stressed *just the three of us,* making it clear that Marcus was not welcome to join us. Never mind that my boyfriend and my grandmother had been close. I knew where this conversation was headed.

"Maybe you could cut back on your late nights on the roof with Marcus," Sheldon suggests. "Try to get more sleep. Your school load is heavy this year with the AP classes, your job with the Douglas family, helping Persephone on a weekly basis, and taking care of Jude's house. It's no wonder you don't feel well."

"I don't spend *that* much time with Marcus," I grumble.

"I beg to differ," Sheldon grumbles back.

Bernard touches Sheldon's arm. They exchange a meaningful look.

Sheldon releases a heavy sigh. "This is not how I wanted tonight to go," he says to Bernard.

"I know," Bernard says. He presses his hand to Sheldon's cheek. Sheldon nods in response. They exchange a smile.

"What do you say we change the subject?" Bernard suggests brightly.

They both fix their attention on me, their dispositions suddenly animated. Bernard is working hard to suppress a wiggly smile. Sheldon starts and stops, trying to tell me something, but struggling to find the words.

"We have something important to share with you," Bernard finally says. His complexion turns rosy. He is working hard to contain himself.

Are they planning another family vacation? *Please no!* Their last attempt had been a fiasco after my father made it clear to me that he would kill them if they tried to take me away.

Sheldon rests his elbows on the table as he shakes his head and grins at Bernard. Bernard beams like a kid who just received the greatest Christmas present ever.

"I give up. What's going on?" I ask.

"You tell her," Bernard says, nudging Sheldon.

"You're a pain in the butt," Sheldon says to Bernard, pushing his plate away.

"You couldn't survive a month without me," Bernard says, crossing his arms over his chest.

Their comic routine, which I don't believe is intentional, provides a welcome distraction from my thoughts about Marcus and my father.

"The suspense is killing me," I push. The sooner we finish this conversation, the sooner I can lie down.

Sheldon reaches for my hand. "Your Uncle Bernard and I are getting married."

"Finally," Bernard adds, pointedly. "It should've happened in 2014."

Sheldon pats his arm. "It's happening. Relax."

"Seriously? That's great news!" I grin.

"That's what I said when he finally agreed," Bernard says with a chuckle, his eyes tearing up.

I move around the table, trying to ignore my headache. I wrap my arms around Bernard's neck and plant a noisy kiss on his cheek. His hands grip my arms and he dots kisses all over my face. Before Sheldon can push out of his chair, I move over to him next and nearly choke him with my embrace.

"Do I get to stand up with one of you? Or both of you?" I ask.

"That leads us to this next part," Sheldon wheezes. He pats my hands and I realize my grip is too tight. Immediately I release my chokehold before he turns purple.

Sheldon takes a deep breath. "We have a question for you," he says.

"Ask away," I say.

"This will be a small affair, so no one is standing up for us," Bernard says before he pulls a white cotton handkerchief from his pocket and dabs at his eyes.

"Instead, we were hoping you would walk us both down the aisle," Sheldon says.

They watch me expectantly—Bernard with his blissful smile and tear-filled eyes and Sheldon, whose hazel eyes and gooey expression remind me so much of Gram it's impossible to stop the tears that brim my eyes and spill onto my cheeks.

I hide my face in Sheldon's neck as I hug him again, gently this time. Maybe it's because I'm not sure when I will see my father again, or the sinking feeling as Marcus's departure approaches, or that two of the most important people in my life are finally getting married and neither Gram nor Momma are here to see it happen.

"There, there," Bernard coos as he rubs my back.

"This is supposed to be a happy occasion, kiddo," Sheldon murmurs.

Once I pull away from the snuggly warmth of Sheldon's neck, I plant another kiss on his cheek and reach out to hold Bernard's hand. "I would love to. When is the big day?"

Bernard pushes his plate away. "We were thinking June of next year. Actually, I would prefer April or May."

"Chicago is rainy in April and May and you want an outdoor wedding," Sheldon points out with a sigh. "We went through this already."

"Do Persephone and Henry know?" I ask. I collect dishes from the table and deliver them to the sink.

"We wanted to tell you first," Sheldon says.

Bernard leaves the table to slice a loaf of banana bread cooling on the stove. When he brings it to the table, I return to my seat. The bread is still a little warm and loaded with walnuts. I spread a generous amount of butter on it before taking a bite.

"If Jude is back from his world tour we would like to invite him," Sheldon says.

If Jude comes to the wedding, does that mean Marcus would skip it? How could I expect him to attend? It would be too difficult for him to hold it together all that time. Marcus will be back by then. Of course he will. Unless something goes wrong. What about Jude? Will he ever come back? I shake off my worries grabbing at the happiness I feel for my uncles. Determined to keep them in the center of the moment, I focus on my smile until it feels genuine again.

"That's nice of you. I will keep you posted once I know when Jude will be home."

CHAPTER NINE

– Lucy Walker –

"My uncles are getting married," I announce to Marcus.

It's too hot outside to sit on the roof. Instead, we stretch out together on the mocha-colored couch in his air-conditioned living room. A bowl of popcorn sits on the coffee table along with two cans of Sprite. I plan to tell Katie the news tomorrow. She will have to help me find a dress.

Aiden is working late at the office, so Marcus and I have the apartment to ourselves.

"Really? I figured they didn't want to or they would've done it before now," Marcus says, pulling his attention away from the Foo Fighters documentary we're watching.

"Bernard wants this big time. Always has. Sheldon was the holdout," I tell him before I scoop popcorn from the bowl.

Marcus laughs. "Big surprise."

He runs his fingers along the length of my arm. I look to the corner of the living room where two duffle bags sit, one piled on top of the other. Seventeen minutes. That's how long I've been in Marcus's apartment. I noticed the bags the moment I walked in the door. A quarter of an hour and he hasn't said a word about them.

"Marcus?" Now is as good a time as any. He should be the one initiating the conversation, but apparently isn't going to.

"Hmmm?" His hand continues to run up and down my arm while his attention is fixed on the rockers on his TV.

"When are you leaving?" I really am trying to keep my voice even.

"In about a week, give or take."

Marcus absently presses his lips against my hair, his attention still annoyingly *not* focused on his packed bags or me.

Here we are going through the motions like everything is normal. How do I get his attention? Why is it that I'm on the verge of freaking out and he's as cool as the soda can on the table?

I shift myself into a sitting position and out of his distracted embrace. Marcus pulls his eyes away from the screen. That's a great start.

"Can we talk about this?" I am way too edgy to sit, so I climb off of the couch. "Can you fill me in on whatever updates you've gotten from Selima, her mother, their connections within the clan? You must've heard something, because your bags are packed."

Reluctantly, Marcus pauses the documentary. He sits up with a grimace and his slumped posture communicates volumes. So does the fact that it takes a count of five Mississippi's before he looks at me.

We study each other in a horrifically awkward, silent kind of way. Marcus looks away first. His gaze drifts toward the sliding glass door. Boy, does that speak volumes. He wants to get away from me? Anger and panic and fear tangle and snarl inside of me. Heat settles in my hands. In an instant, I cross my arms over my chest and tuck my hands beneath my armpits.

"How long are you going to be gone?" I ask bluntly. If Marcus knows me at all, if he is paying attention, he would know that I'm scared and anxious and ticked off.

"Selima said we should be back in two weeks."

"Should?" I ask.

"Lucy..." He rakes his fingers through his hair.

"Where exactly are you going?"

"Come on...I'm not allowed to tell you that," he says.

If our roles were reversed, I'm certain I would tell Marcus where I was going. I don't think there is a secret I could keep from him. Even if I tried to keep one, he would get it out of me.

"So, I can't visit you while you're there?" I ask.

His hair sticks up at crazy angles and he looks at me with that tight expression that tells me he *really* doesn't want to talk about this right now. "I don't even know if that's allowed."

How do I respond to that—his expression and his lame response? He hasn't asked Selima the very questions I'm posing to him now?

I tap my foot on the floor, my arms crossed tight over my chest. The last thing I want to do is go off on my boyfriend, but the dynamic I feel between us is very different than it's been all week. What changed? Suddenly a thought occurs to me.

"Is this information you can't tell anyone? Or just me because I'm a demon?" I ask.

He says nothing. That's all the answer I need to know that I'm right.

I drop my arms. "You know I would never tell anyone. Not even my father."

Marcus looks at me quickly before he averts his gaze. "But you don't have to tell Jude anything for him to find out, do you?"

He's referring to our ability to communicate telepathically.

Anger surges inside of me. "You think you need to protect the clan council from my father?"

The protector council accused my father of slaughtering their kind. It wasn't true. The real monsters in that whole mess were Garret and his army.

"This is no big deal to you—that you're leaving—but I'm losing my mind worrying about it. About us. You don't seem to care." I wait for him to say something.

Marcus releases a heavy sigh. "I won't be away long. You'll see. Plus, you have Katie. You'll barely notice I'm gone."

His statement about being gone for two weeks is flimsy. Even he didn't sound confident when he said it.

If I don't leave now, I'm going to say something I shouldn't.

"I need to go home," I snap.

Marcus nods, his eyes still fixed on the patio door.

I storm out the door and down the stairs to my apartment. There is no way I will allow him to see my tears.

Once in my bedroom I replay what just happened. Then I stop because the thoughts racing through my mind all point to Marcus not caring about me. If he did, he would talk to me about the trip. If he cared about me, we would talk about what Selima told him he could expect, how he feels, how I feel, how much we will miss each other. He is getting ready to leave and he didn't want to talk to me about any of it. He never even kissed me.

What does that mean?

Before I start to hyperventilate, I grab my phone. I need to talk to someone. I text Katie. Sure, there are a bunch of details I would have to leave out, like blood drinking and morphing gargoyles and me killing Marcus's father, but I need my best friend right now.

Can you talk? I ask.

I'm with Trevor. SOS? Katie types back.

Katie would leave her boyfriend, drop everything if I sent her an SOS. Just like I would do for her. With my thumbs paused over my phone, I consider that maybe Katie's not the right person for this conversation. I would have to explain why Marcus is leaving. With how freaked out I am right now, maybe I would slip and reveal details I'm not supposed to. Then it hits me. Dylan. A guy's perspective is exactly what I need.

No. Let's talk tomorrow. I tell her.

I call Dylan.

"I thought you would be hanging out with Marcus," Dylan says.

It's strange that he doesn't say hello to me anymore on the phone.

"Yeah, I thought so, too," I say. "We were together but then I saw his bags packed in the living room. It seemed stupid that we were watching a movie when we should've been talking about this trip. He claims he may be leaving within a week. He doesn't say anything beyond that."

"Selima told me the same thing. She's waiting for a call from her mother," Dylan says. He doesn't sound angry or tense or any of the other normal Dylan moods as of late.

"I'm freaking out," I confess. "He won't open up to me."

"Hmmm..." Dylan says.

"That's insightful," I say sarcastically.

"I'm eating," he mumbles through a mouthful of food.

"What a surprise," I say.

"Marcus is a guy. You get that don't you?" Dylan asks. "We don't share our feelings much. We don't explore emotional stuff like girls do."

"So, what are you saying? He feels nothing?"

"I didn't say that." He chews something crunchy in my ear. I almost complain, but stop myself. A guy's perspective is truly what I need right now. "Other than his psycho dad and his sister and those doped fiends from the battle, Marcus has never been around other protectors. He's about to be and not just a couple, but an entire community of them. If I were him, I'd be excited but also freaking out."

I let that sink in. "Okay. Is he pushing me away?"

"My guess is Marcus is swimming in his own head right now and it's not pretty whatever's going on in there. You should cut the guy a lot of slack. Be there for him. Or give him space. Find out what he needs then give it to him."

"So, he still loves me?" If he makes fun of me tomorrow about this phone call, I will punch him or roast him.

"Head over heels."

I can tell by his tone that he means it.

I smile. "Sometimes you're pretty great, especially when you aren't in one of your moods."

Dylan laughs. "I just worked out for two hours. Now I'm eating through the entire kitchen. I think I'm devouring my feelings. Your dreamboat is not the only one leaving. My girlfriend is, too, and I'm kind of a mess."

He falls silent then I could swear I hear a low moan.

"You okay?" I ask.

"Mint chocolate chip ice cream with a crushed Heath bar on top. So good."

CHAPTER TEN

– Lucy Walker –

"Lucy!" Brandi tackles me as I enter the Douglas penthouse. At eight years old, she is still small enough that she doesn't knock me over. Brandi's dark blond hair tumbles down her back and smells of strawberries. I appraise the little girl's cotton candy pink tracksuit with gold trim. It screams expensive. Leave it to Mrs. Douglas to find designer play clothes in Brandi's favorite color. I will have to watch her like a hawk today to make sure she doesn't spill anything on it.

"Hey, Lucy," Ethan says, his manner more subdued than his sister's. The smile on his face is something I have worked hard to earn. Unlike his sister's preference for Disney princess-colored clothing, Ethan dresses like a mini adult. Today he wears a pale blue Polo shirt paired with navy cotton pants and a brown leather belt. His wardrobe looks clean, practical, and always presentable. Ridiculous words to describe an eleven-year-old boy.

My role as nanny to Dylan's younger brother and sister is the job of a lifetime. Well, sort of. The pay is fantastic, especially over the summer when I work full-time. Initially the money I made was going to pay for a used car, until my father surprised me with a brand-new one. Now I'm banking the money for college and periodic shopping trips with Katie. After fifteen years of wearing a wardrobe built mostly from Goodwill purchases—except for gifts from Gram and my uncles—I am determined to dress in nice clothes. The kind of clothes that allow me to fit in.

The biggest benefit of my job is the time I get to spend with Ethan and Brandi. I love them as if they are my own brother and sister. The downside of my job is interacting with their parents—mostly Mrs. Douglas, since Mr. Douglas is always at work.

Brandi pokes her brother in the arm. "We need to tell her," she whispers to Ethan, her face pulled into an uncharacteristic frown.

"Is something wrong?" I ask gently, unhappy about the sudden shift.

Brandi tugs on my hand until I kneel. "My mom needs to talk to you. She's very serious this morning," Brandi whispers, her breath warm against my skin. Her loose curls tickle my cheek.

I meet her frown with my own, to acknowledge the tone of her message. "Where is she?"

Ethan jabs his thumb behind him and whispers, "In the kitchen. Lucy...It's bad."

His words hit me like hard blows. Bad how? Jude is out of the picture, so he isn't threatening their family. Dylan told me he has been working hard to make nice with his stepmother in order to see his brother and sister on a regular basis without a battle. Did I screw something up last week?

I make my way through the humongous condo decorated with

expensive art on every wall and positioned just so on every surface. Normally Ethan and Brandi would tear off ahead of me. Not today. Instead they stay tucked behind me. That small change causes my stomach to tighten. As quickly as possible I sift through my day with the kids last Saturday. Could I have done something wrong? Or did I neglect to do something I was asked to do? Or is she upset that my full-time schedule is over and she has to be home more? Saturdays are all I can give her. I can't do anything about that. I'm in high school. That knowledge helps me steel myself for the confrontation.

"Good morning, Mrs. Douglas." I keep my voice light as I enter the kitchen.

With her cell phone in hand, Mrs. Douglas holds up a perfectly manicured finger to indicate I should stand mute and obedient for however long it takes her to finish reading a message. I remind myself how much I love the kids as I wait for Her Highness as she continues to read and type. Her white-blonde hair lies silky smooth from her scalp to her shoulders. She wears a loose-fitting pale beige silk blouse together with wide-legged white trousers. With all the white clothes in her wardrobe, I have no idea how she keeps them all stain-free. Maybe Mrs. Douglas has magical powers of her own.

Charlene, the family's cook and one of the nicest people on the planet, is busy at the stove stirring a pot of what smells like oatmeal. Normally she and I would greet each other with a warm hug. Today she casts a nervous glance over her shoulder at me.

"Good morning, Charlene."

"Good morning, Lucy. Breakfast is just about ready."

Charlene's tone is cooler than normal. Another bad sign. Mrs. Douglas has a habit of going after Charlene when she's stressed out.

Mrs. Douglas tucks her phone into her mammoth Hermes camel-colored handbag. The money she paid for the designer purse would have covered groceries, rent, and utilities for Momma and me for an entire year back in Lexington. I keep my expression blank.

"Lucy, I'm glad you are here." She takes a manila folder off of the counter. That's when I see a catalogue for Versace, the cover features young children wearing black and gold outfits. In bold letters, the bottom of the page reads: *Baroque.*

Quickly, I return my focus to Mrs. Douglas. Uh-oh. Those files typically mean one thing: major shifts to the kids' schedules.

"Please review this material. Mr. Douglas and I are taking the children for a visit to New York. We leave tomorrow. You will have next Saturday off."

"We leave tomorrow? For a whole week?" Ethan shrieks, his eyes huge.

The entire time I have worked for this family, this is the first time Ethan has raised his voice to his mother.

"We don't want to go," Brandi whines.

Mrs. Douglas glances at the delicate watch on her wrist before focusing on her daughter. Her face is void of expression; whether that's from a lack of emotion or due to the quarterly Botox injections I am not sure. "Your Barbies will be in New York. You can choose to be with them or not."

Brandi's eyes instantly fill with tears and her entire face crumples.

Ethan takes hold of Brandi's hand. "We heard you and Dad fighting again last night. Is it t...true? You want to move to New York? Are w...we looking for a new apartment during the visit?" He stumbles over his words under his mother's glare. "Our friends are here. My s...swim team is here. Dylan is here and so is Lucy." My throat closes as I watch Brandi's brave protector continue, his voice shaking and his cheeks flushed. "What about college? You know...Northwestern or University of Chicago."

College? Leave it to Ethan to have his entire future mapped out.

Mrs. Douglas smiles and I wince.

"Your opinions are welcome and encouraged. You know that, Ethan. You both need to trust that your father and I will make the best decisions for the family." Mrs. Douglas turns to me. "The information in the folder contains a list of what needs to be done before we leave. Please see to it that those items tasked for you to handle are taken care of before the end of your shift today."

Across the kitchen Charlene silently expresses her frustration by scrubbing the stove, her back bowed. It will shine like new by the time she's finished.

The entire time she speaks to me, Mrs. Douglas fiddles with the watch on her wrist. There is more to this. Unlike Charlene who will not speak up for fear of losing her job, I have to, especially after seeing Brandi's tears and Ethan's heroics. Will Mrs. Douglas fire me? Ethan turns away, his shoulders hunched. Is he fighting tears of his own? Why does she do this? Why does Mrs. Douglas always put herself first? That's a trait she and Momma have in common. While there was no one in Lexington to fight for me, I'm here to fight for Ethan and Brandi.

74

As Mrs. Douglas lugs her handbag from the counter, she delivers perfunctory kisses to the kids on the tops of their heads.

"Ethan and Brandi, why don't you sit at the table and get ready for breakfast. I'm going to walk your mom out," I suggest.

The kids are about to object, but Charlene ushers them to their chairs.

"Mrs. Douglas," I stop her once she reaches the front door, careful not to touch her delicate clothes. "May I ask what happened that you are considering a move?"

She holds her bag to her stomach as if to shield her body from me. Her narrowed eyes remind me of Cruella de Vil from the 101 Dalmatians movie I watched with the kids last weekend.

"Nothing is wrong at the moment, Lucy. Unless you consider the fact that my husband almost lost his eldest child because of your father. That alone caused Mr. Douglas to resume a sleeping pill habit he had gotten over years ago. Then your father proceeded to threaten the lives of my children. I know you are nothing like Jude Morgan"—she cringes as she says his name—"in fact your presence around Ethan and Brandi has been quite positive for them and for us." She takes a deep breath. "Mr. Douglas and I feel this is an opportune time for us to explore other cities, while your father is overseas."

"But Jude has no issues with Mr. Douglas. That's all in the past," I say, a pleading edge to my voice. Dylan can't lose Ethan and Brandi. Neither can I.

The icy smile returns. "For how long? The reality is that your father does business with every large company in Chicago. Most of the small ones, too. If at any point my husband falls out of favor with Jude, what then? I don't believe my children will be harmed. I have you to thank for that—and trust me, I am grateful. What happens if suddenly no one wants to invest with my husband? What happens if anyone of importance stops inviting us to their events or we are shunned from the club? My reputation is valuable and must be protected."

"You've got it all wrong. Jude isn't a member of high society. None of that matters to him," I protest. How did she come to such a wild conclusion?

With a tilt of her head and a flair of her nostrils, possibly the only part of her face that moves, Mrs. Douglas says, "You are overstepping, Lucy. This is a family matter."

Her acidic tone forces me to back down.

Mrs. Douglas closes the door behind her. It's impossible to move. How can I return to the kitchen where Brandi and Ethan sit? The kids I have grown to love are being forced to move because of Mrs. Douglas's fear of my father? Jude will never go after the Douglas family. He promised me. Now Mrs. Douglas worries Chicago's high society will turn its back on her at some point in the future? How can I make her see that she's wrong?

Can I dispute anything she says about Jude and his favors? I know how it works with my father. Every gift, every favor, has strings attached to it. It didn't occur to me that his favors were doled out to so many people. I was only aware of those he granted to me. If his reach extends to all of Chicago, what makes Mrs. Douglas think Jude—with his international conglomerate—can't touch her and Mr. Douglas in New York?

Charlene pokes her head around the corner. "The kids are

asking for you." When she sees I am alone, her expression softens. "Maybe Mr. Douglas will hate New York."

There is no way for me to fake a smile, not even for Charlene. "You and I both know that won't matter. Mrs. Douglas will get her way."

The rest of the day is spent going through the motions. Ethan is dropped off at his swim competition. It is the first time I don't stay to cheer him on through his events, but I have to tend to Mrs. Douglas's list. Back at the condo, Brandi and I pack her suitcase. I sort through Ethan's clothes while Brandi meets with her French tutor in the dining room. I notify the building of the dates the family will be away and arrange to have mail and any deliveries held for the week. I work my way through the long list of phone calls to be made on behalf of Mrs. Douglas.

Once the suitcases are lined up by the front door, Brandi starts on her homework in the playroom. This is the one area of the house where I feel comfortable. The thick gray carpet is exceptionally soft. The artwork that hangs on the walls in this room is rich with colors of red, orange, blue, and yellow and inexpensive according to Dylan. There is also a large map covering most of one wall. The kids put a Post-It note on Tennessee with my name written in pink crayon. The large gray sectional looks more like salt and pepper with the tiny flecks of gray, white, and black. The low black table on the far wall is perfect for jigsaw puzzle projects. Outside of the kitchen, this is the only room where we are allowed to eat snacks. Even Dylan will shed his tension once he's on the couch and Ethan and Brandi pile on top of him for movie time snuggle fests.

That's when it hits me. Does Dylan know about this trip? The potential move? I can't see Mrs. Douglas calling to notify him. She doesn't like him. I suspect Mr. Douglas is too chicken to confront his son with this news. Did Ethan contact his brother directly now that he has a cell phone?

"I need to make another call," I tell Brandi. "Why don't you start on your math problems and I will be back in a few minutes."

From the privacy of the living room, standing a safe distance from anything fragile and valuable—basically everything in the room—I slide my cell from my pocket and punch speed dial.

"Need more advice about your dreamboat?" Dylan teases. "This better be important. I am getting ready to pick up Selima. We're going to race Go Karts."

Maybe now isn't the right time to tell Dylan, especially since he's in a good mood and about to meet Selima. Then again Ethan and Brandi are leaving tomorrow morning.

I pause momentarily, resenting Mr. Douglas. I really had thought that after Dylan's illness that his father was committed to making more of an effort with him.

"It is important, but won't take long," I say stiffly.

Dylan pauses. "You're using that tone. The one I don't like. Did Ethan and Brandi tell you about my father and his wife's fights about New York?"

I sigh in relief. "You know about the trip. Good. I thought you were going to blow up at me."

Dylan is silent for a beat. "A trip has been planned?" His voice fills with excitement which confuses me. "When is it? Are you going to watch the rug rats while the witch and my father are

78

away? Maybe I'll bring Selima over so they can meet her. We'll plan a pizza night."

The nervousness returns. "No, Dylan. They're leaving tomorrow for a week. Ethan and Brandi are going with them. You get that Alana wants to move, don't you?"

"She's serious? This is insane. I was hoping she and my dad would fight about it and the subject would die," Dylan snaps.

"It hasn't died," I say. "Based on what she said to me this morning, she wants this and she's determined."

Dylan falls silent for a tense moment while I hold my breath. "Gotta go. I need to call my dad," he says before disconnecting.

I press one hand to my forehead and close my eyes. This is going to be bad.

CHAPTER ELEVEN

– Lucy Walker –

Any attempt to sleep is a lost cause. Every time I finally doze off, I face Marcus who tells me he's never coming back. He's with his own kind—others who love to fly. The images change and Dylan and I stand side by side at the airport and watch Ethan and Brandi, both stiff and dressed in matching gold and black Baroque clothing as they board a plane with their parents. The dream changes again. I am no longer at an airport. There is no Marcus. No Dylan.

I am in a cave of sorts. The lighting is dim. I shriek in alarm and disgust as something thick and wet oozes between my bare toes. I realize that I am ankle-deep in liquid, a consistency like one of the brownish-green potions Persephone makes in a pot on her stove. While her concoctions often smell like rotting grass and sulfur, this thick goo smells sweet. Chocolatey.

Animals that I cannot see squeak, caw, bark, and moo as they flap through the air or clumsily lumber around the echoey chamber. My eyes slowly adjust to the lighting and I see that these animals are built all wrong. The head of a black bird on the body of a calico cat dashes across the deep puddles, its legs merely grazing the surface. A German shepherd's torso lumbers along on thick tortoise legs. It raises its muzzle into the air and sniffs. The animal pauses, its ears twitching and its tail at attention. The dog's hyper alert eyes take me in and, after determining that I must be okay, the creature continues along. Its legs make a slurping sound as the dog turtle wades through the shallow muck.

Bunnies the color of glow-in-the-dark pink, orange, and turquoise fly overhead. Their floppy ears get in the way of their wings, which are large on one side of their body but half the size on the other. The lopsidedness causes them to fly in circles. A bunny—the turquoise one—has a large, dark spot on its bigger wing. The spot looks a lot like the one on Selima's wing. Suddenly, the spot winks at me. *An eye?*

"Do you know where you are?"

I whirl around, excited by the familiar voice.

"Jude!"

My father looks the same—dark eyes, black slicked-back hair, stern expression—except for his clothing. He wears a brown robe much like the one Lucifer wore the night of the battle at St. Aquinas. He catches me watching and grabs hold of the edges of the drab material, his lips curl with distaste.

"Hideous, isn't it? It is the required uniform for executive-level management. I am working to change that."

My eyes fill with tears.

Jude's expression softens and he holds out his arms.

I attempt to run to him. If his touch shocks me, I don't care.

For the very first time, I want him to hug me. As I try to lift my right leg, the brown gelatinous substance sucks at my limb. The goo has risen so that it nearly reaches my knees. It holds me in place.

"Jude?" I cry out in panic.

The goo surrounds Jude's legs, too. The entire chamber is filled with the stuff.

"Chocolate pudding," he says with distaste. "Lucifer can't get enough of it. That intel is a secret, however. I recommend you not share it with anyone."

The bunnies, in their strange, cockeyed manner of flight, skim the pudding. Surprisingly, they don't splatter any of the brown stuff onto their fluffy, technicolor coats.

"How are you?" Jude asks.

"I miss you. When will you come home?" I plead.

He smiles then, showing teeth. It is a rare sight. "What do you miss?"

"Our lunches together. Training, believe it or not. Movie nights. I'm learning to cook more elaborate dishes. Once you're home, I will make them for you."

"We will cook together," Jude says warmly. He surveys our surroundings with annoyance.

"When will that be?" I demand. In the past if I took a tone with Jude, there was a good chance he would punish me with one of his painful zaps. Not today.

"I am doing the best that I can. You need to know that." Jude struggles against the thick, brown pudding. More slurping sounds. It's no use and he finally stops trying to move.

On a man who runs a bazillion-dollar company who now runs the underworld while Lucifer is on vacation, the wilted look of defeat is not something I recognize.

"It's Lucifer," he says.

Panic floods my entire being. "Does he hurt you?"

Jude smiles and shakes his head. "No. He respects me, views me as a brother."

"Then why won't he let you go home?"

Something thrashes against my leg and I scream, flinching in a useless attempt to scoot away from whatever lurks beneath the pudding.

"Jude!" I screech.

The head of a kitten pokes out from the surface of the thick chocolaty slime, gills open and close against its throat. I reach down to pet the adorable, gooey critter.

"So cute," I murmur.

"Don't!" Jude orders. "They're a breed of Irish *Cattus piscis*. They prefer the taste of blood over anything else."

I jerk my hand back.

"Why won't Lucifer let you come home?" I flinch as the bizarre kitten fish continues to slap its body against my leg under the surface of the muck. The slimy, cute face breaks the surface again.

"Lucifer trusts only two people and I am the one here. I am bound to my obligations here until he returns."

"Bound in what way?" I ask, feeling desperate.

"Unable to leave."

"Who else does he trust?"

"His only living progeny," Jude says.

I freeze. After the battle at St. Aquinas, while Marcus was in his stone form healing from his severe injuries, Aiden and I sat beside him under the light of the moon. That was the night Aiden revealed to me that Lucifer is his grandfather.

"How is Aiden qualified to run things here?" I make a face as I splay my hands in a gesture to include our surroundings.

Jude ducks to avoid a cockeyed flying bunny, and a drop of pudding splatters on his hair. The glow-in-the-dark pink creature nearly slams into his head as it tries to fly in the opposite direction. "Damn *Cuniculus ales!*" Jude says, waving it away.

"Aiden's been working for me for years. Lucifer's instructions to me have been clear from the beginning. Groom his grandson to one day run JM Holdings, which would also equip him to run the underworld. He started in the mailroom and worked his way up to management. Once your grandmother and I convinced him to leave the destructive path he was on, he grew serious about his career track and progressed through the company at rapid speed."

My uncles and Persephone had mentioned Aiden and his reckless years. He had nearly blown up the three-flat performing magic in the attic. Demon magic within sacred witch space.

"You and Gram worked together to help Aiden?" I ask, surprised.

Jude nods.

"But I thought Gram wasn't much of a fan of yours," I say, confused.

"Your grandmother would never forgive me for my relationship with your mother, for hurting her. She was right to be angry with me."

It's the first time I've ever heard remorse in my father's voice.

"Your grandmother kept you hidden, but it wasn't me she protected you from. Have you figured that out yet?" Jude asks.

A psychedelic bunny lumbers over my shoulder and splatters a white pasty substance on my arm. A rainbow glimmers through the white substance. Bunny poop? Suppressing my disgust, I hold my arm away from my body so it won't get on my clothes. A quick peek at my slime-covered jeans and I realize it no longer matters. I drop my arm to my side while I consider Jude's question.

I cock my head. "She hid us—me—from Seamus McAllister?"

"The very same demon who has been trying to kill you since you arrived in Chicago."

Marcus had it all wrong. Persephone too.

"His determination to take you from me began the moment you were born," Jude says.

All the fear and suspicion when I first met Jude was based on misinformation. A wave of fury sweeps over me. "I was stuck in Lexington, away from Gram...away from you...because of Seamus?"

"Seamus was only one of my enemies," Jude says.

Garret was another.

"Vera told me how she, together with Persephone and Henry, could hide you so that Seamus would never find you. The trade-off was that I could not know your location, either."

The memories thud against me like angry punches. Life with Momma. The miserable trailer park. Nightly prayers that Gram would come to rescue me, allow me to live with her permanently, that my mysterious father would come for me—for us.

"I thought..." The words fall away as the sadness—as acute now as it had been then—washes over me.

"Aiden told me about your difficult life with your mother. I am very sorry for that. We all believed it was the best way—the only way—to keep you alive."

"Aiden told you?" I choke, swiping at tears, careful not to use the hand dripping with rainbow bunny poop.

Jude gives a tight nod before changing the subject. "Aiden trains you each week? Dylan too?"

"Yes," I say. I struggle to shed my sadness and give him a summary of our lessons since he's been gone. "Can I ask you something about Aiden?"

Jude nods.

"Why does he hate me?"

Jude considers my question. He glances at the large watch on his wrist, the one from Switzerland that he wears all the time back home, and frowns.

"I'm not ready to say goodbye," I nearly shriek.

Even in this strange place surrounded by bizarre animals, I am happy to see my father. He is safe and will come home eventually.

Jude shakes his head, dismissing my panic. "We have a few minutes." He studies me for a moment. "Look at it this way," he says. "How would you feel if you were Aiden, the child of warring parents, raised amidst constant violence, which resulted in the painful mutilation of your own body by a parent?"

I gasp. Aiden is a half-breed like me, except that he is half-protector, half-demon. While protectors and demons have been enemies forever, I assumed Aiden's parents rose above their differences to be together.

"They hated each other? Why'd they get together in the first place?" I've seen the web of scars on his back. Nausea swells in my stomach at the horror of a parent slicing off his or her child's wings.

Jude deliberates over my question. "Why do two people who are very different ever come together? Attraction? Passion? To defy their parents? To prove they can overcome what no two before them have overcome?"

He pauses before continuing. "Imagine years later when the two people Aiden trusted most—Vera and me—enlisted his assistance to serve as a secret agent to relay confidential information about a child we both loved dearly, one we went to great lengths to protect. Knowing what you do about Aiden's parents, how would you feel in his shoes about the child?"

My body slackens at the same time I close my eyes. I suspect Aiden would feel threatened. Jealous. I suddenly feel bad for Aiden.

"Finally," Jude continues, "along comes the child, now grown. Not only is she precious beyond measure to me and Vera, whom he had lost, but Aiden has to watch as the boy he had come to care for as a brother falls in love with the girl. Tell me, Lucy, do you understand Aiden better now?"

The weight of this visit and the sadness it brings is almost too much.

"His life has been awful," I choke.

"Aiden would likely torture you if he knew you had this knowledge. I suggest you keep it to yourself," Jude says.

I nod, appreciating the truth.

"You have a perception of hell, am I right?" Jude asks. "Whatever it is, you would be wrong. We have a long-established system of hierarchy here. Everyone has his and her role. Demons are task-oriented beings. We are driven."

"Really?" My skepticism comes through loud and clear. For emphasis, I gesture to the bizarre surroundings and the creatures around us.

"An illusion." He draws his eyebrows together, his look stern. "There are those here who strive to become the very best and with good reason. The rewards are plentiful. Many stay here and achieve greatness. Others have been hand-selected for vocations beyond this realm, placed in powerful positions with some of the world's largest companies: Oil. Electronics. Pharmaceuticals. Financial conglomerates."

My head swims as I try to take in the new direction of our conversation.

"There are other demons, those who have no skills for top-tier business. They tend to be bottom-feeders. You have met one of them. Max Vedder."

The image of the red-haired demon comes to mind. I nod.

"Max will prove useful to you. When you find yourself in need of a favor, information, or assistance, go to him. Tell him I expect his full cooperation. He will be paid for his services by Aiden. To be clear, you should utilize Max when needed, but do not trust him."

The ring of a telephone startles me. It's a sound that doesn't belong here among the pool of pudding and the strange animal hybrids.

Jude slides his cell from a discreet pocket in his robe.

"Yes," he says. His expression grows fierce. He listens intently, then simply replies. "Very well."

Jude returns the phone to his pocket.

"I have business to attend to, so it is time for you to go."

"No!" My loud protest bounces off the stone walls. The bunnies, startled, chirp and flap their wings faster in an attempt to get away. "Wait! What about Seamus McAllister? With you gone, he's going to come after me!"

"He's under orders not to touch you. Lucifer's mandate," Jude says.

"Will he abide by those orders?" I ask, a sliver of hope shining inside of me.

"When Lucifer gives an order, a demon must obey."

I don't want our time together to end. I stretch my arms to him.

"But!"

Before I can ask, Jude reaches a hand toward me. Despite the space separating us, the electrical shock hits me so hard my knees buckle. My father's version of a hug. As I collapse into the pool of chocolate goo, my world goes dark.

Chapter Twelve

– Lucy Walker –

"Slow down, Lucy. You're going to make yourself sick," Persephone warns.

It's Sunday morning and my uncles' kitchen is a hubbub of activity and full of mouthwatering smells. Bernard scrambles eggs while Sheldon flips pancakes. The two of them wear their newest matching aprons, candy apple red with the words Kiss the Cook printed across the front. Dylan, Persephone, Henry, and I sit at the table attacking a platter loaded with the most delicious pancakes I have ever tasted. Dylan and I compete to see who can eat more.

"I've got sixty pounds on you, shrimp. You don't stand a chance," Dylan taunts between mouthfuls. He sucks a drop of syrup off of his thumb.

His biceps taunt the short sleeves of his maroon St. Aquinas T-shirt featuring the school's Wildcat mascot. Have his muscles grown larger since last week? How does his wardrobe keep up with his constant growth spurts?

"By the time Aiden and Marcus arrive, there won't be any food left," Persephone says, genuine worry on her face as she spreads strawberry jam on her toast. She looks like she's ready for Halloween in a flowing brown and orange striped blouse paired with brown stretchy pants.

"It's their fault. They shouldn't be late," I say as I fork another pancake from the tall stack. Once I drop it on my plate, I smear butter on it and drown it in syrup. Dylan is six pancakes ahead of me.

"We have plenty of food," Sheldon reassures us from the stove, waving his spatula in the air.

"We have gathered you here this morning to share some news, but first we want to fatten you up," Bernard says with a chuckle.

"I hope they're not going to butcher us." Dylan laughs at me between mouthfuls.

"You have the most meat to offer, so they should take you first," I say with a grin.

"Nice talk for a vegetarian," Dylan volleys back.

I feel a pang of guilt watching my uncles' faces bead with sweat as they work over the hot stove. Even with the central air running full-time, it's warm in the kitchen with so many people. I hope it cools off soon.

"Are you sure you don't want some help?" I ask Sheldon and Bernard for the third time.

"No!" Sheldon and Bernard say in unison.

Persephone's pinched expression focuses on my plate as she dabs sweat from her hairline and lip. "Seriously, Lucy, slow down."

Dylan and I burst into laughter.

Persephone pokes Henry, who is reading the newspaper. His expression is serious. If Persephone is looking for him to back her up, she is mistaken. Whatever he is reading holds his attention.

"Another female high school student has been murdered," Henry murmurs. "That makes three in the Chicago area since June."

"I read about it before you got here. The police have no leads. It's horrible," Sheldon says. He delivers a fresh plate of scrambled eggs to the table, followed by a plate of sausages, which Dylan attacks.

Bernard turns from the stove, pointing his spatula at me, his expression stern. "You, Katie, and the rest of your girlfriends need to be careful. No going out alone at night. Always in groups. Make sure to carry your pepper spray."

Dylan kicks me under the table. "I'll watch over her. You have nothing to worry about." He flexes his arms for effect and I roll my eyes.

Bernard trips all over himself to express his gratitude to Dylan. As if I need Dylan's help. I can take care of myself.

"In all three cases, there is vomit near the body. A lot of it. They were poisoned," Henry says aloud.

Persephone swats his hand. "Not during breakfast!"

Just then the doorbell rings. Sheldon removes his apron. He tosses it onto the counter before making his way to the living room. Bernard tsk-tsks under his breath as he takes the apron and hangs it on the wall hook next to the sink. "That must be Aiden and Marcus."

Bernard glances at the clock. "Sheldon," he calls out, "we need to leave soon if we're going to make it on time." He turns to me, his voice dropping. "We have to make our announcement, then get out of here. I hate to leave such a mess."

"You two just cooked a feast. I will clean up. Dylan will help me," I say, which elicits a scowl from Dylan. Sheldon returns with Marcus and Aiden in tow. I am happily surprised to see Selima trailing behind them.

She rushes over and I stand up to receive her hug. "Hey, stranger," she says.

"I've missed you," I say, hugging her back.

"So, this is the girl we've heard so much about?" Bernard says, hands on his hips. "You are a beauty. Dylan talks about you every time we see him."

Dylan chokes mid-shovel, his face turning red. Selima and I both giggle.

"Please sit and eat," Sheldon orders Selima, Aiden, and Marcus.

Marcus's eyes meet mine. We haven't talked since Friday night. He worked late with Father Bill last night while I worked on a paper for English after watching Ethan and Brandi. It's rare for us to go a whole day without seeing or speaking to each other. I'm not sure where we stand just yet. Looking past him, I do a double take at Aiden's attire. Gone are the black shirt, pants, and shoes that he typically wears. The ninja warrior uniform has been replaced by dark gray dress pants, a crisp white dress shirt, and shiny black dress shoes. I'm guessing this is how he must dress for work, although today is Sunday.

"Sheldon and Bernard, spill the beans. What is this big news?" Persephone asks. She delivers her dishes to the sink. Marcus takes her vacated seat. "You need to get going soon. What time is your meeting for the Restoration Society's annual fundraiser?"

Bernard glances at the clock. "We have some time. The event is all set. We just have a few last-minute details to go over today."

Clutching his plate, Dylan gives up his seat to Selima so she can eat while he leans against the wall behind her. He nods at me. "Might as well give up. I'm eight pancakes ahead of you."

My stomach groans in response. There's no way I can eat anymore. "Fine. You win."

Dylan stabs the air with his fork in victory.

Henry slides the newspaper over to Aiden, taps an article below the fold. Henry works a lot of weekends at his law firm, but unlike Aiden he doesn't have to wear a suit. Today he wears a tangerine collared shirt and navy cotton pants.

"The third one," Aiden murmurs darkly after scanning the newspaper.

Henry nods grimly.

Sheldon clears his throat and we all look to him and Bernard.

"We invited you here because..." Bernard pauses, his lips pursed. Tears glisten in his eyes. "I have said it before and I will say it again. You are like family."

"Because you are important to us, we wanted to tell you in person..." Sheldon says. He nods to Bernard to finish.

"Sheldon and I are getting married. You are all invited to join us on our special day," Bernard says.

"My goodness! Congratulations," Persephone crows. She pushes away from the counter and with a slow limp, moves over to my uncles. The three of them laugh and hug.

Henry leaves the table to join them. He hugs Sheldon then turns to poke Bernard in the chest playfully. "You owe me lunch at Manny's."

Sheldon eyeballs Bernard. "What's this?"

Bernard wipes his eyes as he chuckles. "I thought you would put off the big day indefinitely. Henry disagreed. We bet on it."

The three of them burst out laughing. Persephone huffs and rolls her eyes over the bet. Henry hugs Bernard.

Manny's is a cafeteria-style deli that's been in Chicago for seventy-five years. It's the restaurant my uncles go to for their brisket and pastrami fixes. Their egg salad and special order meatless Reubens are pretty good, too.

"Lunch is on me. I will take the three of you," Sheldon says before returning his attention to the group. "The wedding will be in June. Once we finalize some details, we will send around an e-mail so you can save the date."

Bernard beams.

"I can't believe you bet against me," Sheldon says. He brushes a tear from beneath Bernard's eye before cupping his cheek.

"Don't you dare try to order the pastrami when we go, unless it's the turkey version. Your cholesterol is sky-high," Bernard chastises Sheldon.

Sheldon makes a face and we all laugh.

All of a sudden, I feel like I should say something to honor the occasion. I rise to my feet. Nervously, I raise my juice glass.

"I'd like to make a toast," I say. I swallow in an attempt to ease the tightness in my throat. My gaze is glued on the two men who have taken care of me since Momma died. "I have a lot to thank you for," I begin. The darn lump sticks in my throat again and it takes a moment before I can speak. My glass trembles in my hand. "You've given me a great life, a happy life. Thank you for that."

Sheldon and Bernard both beam.

"This is much different from the life I came from. Your devotion to family, to friends, to caring for each other...caring for *me*." My cheeks flush. I take in the room, looking at all the people who play such an important role in our lives. *I am lucky. We are all lucky.* It started with Gram. She brought many of these people together. My uncles keep bringing them together. With my attention fixed back on them, I continue. "You both understand the power of family. Not everybody does."

Next to Bernard, Persephone swipes a tissue beneath her nose.

"I would like to toast two of the most loving and amazing people I know. Congratulations. I wish you happiness and lots of great vacations together."

Henry holds up his mug, beaming. "Well said. I only wish Vera and Donna were here to celebrate with us."

Dylan glances at me in confusion. *Who's Donna?*

My mom, I respond mentally, surprised that I never told Dylan my mother's name.

He nods and gives me a tender smile.

"Cheers." Aiden raises his own coffee mug.

Everyone else thrusts their glasses and mugs into the air as they toast my uncles with a loud chorus of "Congratulations!" and "Cheers!" The room is suddenly a spirited swarm of activity and booming voices as everyone bumps into each other to get to my uncles.

Aiden is the first to return to the table, his mood somber all of a sudden. Was it the mention of Gram? The newspaper article about the deaths of local kids?

Marcus moves to my side. "Great speech," he says. He quickly kisses me on the cheek. "I'm happy for them."

Dylan hugs each of my uncles. Selima extends her hand. Bernard ignores it and embraces her.

"When we said everyone here is invited, that includes you, young lady," Bernard says as he releases her.

Selima presses a hand to her heart. "Thank you. I wouldn't miss it."

"Will there be dancing?" Dylan asks.

"Of course!" Sheldon says.

Dylan aims a sly glance at Selima. He bounces his eyebrows devilishly.

Marcus leans in close, his low chuckle against my ear causing a pleasant shiver to ripple through me. "Dylan's going to wind up serving as best man. Just watch."

"You could suck up and be a part of it, too," I tease. "Give Dylan some competition."

"He can have your uncles. All I want is you."

Marcus has put Friday night behind him. Recalling Dylan's advice, I decide that I will, too.

"You have me." I meet his gaze straight on.

Marcus slides his arm around my waist. A tingly sensation courses through me as he pulls me against his side.

Persephone cluck-clucks at Sheldon and Bernard. "Look at the clock. You two need to go."

"Did you receive my firm's sponsorship check for the event?" Henry asks.

Sheldon nods. "Yes, last week. Thank you for your generosity."

"There's going to be a fantastic silent auction," Bernard says to Henry. He turns to Persephone. "Did you get a dress yet?"

Persephone smiles broadly. "I have two picked out. Mirabelle insisted that I allow her to make the final decision when she gets to town. She claims I have no fashion sense."

Sheldon nods at Aiden, his eyebrows raised. "We received the check from JM Holdings—or was it JM Industries?"

"One is a subsidiary of the other," Aiden says simply. "The check would've been sent from JM Industries."

"Very generous contribution. Thank you," Sheldon says.

Jude's words from my dream come back to me.

Aiden's been working for me for years. My instructions have been clear from the beginning. Groom him.

It's time I cut Marcus's pseudo brother some slack.

"You're working all the time now with Jude traveling. He must place a lot of trust in you," Bernard says.

Aiden squirms and I realize for the first time that he is uncomfortable in the spotlight, even among friends. His gaze sweeps around the table, his brows scrunched together. "It is a lot of responsibility—and not just for me. Darcy, who some of you have met, works just as hard as I do. So do the roughly twelve

others on the management team. I look forward to Jude's return."
He directs his attention back to the newspaper, one hand
gripping his coffee cup, effectively ending the conversation.

"Darcy?" I whisper as Dylan and I exchange a look of shock.

The woman with long, sleek black hair who looks like she
belongs on the fashion runways of Paris or Milan? The woman
who shape-shifts into a black panther? That creature sought to
take Dylan out the night of the homecoming dance when Dylan
and I went to rescue my boyfriend from my father's house.

Marcus squeezes my hand. "Let it go," he says under his
breath. He fixes Dylan with a long look.

Dylan snags the last sausage link from the platter, smears it in
the syrup residue on Selima's plate, then eats the entire thing in
one bite. "That's the best breakfast I've had in a long time. Thank
you, Sheldon and Bernard." He rubs his stomach, a strained smile
on his face.

"Keep eating like that and I'm guessing your days as the
fastest quarterback in school history will be over," I say with
forced cheer, digesting the fact that Darcy has been in Chicago all
this time.

"You're kidding, right?" Dylan says. He inspects the food
selection on Selima's plate. "I'm burning through five thousand
calories a day like it's nothing."

"You would be good to remember the speed of my reflexes,
handsome fella," Selima says, shooing Dylan away from her
breakfast. Like Aiden, Selima does not wear her typical ninja
attire. She must have changed into her purple sleeveless sundress
at the last minute once she learned she would be meeting my

uncles. Of course, she could also have dressed up because she would be seeing Dylan.

Sheldon addresses the group. "Thank you all for coming and sharing our good news with us."

"Stay as long as you'd like," Bernard says. He hangs his apron next to Sheldon's on the wall hook. "We are off to our meeting."

Sheldon tugs my arm, gently pulling me away from Marcus. He wraps his arms around me and presses a kiss against my cheek.

"I love you, kiddo. Never forget that," he says. "Thank you for your speech."

CHAPTER THIRTEEN

– Lucy Walker –

Once Sheldon and Bernard leave, we all return to the table. Persephone brings fresh cups of tea for Henry and herself. She tops off Aiden's coffee before taking a seat. How can they drink hot beverages on a sweltering day like today?

"Now, Lucy, your dream about Jude. How much do you remember?" Henry asks.

When I woke this morning so exhausted, as if I had run a marathon, I worried that I was coming down with the flu. Once the details of my dream came flooding back to me, I texted Marcus, Dylan, Persephone, and Henry in a group chat.

"All of it, I think" I say. "Most of my dreams are faint. Choppy and fragmented. Not this one."

Henry and Persephone turn to Aiden.

"Could it have been a true visit?" Henry asks him.

Aiden nods thoughtfully. "Jude has visited me, too, in my dreams. However, for him to visit Lucy, a young supernatural, takes a tremendous amount of effort and power on his part. It had to be important."

"You're saying Jude actually communicated with Lucy through her dream?" Dylan asks, incredulously. He leans against the wall behind Selima, his arms crossed over his chest.

"Yes," Aiden says, the word turning into a yawn. He rubs his eyes before resting his forearms on the table. "Few demons have this ability. Then again it's Jude we're talking about."

"It was so weird," I say, focusing on the memory, trying to pull it forward in my mind. "A flood of chocolate pudding and bizarre animals. It was like a psychedelic version of Willy Wonka."

"The pudding fixation is top secret. Jude didn't tell you?" Aiden asks sharply.

I smack my hand over my mouth. Now that I think about it, Jude did tell me that. "Sorry," I say, my voice muffled behind my hand.

"Bizarre animals? What do you mean?" Persephone asks. She gathers dirty dishes from the table. She watches me from the sink as she rinses dishes and loads them into the dishwasher.

Marcus rests his hand on mine. "You should start at the beginning."

"Leave the dishes for now, Persephone. I can clean up once we're done talking," I say. It's bad enough my uncles made such an elaborate meal without my contribution. The least I can do is clean up.

"We will all help," Selima says to Persephone before turning her dark eyes to me. "I can't believe communication through a dream is possible."

Henry points to the newspaper and is about to comment, but Persephone hushes him. "One thing at a time," she murmurs.

So, I tell them about the distorted, trippy dream from

beginning to end. When I get to the part about Aiden being one of two people Lucifer trusts to run hell, I feel like I am dumping a humongous responsibility on his already overloaded shoulders. Aiden's tight nod tells me this isn't news to him. I leave out the part about Aiden's family and why he doesn't like me much. I conclude with the great news about Seamus.

Marcus closes his eyes briefly and releases a sigh of relief. "Best news I've heard in a long time."

"Once Jude made Lucifer aware of Seamus's actions, Lucifer instantly put an order of protection in place. Lucy is his namesake," Aiden says.

"Seamus will honor the order?" Dylan asks, his voice filled with suspicion. "That night on the roof at Jude's house. That nut case was seriously determined."

"Jude said Seamus would have no choice," I reply, not sure if I believe it myself. "He can't touch me."

"Seamus is bound?" Selima asks, wide-eyed, before taking another bite of scrambled eggs.

I nod.

Marcus focuses on Aiden, his eyes dark and serious. "Can we trust this?"

"If he goes against the order, Lucifer will destroy him," Aiden replies.

The statement lingers heavily in the air.

"If Seamus is bound by the order, would that prevent him from orchestrating action against Lucy without being the one to carry it out?" Dylan asks.

Dylan is thinking outside the box and I'm grateful.

Henry nods at Dylan. "That's a good question."

"Seamus knows the rules. If he goes after Lucy directly or through someone else, the consequences would be the same," Aiden says. He drains the last of his coffee cup.

Destroyed. Turned to ash. Lucifer more than anyone would know how to keep Seamus's ashes separated forever.

"I'd say that's motivation enough," Dylan says. He reaches over Selima and snags the last sausage link from her plate.

"Hey!" She swats his hand.

"It sat there for fifteen minutes. I counted. Fair game," Dylan says with a grin.

"Was there more to the dream?" Persephone asks.

I consider the information Jude shared, that it was Seamus who Gram had always tried to protect me from, not Jude, but I would rather fill them in on that later, privately.

"Lucifer put Jude in charge of running hell. It's not a punishment. Lucifer trusts and respects him. Unfortunately, my father has no idea how long it will be before he can come home," I say.

That last part sucks most of all.

"I can't say I'm devastated by his absence," Persephone says. She collects more dirty dishes from the table.

Is it that simple? Lucifer makes a demand and the demon who's been trying to kill me all this time suddenly backs down? If so, would this be considered a favor from Lucifer? Mrs. Douglas wasn't wrong when she mentioned people owing Jude. Any favor I ever asked of my father had strings. What will I owe Lucifer in exchange for my life? Will my father be required to run hell for eternity?

"Selima, have you made progress with clan members and the council, gathering information on Camille's behalf?" Henry asks.

Selima nods. "The members I've talked with are pretty divided. Some believe the plan to dope protectors and build an army was hatched by Garret and that Camille stood obediently, but quietly, by his side. Others feel they both were invested in the plan and that Camille had a strong voice in every decision," she says. "If they had some solid evidence, perhaps a vial of demon blood in her purse, it'd be a different conversation. But they don't have that." She turns to Dylan, who is eyeing the last pancake on the platter. "What did you tell me right before I left last time?"

Dylan shifts his focus to me for a moment. He keeps his expression neutral. "I was there that day. During the battle." He looks at Marcus for a moment. "Camille had authority over the morphed gargoyles. They respected her. Maybe even feared her."

Without looking at Marcus, I feel his whole demeanor deflate. He was barely conscious by the time his mother arrived that day. I filled him in later, when he was on the mend and demanded to know everything. His mother probably saved his life. Dylan is right, though. The atmosphere in that room changed the moment Camille arrived. She had command over them, until Garret's jealousy over Marcus got the best of him and he ordered Camille's death. I think that's when Selima realized her father had lost his mind.

"You spent a lot of time with your mother while she was here. Based on your conversations and observations, what do you think?" Persephone asks Marcus. Her voice is void of judgment.

"I didn't know about the soldiers or demon blood when she and

I spent time together," Marcus says. "When Selima and I go to see her, I have questions to ask her. I hope she'll tell us the truth."

"We need to talk to clan members who know how these investigations work. Perform our own due diligence so we are prepared before the Clan Tribunal questions you," Selima says to Marcus.

"Are you entitled to legal representation during the questioning?" Henry asks.

Selima shakes her head. "It doesn't work that way. He can have up to two witnesses present, but our system doesn't involve attorneys."

Marcus focuses on Henry and Persephone, a scowl on his face. "Garret came to Chicago to kill Jude. He admitted that to me. To us," he says, gesturing to me. "Beyond that, I didn't know anything that he and Camille were up to."

"Protectors don't lie," Persephone adds. "That has to make the whole Tribunal process efficient."

Protectors don't lie, but humans sure do, I consider gloomily, envisioning Camille's face.

"According to my mother, who has a friend on the council, in addition to their inquiries about Marcus's interactions with Camille and Garret since they came to Chicago, what happened at the battle, and if he witnessed any blood drinking, they are also very curious to meet Garret's son who has lived outside of the clan his entire life," Selima says.

Marcus turns to me. "I'm sorry I didn't tell you this on Friday night. I was taking it all in. This isn't the introduction to the clan that I wanted."

I nod and squeeze his hand. Marcus has to deal with a lot. I feel like a jerk for making Friday night all about my feelings. Now that I know Seamus isn't going to try to kill me, I can live without my protector. The sense of relief is massive.

Aiden stands. "I'm going to take a shower and change. Meet me at Jude's house in two hours," he says to Dylan and me. He taps the newspaper. "Could you continue to keep an eye on this?" he says to Henry.

Aiden looks to be nearly asleep on his feet. I can't believe he doesn't cancel training for today, especially after the good news Jude delivered to me in my dream. Aiden also looks crabby, so I keep my mouth shut.

"I have a friend at Chicago PD who is reviewing the files for me. I will call you if there is new information to share," Henry says to Aiden.

Aiden nods. "Two of these girls were found in the woods. There are a lot of similarities. These murders strike me as the work of a dark witch or a demon."

Everyone falls silent.

Breakfast suddenly feels like lead in my stomach. "Could it be Seamus?" I ask.

Aiden and Henry exchange a look.

"Could be," Aiden says.

"In my dream...Seamus has orders not to come after me. Jude said so. Why would he kill those other girls?"

"When was Lucifer's order issued?" Dylan asks.

"Aiden, can you find out?" Henry says.

Aiden nods grimly and leaves the kitchen.

Chapter Fourteen

– Ella Rosenthal –

Monday morning English class is a major snore. It's exactly four days since old man McAllister visited me. Maybe I overreacted a little to his magic. He didn't hurt me. Sure, that freezing thing was scary and I was freaked out about my car and arriving late for school. My dad put the fear of God in me over the last couple of years that if I screw up with tardiness or absences, my days at St. Aquinas with its expensive tuition are over and I will be thrown into public school. I've worked way too hard on my high school career to blow it now.

McAllister promised he would share his magic with me. What kind do I want? Surely, I have options. Or maybe if I do exactly what he wants me to do, he will share all of his powers with me. I could be his protégé. I could be Robin to his Batman. Then I could dole it out to whomever I want to. The recipients would have to earn it, though.

Now, I just need to snag a couple of items from Lucy to make it happen.

Seamus McAllister wants to know Lucy's class schedule. I

know for a fact that she still carries a printed copy around with her. She refers to it nervously all the time. Her hick high school must've been pretty small if she can't memorize the order of her classes and their room numbers here.

The second item has to include a photo of Lucy, one that she has touched multiple times. That's not an easy request. All the photos I've seen of Lucy are digital. Maybe I could get a couple printed then show them to her over lunch. Once she viewed them, I would ask for them back, claim I am making a scrapbook. Katie would love that idea. That's one of those cheesy things she and her mom do together after every school year. I would have to make sure that Katie—and the other girls—don't get all handsy with the photos. Did McAllister say no one else could touch the item? I don't remember. I don't want to screw this up, though. Then there's the third item, the other photo—

"Crap!" Lucy exclaims in a whisper from her seat in the front of the classroom. She's such a Goody Two-shoes with the language. She bends over to retrieve her school ID, which has clattered to the floor. The boy next to her bends to grab it at the same time. People always offer to help the pitiful Lucy Walker. She clips the hard plastic card to the waist of her black uniform pants.

An idea occurs to me just then and I tingle with excitement. I lean just a little to get a clear view of the white and maroon rectangle hanging from Lucy's hip and smile just a little. Our school ID cards include a photo. Lucy has touched it lots of times since the beginning of the school year. *It's perfect!* If it goes missing, Lucy will simply assume she dropped it. McAllister is going to be pleased and eager to hand over my reward.

For the next forty minutes while Mrs. Lyerly blathers on about the comparison between The Grapes of Wrath and Steinbeck's later novels, I've come up with a simple plan.

My backpack is zipped by the time the bell rings. I stroll over to Lucy who is swinging her pack over one shoulder.

"Hey, Lucy, can I ask a favor?" I say. The rest of the class rushes for the door, bumping and jostling their way out of the room to reach their second period class.

Lucy's hazel eyes widen at me, then narrow. "What's up?" she says. "This isn't about the séance is it?"

I plaster a pathetic look on my face. "What will it take to get you to join us? It really will be fun, I swear." I am begging Lucy Walker to hang out with me and the other girls. McAllister's powers had better be worth it.

"Tell you what, come up with another plan—shopping, skating, laser tag, the beach—then I'm in," Lucy says, her expression hopeful.

"I'm sticking with the séance," I say, playing it sweet but firm.

"Then I'll pass," Lucy says, turning away from me. She walks away too fast for me to snag her ID.

"Wait, Lucy. I want to talk to you about class. I'm a little lost right now. Any chance we could work on the assignment together?"

Lucy glances over her shoulder, tugging her pack higher onto her shoulder. Our passing period is short. "It's the beginning of the year. How can you be lost? Have you done any of the reading?"

I bristle. "Not all of us can be a brainiac like you."

She hesitates for a brief moment. "Sure, I'll help you, but can we talk about it later?" She takes a step toward the door.

I give her a big smile. "That would be great. Thanks," I say, hurrying toward the door.

Lucy and I collide as we exit the classroom door at the same time.

"Really Lucy? You're so klutzy!" I follow my admonishment with a playful laugh. Lucy turns beet-red. The girl embarrasses so easily. While Lucy races off to second period, I tuck her ID into the lower pocket of my pack. Next on the agenda is to get her class schedule. As I rush down the hall to second period, I wonder if the magic that the old man plans to share with me will work on social media.

Chapter Fifteen

– Lucy Walker –

"Jude won't do anything to them. Maybe New York has better shopping and country clubs and that's what this is all about," I rant to Marcus.

It's Tuesday night and Marcus sits on my basement floor combing through a bin of Gram and Uncle Zack's old records while I spill the contents of my backpack onto the couch. My boyfriend wants to supplement his music collection before he and Selima go wherever the protector clan is located. I remind him that Spotify has a huge selection of music, but this is Marcus's ritual. He enjoys looking at the old records, appraising the covers. "Works of art," he calls many of them.

"You realize this is out of your hands don't you?" Marcus asks. He pulls another album from the bin, flips it over and reads the song list. He adds it to the pile on the rug next to him. "You have other things to focus on."

"We're talking about Brandi and Ethan. You know how much I love them," I point out.

Marcus looks at me. Finally. "You love them. I get it. They love you, too. Their parents, as messed up as they are, will make the right decision in the end."

I stare at my boyfriend as if he just grew a third eye. "Right decision for who? Do you hear yourself?"

Marcus sighs as he climbs to his feet. He checks out the mess on the couch before pulling me to my feet. His hands on my arms have an immediate effect. My anger reduces to a low simmer. "You need to consider this from another angle. If they actually move, who will take care of those kids?"

"That's my point!" I say. "They're not even thinking about the kids!"

"No, what I'm saying," Marcus says soothingly, "is that the parents need you. What have Ethan and Brandi said to you about all their former nannies?"

I think back to when I first started watching them. While we played games, assembled puzzles, and colored together, the kids would open up and talk. They told me lots of things about their parents, their friends, their school, their parents' friends and *their* kids, and the former nannies. "There were lots of problems, mostly because Mrs. Douglas didn't stick to timelines. She broke promises and overworked them. Gita lasted the longest. A year, maybe."

"Do you honestly believe Mrs. Douglas will leave the sweet gig she has with you? She likes you and the others she employs." Marcus folds me into his arms. "Now isn't the time to freak out. Let her start to look for help in New York. Let her find a nanny, a cook, a chauffeur, music teachers, art teachers, a swim coach, and whatever else she does to keep those kids so busy she doesn't have to deal with them."

I press my face to his chest, wrapping my arms around his waist. "I hope you're right."

Marcus trails kisses along the top of my head. "I wouldn't rule Mr. Douglas out, either."

The sound of Marcus's heartbeat, together with his calming touch, lull me to the point I am nearly hypnotized. It takes a moment to register his words.

I pull back to look at his face. "What do you mean?"

Marcus grins. "He's a workaholic which conveniently allows him to avoid his wife as much as possible. I bet the idea of moving to New York without that great support system in place, where he may have to spend more time with Mrs. Douglas scares him to death."

I burst out laughing. "I bet you're right." The amusement fades almost immediately. "I hope Dylan figures into Mr. Douglas's decision, too."

Marcus rubs my arms. "We're not in Mr. Douglas's head. Maybe Dylan does figure into his thoughts."

"They've been gone for three days. I wonder how it's going," I say, mostly to myself.

Marcus raises my chin at the same time his lips descend on mine. I put thoughts of Dylan and his brother and sister away for now. Marcus is right, and I should focus on the things I can control. Like spending time with my boyfriend while we're still in the same city. My arms slide up and around Marcus, grabbing hold of his shoulders, massaging his muscles before I move on to his neck.

"Lucy and Marcus! Time to call it a night," Sheldon calls from the top of the stairs.

I pull away from Marcus, aiming an annoyed glare toward the stairs.

Marcus grins as he shakes his head. He grabs the stack of albums from the floor. "I'll record these over the next few days, then get them back to you."

I nod, feeling glum that our evening together is ending.

"You will be happy to know that I'm also tackling a stack of college applications. I have to get them submitted by the January deadline. Persephone is going to cast a horrible spell on me if I don't get them done. She made me promise to show them all to her by November first."

"Have fun writing all those essays." I run my hand along the length of his arm. "Why are you being so secretive about the schools you're applying to?"

"Secrecy has nothing to do with it." Marcus grimaces. "I have big fat envelopes from thirty schools piled on my kitchen counter. Imagine facing that every day."

"Thirty?" I ask, incredulous. "That sounds horrible."

"Aiden. He determined a list of ideal schools for me after asking me a bunch of questions then having one of his interns crunch my data. The applications started showing up in the mail," Marcus says, his expression full of disbelief and annoyance. "Just give me some time to read through them and figure out my top five—eight max—then I will fill you in."

He sounds tired and he hasn't even opened the first envelope yet. He stares past me, lost in thought. A flicker of worry or maybe fear crosses his face.

"College and having to deal with Camille's situation and not knowing when you have to leave," I say as I rub his back. "It's a lot. What can I do to help?"

Marcus blinks and the look disappears.

"Lucy? Marcus?" Sheldon calls. He pokes his head through the doorway, eyeballing the two of us at the bottom of the stairs.

"We're headed up," I announce loudly, frustrated by his interruption. I move around Marcus in a huff as I shove the mess on the couch back into my pack.

"What are you doing with all of that anyway?" Marcus asks. He chuckles at my little tantrum.

"My school ID is missing. Maybe it fell in my locker. *Hopefully.* I have until tomorrow before my loaner badge expires. I really don't want to spend fifteen dollars to buy a new one."

Given that Sheldon stays within eyesight as I walk Marcus to the door, our kiss is more of a peck. After I hug my uncles good night and wash up, I grab the feather I have tucked in the back of a drawer in my desk. Once I have it in hand, I sink onto my bed. The white feather belonged to Marcus. As I twirl it in my fingers, I consider the many sides of my protector boyfriend. He is analytical, thoughtful, intelligent, brooding, sometimes moody, and even angry. What about the look I saw on his face tonight? What is he worried about or afraid of? The investigation into Camille's actions? College? Does he worry about fitting in with other protectors? Leaving me? What can I do to help my boyfriend?

CHAPTER SIXTEEN

– Lucy Walker –

Katie joins me in the lunch line in the school cafeteria. Wednesdays are spaghetti day at the St. Aquinas Café. The smell of zesty red sauce hits me full on and I nearly drool. It reminds me of my father's cooking, although his dishes taste a lot better than those served at school. That says a lot because the lunches at St. Aquinas are so much better than the lunches at my old school. I glance over my shoulder as Katie stuffs a Ziploc bag of crackers into my backpack. The racket of several hundred voices talking and laughing forces Katie to yell at me.

"My mom bought a jumbo container of Goldfish crackers yesterday. Told me to share them with you," Katie says as we grab our lunch trays.

Fish. Gills. Cats who swim in pudding and like the taste of blood. *Super weird.* In the sea of students, I suddenly miss Jude. I turn to Katie and want to tell her about the visit from my father. How his expression, usually dialed toward stern, which used to scare me, was gentle in my dream. I want to tell her how, after a year of believing Jude was the baddie Gram hid me from, what a relief it is to know it was Seamus McAllister who was the problem. In my mind I can see the psychedelic animals so clearly. Katie would get a huge kick out of them. With a heavy heart, I know that I can't tell her any of it. She is my best friend and the inability to share my supernatural life with her makes me feel like a terrible friend.

I follow Katie to our table, feeling irritated and nearly overwhelmed by the noise in the lunchroom today. More than anything I want a small quiet place where Katie and I could go—Cloe and Suzy, too. It would be nice to talk without having to holler at each other. Ella eyeballs our overloaded plates and I brace myself for her commentary. She can't help but give Katie and me a hard time about how much we eat. As if being short, skinny, and boob-deficient is something I would actually choose. Maybe since she wants my help on our English assignment, she will give us a break today.

Katie and I take seats across the table from Ella and Caroline. The table next to ours has five junior boys playing Dungeons and Dragons with cards and dice. The game is pretty animated and we're only ten minutes into the period.

"Nerds," Ella declares, catching me checking out their game.

Caroline giggles.

As I survey the gaming at the neighboring table, I recognize several kids from my classes. "They're super-smart. If I were organizing a study group, I would invite all of them to join. I bet they could bring you up to speed in English in no time."

Suzy and Cloe arrive with their lunch trays, sitting next to Caroline and Katie.

Ella looks like she's about to say something but presses her lips together and stays silent.

"I hereby anoint you as Queen of the Dorks," Caroline says to me, making some fake royal gesture with her fork.

Ella bites back a laugh.

"Whatever," I mutter, rolling my eyes.

"I want to be Queen of the Dorks," Suzy complains. "Could Lucy and I be Co-Queens?" She told Katie, Cloe, and me over the summer that she was going to turn the tables on Ella and Caroline every time they made fun of someone. She was tired of their constant criticism of people they viewed as less than them.

"I am probably the most qualified to fill those shoes," Cloe says. She pulls her cell phone from her backpack and logs into whatever game she's playing.

Ella huffs with disgust. "You can all be queens together for all I care."

"Like the Three Musketeers," Suzy says with a self-satisfied smile. "But better."

Ella attacks her salad and refuses to look at any of us. I decide it's time to change the subject.

"Hey, did you find your ID?" Suzy asks. "Katie told me you lost it."

I shake my head. "Had to buy a new one."

"That sucks," Suzy says.

"Are you all ready for the séance this weekend?" Caroline asks. She grins excitedly.

Ella's gaze flits my way. "Too bad Katie can't convince her BFF to join us."

Katie loops her arm through mine. I wait for her to start in on me again.

"Think of how amazing it would be if you were able to connect with your mom or your grandmother," Katie had said last week, in another attempt to convince me to attend Ella's supernatural sleepover.

I had stared open-mouthed at Katie. "If a miracle occurred and I was able to make that kind of connection, what makes you think I would want to experience it—something so personal—in front of Ella and Caroline or anyone else?"

Today Katie faces Ella across the lunch table. "Lucy doesn't want to go. Let it drop."

Ella blinks at Katie. A look of surprise flutters across her face. The rest of the table falls silent.

"Make sure to bring a photo of someone you want to connect with," Ella says, finding her voice. She continues as if Katie hadn't spoken. "Don't forget it's a slumber party. Bring your pajamas and toothbrush." Ella smiles at me and I can tell it takes effort. "If you change your mind, I would love for you to come."

"Forget it," I say before twirling spaghetti onto my fork and shoving the golf ball-sized bite into my mouth. The lunch ladies were generous today and gave me extra pasta. I think they take pity on my puny size and want to fatten me up. I'm totally okay with that.

Katie turns to me. "You do believe in supernatural stuff, don't you?"

Suzy pokes her head around Katie waiting for my response.

After a long pause while I chew and swallow, I respond. "I think there's something to it."

"I would love to connect with my Uncle Don. I wish you were coming, Lucy," Suzy says with a smile, batting her ridiculously thick lashes at me, "but I won't pressure you at all."

"I was super close with my grandmother. I'm going to bring a photo of her," Katie says. She shoulder-bumps me. "I really do wish you were coming. Not to participate. It's just that, if she visits, I want you to be there so I can introduce you." She looks over at Ella with a frown. "My grandmother wasn't a big fan of your mom, so I'm not sure introducing you would be a good idea. Don't be upset, okay?"

"Whatever," Ella says. I could swear a flash of hurt crossed her face.

"I hope we connect with a movie star on the other side," Caroline chimes in. "Heath Ledger would be pretty cool."

"That would be a-mazing!" Suzy exclaims.

"You're all crazy," Cloe says. She arches an eyebrow and the corners of her mouth tug slightly, all without lifting her eyes from her phone.

"The evening will be epic. You're welcome," Ella says, a smile finally breaking through her cranky expression. "Hey, Lucy, while the rest of the girls work to convince you to join us, could I see your class schedule? I'm hoping we can form our own study group. I'm going to need help beyond English class."

"You should check with our neighbors. They could help you a lot more than I could," I tell her, nodding to the D&D players.

Ella ignores my comment as she holds her hand out expectantly.

I retrieve my schedule from my backpack. As I hand it to Ella, she grasps my fingers. I try to pull away but she holds tight. The hopeful look in her eyes startles and confuses me.

"You really should come on Saturday night. My boss gave us special thirty percent off friends and family coupons at the store. I plan to give each of you one at the party. Plus, I'm giving away one of my purses. You could use an upgrade."

I yank my hand free, my cheeks burning. "I don't need your charity."

"Don't be offended," Katie gushes. "Ella does this once a year. We all look forward to it." Katie turns to Ella. "Which purse are you giving away this time?"

Ella smiles regally as all eyes fix on her. "The black Michael Kors bag."

Caroline gasps. "But I love that bag!"

"I've given you, like, three bags. Don't be greedy," Ella says to her.

Katie slips her arm through mine again, tucking herself to my side. "For Ella to offer you a chance at one of her purses means a lot. I finally got one last year and I've known her forever."

Caroline and Ella freeze at the same moment. They both focus on something or someone behind Suzy, Katie, and me.

"Dylan Douglas is headed our way. I know for a fact he's not in our lunch period," Caroline says. She pushes her salad to the side and smooths her hair with both hands.

"You mean the Incredible Hulk," Ella purrs. The glint in her eyes and the slow smile remind me of a hungry shark.

I twist in my seat as Dylan arrives at our table. He plunks his lunch tray next to mine and sits. The chair creaks under his weight. Suddenly I am squished between his massive body and Katie.

"If anyone tries to bully me, I will call you," Katie says. Her eyes bug as she takes in his size.

Dylan and I tell people his growth spurts are due to all of his time in the gym training for football and the protein shakes he's always guzzling. He and I both suspect it's the demon blood coursing through his veins. Dylan looks like he's going to burst out of his white button-down shirt if he flexes his muscles. He will need new uniforms before the end of the month. Good thing his dad is rich.

"Slumming with the juniors?" I tease.

Dylan's expression tightens. He leans toward me, his voice low. "It took three messages before my dad finally called me back. He said he'll try to meet me for breakfast when they get back to town. When I asked him point blank if he and Alana are planning to move to New York he nearly bit my head off." Dylan grabs one of the sub sandwiches—the backup lunch option featured at the café—from his plate and devours half of it quickly. Across the table Cloe watches him, her lips parted as he finishes the sandwich. "That's a tactic of his, getting all pissed so that other people back down. I kept asking, though. He downgraded the seriousness of the move, which he does about everything orchestrated by my step-monster. The thing is, during the entire call he never said it *wasn't* going to happen."

The ferocity in his tone—even as he attempts to whisper— causes all the girls to stop eating and gawk at him.

I touch his arm. Through the fabric of his shirt, his skin feels hot. "Calm down. Your dad never said they were definitely moving. Nothing is certain—okay?"

"I can't stand her," Dylan snaps. He pounds his fist on the table. I jump.

Katie tugs on my arm, pulling me away from Dylan.

"Stop it, Dylan!" I hiss, shocked by his outburst.

"Nothing new about that, right?" Ella asks. "What did she do now?"

She acts unfazed by Dylan's anger. Meanwhile Katie and Suzy cast nervous glances at him. Cloe eats her potato chips while she watches Dylan and me over the top of her phone. With my demon powers combined with my witch powers, I could probably take Dylan. It's not something I want to do in the middle of the busy cafeteria.

"Before you totally freak out over a possible move," I say, remembering Marcus's words, "consider that Alana will first need to find a nanny she likes, a swim coach for Ethan, and piano and art teachers for Brandi. All that plus a new driver and a cook. And tutors. A lot has to come together before they can move."

Ella leans forward and fixes Dylan with a look that is equal parts flirty and sympathetic. "If you ever want to talk about it, I'm here for you, Dylan."

It seems like an appropriate time to bring up Dylan's girlfriend, to remind Ella that he's not available and to improve his mood.

"How's it going with Selima? Has she met your mom yet?" I ask.

Dylan's grumpy face softens just a little. "Not yet. They'll hit it off, though."

Dylan and Selima have grown close in a short period of time. Maybe the drama of the battle helped intensify their relationship early on. It's a relief to have Dylan's romantic attention diverted. The pressure he placed on me in the past to consider him over Marcus nearly forced me to end our friendship.

"Unbelievable! You have a killer following!" Suzy gushes.

I pull my attention from Dylan to see Katie, Suzy, Ella, and Caroline crowd over Cloe's phone.

Over Katie's shoulder I watch as Cloe shows off her YouTube channel on her cell.

Dylan leans over the table to get a look.

"You totally need to show me how you did that. I'm starting a blog about fashion and makeup," Ella says, impressed.

"*We* are doing that together," Caroline corrects her.

"Well, yeah. A joint blog," Ella clarifies.

I jump at the sound of Dylan's voice in my head.

Selima got a call from her mother last night. The investigation isn't going well.

"You make it look so easy, not that I know what all this gaming stuff is about," Suzy says as she and Katie watch the episode.

I pretend to watch, too. *Did Selima give you details?*

Katie giggles, says something about her challenges with technology.

Whoever was backing Garret in the past is a ghost. Camille is hostile, so she's not gaining much sympathy or support. Selima won't tell me how long she and Marcus will be gone once they

125

leave. That's really eating at me. She said it's impossible to gauge the progress of the inquiry. Now my dad is planning to leave and take my brother and sister with him. If Alana has her way, the move will be permanent. My life is turning to shit, Lucy. I can't...

What? I ask.

I can't hold it together much longer.

I turn away from Cloe's phone. Dylan's expression frightens me. The cords of his neck stand out. His hands curl into fists. All those years his dad focused on working and making money, Dylan rarely saw him. Worse still, Alana exerted her influence to keep Dylan away from his dad and his brother and sister.

What can I do to help him? There's nothing I can do about Selima. She and Marcus have to go help Camille. As far as his family, I had hoped Marcus's feedback would prove to Dylan how hard this will be for Alana to achieve. If only I had the magical calming influence of a protector, then I could truly help him.

If only my dad could develop a backbone and stand up to her. That would solve a lot, Dylan says.

I nod. At the same time, I wonder what's going wrong with Camille's investigation and what that means for Marcus.

CHAPTER SEVENTEEN

– Lucy Walker –

"I can't get together tonight," Marcus says breathlessly over the phone after school on Wednesday.

I shut my bedroom door in case my uncles get home early, moving my backpack off of my desk chair so I can sit down. The *Taking Your Spell Work to the Next Level* book sits open on top of *Herbs A-Z* beside my laptop. Using magic on Ella is something I am prepared to do if she performs some boneheaded, accidental magic on Saturday night. While I haven't agreed to attend Ella's reckless idea of a slumber party, and I *really* don't want to go, I can't escape the nagging feeling that I *should* go. What if Ella conjures someone or something dark? Was it responsible of me— the only real supernatural in the group—to stay at home while my friends were potentially exposed to danger? If the night turns out to be harmless, it will be a chance to hang out with Katie, Suzy, and Cloe. If I do decide to go, I better have a spell prepared just in case.

"I'm still at St. Pat's. *'These projects aren't going to finish themselves,'*" Marcus says, mimicking Father Bill, his employer.

Marcus's amused tone is laced with irritation. "He reminded me again about the letters of recommendation he will write for me for college."

"Sounds like blackmail," I say.

"That's what I told him." Marcus laughs.

"Will your project take all night?" I ask.

"Normally, Father Bill is an early-to-bed kind of guy, but with my upcoming trip, he's breaking all of his routines. I think he's trying to work me to death before I go."

"Bummer, I really wanted to see you tonight," I say.

"I know and I'm sorry, but when I'm done here I have to meet Selima. We're going to have a Zoom call with her mother. She has an update about Camille."

"Fill me in later?" I ask.

"I will, but I have to go. Father Bill and I are hauling lumber. It's heavy."

"Good luck with the job and your video call," I tell him.

"Thanks. Talk later," Marcus says before ending our call.

Tonight, Marcus will learn what's going wrong with his mother's investigation. If it's a problem on the side of the council, maybe that means they don't have enough evidence or information to keep Camille on house arrest. Will they end the investigation? Or is it the opposite? What if the council did find evidence against her? What happens then?

CHAPTER EIGHTEEN

– Dylan Douglas –

The guidance counselor's offices, like those of the rest of St. Aquina's administrative staff, are located in a part of the school where the waiting area is dimly lit, with overstuffed chairs, woven rugs, and oil paintings like you would see in some wealthy great-uncle's house. Or in my case, in my father's house. Classical music plays softly over some hidden sound system. I sink into one of the comfy chairs and stretch my legs. It's Thursday afternoon and I find it strange that I am the only one in the waiting room. The music lulls me into a pleasant state of mellow. If only they served beverages the whole "zen" theme would be complete. Not that I'm an expert. I just happen to be thirsty.

There is no receptionist for the counselors or the deans. They simply come out to retrieve you at your appointed time. Timeliness is valued here at St. Aquinas. I've always been curious about what happens when a student is sent to the dean for some rule violation. Do the teachers and admins text one another?

My phone vibrates. A text from Aiden. It's about time.

Explain what you mean by rage and scary strength.

129

"Ignoramus," I mutter.

Every time I get upset; it escalates. I break stuff. Don't want to break PEOPLE.

The soft crunch of heels on carpet—a sound normal human ears would never detect—alerts me to Mrs. O'Shaughnessy's approach. "Dylan?"

I give the middle-aged woman with Irish-red hair, pale skin, and green eyes the famous Dylan Douglas smile. Her return smile is tight and does not reach her eyes. I groan mentally.

"That's me."

"Won't you please follow me?"

We pass through a door and proceed down a hall covered with more of the same carpeting until we reach the third office on the right. Mrs. O'Shaughnessy's walls are covered with lush green landscapes. Ireland maybe? It's not at all what I expected. Where are the posters with inspirational quotes, professionally rendered college campuses, and the ROTC posters?

"Please take a seat," she says, gesturing to the chair across from her desk. Picture frames—six to be exact—featuring her dog against different backdrops are set in an arc between her phone and a tea cup.

"I wanted to talk with you about college options. My mom and I need to start scheduling campus visits and I'm hoping to get some advice from you," I say.

"I'm surprised you didn't come to see me last year, Dylan. Most seniors are further along in the process by now." Mrs. O'Shaughnessy taps on her computer keyboard with short stubby fingers. "What schools are you interested in?" She asks the question while her eyes study whatever information appears on her monitor.

Further along? *Yeah, well, there's been a lot going on over the past year.*

Once she pulls up my information and sees I have already taken the SAT and ACT, she will back off. I puff out my chest with pride. "Northwestern and UIC...but I may also want to add some New York schools," I say. If Alana gets her way and moves Ethan and Brandi, I will follow them after graduation.

"Hmmm..." she says, her brow tight in a frown.

That didn't sound encouraging. My chest deflates a bit.

Mrs. O'Shaughnessy clears her throat as she shifts in her seat. The loose flesh below her jaw jiggles with the movement. "Both are very good schools."

I flash the Dylan Douglas smile her way. Meanwhile my body tenses at her tone. Is she trying to insinuate something here? "They've been my top choices as far back as I can remember. My kid brother plans to follow in my footsteps."

"But..." she draws the word out.

"But what?" I work for a light easy tone, to keep a lid on the growl ready to tear free from my throat. The smug, knowing look on her face sends my hands grasping for the arms of my chair. I don't think I can stand one more piece of bad news.

The counselor eyeballs me over her computer. "Your grades last year, Dylan. You struggled a bit. I'm sure you recall that."

I grip the arms of my chair harder. In ten seconds I could tear the chair apart...destroy this entire office. *Tamp it down, Dylan.*

"I was hospitalized last year. Several of my instructors gave me a pass on missed assignments so long as I aced finals, which I did." The last three words are punctuated like a hammer on a nail.

"Can I take a look?" I ask, coming around to look at Mrs. O'Shaughnessy's computer screen. Her green eyes grow wide and she swiftly snaps her laptop shut.

"These are private school records," she sputters.

"They're *my* records," I counter.

"Dylan, please sit back in your chair."

I resist the urge to snatch her computer, which would happen so fast she wouldn't be able to stop me. Instead I sit down. I've gone all these years without a single demerit, a fact that astounds my friends and my mother. I can't blow my standing now.

Mrs. O'Shaughnessy clasps her hands together on her desk as she takes a deep breath, a practiced delivery. "Your football history here at St. Aquinas is impressive and for that, I thank you. Your grades are good—as are your ACT and SAT scores—but... The schools you are aiming for, I'm afraid they are out of your reach."

The simmering inside climbs up a notch.

"What are you talking about? My freshman and sophomore years are stellar. I've loaded up on AP classes every year. What's the issue?"

"All that time you were out last year, I am sorry for your health issues but it's a significant blemish on your record."

"I was in a coma," I remind her. Pain radiates in my head. Too much pressure.

She tilts her head toward the computer, her lips pursed. "Nevertheless. You should consider other schools. DePaul or

Loyola, perhaps, if your goal is to stay in Chicago. Focus on more realistic options."

"Again, I aced all of my exams last year. I worked my butt off to do that despite my time in a *coma*."

Mrs. Dog Lover-Student Hater peers at me over her stupid laptop. "I'm not sure we're seeing eye to eye here, Dylan. I think it's time you go to class." She smacks her lips together.

The low boil inside of me gathers momentum, turns into something hotter and dangerous. Mrs. O'Shaughnessy doesn't mention any New York schools and for her sake, we really should end the meeting.

I push from my chair so fast it slams into the wall and tips over. I don't bother apologizing. If she wants to give me a demerit, she can add it to my abysmal record.

An hour later I join Lucy and her friends at lunch feeling better. The pressure in my head is gone. My anger level is back in normal range. Forty minutes in the weight room is the best anger management strategy for me.

"A little hungry?" Lucy frowns at my tray, taking in the two hamburgers, a loaded baked potato, a double portion of French fries, two bottles of water, and a Coke. She ruffles my short, wet hair at the same time she meets my eyes. The grin on her face is forced. "You skipped Latin class to work out?"

"Uh-huh," I mutter through a mouthful of food.

Lucy jumps into my head. *What's wrong?*

Better question: what isn't wrong? I shoot back. *Is it illegal to kidnap someone's dog?*

Lucy gives me a quizzical look.

"It must be nice to have a bionic metabolism," Ella remarks from across the table.

"Yeah," I say as I shove more fries into my mouth.

Is it Alana? Ethan and Brandi? Selima? Lucy asks.

Four bites and one burger is annihilated. A quick glance at Ella as I dunk three fries into a mound of ketchup on my plate, I plunge into the same mental debate that plagues me every time I see her. She's smoking hot. She throws herself at me all the time. Yet, as I dig deep for the fantasies I used to have about her, they're gone. All I can think about is Selima.

"You had your appointment with the counselor!" Lucy says finally figuring out the cause of my foul mood. She elbows me. "Colleges? Fill me in."

"Mrs. O'Shaughnessy claims I'm not good enough to get into Northwestern or UIC, that I should set my sights on something more realistic," I tell her, impressed that my mood stays chill. The weight room should qualify as a chapel or a powerful sedative. For a moment I wonder what would happen if I didn't have that outlet.

"No!" Lucy says, her expression fierce. "Your teachers were all so great to you last year."

"That's crazy, Dylan," Katie chimes in from Lucy's other side.

"All your work studying for finals," Lucy adds, dropping her burger onto her plate. "They can't hold an illness against you."

I nod. "That's what I thought, but she wouldn't let me see my information. Students are allowed to see their own records, aren't they?"

Suzy snickers. "Maybe she wasn't looking at your records, but more photos of her beloved dog."

Lucy's cell phone buzzes on the table next to her tray. Her heartbeat quickens.

Marcus? I ask.

No. It's from Cloe. She can help you get access to your records. Can I give her your number so the two of you can talk?

Cloe catches me watching her. She returns my look with a curious one of her own. I nod at Lucy's cell phone. Her return nod is barely perceptible.

Yeah, sure.

"I have to put off a conversation with my mom about this until I figure out what's going on," I say to Lucy, loud enough for Cloe to hear.

"Just sweet-talk her like you do all the other girls," Caroline teases.

I laugh absently. "Yeah, if only that was possible."

After working my butt off on my grades and sports all through high school and the fact that my dad could afford the tuition, it never occurred to me there could be a problem getting into one of my colleges of choice. Whatever that weirdo counselor saw on my records has to be an error. With Cloe's help, I hope to figure out what it is.

CHAPTER NINETEEN

– Ella Rosenthal –

"I can't believe your dad lets you buy whatever food you want," Katie says as we unload bags onto the counter after school on Thursday. She helped me grocery shop for the séance and sleepover on Saturday night. "He's so generous."

"Yeah, he's awesome."

After all this time, Katie is still so dense, living in her little girl world where everything is milkshakes and lollipops. Her parents' divorce didn't make a dent in her naïve spirit.

A blast of cold air hits me as I open the freezer and shove two frozen pizzas, a tray of jalapeño poppers, and a pint of Ben & Jerry's caramel chocolate cheesecake ice cream inside. The ice cream is leverage. Junk food is the way to Katie's heart. Tonight I will do whatever it takes to get information. I am close to getting Seamus McAllister everything he asked for.

"Oh, my God! Thank you so much for buying these. Can I open them?" Katie asks, clutching the bag of Cool Ranch Doritos. Since Ms. Stevens limits junk food in their house, I made sure to get all of Katie's favorites.

"Go for it," I tell her. "Let's save the cheese popcorn and chips and salsa for Saturday night."

The poor girl is about to drool on her powder blue T-shirt, which I know for a fact she bought on the sale rack at American Eagle. As a gesture of good will, I crack open a can of Orange Crush and set it on the counter near her.

I release a heavy sigh and don what I hope is my most convincing look of concern. "We need to have a serious talk about Lucy. I'm worried about her."

Katie's smile is as bliss-filled as a puppy getting a belly scratch as she crunches on chips and downs Orange Crush. "Worried? Why?" she says, stuffing another Dorito into her mouth.

"It's about her dad," I say after a dramatic pause.

"What do you mean?" Katie asks. The smile disappears from her face as she takes in my grave expression. She brushes her hands off on a napkin and gives me her full attention.

"I'm going to share a secret with you, but you have to promise not to tell anyone."

Katie leans against the counter, suspicion flickering across her face.

"Lucy is in danger," I tell her, my voice grave.

Katie narrows her eyes at me. "From who?"

I crack open a Diet Coke and propel her to the slate-topped kitchen table. Katie grabs the chips and her soda from the counter and takes them with her.

"Tell me everything," Katie says. She points a finger at me. "If this is a stupid trick to somehow hurt Lucy, I *will* get you back. I'll make sure Dylan knows about it, too."

That makes me pause. Dylan? My plan with all of this is to get rid of Lucy and hopefully the goth girl so I can have Dylan to myself—and to load up on magical powers. I shake off thoughts of Dylan for now. I have orders from McAllister.

"I met a man recently, an old friend of Lucy's family. He was close with her grandmother," I tell her.

"Lucy's Gram? Vera?" Katie asks. She begins eating the chips again.

I nod as I continue. "He told me about a secret history in their family. While he didn't tell me much, he did say that part of it involved the death of Lucy's uncle years ago and that Lucy and her mom had to hide from Lucy's dad all the way in Tennessee." I let the revelation hover in the air between us.

Katie becomes more engrossed in her Doritos than a starving kid in those ads on TV.

I pull the bag of chips away from her. "I'm guessing you know something about this."

"Um, no," Katie says, unable to meet my gaze. "Talking with you about Lucy...it doesn't feel right."

I grab hold of her wrist before she can reach back into the crinkly bag again. *Hello future fatty!* "This man I met, he told me that Lucy's dad is dangerous, that he intends to hurt her."

Katie's eyes bug out of her head. "Mr. Morgan? That doesn't make sense. Lucy hasn't said anything about him being scary or mean or anything. They spend a lot of time together. Well, before he left the country." Katie quirks her mouth as she thinks about what I said.

When I first met with Seamus McAllister, he filled me in on

Jude Morgan, that he's a super bad guy. He said that Lucy was following in her dad's footsteps. So long as I do my part, McAllister will handle Lucy and her dad. All I want is to have Dylan and my friends focus on me again and not *her*, for everything to return to the way they had been. Plus, once I launch my beauty blog, I also want a million followers. Magic will help me achieve that goal.

"I don't know, Ella. This all sounds way too weird." She yanks her wrist free from my grasp and pushes away from the table. "Listen, I helped you shop for the party. Can you take me home now?"

I put a hand out to stop her. It's going to be harder than I thought to get Katie on board. Her protectiveness of Lucy rattles me. "Lucy is your friend—not mine. We both know I don't like her much, but if her dad is going to hurt her, don't we have to do something about it?"

Katie wipes her hands on the napkin again. She tucks her legs beneath her. "I'm listening."

"Lucy's dad is not the great guy he pretends to be. I thought *you* of all people would want to know that," I tell her. "If Lucy is your best friend and you want to help her, we need to have an honest conversation, be transparent with each other. That way we can protect her together. If you think you can protect her by yourself—fine—I will back off and keep my mouth shut. All I can say is that if Caroline was in this situation, I would want help confronting someone as horrible as Lucy's dad. I wouldn't be able to handle it by myself. I definitely wouldn't stand by and do *nothing*."

"How can we help her?" Katie asks, cautiously.

She's a little afraid. That's good.

"This man—the family friend—he was in town. He came to Chicago because he wants to help Lucy but he hasn't been able to talk with her. He promised Lucy's grandmother on her deathbed that he would look after Lucy." I reach out to touch Katie's knee. "He wants to help."

Katie cocks her head as she studies me. "This doesn't make sense. Why did the guy—Lucy's Gram's friend—talk to *you*? You don't like Lucy. Never have."

Damn. That's a great question.

"Because," I say, my mind racing. "I ran into him outside of school. He was looking for you. He knows you are her friend and neighbor and he wanted to talk to you. You and Lucy were already gone. So, instead he got me."

Pleased with my dramatic flair and my knack for thinking fast, I suppress a smile and instead do my best to look somber.

"What does this guy want to know?" Katie asks.

"Tell me about Lucy's dad. You said he's traveling?"

Katie doesn't look totally convinced, but I can see it won't take much more. Slowly, she nods. "He's going to be gone for a while. Lucy goes to her dad's house every weekend. She gets the mail, waters his indoor plants, makes sure the landscapers are doing what they're supposed to. Stuff like that."

It would be so easy to blow Katie's trust. I have to play this carefully, take my time and pretend to consider the information she just laid on me.

"Doesn't that strike you as strange? Her dad lives in Lake Forest. Daddy Warbucks could hire a service to water his plants

140

and get the mail." As the information sinks in for Katie, her expression darkens. "What's the real reason Lucy's trekking all that way every weekend?"

Maybe Lucy and her boyfriend hook up at her dad's house. That's what I would do with a specimen like Marcus Turner. The old magician mentioned Lucy's trips to her dad's house. He wouldn't care about teenage hormones. There must be something more to it. Or maybe he plans to confront Lucy at her dad's house.

"What if something else is going on?" I say.

Katie absently rubs her fingernail along her can of soda, scratching at the big, fat "O" in the word Orange. She chews on her bottom lip.

"I might know what's going on," she says after an annoyingly long pause. "At least part of it."

It takes great effort on my part not to jump out of my chair and shake the information out of her. I'm guessing her feelings are hurt. It looks like Lucy is keeping secrets from Katie.

"What do you mean?" I ask with genuine curiosity.

Katie focuses on me. Her big troubled eyes search mine. "You have to promise me that you won't tell anyone what I'm about to tell you."

With dramatic flair, I cross my heart with my index finger. It doesn't matter that she's mad at Lucy, she still wants to protect her BFF's secrets. That's loyalty.

"I'm not joking, Ella. This is big," she says, urgently.

"When are you going to get it through your thick head? We have to stick together, help each other. You and I have known each other since we were babies. You can trust me," I say.

"Okay," Katie says, resolved. She's slow to get the words out. I consider punching her on the leg to help her along, but she finally gets her thoughts together. "About a week ago, Lucy and Marcus spent a bunch of time on the roof at her place. They came down without using the stairs and he tucked her into her bedroom window around midnight."

I blink several times waiting for the punch line. "So what?"

"No stairs, Ella. Three stories plus an attic." Katie looks at me like I'm dense. "Marcus *flew* off the roof, carrying Lucy."

I cock my head, a tingly sensation running down my body. "He flew?"

"Marcus has wings," she says.

"Wings?" I draw the word out. My face burns hot as I digest this shocking news.

Katie merely blinks and nods. Clearly, she has had time to adjust to this shock.

A dark magician and a guy with wings. What the hell is going on in Chicago? All this time I had been eager for the scoop on Lucy, it never occurred to me that I would find out Marcus is some kind of birdman.

"How is that possible?" I say, more to myself.

Katie sits motionless in her chair. She doesn't respond.

"Do you think he's dangerous? Have you talked to Lucy about it?" I ask, reeling from Katie's revelation. Marcus is one of those guys who is the perfect mix of gorgeous and aloof. He plays guitar which bolsters his sex appeal in a big way. While he doesn't come from money, that never seemed to bother him. Lucy is dating a freak, her father is bad news, and, according to McAllister, she is following in Mr. Morgan's footsteps.

Katie chews her bottom lip again. "I want to talk to her, but I don't know how to bring it up. What I keep wondering is why hasn't *she* told *me*? Is she afraid I won't be able to handle it? Sure, it's super weird, but I'm her best friend. We're supposed to tell each other everything."

Right then and there I make a decision.

"If you truly consider yourself to be Lucy's best friend, we need to follow her to Jude's house this weekend. It's possible she's being influenced by others and is in danger. Maybe her father didn't really leave the country. Or maybe it's someone else."

"But who? Not Marcus..."

"How do we know she's safe with Marcus? He has wings. That's not normal, Katie. Who knows what kind of power he has over her?"

Katie scowls at me. "Marcus would never hurt her, even being different. He's crazy about her and he's always been nice to me."

"Of course, he's nice. Villains are always nice until they drop the big boom on everyone."

Katie sucks on her bottom lip, mulls it over. Finally, she nods. "Maybe you're right. Maybe we should go check things out."

"It's the right thing to do, especially since you are her *best* friend." I lay it on thick. "Keep this just between us, okay? Also, you should keep trying to convince Lucy to come to the séance. We have to stay close to her in order to help her." I touch Katie's arm and she nods solemnly. I take another drink from my Diet Coke. "Ready for some ice cream?"

"Maybe I was wrong about you," Katie says, rubbing my back as she passes by me to grab the Ben and Jerry's out of the freezer. "Maybe you do have a heart."

I cringe at Katie's touch. If she smeared any Dorito grime on my blouse, I'll make her pay the dry-cleaning bill.

CHAPTER TWENTY

– Dylan Douglas –

It's early Friday morning and scorching hot by the time practice starts. So much for my hope that the temperature would cool off in time for tonight's game. The players are padded up and guzzling Gatorade as they sweat through their practice gear.

"Elba, Stemple, Lopez, Douglas. Wait—where's Douglas?" Coach Skillman's face turns red with effort as he barks, his voice hoarse from a career of yelling his way into five straight championship wins for St. Aquinas.

My head throbs in time to my heartbeat, a phenomenon that began only recently. I've grown used to both the pain and the sensation. Deep breathing and de-escalating self-talk. That's what Aiden suggested when this comes on. Keep my inner psycho in check. That's hard. A brief scan of the field and I understand I could take out every person visible with my bare hands in thirty minutes, probably less. The fact that I know that scares me.

"Where the hell is Douglas?" Coach Skillman yells.

Coach would be the easiest. He can't outrun me. I could snap his neck in five seconds. *Jesus, where do thoughts like that come from?*

Several players frown in my direction. Coach calls my name again.

Slow, deep breaths.

"Over here, Coach," I say, grabbing my helmet from the ground.

"We don't have all day. Just because you won MVP doesn't make you the Prom Queen. Get your ass in gear," Coach growls.

You should really watch your mouth, Coach, I want to warn him.

I trot over to Nick and Chad as they line up behind the sled on the field. The throbbing in my head continues. My heartbeat's right there, too. It's a freaking symphony. *Just need to get this over with.*

Coach blows his whistle and Nick rushes toward the sled, his pads making a *chlatter-thunk* sound upon impact with the metal contraption. He grunts as he thrusts the sled down the field. He repeats the move to bring the sled back, then jumps out of the way as Chad takes position. *Chlatter-thunk!*

Chad returns the sled. Coach checks his stopwatch.

I don't need a stopwatch to know that Chad was nine seconds short of Nick's time.

"Don't stand out. Temper your anger, your strength. Whatever you do, do not draw attention to yourself," Aiden said during training last weekend and the weekend before. Nag, nag, nag, like my stepmother every time she lectures me on how to be a better son and brother.

This power-morphing thing—or whatever it is that Jude's doing to juice up my power—is kind of cool on the field, but I worry...*What if I lose control?*

Chad and Nick stand off to the side, behind Coach. It can be difficult to read a player's expression when he's wearing his helmet, but I zoom in on my boys and can see the challenge posed on their faces.

Temper your anger, your strength.

Jude always said I didn't push myself as hard as I should.

Do not draw attention to yourself, Aiden had ordered.

"Any day now, Princess," Coach says, his stopwatch in hand.

A chorus of chuckles breaks out.

Is it possible to beat every guy's time enough to remind them who dominates the team without drawing too much attention? Would I be accused of taking performance-enhancing drugs? That would get me kicked off the team. Worse still, if my blood gets tested, what would the doctors find? Jude is gone. Marcus will be soon, too. It'll just me watching out for Lucy. I can't risk getting locked up somewhere, probed by a team in white coats.

I lower my body and, holding back as much as my ego will allow, collide with the metal sled. *Chlatter-thunk!*

The sound excites me. Adrenaline rushes through my veins. My worry fades.

I reach the other side twenty seconds faster than any other player.

Tamp it down, Dylan. Your strength, your speed, or others will notice.

I force myself to step away from the sled, bend at the knees to appear winded, and cough a couple of times. I push the sled back down the field holding back *a lot*. The exertion feels like nothing more than a walk down the halls at school. In the end I am fifteen seconds ahead of Nick.

Coach smacks me on the back. "Great job, Douglas. I can see you've been working on your conditioning." He turns to the rest of the players. "Maybe the rest of you could step up your efforts. Show me you're invested."

After a quick shower, declining Chad and Nick's invitations to grab a burger, I head out to my car. As I plug my phone into the power adapter so I can sync to my car stereo, my speakers blast static.

I flinch from the noise and rush to turn the volume down. Suddenly I hear a voice through the static.

"Dylan!"

"What the hell?" I gasp. I release the knob as if burned.

Spooked, I whip around to check the backseat. No one there. Was it in my head? A result of too much adrenaline these last couple of weeks?

"Dylan!"

I'm sure this time. It's coming through the speakers. In an instant, I flick the power button on the door to roll up my windows.

"Who's there?" I ask, feeling totally stupid. The prickle of goose bumps spreads like wildfire along my arms.

I toss a wave at several players as they pass my car. To anyone walking by, I hope I look like I'm on a hands-free call.

"It's Jude. Can you hear me?" his voice demands through the white noise.

No way. This is one hell of a long-distance call. Pun intended.

"You there?" Jude yells.

"Yeah, I'm here," I yell back, flinching from the ear-blistering static. "How are you able to call me through my car radio?"

"Listen up. I've got a lot to tell you and I can't maintain this connection for long. Don't disappoint me, Dylan. I can kill you from here."

CHAPTER TWENTY-ONE

– Lucy Walker –

"What's so urgent that we had to meet now? If you would have waited until later, Marcus could've joined us." I say to Dylan as he blasts past Aiden into Persephone's apartment.

My boyfriend's brother walks past me with a tight nod of greeting as he stands near the window.

"Dylan. Aiden," Henry says, perched on the arm of Persephone's couch. "You said it was urgent. I came straight from work."

"It couldn't wait," Dylan says. "I have a game tonight, so this won't take long."

Persephone sits in the middle of the couch, her brows knit into a frown.

"You know the static coming through your car radio that you've been complaining about for the past couple of weeks?" Dylan asks me.

I shrug, not sure why my malfunctioning stereo is relevant. "Marcus hasn't been able to fix it."

He levels his gaze at me. "I have that same static problem in my car all of a sudden. It's not a coincidence."

An eerie feeling causes me to shudder. Dylan wouldn't bring all of us here just to talk about defective stereos.

"What's going on?" I ask.

"It's Jude. He contacted me today through my *radio*," Dylan says. He shakes his head in amazement.

Henry pushes off of the arm of the couch. "Through your car stereo? From another dimension?"

Dylan nods. "Today it was specifically to warn us."

"About what?" I ask.

"Seamus. Who else?" Dylan says, grimly. He turns to Persephone. "Do you still have that old boombox?"

Persephone nods. "Of course. I'll get it."

She pushes off of the couch. I cringe as she limps across the room.

Henry shakes his head as he touches her arm. "I'll get it." He heads to her second bedroom as Persephone returns to the couch.

"What about Seamus?" I ask slowly. My knees wobble and I sink onto the couch next to Persephone. She pats my knee. I take comfort in the gesture.

Dylan paces the room. Veins stand out on his arms. Is that from working out or stress?

"You may want to stay away from Dylan," Marcus said a couple of days ago. *"Aiden said he's working through some stuff. He's not exactly stable."*

Henry returns and sets the boombox on a side table after moving a large potted plant to the floor, struggling under its weight. Dylan kneels in front of the stereo. He hits the power button and twists a knob, moving from station to station. Suddenly, static blasts through the speakers.

"Jude!" Dylan hollers. His voice booms so loud I jump in my seat.

There's no way Jude can communicate through radios. It's the craziest thing I've ever heard. Had Dylan has lost his mind? Aiden studies Dylan, his face expressionless. Does he suspect it, too? What if Jude's magic is too much for Dylan? What if it's caused his brain to short-circuit?

"Jude! I'm here with Lucy. You there?"

I press my hands to my ears, against the loud blasts of static.

"Power up the connection, Jude," Dylan hollers. He leans close to the black stereo speaker. "You're not coming through."

"Aiden? Is this possible?" I ask, not trusting the sanity of my demon BFF at the moment.

Aiden glances at me, but quickly returns his attention to the noisy electronic.

The static blasts again.

"...Lucy with you?" a voice says, sounding very far away.

On reflex, I clench my fists to quench the rip of heat that surges down my arms.

Is this a joke?

"She's here. Persephone, Henry, and Aiden are, too, just like you asked," Dylan says, leaning close to the speaker. "What have you got?"

How is this possible? In a flash, I am off the couch and scrambling across the floor on my hands and knees to crouch beside Dylan. I lean close to the speaker.

"Jude? Is that really you?"

The static blasts again and I rock back on my heels. Jude's voice comes through. "Seamus has gone rogue. No one can track him down in our dimension or yours," he says.

My father's voice sounds gravelly and staticky and so faint. His visit in my dream, as much as I welcomed it, hadn't felt real. Hearing his voice now among a room full of others, feels real. There's no way he would go to so much trouble for a friendly check in. This is a warning.

"What about Lucifer?" Dylan asks. "Did you communicate with him?"

Static again. Persephone, Henry, and Aiden close in behind us.

"Lucifer is out of contact right now. I will make him aware of the situation as soon as possible, make sure he places the order."

"What order?" I ask, yelling over the grating noise.

"To destroy Seamus," Jude says. "He's trying to share his magic—to recruit others. He is using dark magic. We are now certain of it."

Soul magic.

"Once Seamus empowers others, your gargoyle won't be able to detect it," he says.

Jude doesn't know that Marcus is about to leave town. I have no intention of telling him, either. For all I know, he would arrange to have Camille taken out to eliminate Marcus's need to leave.

Henry kneels beside Dylan and me. "Aiden updated Jude on evidence I received from my connection at the Chicago PD."

"Lucy and Dylan, do you remember when we were in the forest and we found the ash on the ground and the symbols burned into the tree?"

"Yes," I say, recalling that Dylan and I both nearly puked after smelling the ash—the remains of a baby lamb sacrificed in Seamus's wacked-out magical ritual.

"I had previously confirmed it was soul magic, that it was Seamus's magic. The recent crime scenes have some of the same trademarks."

Persephone gasps. "He's robbing people of their souls to strengthen his power?" she cries. "No human could withstand that."

"That's his plan. Seamus is trying to share his magic, to empower those girls. It killed them," Jude says. "My guess is they never made it to phase two."

"The soul magic phase," Aiden says.

"Seamus is delving into dark territory," Henry says. He and Aiden eye each other grimly.

"Jude?" Aiden calls out from behind me. "What do you want us to do?"

"Lucy!" Jude barks through a hissing, crackly blast. "Don't turn off your car radio again. I am using tremendous power trying to get through to you."

"I'm sorry," I yell into the speaker. My fingers clutch the boombox. "When are you coming home?"

"Not soon enough."

"How do we find out who Seamus is working with?" Persephone asks.

154

"Most humans can't withstand demon magic, as you are learning in your newspapers. Given that this is forbidden magic, I doubt Seamus would find another supernatural willing to work with him. The consequences are too severe. I suspect he's going to keep trying to create supernaturals. If he is successful, he will try to perform soul magic on them."

Persephone gasps behind me.

"Lucy—be suspicious of everyone. Always have your guard up. Seamus will come for you."

The faces of Katie, Suzy, Cloe, Ella, and Caroline flicker through my mind. Are they safe? Will Seamus come for me and for them? The room suddenly feels too hot and I plunk back on my butt with a thud.

Another blast of static, then silence.

"Jude?" Dylan calls out.

I crawl back to the stereo in a hurry. "Jude? Are you there?"

No response. My father is gone.

CHAPTER TWENTY-TWO

– Lucy Walker –

Once home from Persephone's apartment, I head to my room to call Katie. I sink into my desk chair. Absently, I trace the letters on the cover of a spell book Persephone lent me. First my father told me Seamus was out of commission. I was free to live happily without the crazed, revenge-seeking demon coming after me. Now he tells me Seamus has gone rogue and is creating more demons, and I'm their target. The freedom was short-lived.

I call Katie on her cell.

She answers on the second ring. "Hey."

"Hey back." I try to keep my tone from sounding glum.

"I thought you were getting together with Marcus," Katie says.

"We're getting together later." Based on Katie's gloomy tone, you would think she just learned that a demon is hot on her tail. Maybe she and Trevor are fighting? I don't have the energy to go there right now. "I'm calling with good news. I'll go with you to Ella's séance if I'm still invited."

"Really?" There's life back in Katie's voice. "You're definitely still invited. Do you want me to call Ella and let her know?"

I don't want to call Ella. "That would be great. Thanks."

"Ella's going to be so excited you're coming. She's changing. Really, you'll see." Katie genuinely believes what she's saying. That stumps me. Ella doesn't like me. Never has.

The bottom line is that I don't have a choice. I have to attend the party to keep Ella from inviting unwelcomed supernatural guests to the evening. Seamus is a very real danger again. I have to make sure he doesn't show up and try to turn them into demons, so that he can later suck out their souls.

CHAPTER TWENTY-THREE

– Lucy Walker –

Since Mr. and Mrs. Douglas and the kids are in New York and I am off work today, I had hoped to have a weekend off from my lessons. Persephone wouldn't hear of it. Neither would Aiden. They should be giving me credit for reading up on herbs, going to the store to buy bay leaves, burning them in a fireproof bowl in the backyard and bottling up the ashes to take with me to Ella's party tonight. I also have a sandwich bag full of rosemary. Instead they felt the need to remind me that Seamus is on the loose. Like I need reminding.

My witch mentors were *generous* enough to let me switch my lesson to today. By the time I get home from Ella's tomorrow, train with Aiden and Dylan, and finish homework, I will barely have any time with Marcus. There are valid reasons for my bad mood.

"Our last session got me thinking," Henry says once I arrive at Persephone's apartment. He hurries out of the kitchen, leaving Persephone and me at the counter. He continues from the living room, his voice loud. "Lucy's ability to manipulate the water, the wind...How did that strike you, Persephone?"

The plate on the counter next to the stove piled high with snickerdoodles is far more interesting than whatever Henry has to say. The scent of cinnamon beckons.

"I made them for Mirabelle. We are seeing her tonight before Henry leaves for Los Angeles. Help yourself and be quick about it. Once Henry's back, he will want your full attention. He's been looking forward to today's lesson."

"Why's he going to LA?" I ask as I snag a cookie.

"A case he's working on for a client. It's a big one," Persephone says. She wiggles her fingers for a cookie. I hand her one while stealing a second one for me. "Tell me more about this séance at your friend's house," she says between bites.

"Ella is not my friend. She's someone I have to tolerate for the sake of my friends," I clarify. "I don't know if tonight is just her trying to entertain the girls, like telling scary stories after dark. I guess I'll see when I get there."

I fill her in on my preparations: the herbs I'm bringing with me and the spell I prepared, just in case. I play it down, though. There's no need to worry Persephone. Tonight could turn out to be nothing. Then again, with Seamus on the loose, there is some heavy-duty magic out there and the fact that Ella is diving in blind is typical of her. What if she summons him or another demon? What if her made-up séance procedures together with the energy of six girls are enough to conjure someone? Because of Ella's idiocy, I am forced to attend her party instead of spending time with Marcus.

In the living room I hear the clanking of glass objects against wooden surfaces.

"These are good. Probably the best part of my entire stinky day," I say, munching away, not bothering to hide my grumpiness. If Persephone had mentioned cookies when she called, I would've been less crabby about meeting her and Henry.

"I'm proud of you. Crafting a spell and preparing herbs for tonight on your own without instruction is commendable. She takes another bite of her cookie, holding her hand beneath to catch any runaway crumbs. All the while she watches me intently. "Do you think there will be a need to use them?"

"No way for me to know," I say with a shrug. "I have to prepare just in case."

My father is gone. Marcus will be gone soon. Persephone has a bad hip. It's time I learn to manage situations on my own.

Persephone takes the last bite of her cookie as she nods. "Keep up the good work."

Henry returns to Persephone's side. He brought with him one of the many small glasses that decorate the windowsill in the living room. The glass holds a couple of inches of water and a small stem from a large pothos plant, one of the many cuttings Persephone has all over her apartment taken from the larger plants whenever she feels they are growing too long. With Persephone's green thumb, her plants grow at an alarming rate—particularly the pothos. It will only be a matter of time before the plants take over her apartment.

Henry slides the small glass over to me. "Let's try another spell. I want to test a theory. I picked the smallest cutting from the living room. Can you attempt to help this little one grow roots at an accelerated rate?"

"I can try," I say, doubtfully.

"Henry, that's beyond her magic," Persephone says with a frown.

"Did you feel it when she was working with the rainwater last weekend?" he asks Persephone, his eyes shining with excitement behind his glasses. "Did you feel the same hypnotic, soothing power that I did?"

His words startle me. "That's what I felt while I was performing the spell," I say.

Henry looks to Persephone with raised eyebrows. "And you?"

Persephone heaves a sigh. "I did as well. It wasn't strong, but I did feel it."

He pushes the small glass closer to me. "Let her try," he urges.

A lot was different during my last lesson. Mainly, my emotions. There's no way I can replicate that. Words don't come as easily as they did last weekend. I was in some kind of a zone. The rainwater. My tears. The sadness.

Today is different. I'm worried about a lot, but mostly my friends attending Ella's séance. What brought on Ella's curiosity about the supernatural? What happens if she unleashes some bad magical mojo upon my friends? I can't allow anything bad to happen to them.

"Lucy—be suspicious of everyone. Always have your guard up."

What did Jude mean? Should I be suspicious of people already in my life or strangers? Cryptic messages won't help me. Once I finish my lesson, I will go home and practice my spell so that I have it memorized for tonight. If any uninvited guests show up—of the supernatural variety—I'll need to focus harder than I ever have before. I'll have to rely on my magic, alone, to keep the girls safe.

"Lucy?" Henry says. His green eyes watch me expectantly.

Focus, I tell myself.

Needing some help, I grab my phone and Google words that rhyme with roots and grow and thrive, a process I have practiced many times in my bedroom and on the roof while reading through Gram and Persephone's spell books. Henry grabs a pen and a pad of paper. He flips to a blank page and sets it in front of me.

For months I had created spells, practiced weaving together words that communicated the intention I was trying to achieve all while rhyming. Nothing much came of it, except for those rare times when my emotions escalated.

Tick-tock, tick-tock, tick-tock.

I take a deep breath and will thoughts of Marcus's impending departure away. I can't carry that weight today. *My boyfriend will be around his own kind. I want that for him. I want him to be happy.* Henry and Persephone watch me intently. The pressure of being watched while I try to construct a spell unnerves me, but I persist.

"What purpose are you trying to achieve?" Henry asks as he watches me scribble words onto the paper then scratch them out.

Little plant. It's a shrimp like me. I want it to grow, to thrive, to double...no *triple* in size.

A couple of lines farther down the page I write the words: roots, growth, thrive.

"What are you doing?" Persephone asks. She cranes her neck as I pick up my phone again.

"Once I commit to the words that represent the basis of my spell, I look up other words that fit the actions I'm trying to achieve and that rhyme."

Out of the corner of my eye I see Persephone turn to Henry with a puzzled frown. "We don't rely on rhymes or the Internet. Did you teach her that?"

Henry's chuckle makes me smile.

"If the spell is effective, I see no issue with it. Be open-minded," he says to her.

Henry peers over my shoulder, watching as I write more words.

"Rhyming was never our goal. The intention should be enough. It was always about the purpose and layering in the structure of the spell to achieve our objective," Persephone continues.

I have read Gram's books, both the official content and her notes scribbled in the margins. For years Gram didn't rhyme her spells, but I did see a pattern in her later notes. She remarked in one of her herb books that rhyming *did* make the spells more powerful. She also found them to be more lyrical. Like a song or a poem. That resonated with me.

"I determine my goal," I tell Persephone, tapping the pen against the paper. "Then I weave in the instructions."

Little plant with little roots
Allow yourself to recruit
My energy to enhance your attributes

I clear the search on my phone's Web browser, then type in grow.

"Borrow?" Persephone clucks her tongue. "I don't see what that has to do with grow."

The judgment in her voice annoys me. Why can't Persephone give me a chance to do this my way?

Henry clears his throat and I hope he is fixing Persephone with a reproachful glare behind my back.

As I scan words for those that connect with my objective, I keep glancing back at the plant cutting. More than anything I want to do right by the stem; my worry for my friends can be channeled into my worry for the cutting. That sounds crazy for sure, but if emotion helped my spell work last weekend, maybe it'll help me today. *Feelings as fuel.*

I have seen all those little glasses on Persephone's window ledge, and those on the bookshelves, and the kitchen window sill, and cabinets less than ten feet from where I stand now. There are probably more than thirty throughout the apartment. They are all thriving, except for this one. Henry brought me the runt of the litter. From time to time Persephone will throw away stems that don't grow roots. Will I be able to save this one? What would a runt need more than anything to grow big and strong? The next line comes to me without the need for my phone. I can feel myself growing protective of the struggling little plant.

"Nice...I like that," Henry murmurs, pressing his index finger to his lip as he reads over my shoulder.

Grow...grow...grow
My magic is yours to borrow
Like oxygen and blood allow it to flow
Through your stems, to plow...
Through your cells until you are the opposite of micro

I don't pause and immediately go to work on a third verse. It comes to me faster than the prior two. I have found my groove.

Feel my essence as you thrive
As you triple your original size
Use the energy from those in this room
as you come alive

Once finished, I put my phone aside. I cup the glass with both of my hands. I recite the entire spell, peering at my handwritten notes on the counter. As I work my way through that first round, my mouth, tongue, and lips forming the words, I focus on the intent behind my spell. It's not so easy with my mentors literally breathing down my neck.

Mentors. The word makes me pause.

Images of the huge, beautiful oaks and maples in my uncles' backyard appear in my mind. Tall and lush and green, providing shelter to so many birds and squirrels. What about the imposing giant ogre-like trees in Jude's football-field-sized backyard in Lake Forest? They used to scare me, but not anymore. Now they remind me of my father. Rough exterior, otherworldly, but solid and reliable.

I repeat the spell while I mentally present the images of these examples of thriving trees to the cutting, showing it what is possible. Sure, the plant itself can't *visualize,* but it's all about the energy I send to it.

Halfway through my third round of the spell, I am struck by the scent of wet earth. It's exactly the smell that fills the air after a storm—like the one we had earlier today.

Persephone's sharp gasp yanks me out of my thoughts. "Lucy!"

I had been focusing so hard on the written spell envisioning the trees that I hadn't noticed the transformation of my little plant.

The original cutting was only about four inches long. Now it was nearly twice its original size. With five...no, six little root shoots.

Henry grins enthusiastically. "Your modern spell writing techniques are effective."

I suspect that was a jab directed at Persephone.

"I am impressed." Persephone's voice swells with pride, her head bobbing in an affirming nod. "Forgive me for doubting your methods."

"I doubted myself," I tell her honestly.

Henry chuckles as he pats my shoulder. "So much like Vera in her early years."

Persephone holds the little jar up to the light, inspecting the roots. "It's uncanny."

"We'll tell Mirabelle about this when we see her tonight," Henry says to Persephone before turning to me. "Your grandmother and Mirabelle were close. We'll arrange for you to meet her."

The other witch in Gram's life, the one from New Orleans. Persephone and Henry have mentioned her a couple of times. Had Gram talked about her? Surely, I would've remembered her name.

While they marvel over the root—so impressed that I'm given permission to leave our lesson early—I snag two more snickerdoodles and make my escape. I've got a spell to memorize for tonight.

Chapter Twenty-Four

– Lucy Walker –

Ella's house is twice the size of the large apartment I live in with my uncles. All the walls are white. The carpet is beige. Even the décor that hangs on the walls is neutral and bland. While her living room and kitchen are clutter-free and ooze fancy with expensive countertops and stainless-steel appliances, I prefer Sheldon and Bernard's rooms with walls the color of lightening bug yellow, candlelight orange, honeydew melon green, with hardwood floors, dark wooden furniture, and piles of books everywhere.

"Help me move this into the living room," Ella says. She grabs one end of the kitchen table. Ella, Katie, and I groan under the weight of the slate-topped piece of furniture and shuffle into the living room.

"You wanted the yellow tablecloth?" Caroline calls from the stairs leading to the second floor, her body half hidden by a closet door.

"Yes. Spirits...are...attracted to bright...colors," Ella grunts out. She nods for us to set the table down. "It has to be equal distance from the couch, the armchair, and the fireplace." She frowns. "Do you think it's warm enough in here? Too cold? Spirits will only come if it's comfortable. You know...*inviting.*"

Jeez. Where did she learn this stuff? Martha Stewart's *Guide for Hosting Spirits*? That must explain the orange sundress Ella wears. It's pretty, but it's so bright it hurts my eyes. When I summoned Lucifer, it took a group of supernatural beings around a table, a Ouija board, and a summoning spell. I can't speak for everyone else that night, but I put every ounce of effort and focus into my intention and didn't care one bit about the feng shui or ambience of the space.

Caroline returns with a tablecloth. "Got it!" Her lime-green jumper is bright, too, but less painful to look at than Ella's outfit.

The doorbell rings. Caroline tosses the tablecloth onto the table before she dashes off to answer the door. Katie and I cover the table with the crinkly fabric.

Caroline returns followed by Suzy.

"I brought a photo of my Uncle Don," Suzy announces. She holds up an image of an older man with huge brown eyes, wearing a charcoal-gray fedora on his bald head. He flashes the peace sign. "He died when I was in middle school. I owe my killer taste in music to Uncle D."

"I brought a photo of my grandmother—my mom's mom." Katie holds up a picture of a woman with a gap-toothed smile, curly gray hair, her arms wrapped around a much younger Katie. She looks like an older version of Katie's mom.

"She's pretty," I say.

"Lucy?" Ella asks, cutting Katie off before she can respond. "Did you bring a photo?"

They all turn to me. I know what they're thinking. I lost my mom, my grandmother, and my uncle. Whose photo did I choose?

I clear my throat. "I did some research on séances and read that so long as you focus clearly on the image of your lost loved one, that's as good as having a photo."

Ella and Caroline exchange a look of exasperation.

"Why can't you follow simple instructions?" Ella scolds me. Her face turns crimson. "Everyone else brought a photo."

Katie gives Ella a long look that I don't understand. "If Lucy looked it up, I'm sure it's fine," she says finally.

I appreciate that she's always supportive of me in situations like this with Ella, but what was it she said last night about Ella changing? I didn't believe it then and I don't now.

Suzy rubs her hands together with excitement. "I'm warning you all up front that if I'm able to connect with Uncle D, I'm gonna hog the séance."

The doorbell rings again. Ella and Caroline leave to answer it. Ella doesn't make much of an effort to whisper as she complains about me trying to ruin her event. Why is she being such a stickler about rules she doesn't really understand? Because she's a control freak? *Whatever.* I'm already regretting coming tonight. If I wasn't so worried about Ella and her dangerous plan, I would pack up and go home. Instead, I have to focus my energy on keeping uninvited guests from joining the party.

A moment later Caroline and Ella return with Cloe in tow. She joins me on the far side of the room. She shakes her head, lips twisted into a lopsided grimace. "Such a dumb idea," she whispers. "Halfway here, I almost told my dad to turn around and take me back home."

"I agree," I whisper to Cloe.

"She's inviting trouble," Cloe says. "I didn't want to come, but if trouble shows up tonight, I'd like to think I could help somehow."

"That's how I feel, too," I say, surprised.

"Cloe, did you bring a photo?" Caroline calls across the room to her. She pulls her own photo from her purse and presents an image of an older woman to all of us.

"Nope. I'm just a bystander tonight," Cloe says.

Ella huffs on her way to the kitchen. She glares at Cloe and me as she passes by.

It's good to know one person here agrees with me. "Could you do me a favor?" I whisper to Cloe. "This is going to sound strange, but I'm asking you to trust me."

"Tell me the favor first." She mimics my whisper.

"If something goes wrong tonight, I need you to imagine sending all of your mental energy to me. Don't overthink it, please. When I signal to you, just focus with every ounce of effort you can."

Cloe narrows her gaze. "Let's pretend I understand what you're saying. Why would I do that?"

"It's like I said before, I side with your grandmother on this stuff. We need to shut down whatever bad juju Ella accidentally or intentionally invites in tonight," I say darkly.

Cloe fixes on our redheaded host who returns carrying a vase of white roses and sets them on a cabinet behind the table.

"The spirits are drawn to white roses," Ella tells Caroline. Her voice rings with haughty authority.

"I can see why. They're beautiful," Caroline gushes.

Cloe rolls her eyes at Ella and the roses. "I trust you a lot more than I trust her." She nods. "I'll do it."

"Make sure all of your cell phones are off. Let's take one group photo with my camera. Everyone hold up the photo you brought, if you brought one," Ella's voice is full of irritation when she utters that last part.

We crowd around Ella. I notice the black-and-white photo Ella holds in her hand. It features a dark-haired woman with a stern expression who looks to be roughly the same age as Katie's mom. According to Katie, Ella's grandmother on her dad's side is still alive. I'm guessing it's her mom's mom in the old photo.

Ella snaps a few photos until she and Caroline are satisfied. Next, she lights a trio of short, fat navy candles she places in the center of the table before moving to light a stick of incense in a brass holder on the mantel. She carries her phone with her, nodding as she reads the information on the screen. Her lips move silently as she moves from item to item. I squint hard, trying to read her lips but am not able to.

"Draw the drapes," Ella instructs Katie. Her voice takes on an edge of dramatic flair.

"I'll do it," I offer, touching my pockets. As I move through the living room, I quickly and discreetly spread ashes of the bay leaves I burned earlier along each window sill before closing the drapes. Once at the door, I kneel and sprinkle needle-like rosemary leaves along the entryway. I already treated the kitchen windows and back door earlier while Ella and Caroline were getting dressed and Katie complimented them on their new outfits. Doubt begins to nag at me. Will the two herbs be enough? Should I have asked Persephone for some nettle to increase the strength of the protection?

Caroline flips off the lights and takes her seat. My time is up. I scoot over to the table and slide into my chair.

So far Ella follows the basic steps I found online to conduct a séance while adding plenty of her own stylistic enhancements. I had no idea it's such a popular thing for entertainment purposes.

Cloe sits on my right while Katie plunks down on my left, jittery with excitement.

"Now hold hands so that we are all linked," Ella orders.

Cloe exhales an annoyed breath beside me. Ella doesn't notice. She's focusing on whatever steps are outlined on her phone. Katie immediately grasps my hand and holds tight. Cloe pinches my palm and I jerk my head in her direction. She gives me a wink before grabbing my hand.

Katie and Suzy both admire the photos they brought.

"Finally!" Suzy whispers impatiently.

Ella begins, "Spirits of the earth, of the sky, of the sea, please empower us as we call upon our departed loved ones."

Suzy flashes two fingers in a peace sign gesture at all of us around the table.

"Remember. Never break the link. We must hold hands until the séance is over and I tell you to let go." Ella says in a tone that suggests she is a teacher in a classroom full of difficult children. "Katie, would you like to start?"

"Um...sure," Katie says nervously. Her hand is damp in mine.

"Why don't you or Caroline go first?" I suggest. This was her dumb idea after all.

"I'll go first," Suzy says quickly. She bounces in her chair with excitement.

If Ella were magical, the glare she laser beams my way would turn me into a pile of ash for sure.

"Uncle D—Uncle Don—if you can hear me, I want to thank you for everything you taught me. I would never have been exposed to the Ramones if not for you. Or the Pretenders. Or Patti Smith. I try to make you proud with every one of my blog posts. With my art. Remember when you told me to always be true to myself? I finally understand what that means." She pulls her hand to her face, her fingers still laced through Cloe's, and scratches her nose.

A chill snakes through the room. I open my eyes as I register the decrease in temperature, to see if anyone else noticed. With a jolt I catch Ella watching me. What is she up to? The candles begin to flicker. Probably just the central air kicking in.

Suzy continues, her eyes closed tight in concentration. "I miss you so much. You were the only adult in my life who always gave it to me straight. You didn't treat me like a kid. Thank you for that. I invite you to visit me any time. I sure would love to talk with you."

Suzy finishes and the room falls silent.

"Good job, Suzy," Caroline says. "Smart of you to invite the spirit of your uncle. I didn't think of that."

Suzy raises her shoulders high, a crazy grin on her face. "That was cool," she says before dropping her shoulders.

"I'll go next," Katie volunteers, her voice stronger this time.

"Great! Let's keep the energy going. Everyone close your eyes again," Ella says with the enthusiasm of a drill sergeant.

A strange request since she doesn't close her own. I keep mine open, too.

Katie concentrates on the photo of her grandmother for a long moment.

"You have to talk out loud, Katie," Ella says. "It won't work if you keep it in your head."

In the glow of the candlelight, Katie squirms. She squeezes her eyes closed tightly.

"Hi Grandma. I...I wanted to say hi and let you know how much I miss you." She pulls her bottom lip into her mouth and chews for a moment. Her hand trembles in mine.

I want to squeeze her hand, to comfort her, but I resist. I don't want to distract her.

Katie begins telling her grandma about school, Trevor, and her mom.

I shiver as the room continues to grow colder. Peering around the table, I see the thick white exhales of every girl in the room. Caroline draws her shoulders up to her ears in response to the chill. Ella surveys the room, not paying any attention to Katie.

My throat feels dry, scratchy. I clear it as quietly as I can. Had Ella set the digital control on her central air to drop during the séance? Is it part of the show?

Ella and I both notice the candles as they continue to flicker. She appears transfixed. Is she so attached to her séance rituals, that she won't pause them for a few seconds to turn off the air conditioning? Cloe squeezes my hand and our eyes meet. She shivers against the cold at the same time she aims a dark look at Ella. Katie wraps up her chat with her Grandma, stuttering over her words because she, too, is cold. I clear my scratchy throat again and am about to call Ella out for being the worst hostess ever when suddenly all three candles go out.

Gasps ring out around the table.

"Could it be Uncle D? Is he visiting?" Suzy whispers.

I attempt to swallow past the sandpapery feeling in my throat, but can't. I try again. My throat constricts. With a silent cry of panic, I yank my hands free from Katie and Cloe's. I clutch my throat. *I can't breathe.* In the dark room, no one sees my distress.

"Lucy?" Cloe reaches for my hand. I thump her on the shoulder, tug her arm, desperate to get her help.

I pull and claw at my throat, stretching my neck, moving my head, *anything* to get air. Without thinking, I kick my feet, flounder, and send my chair flying backward. Pain bursts through my head and back upon impact with the floor. The room is suddenly bright as someone turns on the lights.

Cloe appears and hovers over me. She focuses intently on my face. I clutch my neck, stick my tongue out. I...CAN'T... BREATHE, I scream silently to her. She grasps my hands in hers.

"Lucy can't breathe!" Cloe yells.

Silently and quickly her lips move, her eyes round and full of fear.

I barely notice the gasps and cries around the table as the girls jump out of their chairs.

Katie drops to her knees at my other side. "Should I do the Heimlich?"

Cloe ignores her.

I stretch my neck. My eyes roll back in my head. I beg the Goddesses, God, Gram, Momma, and anyone else who'll listen to open my throat.

"What's happening?" Caroline cries out.

"She can't breathe, idiot!" Suzy screams.

"Call 911!" Katie cries.

"Calling now," Caroline shouts.

In my panic, I try to yank my hands free from Cloe's, but she tightens her grip. My heart thunders in my chest. I pull and pull and pull, but my throat is closed.

Katie sobs as she clutches my arm, my leg. Suzy's face appears next to her. Cloe's lips move so fast. I try to suck in a breath. Like a stalled hiccup, the attempt fails. I try again and again. A low sound like humming powerlines fills my head. Foreboding seeps through me like black smoke.

A surge of current zings through me. Suddenly, my throat opens the tiniest bit. Enough to get slivers of air. I lock my eyes on Cloe's. Her expression hardens. Her lips flatten. Sweat beads across her brow in effort.

A surge zips through me. My throat opens more. I inhale delicious bits of air.

"Go get her some water. NOW!" Cloe hollers to the group. We never break eye contact.

Katie chokes out another sob as she pushes to her feet and runs off.

I suck in a big, deep breath. Too much too fast. I cough and splutter, nearly gagging. Cloe continues to clutch my hands tight which forces me to remain on my back. In the kitchen Ella shrieks. With my eyes locked on Cloe, I struggle to get my coughing under control. Her mouth never stops moving. Both of our bodies tremble.

"Suzy, turn the freaking air conditioning off. Get me a blanket for Lucy," Cloe says, her own teeth chattering.

Her lips move silently again.

Suzy nods and rushes off.

I struggle to relax, to ease the muscles in my throat—which is impossible. My heartbeat continues to beat too hard, too fast. I will it to slow down. My throat opens a little more. *You're not going to die,* I tell myself.

Cloe leans close to me. "Who's doing this?" she whispers. "Whoever it is, they're strong and they aren't done yet."

I open my eyes wide.

"How...?" I mouth the word.

"Don't try to talk!" she hisses. "You knew tonight was a bad idea. Do you have a plan? A spell?"

I nod then gasp as the small movement sends a blast of pain through my head from my fall.

Cloe pulls her eyes from mine and peers around the room. "You ready to use it?" she asks when her gaze returns to mine.

Katie arrives at my side with a glass of water. Her eyes wet and her nose red.

"Can you breathe? Please tell me you can breathe," she says. She clutches the glass with one hand and rests her hand on my leg. "Paramedics are on their way."

EMTs aren't going to be able to help me. I know what caused this and it has nothing to do with shellfish or peanuts. I don't bother to respond and focus on small breaths instead. How does Cloe know about spells? How does she know about my magic? Then I remember that I asked her earlier to send her energy to me. Probably a good clue that I'm something beyond plain human.

"She needs to lay here for a little while. Give her time for her throat to fully open," Cloe says, her teeth clenched with effort. Is she fighting off whatever intruder is trying to get in? Or focusing her energy to help me breathe?

Katie nods quickly in response. Suzy returns with blankets. She and Katie spread one over me. Suzie wraps a blanket around Cloe.

I stretch my neck as I continue to draw in small inhales. More than anything I want to gulp big, greedy breaths. It takes all my restraint not to. I don't want to experience another choking fit and lose my ability to breathe again.

Another zing pulsates through my body. My throat opens a little more. Is Cloe hurtling magical mojo at me? With oxygen comes clarity. The spell I had prepared for tonight filters back into my thoughts.

With my hands grasped tightly in Cloe's, I visualize myself pulling energy from her to help to fuel my spell. I concentrate on the words.

Attention all spirits
Cancel your visit
Even those of you nearest
And dearest

Do not attempt to appear
Evil is near
So, please steer clear

For those who are wicked
You are not permitted
To be explicit
Any invitation has been lifted

Fear of my throat closing again prevents me from slipping deep into focus. What if the spirit's proverbial grasp on my throat tightens again? He or she could crush my windpipe. He or she would have access to Katie, Cloe, Suzy, Caroline and Ella. Cloe squeezes my hands, urging me to continue with my spell.

Trust. The word floats into my mind. Trust Cloe? Trust myself? Both? A calm begins to settle over me. The fear needs to go. Dark spirits can manipulate fear, use it to their advantage. That note was scrawled in the margin of one of Gram's books, in her own handwriting.

Cloe watches over me. I am safe in my spellcasting. *Go deeper,* I tell myself.

Slowly, I slip into focus. I visualize Ella's house. Around the exterior, I envision bricks. They are thick and strong. Lots of impenetrable bricks. Layer upon layer of them. I repeat the spell. The more I can breathe, the angrier I get. A spirit...Who am I kidding? It was Seamus McAllister who did this to me. There's no way he's getting inside this house. Finally, the brick wall is finished. Next is the roof. Forget asphalt. I focus on slate tiles. Row after durable row.

Attention all spirits
Cancel your visit
Even those of you nearest
And dearest

Do not attempt to appear
Evil is near
So, please steer clear

For those who are wicked
You are not permitted
To be explicit
Any invitation has been lifted

I repeat the spell while pulling all the energy I can from Cloe. I turn to Katie and Suzy and pull energy from them, too.

A jackhammer appears. It attacks the brick along the front of the house. I lose my grasp on the spell. I squeeze Cloe's hand in alarm. Katie gasps. Did I squeeze her hand, too?

Jackhammer?

I take several shallow breaths. Try to sharpen my concentration.

A second jackhammer joins the first. Bricks go flying as the huge tools blast through my protections. *No room for fear. That will give him access to my friends. Access to me.*

Suddenly, a metal wall appears behind the demolished brick. I pause for only a moment before knuckling down, reinforcing my concentration and the strength of my work. Where did the metal come from? The jackhammers attack the east wall next. Once they break through the brick, another metal wall appears.

I repeat the spell.

The jackhammers attack the back of the house. Another metal wall appears as they demolish the bricks. Not just any metal. Steel. No, not steel. Not chromium, either. *Titanium.* It will protect the house best with a strength of 434 MPs.

I am thrown off kilter then. I don't know anything about steel, metal, or MPs. *Never mind.* Must focus on protecting the house, keeping the girls safe. Don't allow the jackhammers to get through.

Katie removes her hand from my leg. My energy dips just a little then returns when she sits next to Cloe. Heavy footsteps cause the floor to bounce beneath me.

What's happening? I don't dare break my concentration.

A hand clutches my shoulder, shakes me.

I open my eyes and squint against the offensively bright lights. Loud voices. A black woman in uniform. Her gloved hand gingerly and expertly explores my throat. A Hispanic man with a shaved head and a dark goatee, wearing a nearly identical uniform, squats behind her. He sets a large bag on the floor. In his hand he holds an oblong beige contraption. An Epi Pen?

"Can you breathe?" the woman asks.

I nod, not trusting myself to speak.

"Good. My name is Tracy. This is Esteban."

She lifts my hand, presses two fingers to my wrist.

"What did you eat tonight?" she asks.

"Nothing. We were planning to eat in a little while," Katie answers for me.

Cloe's posture remains rigid as she concentrates.

"Can you tell us what happened tonight?" Esteban asks.

Suzy explains to them that we were having a séance, that I had rocked back in my chair and tipped over. When I landed on my back, it knocked the wind out of me and everyone panicked. Behind the paramedics, Ella looks dazed. Her eyes are red-rimmed. Beside her, Caroline looks confused and unsure as she listens to Suzy's explanation. She wraps her arms around herself as if she's still cold.

After answering a dozen more questions—through Suzy and Katie—I am moved to the couch. Capable fingers examine my head, shoulders, and—again—my neck from my fall. Finally, the paramedics leave.

"You scared me," Katie says. She sits next to me, her legs tucked beneath her as she holds my hand.

Suzy sits cross legged on the floor.

"Me too," I rasp, my throat raw.

"You choked on...nothing?" Katie asks, peering at me disbelieving.

I shrug and point to my neck, trying to communicate to her that talking hurt. Any explanation I could give her would sound lame, but I can't reveal the magical influence that showed up tonight.

Katie nods. "No visit from my grandmother," she says sadly. "I didn't really believe she would come, but it would've been nice to talk with her."

Cloe appears carrying a cup of hot tea. She sets it on the coffee table in front of me. "You need to drink that," she instructs me. An ice cube floats on top, melting.

"Pizza's going in the oven," Caroline calls from the kitchen. "Chips are on the table."

Katie looks past me longingly.

"Go," I croak.

"You sure?" she looks guilty.

I nod.

Suzy jumps up from the floor, casting a worried look at me. She and Katie head to the kitchen.

After tonight, I'm going to live on mashed potatoes and macaroni and cheese for the next several days.

Cloe glances after the girls until they're out of sight. She takes Katie's place on the couch.

The conversation in the kitchen sounds subdued.

I take a cautious sip of the tea and swallow. All the while I review what happened tonight: the attack, the appearance of the metal walls behind my destroyed brick, some invisible force closing off my windpipe, and Cloe's whispered words while I was sprawled on the floor unable to breathe.

I decide to focus on that last part first. "You have...powers?"

Cloe glances toward the kitchen before leaning close. "The

girls won't be gone long. Answer my questions first. What—or who—was that?" she asks. "Something or someone was trying to crash the party. What were those visions in my head? Those jackhammers scared me to death. The magic behind them was strong. Dark. Demon magic? It had to be."

I gasp then regret it as my throat burns in response. "You saw that?" I ask after a long pause. Gently, I clutch my neck until the pain fades.

"Saw it and got involved. What were you thinking?" Cloe asks in a shrieky whisper. "Titanium is a better option than brick. Why would you ever choose brick? It's better than wood, sure, but it's porous. Spirits could get through without much difficulty."

After going so deep in my spell—and nearly being strangled to death—I struggle to make sense of her words. "Titanium—that was you?"

"It's stronger than steel," Cloe says impatiently. "What I want to know is who brought the jackhammers?"

I take another sip of tea. The hot liquid helps to ease my throat.

"I have a good guess," I say bitterly. How do I explain Seamus McAllister to Cloe? Instead, I nudge her knee. "How did you know what to do?"

"You're not the first witch in my life," Cloe says gruffly.

My eyes nearly pop out of my head.

Cloe rolls her eyes. "My grandmother has been spell-casting my whole life. She pushes for me to develop a practice, that I'm a natural, but it's not really my thing."

All this time, sitting across the table from her every day at lunch, why didn't I pick up on her magic? Detect her energy somehow? Or maybe there's a website or Facebook group I could've checked? A registry? Scratch that. A vision of witches burning at the stake comes to mind. A registry or database would be a terrible idea. Persephone, Aiden, and Marcus have always crammed it into my head that our supernatural identities had to remain secret.

"Your grandmother?" I ask.

"She doesn't live around here, but she's visiting." Cloe smiles slyly. "She knows about you."

"What's her name?" For the first time tonight, I begin to feel excited.

"Mirabelle Porter. She was good friends with your grandmother."

The name sends a zing of energy through me. Not the magical kind. More of the recognition kind. Persephone and Henry have talked about their good friend, Mirabelle, since I moved to Chicago. The fourth member of my Gram's original group of witches.

"From New Orleans." I say it more as an acknowledgment and less as a question.

Cloe looks surprised. "You've heard of her?"

Someone's cell phone rings in the kitchen. A moment later, Katie returns to the living room and hands me a cell phone that isn't hers. "Dylan," she mumbles around a bite of pizza.

"You almost choked to death?" he asks angrily. "I'll be there in fifteen minutes. Get your stuff together. I'm coming to get you."

CHAPTER TWENTY-FIVE

– Lucy Walker –

It took a little while to calm Dylan down. Cloe and I left with him while Katie and Suzy stayed behind at the slumber party to appease Ella. I was shocked when he told me Caroline was the one who texted him about my incident.

Twenty minutes later we arrive in the parking lot of a late-night diner. Dylan insisted on driving me. Cloe followed us in my car. A bell chimes as we enter the restaurant. I take in its fluorescent lights, the faded black-and-white checkerboard laminate flooring, and booths with red vinyl benches—some which wear strips of silver duct tape like bandages—and black tables. The heavy scents of greasy food and coffee fill the air. My stomach growls in response. Neon signs hang on the wall behind the main counter, which is covered in black-and-white tiles and lined with black stools. "Fever" sung by Peggy Lee plays on a dimly lit jukebox off in a corner. It's dingy but still a couple steps up from the diners Momma used to work at in Lexington before she went on disability fulltime. I am surprised by Dylan's choice, but take an immediate liking to the place.

A waitress with olive skin and dark hair dyed purplish-red and pulled back into a ponytail, greets us. She has a small sparkly stud in her nose. Her uniform is a powder-blue dress with white buttons down the front and she wears a white apron tied around her waist.

Dylan points to a booth in the back, far from other customers. The waitress escorts us to our table.

"You want coffee?" she asks once we're seated.

"Desperately," Cloe says, her tone pleading.

Dylan and I both grin at her.

As the woman walks off to grab her coffee pot, Cloe adds, "With this conversation, I'm going to need it."

The waitress returns to our table after checking on other customers along the way. She delivers glasses of water, fills Cloe's cup with steaming hot coffee, and hands each of us a menu. We only need a minute to decide what we want and quickly place our orders.

Once we're alone, Dylan turns to me. He's angry. "Tell me what happened."

Cloe nods in agreement, one eyebrow raised sharply. "Spill the beans. I want to know the deal with the jackhammers. Who's behind them? Who tried to strangle you?"

"Had intruders," I say. Talking still hurts. I sip the ice water. It feels good on my throat. The neighboring tables are empty. Still, I keep my voice low. "Supernatural." I let that sink in for Dylan.

"How much does she know?" Dylan asks abruptly. He points a finger toward Cloe. "What about the secrecy rules?"

"My grandmother is a witch," Cloe whispers. "She's good friends with Henry and Persephone. Lucy told me tonight."

Dylan pulls back in surprise. "Really?"

I nod.

He appraises Cloe. "You and your grandmother, both?"

Cloe nods. "Much to my grandmother's disappointment, I'm not into it like she is. I'm too busy with my own stuff."

"She's good," I say to Dylan.

Cloe shrugs humbly.

Dylan nods thoughtfully at Cloe. After a moment, he turns his attention back to me. "Supernatural intruders?" he says, urging me to continue.

I sip my water, wishing I had a cup of tea.

"Tried to strangle me." The fear returns. Tears spring to my eyes. "Couldn't breathe." Tentatively, I touch my throat.

Cloe jumps in. "Lucy was on the floor, obviously choking, or being choked. I used a spell to try to block whoever was hurting her. The intruder was *strong*."

I recall the metal walls Cloe erected once the jackhammers broke through the brick. "Cloe saved us."

She doesn't bother denying it. "Titanium. That's what I provided. Who builds a protective surrounding out of brick?" Cloe razzes me, mock disgust in her voice. "Your defensive skills aren't so hot."

Dylan's nods thoughtfully. "I like how you think," he says to Cloe and they fist-bump. When he turns to me his appreciative smile fades. "But I don't get it. Give me context."

I lean in close and tell Dylan about my spell and constructing protection around Ella's house. Cloe adds her own details, which gives me a break from talking. It takes a while to recount it all.

"Ella was watching you. Weird, right? She was so bossy about us having our eyes closed," Cloe says.

"Could it have been *him*? Or others?" Dylan asks. "I don't know how these things work. Did Ella's event appear like a neon sign inviting supernaturals?"

"Him who?" Cloe asks. Her eyes dart from Dylan to me. "What others?"

"Seamus McAllister. He's a demon," I whisper to Cloe as we huddle.

Cloe nods thoughtfully. "It's like I told Lucy earlier, the magic felt dark to me," she says to Dylan. "My grandmother talks about demons, but I've never had an up close and personal experience with one before."

"You hit the jackpot tonight," Dylan says sardonically. He raises his eyebrows at me. "Have you filled her in yet?"

"Getting to it..." I say.

He scans the diner. "Before you do, will A-Man or P and H have a fit for revealing secret information? Or does her grandmother connection automatically cover us?"

His use of coded names shows he really does respect the rules. I appreciate that. I need to do a better job myself.

"We're covered." *Besides, it's a little too late,* I tell him mentally.

"Welcome to our supernatural tribe," Dylan whispers, extending a fist.

"Thank you," Cloe says, bumping his fist with her own.

I roll my eyes.

The waitress comes by and refills our water glasses and Cloe's coffee cup. I order a cup of tea, eager for the relief on my throat.

"Your orders will be up in a couple of minutes," she says.

Once the woman out of earshot, I turn to Cloe. "What do you know about me?"

"That you're a witch like me, that the gene skipped your mom and went to you—which is what happened with my mom and me," she says. She eyes Dylan and me suspiciously. "Is there more?"

"My father's a demon," I whisper.

Cloe's eyes bug out of her head. "You're a half-and-half? I've never met one before."

I nod and point to Dylan.

"I'm part demon. Mostly human. Don't know the percentages," Dylan says.

Cloe studies me curiously.

"We're nothing like Seamus McAllister," Dylan adds quickly. "SM for short."

She smiles. "I'm good at reading vibes. I can tell you're both good." She sips her coffee again. "When this whole mess with Ella and SM is finished, I'd like to ask you questions. Both of you. Probably a lot of questions. I've never met demons before, never mind the percentages. Would that be okay with you?"

"Fine by me," Dylan says, shrugging his massive shoulders.

I nod, although I feel little uncomfortable as Cloe continues to gawk at me.

"Let's get back to SM," Dylan suggests. He finishes his glass of water before carefully setting his elbows on the table.

I stare at him questioningly while pointing to his elbows.

He sighs. "Just trying not to tip over the entire table."

I nod, curious how much destruction Dylan has left in his wake recently.

"SM is my father's enemy," I tell Cloe.

"One of them," Dylan mutters under his breath.

I glare at Dylan. "Focus." I take a shallow breath before continuing. "Did SM get to Ella? Was this a set up?"

Cloe blows on her coffee and tentatively takes a tiny sip. "See, that doesn't make sense to me. Ella messing with this badass demon? It doesn't seem like her thing at all. What about the hypothetical neon sign Dylan mentioned?" She shifts in her seat as she digs into her pocket. "Let's hold off on SM and Ella for a moment." She sets two black stones onto the table. Dylan and I both inspect them.

"Do you carry crystals?" Cloe asks me.

I shake my head, intrigued. "May I?" I respected magic enough to ask permission before touching another witch's items.

Cloe pushes them toward me. "They're black tourmaline, powerful protection crystals, especially against dark magic."

I recognize the stones. When Persephone and I had performed a protection spell to help Jude, Persephone had incorporated two large chunks of black tourmaline. While she had felt a vibration from the crystals, I had felt nothing. Palming these much smaller stones now, I concentrate for a moment. Maybe I would feel something now as a more experienced witch. After what seems like a full minute, I feel nothing.

I nod at her stones. "Do you always carry them?"

"I didn't before I met you." Cloe says, her gaze narrowed. "My grandmother taught me about crystals from a young age. I learned from her to tune into my senses, my gut. I carry crystals with me when I sense trouble or if I need a boost to my psychic energy." Cloe grimaces. "Since you moved to town, my gut and my senses have been pinging my nerves like one of my video games when I hit level three hundred. They're with me all the time now."

"I'll get some," I say, handing the stones back to her.

Cloe pushes my hand away. "Keep them. I brought twice the amount I normally carry to Ella's tonight. Carry them on you fulltime, in the pocket of your clothes. Not in a purse or backpack."

Her tone is serious and I immediately slide the stones into my pocket.

I quickly fill them both in on the clove ash and rosemary I used at Ella's house.

Cloe shudders. "I don't even want to know what would've happened tonight without your herbs and my stones."

I check the time on my phone. I had texted my uncles on the drive to the diner to let them know the slumber party was canceled, claiming Ella had come down with the flu, and that we were grabbing a late dinner. The sooner we eat, the sooner I can go home, take a pain reliever, then go to bed.

Our waitress delivers a tray piled high with delicious-smelling food and my cup of tea. She refills Cloe's coffee cup.

Dylan grabs his knife and fork and dives in. Cloe smears a thick layer of butter on each of her pancakes. I take a cautious bite of scrambled eggs with cheese and wince. Swallowing food hurts which sucks because I'm hungry. I focus on my water and tea instead.

While Dylan and Cloe eat, Dylan and I take turns explaining the feud between Seamus and Jude, Seamus's subsequent beef with me, and the dark magic—soul magic—he had been practicing in the woods which he has taken further with local high school students.

Cloe looks horrified. "The dead girls around the city? You think that was SM?"

"It's him," Dylan says after swallowing a mouthful of his omelet.

She takes a bite of her pancakes, chews, and swallows. "If there is a connection to those girls, why isn't Ella...you know." She casts an ominous look at us.

"Good question. Working with SM will end badly. As much as I can't stand Ella, we need to confirm if she's involved with him. If she is, we need to convince her to end it quickly. I don't want to see her hurt or worse," I say.

I try another bite of eggs and nearly choke on them. A quick sip of water helps to wash them down. I push the plate away.

"Too painful?" Dylan asks, his voice hard as nails.

The anger in his voice catches me by surprise. I remind myself that his reaction is fueled by worry. Keeping up with Dylan's mood swings and exaggerated emotional reactions has become difficult. Suddenly, the emotional weight of the evening hits me and I feel exhausted.

I nod. "I'll try an ice pack on my neck tonight. Hopefully, that'll help."

He attacks his food with a vengeance, taking his frustration out on the eggs and pancakes as he eyeballs my throat from time to time. I know Dylan well enough to know that he feels he should've been there to help. It's not his job to protect me, but there's no sense telling him that now. He needs time to calm down.

After several minutes, he wipes his face with his napkin as he looks over at Cloe. He appears to have gotten himself under control. "I've known Ella a long time—we both have. She's never been into supernatural stuff. Let's put aside my neon sign theory for a minute. If they're working together, SM had to offer her something. Ella wouldn't help him without a big incentive."

"Like what? Money?" Cloe asks.

Dylan considers that. He shakes his head. "Recognition, maybe. Or status."

I consider how Ella likes to put me down, how she picks on others, making them feel small or at least beneath her. "Power," I add.

Seamus and Ella have nothing in common. He is old. She is young. He is bent on revenge. Ella wants attention or power, maybe both.

"Let's keep at this. What else does she want?" Dylan asks before he folds half a pancake into his mouth.

Cloe watches him in fascination. Her eyes are bright. Is it the conversation that jazzes her up or the coffee? She mulls over Dylan's question for a moment. I notice that not once tonight has she pulled her phone from her purse to log into one of her games. "You don't think she wants money, but that girl is addicted to shopping. She can never have enough clothes and makeup."

I stick with my line of thinking and consider how to translate power into something tangible. Cloe's right. Fashion and makeup mean a lot to Ella.

"She wants to be crowned Prom Queen," Cloe adds.

No big surprise about that. I think about what would be most important to Ella. Is it really only the superficial desires that drive her? Then it hits me.

Katie told me that Ella's dad is in New York all the time, how much she resents it. "Would she strike a deal to get her dad back home?" I ask.

"Good question," Dylan says, mulling that over for a minute. "She misses him, but on the flip side, he gives her a lot out of guilt. She likes that leverage."

Back to the subject of fashion and makeup. "The beauty blog. It's important to her."

Cloe nods. "Ella talks a lot about young influencers in the fashion and makeup world that she follows online. I think that's a title she wants for herself."

"Of course she does," Dylan says sarcastically.

"I would put that at the top of her list." Cloe says after a moment. She takes the last bite of her pancake, chews thoughtfully. "There's one other thing that needs to go at the top of the list. That girl has never stopped wanting *you*." She points at Dylan.

Dylan drops his fork. It clatters onto the table, then bounces to the floor.

"SM can't use a spell to force us together, can he?" Dylan asks, looking at me with horror. "Is that *allowed*? What about free will?" He grinds out the next words through clenched teeth. His fists curl on the table. "My father already negotiated me over to your *father*. Now I have to worry about *this*?"

The night has already gone on too long. The ache in my throat and the pain in my head from my fall are getting worse again. I want to go home, but Cloe just hit a raw nerve with Dylan.

"Please relax," I say, nervously, watching his hands grip the edges of the table. "It's a theory."

Cloe stares openly at Dylan, at the rise and fall of his chest as he takes huge gulps of air, at his reddening complexion. She sets her fork and knife on her plate delicately and wipes her mouth with her napkin. "I think it's time to call it a night," she says. "My grandmother's in town and I'm going to see her in the next few days. I'll find out what she has to say about free will."

Her words have an immediate, positive effect. Dylan's mood mellows a little. "That's good. Let me know what she has to say."

Dylan checks out my plate of unfinished food. I slide it over to him. While he devours my leftovers using my fork, I realize—not for the first time—that while I have Persephone and Henry to talk to about magical issues, Dylan only has Aiden and Aiden has been very busy. I wonder if that's part of Dylan's problems lately.

Dylan insists on taking Cloe home so I don't have to. They both hug me gingerly.

During my drive home I review the evenings events. Is it possible that Ella orchestrated tonight for Seamus's benefit? If so, does she understand how dangerous he is to me *and* to her?

Assuming it was Seamus trying to break through my protection spell, what would he have done if he'd gotten through? Was I his only target? Or would he have gone after everyone else, too?

Could there be any evidence at Ella's house that she's working with the demon?

First things first: I need sleep. Next, I need to go back to Ella's house and try to find clues to her involvement.

My uncles are asleep when I arrive home. After I swallow two Ibuprofen, I fill a Ziploc bag with ice and wrap it in a small towel. Once in bed, I apply the pack to my throat. My body begins to tremble as the weight of the evening hits me full on. At the diner, I kept it locked up. I was detached enough to talk about Seamus and Ella and demons and witches and magic with Cloe. Now that I'm alone, I begin to cry. Seamus—or someone else with a grudge—tried to kill me tonight. When will it end? The pain in my throat from the near strangulation is intensified by my sobs. To calm myself, I visualize confronting Seamus. Dylan and Cloe flank me as I hurl an endless supply of fireballs at him. The demon erupts in a burst of flames. His hands turn charcoal black and flake away. His face melts. The smell of his burned flesh doesn't bother me at all.

Right as I am on the verge of deep sleep, a random thought nudges me: *soul magic.*

CHAPTER TWENTY-SIX

– Ella Rosenthal –

"You say her lips were moving during the séance?" Seamus McAllister asks.

I had assumed it was Cloe and Lucy ringing my doorbell bright and early Sunday morning, so we could talk about what happened last night. That they brought coffee and donuts for Caroline, Katie, and Suzy so I wouldn't have to feed them. Panic bolted through me when I answered the door and saw *him*. When Seamus McAllister started to take a step over the threshold, I rushed us both outside onto the porch. Without makeup and my contacts, I hoped no one I knew walked by.

"Actually, it wasn't during—but after, when she was on the floor, after she fell." I squint at him, filled with unease. "Do you know anything about that? Lucy's choking incident?"

"Tell me about her hands," McAllister says, ignoring my questions. "Was she gesturing with them?"

Guilty as a snake.

"We all held hands," I say stiffly.

The old man eyes me suspiciously. I widen my eyes in

199

response to his probing glare. Immediately, I regret it as the sunshine jackknifes through my skull. Maybe three Jack and cokes last night was too much. Katie and Suzy were super judgy when I broke out the booze, but I needed some help going numb. The terror on Lucy's face as she clutched her throat scared the hell out of me. She nearly died right there on my living room floor.

"What?" I ask, his look putting me on the defensive. Then I remind myself to swallow the snotty attitude. The geezer's mood could escalate my hangover to something much more painful.

"Lucy's father is an evil man. A powerful man. He is teaching his daughter to follow in his footsteps. When I explained this to you the first time, you were eager to help me in my quest to stop him. To stop both of them. Has that changed?"

The ferocity in his expression, in his ancient papery voice causes me to back away. In that one step, I am pressed against my front door. Trapped. McAllister towers over me, his frame broad. He has to be—what—six foot five? Up close, he's scary.

"I'm new to this whole supernatural scene. What else should I have watched for? I never took my eyes off of her. Well, not until the paramedics showed up."

That's when I really started to freak out. Caroline rubbed my back when I burst into tears in the kitchen. Had I caused whatever happened to Lucy?

"Miss Rosenthal, it took tremendous effort for me to join your magical party—more than it should have. After only a brief time, I was blocked. I would like to know how that happened," McAllister says, unblinking. "I don't believe Miss Walker could have blocked me from entering your party. She was briefly incapacitated, was she not?"

I nod weakly.

"What I am trying to understand is who *else* at your home last night had powers?"

I blink stupidly at his question. It doesn't help that my head is throbbing. "No one."

The old man cuts me off with a wave of his hand. "Who else was present?"

If I get all the details out in a hurry, maybe he will leave. I need to go back to bed.

"Suzy Rodriguez, Cloe Gardner, Caroline Appleberg, and Katie Stevens."

He narrows his eyes as he considers the names. "None of them are supernatural? You are certain?"

"They're all perfectly average. I should know. We've been friends forever," I tell him.

He nods, appearing to accept the information. "What about the three items I asked for? Did you obtain them from Miss Walker?"

"I have two of the three items," I lie. Where does he get off with all of his demands? "What about the powers you said you'd give me after the séance? That was our deal."

The magician stares down at me with his beady black eyes and I shiver. I remember what happened the last time he was here. How he paralyzed my body. I blink several times, relieved my eyelids still function.

"It would be wise to remember to whom you are speaking,

Miss Rosenthal," the old man says. The threat in his ancient voice is clear. I shudder.

I nod quickly as he lays out his instructions.

"Bring me the items we discussed. Once you give them to me, I will determine whether you have earned the right to my power."

I was able to snatch Lucy's school ID, which includes her photo, and I did copy her class schedule. It's the third item that bugs me.

"Why do you need a photo of Lucy with her friends?" I say, trying to sound respectful so he doesn't turn me into a statue.

I have a bunch of group photos that feature Lucy. Every one of them also includes me.

"I need all three items for an important ritual. You have one week." His black eyes look past me into the living room. "Such a shame that your father is away so much. A young girl like you, unattended, in this big house. It must be frightening."

I flash back to Lucy, sprawled out on my floor, terrified as she clutched her throat. I press my back firmly against my front door.

"Today is Sunday. Get over to Jude Morgan's home and observe. I want to know what Lucy does during her visits—and who keeps her company."

"Okay." I choke.

"Do as I ask, Miss Rosenthal."

"Yes," I whisper. Tears sting my eyes. More than anything in the world, I want to get away from Psycho McAllister.

CHAPTER TWENTY-SEVEN

– Lucy Walker –

"Imagine your worst enemy, Lucy. Now focus," Aiden says standing off to my side. Training sessions take place every Sunday in the backyard of Jude's Lake Forest home. Backyard is a grand understatement—this one is the size of the football field Dylan plays on.

"We're all imagining the same supernatural psychopath," Dylan says from the sidelines. He tears his attention from a selection of knives in an unrolled pack on the ground and glares at Aiden.

Dylan and I updated Aiden on the events of last night's attack. He deemed me well enough to train, although he switched our agenda to knife skills to reduce risk of further injury to my neck.

Aiden ignores Dylan and gestures for me to continue.

With the metal blade gripped between my thumb and forefinger, I balance on the balls of my feet then fall back onto my heels. I step forward. My eyes zero in on the bullseye drawn on the center of the cardboard. Seamus's face appears in my head. So do the jackhammers. I remember the feeling of my neck being squeezed. My body freezes in fear. It *had* to be Seamus last night. What would he have done if he'd broken through?

If Ella is working with him, does she know he's a demon? Why would she give him access to her friends? My resolve crystalizes. I level my gaze at the bullseye. I throw the knife and it misses the target and lands in the grass.

"Where's your head at right now?" Aiden reprimands me.

"Maybe her focus is a bit messed up after Seamus tried to kill her last night." Dylan snaps. His eyes drop to my neck.

I dug through all of my clothes this morning until I found a shirt that had a high neck. My primary goal was to get out of my house without sending my uncles into cardiac arrest.

"Aiden's right," I say to Dylan. If my father were training me right now, he wouldn't accept an excuse. Then again, my father would help me kill Seamus or whoever else attacked me last night.

Once I retrieve the knife, I return to my spot and the mental image of the gray-haired demon. If he and Ella are working together, I need to figure out why. I need to blast through his plan before he comes for me again. Resolve fuels me. I take my position, aim, and throw the knife. It sinks into the box, four inches to the left of the crimson circle.

"Take that, pizza box!"

I turn to meet Aiden's grimace and my smile fades. I drop my arm to my side mid fist pump.

"That's the best I've done yet," I say defensively.

"The blade was pitched downward. Do it again. This time stand a foot closer."

I bite back my sarcastic response.

"Why does she need ninja knife-throwing skills when she can blast Seamus with fireballs? She took out Garret with magic, too. I should be the one to concentrate on non-magical maneuvers," Dylan says. He tosses a knife into the air and catches it one-handed, his eyes on Aiden and me the whole time.

Aiden glares at Dylan. "Leave the training protocol to me." Aiden clenches his own knife, which looks like something used to inflict torture in horror movies. The weapon together with the black T-shirt, jeans, and black Dockers, screams: *Beware of the assassin!* I step away from him. I kind of liked his professional attire at breakfast last weekend.

"Jude said that Seamus is involved in soul magic—dark even for demons. Let's assume that it was Seamus trying to break through last night. What if he's planning to use that dark magic on Ella, or my friends, or me?" I say, verbalizing the idea that came to me last night.

Is Seamus tethering his magic to Ella? As much as I despise her, especially if she gave Seamus access to me last night, I don't want her to die. There's no way she could survive Seamus's dark magic.

"Does soul magic work if Seamus is sucking souls from non-supernaturals? Would that still fuel his power?" I ask.

"Yes, but the pain would be unbearable to his victim," Aiden responds through clenched teeth. "It's sadistic. I can't believe anyone—even Seamus—would go that deep in the dark arts."

"Sorry to burst your Boy Scout vision of Seamus and demons, generally, but he's gone off the reservation. You heard Jude,"

Dylan raises his voice. "Rule following and Seamus don't belong in the same conversation."

Dylan grasps his knife and throws it at the target, nailing the bull's-eye.

"You want a chance to throw with a real knife?" Aiden asks, offering his massive blade to Dylan.

"Don't you dare point that butcher knife at my muscle man!"

We all turn as Selima jogs over to us from the far end of Jude's house, Marcus not far behind her. Selima wraps her arms around Dylan and plants a kiss on his mouth. Dylan's smile is immediate.

"Good thing I came along to save you," she teases.

"Good thing," he agrees.

I turn my attention to my own boyfriend, trying to ignore the tension causing an ache between my shoulders.

Marcus slips his arm around my waist and plants a kiss on my forehead. I would've preferred his lips to press against mine, but I'm not complaining. A surprise visit from Marcus is a welcome break from Aiden's constant criticism. I can't help thinking about Katie. What would've happened if Seamus had gotten through? What if he'd hurt her? Or any of the other girls?

Marcus's touch works its magic. My tension begins to ease. I catch a whiff of his amazing scent and want to nuzzle closer, until I notice his clenched jaw. He doesn't know what happened last night, so his mood can't have anything to do with Ella's séance.

Dylan's light mood disappears, too. I don't have to see the shift. I feel it. "Something's up. What is it?" he asks Selima.

"Yes, what brings you to the enemy's lair, little brother?" Aiden asks, sheathing his knife.

"Selima received news about Camille this morning." Marcus's grip on my waist tightens. "The council set a date for the tribunal. It'll be held in a week."

"Which leaves us with very little time to prepare," Selima points out. The stress in her voice is plain. "A sneaky tactic."

Aiden studies Marcus. "I thought they were holding off on any decisions until they interviewed you?"

Marcus's expression pinches. "That's why we're here. They want to interview me in two days."

My heart sinks. I expected this, knew he was leaving. A part of me had hoped either the charges against Camille would be dropped or Marcus's testimony wouldn't be needed.

Selima's expression is grave. "According to my mother, they want to charge Camille as an accomplice to Garret's crimes. They have witnesses who will come forward to testify that the two of them worked together to dope protectors and build Garret's army," she says. She pulls out of Dylan's embrace, suddenly all business. Her formfitting, steel-gray outfit makes her look like a member of Team Aiden. Her short, spiky hair completes the look. "Possession of demon blood is a crime. Worse, administering it to protectors is forbidden. The punishment is severe."

Aiden nods. His expression is tight, his voice grim. "Despite all of their good deeds, protectors are inflexible and ruthless when it comes to their laws."

Dylan shakes his head. "Call me crazy, but facts are facts. She and Garret were dosing protectors with the blood of demons they slaughtered, building a mutant army. Or have you all forgotten that part?"

"But—" Selima begins.

"Those mutant soldiers tried to kill us," I add, baffled by Marcus and Selima's bleak attitudes.

If the clan proves she was as involved as Garret in building that army, then she needs to be held accountable. I can't help but think that if they hadn't created the whole mess, I wouldn't have Garret's death on my hands, fueling my nightmares.

"Lucy, you don't know what you're saying," Marcus says, shocked.

How many times did I get defensive when people criticized Momma? Then it hits me. This visit isn't merely an update. I touch his arm, aware that three pairs of eyes watch us. "If the interview is in two days, when are you planning to leave?"

"Tomorrow morning," Marcus says, stiffly.

Selima comes to my side. Up close I notice she isn't wearing makeup and her eyes are red. "I don't think you understand. If she's convicted, her punishment will be death."

I whip my head around to look at my boyfriend and immediately regret the movement. I grind my teeth against the pain in my throat.

"Marcus, I'm sorry. I didn't know."

I reach for him, but his grimace stops me.

"How long will you be gone?" Dylan asks.

Selima returns to him, takes his hand. Is she working her calming mojo on Dylan? "Two weeks, I think. I can't be sure."

I work to keep my expression blank. The grief will hit me later. Camille's life is on the line. For now I need to support Marcus.

"I'll let you know our progress," Marcus says. His tone is cold, detached. I search his face, attempt to meet his gaze, but his words are directed at Aiden.

Selima cups Dylan's face with her hands as she plants another kiss on his mouth.

Marcus doesn't kiss or touch me before he turns and stalks off. I watch as his long strides take him away from me. More than anything, I wish I could hit a rewind button and redo the last fifteen minutes. Instead, my heart hurts as the distance between me and my boyfriend grows.

"Please try to understand what he's going through," Selima says as she wraps her arms around me. "I will keep in touch. Promise."

I hug her tightly. "Tell him I love him."

"You will see him before he leaves. Tell him yourself."

She jogs after her brother.

Marcus is leaving, I think to myself. *He will get what he has always wanted—his family and acceptance from others like him. He'll no longer be an outsider. He can escape his selfish girlfriend, the one who killed his father, and despises his mother.*

The dark energy fills me fast. It is frenzied and angry and threatens to consume me. Camille will get what she wanted from the beginning. Her son. Never mind that she threw him away all those years ago. They are a ready-made family. The two of them. I wonder if Camille is relieved to have Garret out of the picture. After all, he was jealous of her affection for Marcus.

My grief is dark and desperate. My body trembles as heat radiates along my arms. I spin around looking for a target, something to burn. I spot one of the ogre-like trees that decorate

Jude's mammoth backyard and hurl three fireballs in quick succession. Aiden grabs my shoulders and whirls me around, furious. The fourth fireball balancing on my palm tumbles off. Aiden stomps it out.

Sweat trickles down my scalp, beneath my long black hair. "Jude put...some kind of protection spell...on the trees. It's not like...I'll do any damage," I pant, a combination of my effort not to cry and expended energy.

I wince as Aiden's fingers dig into my shoulders. While the wounds inflicted by Garret's claws the night of the battle healed, faint scars remain and right now it feels as if Aiden has angry claws of his own. "What did you do?" he growls.

"What?" I blink at him.

"Your friend, the Stevens girl..."

The pain in my shoulders together with the pain in my heart paralyze my brain. Aiden's words make no sense.

Aiden shakes me hard. "What's her name?"

"Get away from her. She was choked last night, remember?" Dylan yanks Aiden off of me. He confronts our mentor. "Are you talking about Katie?"

Aiden glares at Dylan. "She was there, watching." He points to the edge of the house, the corner where Selima and Marcus originally came from. He turns to me. "Why was she here? Did you invite her so you could show off for her?"

Is he making stuff up just to pick a fight since I upset Marcus?

"She saw you, Lucy. She was there, watching. *Spying.* She saw your target practice with the tree." Aiden glares at me. "Go find her, talk to her. Make sure she keeps her mouth shut. I will talk to Persephone and Henry. One of them will need to erase her memory."

Aiden is serious. Katie was spying on me? Why would she do that?

The sound of screeching tires on the street in front of Jude's house causes all three of us to freeze.

Oh, no. What have you done, Katie?

Dylan lunges around Aiden, grabs hold of my hand. He tugs me across the yard. "We're on it."

CHAPTER TWENTY-EIGHT

– Lucy Walker –

"Do you think Katie was spying on us?" Dylan asks as we climb into my car.

My pile of problems keeps growing and growing.

"Aiden saw her. That she took off in such a hurry...How else would you categorize her visit?" I glance over at Dylan before I pull out my phone. My hands shake as I call Katie. Her voicemail kicks in. I disconnect. "Did you see how mad Aiden was? Do you think he would do anything to Katie, to keep her quiet?" I ask as I pull out of Jude's driveway.

What was Katie thinking, coming over here without talking to me first? Sure, she seemed upset the last time we talked about my visits to Jude's house. She was hurt that I hadn't invited her, but it's not like I can have her stop by for show and tell on training day. Plus, keeping her away is for her own protection. What if Seamus were to appear?

Worst of all is that Katie saw Dylan and Aiden here with me. Did she see Marcus and Selima, too? She's got to be doubly hurt that I've excluded her. How will I explain this to her without revealing secrets that I am forbidden to share?

"Hopefully Aiden won't do anything. He should leave it to Persephone and Henry to handle. Like we talked about at the diner, secrecy in the supernatural world seems to be Rule Number One. Kind of like Fight Club. Now that it's just you and me," Dylan says, his voice edged with nervousness, "you can come clean. Have you talked to Katie about any of this?" Dylan makes devil horns on top of his head with his fingers and his expression morphs into mock rage.

I give him a tight smile and shake my head.

"I've never said a word to Katie about this part of my life," I say. "I feel super guilty about it. Best friends aren't supposed to hide things from each other, especially the big stuff."

Dylan looks at me skeptically. "If you've never said anything to her, how did Katie know where Jude lives?"

"Good question. It's not like my demon father is listed on whitepages.com." I consider that for a moment. "Do you think she followed Marcus and Selima?"

Dylan mulls that over. "Either that or she followed us earlier."

"Marcus and Selima didn't see her or they would have said something, don't you think?"

Dylan shrugs. "Dunno. They had a lot on their minds. They could've missed her."

"I doubt it."

"I finally find a kickass girlfriend and she's taking off to help your boyfriend," Dylan grumbles as we stop at a red light.

I can't allow Dylan to place all the blame on Marcus.

"It's Selima's stepmother. She has more of a relationship with the wicked witch than Marcus does," I say, my throat burning with the effort to get all the words out.

I glance at Dylan in time to catch his twisted grin. It only lasts a second.

"There are now two evil stepmothers in our lives," he complains halfheartedly.

Silence fills the car as we put more distance between Jude's house and us.

"At least your girlfriend's mother doesn't hate you."

Dylan grins, but it fades almost immediately as he glances at my neck. "I wish you weren't losing your protector boyfriend." He reaches for the neck of my shirt, tugs at it gently. "Why didn't you tell Marcus about the attack?"

I keep my eyes fixed on the road. Marcus didn't ask about last night and that stung more than anything. I can't hold it against him. Not when Camille's life is in jeopardy. "I can take care of myself."

Dylan frowns focusing on my covered neck. "We both know you can take care of yourself, but..."

I glance at him with raised eyebrows.

Dylan slinks lower in his seat. It's a strange sight considering his bulky mass. His expression twitches at the same time he rubs his jaw. "You could handle yourself in the past. I'm not so sure that's true anymore."

"Last night...I beat him—with Cloe's help," I say. My point is a weak one and Dylan and I both know it.

After a lengthy silence, Dylan turns to me. "Jude had hoped to be back home by now, but Lucifer refuses to commit to a return date. Seamus has gone rogue and won't abide by Lucifer's orders. Jude's worried about you and he's angry. Scary angry."

I focus hard on the road. My nerves are jumpy and I can't risk an accident. I clench the steering wheel so tight my knuckles glow white.

"I have your back. You know that, right? Jude is fueling my powers. You and me—we can handle this," Dylan says.

First Jude leaves with Lucifer after the big battle between the demons and gargoyles at my high school. Now Marcus and Selima are leaving. I thought I could handle whatever came my way. Ignoring Lucifer's order, Seamus will keep coming for me. What then? It's great that Dylan will fight beside me, but will he be enough? Training and pretending to be okay in front of Aiden took way too much out of me and my throat hurts.

With a heavy heart, I think through how I'm going to deal with Katie. What did she see and hear while watching us today? What would she do if she knew about Seamus? Maybe if she hadn't taken off...if she had announced herself, then maybe this would've turned out differently. The squeal of tires in her rapid departure was a dead giveaway that she had come to spy. Just then a horrible thought occurs to me.

"Dylan?"

He turns to me, eyebrows raised.

"Katie doesn't have a license."

Dylan smacks his forehead with his palm as he groans. "Someone body drove her to Jude's house. Aiden will freak. You—we—need to find out who it was. ASAP."

I jerk my head up and down in agreement while mentally running through a list of suspects. Trevor worked a DJ gig today. Caroline was scheduled to work at Cheesecake Factory all weekend. Suzy is on shift at her family's store. Cloe planned to spend the day on homework and creating material for her YouTube channel.

That leaves Ella.

I accelerate toward home.

Chapter Twenty-Nine

– Lucy Walker –

Once Dylan and I arrive back at my place and he leaves, I go inside and grab Ibuprofen from the bathroom medicine cabinet. More than anything, I want to put another ice pack on my throat and climb into bed. There's no time for that right now, though. While my uncles are occupied—Sheldon reads a book on the back porch while Bernard grocery shops for food to bring to their monthly poker party tonight, I head upstairs to Marcus's apartment. His car is out front, so I know he's home.

He answers the door and while his expression is not anywhere near happy to see me, he doesn't appear to be angry anymore, either.

"I'm sorry," I tell him as I shut the door behind me and follow him into the apartment.

He nods, his hands stuffed in the pockets of his slate gray cargo shorts. "You didn't know."

"Do you want to talk about it?" I ask.

This is where Marcus would normally lead me to the couch and we would sit, our hands automatically reaching for each other as we talked through whatever we needed to. Marcus remains standing.

"Not really," he says. There's a lot of emotion broiling beneath the surface. I know it has everything to do with what's going on with the council and his fears for Camille. Marcus is keeping a tight lid on it all. After a pause he switches topics. "Do you want to tell me about last night?"

I'm still wearing my high-neck top. He catches me by surprise when he nods to my throat.

"The séance turned out to be...dangerous." I utter the words hesitantly, unsure about my boyfriend's mood.

Marcus gently touches the fabric at my throat and pulls it away from my skin. Shock registers on his face, followed by anger.

"Tell me what happened."

I recount the entire evening to him.

"Seamus tried to strangle you?" Marcus says furiously. His fingers probe the bruises. I try not to flinch.

Tears well up in my eyes. I'm not sure if it's reliving the whole experience, the painful pressure of his touch, or that my boyfriend is giving me sympathy that I desperately crave. Not very kickass demon-like of me, but it's the truth.

"We assume it was Seamus," I tell him. "That's not all. After you and Selima left Jude's today, Aiden saw Katie watching us. He flipped out. I've been trying to call her and all I get is her voicemail."

His fingers cease their inspection. "What was she doing at Jude's?"

"I don't know." I raise my eyes to meet his. "Aiden was so angry. Do you think he would do anything to her?"

Marcus shakes his head. "Not hurt her, but I could see him getting Persephone or Henry involved. Keep trying to reach her."

Just then my phone pings in my pocket. I retrieve my cell and read the message. "It's Katie. She agreed to come over tonight so we can talk."

"You want me to join you?" Marcus asks.

Katie likes Marcus. Trusts him. If the situation escalates, Marcus could use his calming power on Katie. That would definitely help.

"Yes, please."

I message Katie back. A few minutes later Marcus and I sit together on his couch after I accept a glass of water and an ice pack for my neck.

CHAPTER THIRTY

– Lucy Walker –

The backyard at Gram's house, now my uncles' house, has always been a special place for me. The brick three-flat hasn't changed since I was small. No matter how scary life gets, I feel protected here. I felt safe with Gram from the horrors of life with Momma. Even now I feel safe from other horrors.

The cool evening breeze passes over my skin and lifts my hair and I sigh with pleasure. At the same time, it rustles through the leaves on the tall oak, maple, and ash trees surrounding me. Do they enjoy the refreshing chill like I do? We are connected—like kin—born of the elements. That's what Henry and Persephone said. Not every witch is able to manipulate the elements. Gram could. On a teeny tiny level, so can I.

Lola calls out from one of the treetops. I raise my chin and study the dark foliage looking for Gram's raven. Another call from a neighboring tree. Serenity—Persephone's raven—communicates with Lola. A rustle of leaves, then Lola launches from her branch and swoops over to where I'm guessing Serenity is perched. They could do this for hours, chatting, and moving from tree to tree.

The night is cool. It makes them playful.

I feel Katie's presence before I see her. Is it possible that I have a connection with her like I have with Dylan? Doubtful since Katie doesn't have any of Jude's magical blood swimming in her veins. Probably just heightened senses on my part. Katie is my best friend and I love her. Is she super mad at me now that she knows I've kept secrets from her? Katie hesitates at the corner of the house.

"Why are you standing over there?" I wave her over to me.

Katie's shoulders rise, but don't drop to finish a shrug. She wears her favorite pink sweatshirt with the hood pulled over her head.

"Thank you for coming over," I say, stuffing my hands into the pockets of my jeans. I kick at the thick, long leather glove on the ground, the one I wear when bringing the ravens outside to protect my arm from their talons. In the dim evening light, I try to search Katie's eyes for a sign, something that will tell me she's ready for what I am going to reveal to her tonight. Because of her hooded eyes, I can't read her expression.

"Your uncles home?" she asks with a tilt of her head toward our first-floor apartment.

"They're out with their poker friends. Won't be home for a couple of hours," I say. "Marcus will join us in a little while, though."

"Where's Dylan?" Katie asks, sarcastically.

"He went home."

"Then why did I see his car parked out front?" Her tone is snotty, distrustful.

"Because I decided to come back," Dylan announces as he strides over to us. He looks past Katie to me. "I know you told me not to come back, but this involves all of us."

After leaving Marcus's apartment earlier today, I had called Dylan to let him know I would be meeting with Katie tonight.

"You're prepared to open up and tell her about yourself?" I ask, bluntly.

"It's only right since you are, too," Dylan says. He stands beside Katie, arms crossed over his well-developed chest.

That statement shocks me given his staunch statements to Cloe and me at the diner about maintaining the secrecy of our supernatural lives.

"Are you ready for this?" I ask Katie.

This isn't how I wanted to spend my boyfriend's last night in town, but he promised to help convince Katie that our secrets need to stay secret. Not just mine and Marcus's, but now Dylan's, too.

Katie nods.

"Why did you come to Jude's house today?" I ask.

Katie snorts. "To find out the truth. Ella said you would be mad now that I know some of your secrets."

Her harsh tone causes me to rock back on my heels.

"You're my best friend, Katie. I shouldn't have kept stuff from you. I was ordered to keep certain information confidential, so that's what I did. I'm sorry." I tread carefully. Somehow Ella has gained Katie's trust. Once I show Katie my magic, will I scare her? Repel her? At this point, I don't feel like I have much choice. She already saw what she saw. "You know Ella better than most

222

people. She's no friend of mine. I will tell you the truth, but you have to promise not to share it with Ella or anyone else. You have to promise me before I show you anything."

"Fine. I promise," she says after a long pause.

"You're going to see some crazy stuff tonight," I say, fighting the tremor in my voice. "None of it will hurt you, though. I promise."

Crazy stuff. I remember when Persephone first told me that Gram was a witch. After that, I learned my father was a demon. Tonight I am going to reveal my family's secrets with my closest friend. My boyfriend is going to share his as well. He doesn't agree with me that this is the right thing to do. He's doing it for me.

"Do it then. Show me," Katie says. Her normally upbeat voice is filled with animosity. She slides the hood from her head.

My throat tightens. Will my revelations tonight be enough to mend our friendship? Can I believe that Katie won't tell anyone what she sees tonight? I have to trust her. With a nod, I slide my cell from my pocket and text Marcus to join us. He was probably watching us from a window in his apartment because he crosses the yard to join us within minutes of me shoving my phone back into my pocket.

"Hey, Katie," Marcus says as he stops beside me.

"Hey," Katie mumbles, flicking her gaze over his body.

Marcus glances at Dylan. "Back for the show?"

Dylan nods. "Lucy wants to tell Katie the truth. She and I share Jude's blood, so I'm part of that truth."

Katie gasps. "You two are related?"

Dylan squirms at the question. Marcus smirks.

"No," I say quickly. "Mr. Douglas drank a goblet of my father's blood a long time ago as part of a magical deal."

Katie's mouth pulls down in disgust. It takes a moment as she digests the information. "What's so special about your dad's blood?" she asks me.

Suddenly, my voice and lips refuse to cooperate. When I told Katie that Momma was an alcoholic and drug user, I was scared the revelation would turn Katie off and end our friendship. It didn't. Here I am about to tell her that my father is a demon. Keeping secrets is something I've done my whole life. Breaking them wide open like this is one of the hardest things I've ever done.

"My father is supernatural," I tell her. "He is a demon."

Katie's eyes widen. "A demon?" she gulps. She pauses several beats as she digests this information. "Like that one from the Paranormal Activity movies?"

I throw my hands up as if to stop an approaching robber. "No! Oh, gosh, no. Nothing like that."

Dylan bursts out laughing.

Katie and I both whip our heads toward him. I cringe as pain radiates along my neck.

"I'm not laughing at you," Dylan gasps before bursting into another round of laughter. "Jude insists on watching all the popular teen shows with Lucy," he clutches his stomach he's laughing so hard, "and he asks all these questions about sex and drinking and drugs. I mean, he's so paranoid. He thinks all guys are bad boy sex addicts and stalkers." He looks over at Marcus with a grin, wiping tears from his eyes. "It's amazing he allows Lucy to date at all."

I can't stifle my own laughter. "It's true." I roll my eyes. "The interrogations are embarrassing."

"Remember how he tried to forbid you from sleepovers at Katie's house early on? He was sure you were going to sneak out to meet boys," Dylan says, slowly getting himself under control. He jerks his thumb over at Marcus. "That was before he understood that you two were serious."

Dylan's dose of comic relief lightens the mood. Even Katie cracks a smile.

"Did Mr. Douglas have magical powers after drinking the blood?" she asks.

Dylan's humor evaporates. "That wasn't what he was after. My father wanted success and wealth. He offered me up in exchange for that."

Katie blinks. "What do you mean?"

"The blood drinking happened a long time ago. Before I was born. Jude's blood passed to me. I have powers—nothing as cool as Lucy's or Marcus's, but still..." he shrugs his muscled shoulders. "My dad is loaded and massively successful. He got what he wanted."

"Dylan went through hell physically and emotionally," Marcus adds. "He's now part demon and a member of Team Jude."

Marcus's explanation on Dylan's behalf is a surprise. I squeeze his hand to express my gratitude.

Katie nods slowly as she takes it all in.

It's time to get to the point of our meeting. "We should talk about your trip to my father's house."

Katie's lighthearted mood disappears. She looks tired. "You make fire with your hands. I saw you. Will you show me?"

"Okay."

Marcus takes a step toward Katie. "Before we begin," he extends his hand. "Could I have your phone until we're done? We can't risk any photos or video."

He told me ahead of time he would do this. I protested then. It's Katie. She wouldn't betray me.

Katie focuses on Marcus's hand for a moment. Her brows pull together as she considers his request and I wonder if she will turn and leave. Instead, Katie smacks her phone into Marcus's palm.

"If you break it, you're buying me a new one," she says.

Her sharp tone surprises me. Dylan meets my gaze with raised eyebrows. Was she going to try to film me? Would she show evidence of my secrets to Ella? To others? It's impossible to see past her angry expression. I force myself to exhale. Marcus has her phone now.

Just get it over with, Dylan says.

Will this demonstration save my friendship with Katie? Was Marcus right when he said revealing the truth—my magical truth—to Katie was a huge risk? Fear and suspicion chew at my insides. It doesn't matter, though. I promised to show her. Marcus spoke with Persephone and Henry. If things don't go well during the demonstration, my witch mentors will erase Katie's memories from today and tonight. Once we find out who drove her to my father's house—Ella, probably—we will deal with that person next.

With all of my practice, I don't need to embrace darkness to conjure my demon magic. Aiden helped me to understand that. Henry, too.

As I face the trees, Lola and Serenity no longer chatter. The only sign of their presence is the rustle of leaves as they move from tree to tree. I lift my palm and will the fireball to appear. It's instantaneous.

Katie inhales sharply.

"How...How do you do it?" she asks.

Her tone—a little wobbly and hesitant—gives me a glimmer of hope. It is the voice of my inquisitive friend and not the judgmental, accusing version who arrived at my house tonight.

"Come closer," I say. I turn my body to give her a better view while balancing the ball of flame on my hand.

Katie's eyes grow wide as she steps forward. She clutches her hands to her chest.

Marcus and Dylan watch Katie.

"Does it hurt?" she asks.

"No," I say, bouncing the fireball from one hand to the other. "My hands turn red, but that's just a protective response of my skin."

Katie holds her hand several inches above the fireball. "I can feel the heat."

"Don't get any closer," I caution. "It will burn you."

We watch the fireball in silence, transfixed. Magic is no longer something I fear. The gold, orange, and red flames are beautiful and they're a part of me. The crackly hiss captivates me.

Katie's eyes glow with the reflection of the ball of light. "What do you do with it? I mean, we aren't in the Stone Age. We don't need fire to cook our food—although I kind of wish I had a marshmallow on a stick right now."

She and I both chuckle.

"I could go for some s'mores," Dylan says, grinning.

Marcus narrows his eyes at me. I read the caution in his eyes, but I have already revealed so much. What does it matter if I tell her more? It's a relief to let the secrets out.

"Jude—my father—has been teaching me to fight, to defend myself," I say. "Creating fireballs is my most potent demon skill."

Katie's face remains pointed toward the fireball, which I slide from my left hand to my right, back and forth, back and forth. My own magical Slinky.

"Why do you need to defend yourself?" she asks slowly.

"Lucy—" Marcus warns.

"This is my decision, Marcus," I remind him before turning back to Katie.

"My father trains me to defend myself against Seamus McAllister, a demon who keeps trying to kill me," I tell her. "Jude trains Dylan, too, so he can help me."

Marcus's exhale sounds like the rasp of an angry snake.

Katie's huge eyes focus on my face instead of the fire in my hands. "Another demon? Trying to kill you?"

"That's enough," Marcus says, clutching my arm.

"Marcus, what is your issue?" Dylan snaps. "Let her finish."

"Trying to kill you?" Katie says again.

I press my fingers to Marcus's arm while balancing the fireball in my other hand. "Secrets suck, Marcus. I can't hide them from Katie. Not anymore." He is about to interrupt me, but I charge on, my voice strong, pleading for him to understand. "You are leaving to go help your mom. I can't talk to my uncles about any of this. I have Dylan—which is awesome, but I need Katie to understand what I'm going through, so I can puke out all the garbage eating me up inside, so I don't lose my sanity."

Marcus takes an exaggerated breath and backs down.

"Trying to kill you?" Katie glances around the yard nervously. "Is he here in Chicago? Does he watch you?" She backs away from me, no longer interested in the ball of flame. She moves in a circle, studying our surroundings. Her voice wavers. "How do you know he isn't watching you...us...right now?"

I drop the fireball to the ground. It sizzles and dies out.

"That's where I come in," Marcus says, his voice flat.

Katie whips around to face him. "What do you mean?"

Marcus and I take turns explaining his ability to sense demons and see their auras. The grumpy expression on his face reminds me that he is unhappy about it.

Katie listens attentively, still looking completely freaked out about a killer demon on the loose. Her arms wrap around her body tightly.

"I'm such an idiot," Katie says finally. She shivers and I feel bad for her. This is a lot to take in all in one night. "I was convinced you were in danger from your own father. After seeing you at his house, with Marcus and Dylan and the others earlier today, I was angry that you were hiding stuff from me, having a fabulous time hanging with your other friends and excluding me. I should have asked you what was going on instead of buying into Ella's theories."

A chill races up my spine. "Ella?"

Katie bites her lip. "She told me you were in danger, at least that's how she sucked me into her web of lies."

"What does she know?" Marcus asks Katie.

He presses his hand to the small of my back. His touch keeps me from totally losing it right now.

"She got into my head, told me she was worried about you, that we needed to figure out what you were doing in order to protect you. Some friend of your grandmother's approached her. He said your father was going to hurt you. After I saw you at Jude's today and explained to her what I saw, she freaked out." Katie says, sounding nearly hysterical. "She said you were doing bad things just like your dad." She fights to catch her breath, her eyes shining with tears. "I know Ella better than anyone. Should've seen through her. She totally played me."

"Ella drove you to Jude's?" I ask.

Katie chokes back a sob and nods.

"What I don't get is how did you two get through the gate?" Dylan asks.

Katie shrugs. "Ella knew the code."

I inhale a careful breath. "Katie, what exactly did you tell Ella?"

"She knows Marcus has wings—which I saw one night out my bedroom window. She knows what I saw at your dad's house. The fireballs, who was there. I told her everything."

I drop my head in my hands. I had suspected it was Ella who drove Katie to Jude's house. Now she has information about Marcus, too.

"You mentioned that a friend of Lucy's grandmother's spoke to Ella. Who is it?" Marcus asks. There's not an ounce of gentleness in his voice.

"I don't know," Katie says tearfully. "Lucy, please don't hate me. I'm so sorry!"

St. Aquinas's resident mean girl is going to try to ruin my life. The problem is, she may be teaming up with Seamus McAllister to do it. Scenes from Ella's party flicker through my mind. The freezing cold room. The flickering candles. The invisible grip on my throat. We need to confirm whether Ella and Seamus are working together. If they are, then we have to do whatever it takes to make Ella break her alliance before they kill me or anyone else.

CHAPTER THIRTY-ONE

– Lucy Walker –

The next morning Marcus and I stand side by side on the roof, our shoulders touching. We lace our fingers together as we watch the sun rise.

"Two weeks will fly by," I tell him. The strong line of his jaw begs to be touched, so I pull my hand free from his and trace the angle of his face. My fingers brush his cheek, stroke his ear then move along his jaw down to his neck. Marcus wraps his arm around me and pulls me against him. I hold him tightly.

"Will you be okay today, not having spent time in your stone form?" I ask.

Marcus spends every night on the roof in his stone form. It's the only way his kind—protectors—maintain their powers, energy, and good health. He spent last night with me after he finished his homework instead.

We laid in my bed, our legs tangled. While his fingers traced the outline of my face, his lips trailed small kisses on every spot his fingers touched.

"It's going to be incredible for you, being around all those protectors. People just like you," I said to him.

He kisses me now as the sky brightens. The birds chirp and sing their morning greetings. Down below, car doors slam and my neighbors leave for work or school.

"Two weeks. Worst case it runs a little longer, but I will be back," Marcus says, pulling away just a little. His eyes meet mine. He leans down and presses his lips to mine.

"Hmmm," I murmur as I kiss him back. His arms tighten around me.

I believe Marcus is telling me the truth as far as he knows it. The thing is...I don't believe Camille will let him go so easily. On top of that, I don't think her case is going to run all that smoothly given her crimes—not that I know anything about the criminal trial system—the regular kind or the supernatural kind. The miserable cherry on top is if Marcus changes his mind once he's around his own kind. If he decides that he's happiest around other protectors. Add all that together...I don't allow myself to finish that thought.

Dylan and I have a plan for this week. One I don't plan to share with Marcus. We need to figure out what Ella is up to and keep her from exposing me and the other supernaturals in my life. While I trust Katie, I need to make sure she keeps her lips sealed about everything I told her last night. Dylan promised to help me keep an eye on her.

I unwind myself from Marcus's embrace. "I have to get ready for school."

"Will you be okay today?" Marcus asks. He eyes my neck.

I have a handkerchief-type scarf wrapped around my throat that I borrowed from Katie—maroon and gold, our school colors. St. Aquinas sold them as part of a fundraiser two years ago, so it's not like I could get a demerit wearing it. At least I hope not.

"My bruises? Or facing Ella who has probably revealed to half the school that I shoot fire from my hands?" I chuckle bitterly. "Maybe she'll publish an expose in the school yearbook."

He grips my shoulders. "I could give you another dose of blood. You would heal faster."

Marcus had given me a small dose before I met with Katie. It allowed me to speak to her without pain. "Just the one was enough. Thanks. Besides, a little pain and the bruises keep me motivated and focused." I touch my neck. "It's a reminder that Seamus—or someone else—is after me."

Marcus's grip tightens. His eyes burn into mine. "What's the code?"

While wrapped in each other's arms last night after talking for hours, we decided on a phrase. We would use it in a crisis, to signal to the other person to return home quickly. In this case, that would be Marcus.

"Vera always loved you."

"She always loved you, too," Marcus says softly. He kisses me so tenderly tears spring to my eyes.

"I really need to go," I say, sadly. "Call me Wednesday night?"

"I will," he says.

I turn to leave but not before I notice the load of guilt distorting my boyfriend's face.

CHAPTER THIRTY-TWO

– Dylan Douglas –

Standing in Ella's kitchen is the last place I want to be tonight, but Lucy and I are on a mission. My mood boils over with resentment between Selima leaving this morning and having to be here. Instead of working out with Chad and Nick, I'm making nice with a superficial monster who conspired to hurt Lucy.

"I'm surprised you're here. Shouldn't you be at home pining away over that weird goth girl?" Ella says as I lean against the counter. She retrieves a bag of eggrolls from the freezer before grabbing me a Coke from the fridge. I glance at the package to make sure she followed instructions. They are vegetarian for Lucy's sake. "You want some Jack to spice things up?" she asks with a provocative smile, opening a cabinet stuffed with her father's booze collection. The large bottle of Jack is half empty. I'm curious if it was full the last time her dad was home. Ella presses her finger to her lips. "Don't tell Goody Two-Shoes."

"I'm standing right here, Ella," Lucy says, standing by the kitchen table. She pulls her attention from her frayed cuticles which she continues to pick. She doesn't wear a scarf or high-neck shirt. She wants Ella to see her bruises.

I need to go search for stuff. Can you manage her?

While Ella dumps eggrolls onto a cookie sheet and slides them into the oven, I reach for my throat with both hands and cross my eyes.

Kill me now.

It's an inappropriate gesture given Lucy's recent attack in this house. I immediately feel like a total jackass, but she grins at me.

"It's like Lucy told you, she thinks she left her earbuds here Saturday night."

Ella's playful smile transforms once she glances at Lucy. Lusty flirtation turns to...what? I'm used to her ice queen, condescending attitude toward Lucy. Her eyes travel to Lucy's throat and the smile quivers and disappears. "I haven't seen your earbuds," she says softly.

"Could we check? I really need them and don't want to buy a new pair," Lucy says.

"Ella just put food in the oven. Could you check on your own?" I ask, sticking with our prearranged script. I turn to Ella. "If that's okay with you."

Ella hesitates. "I'm not a big fan of Lucy nosing through my stuff."

I laugh. "She's looking for earbuds. Not a big deal. Besides, it'll give us time to catch up."

Ella studies Lucy, her expression worried.

Lucy clears her throat then winces. She fingers her throat with a pained expression.

Ella's posture hunches slightly. "Sure, I guess that's okay."

Have fun, lover boy, Lucy says before she slowly exits the kitchen, her fingers fluttering at her throat.

You better hurry! I holler at her.

Ella grabs the bottle of Jack from the cabinet and holds it out to me. "The offer still stands."

"I'll pass. Have to keep my system clean or Coach Skillman will bench me." My pout wins her over instantly. She'd better leave Selima out of the conversation. I don't want to lose my cool. "Give me an update on the colleges you're looking at. You thinking of staying in state?"

Ella cracks open a Diet Coke and takes a sip. "My dad keeps talking about New York. He loves it and wants me there with him. Honestly, I've been so busy, I haven't researched any schools yet. You still planning to stay local? You have to firm up your plans ASAP, senior."

"That's my preference." I would rather not go into my dad and Alana's potential move to the Big Apple, but I have to buy Lucy time. This used to be easier—hanging with Ella. I grind my teeth and proceed. "Like I mentioned at lunch recently, my dad and his wife are thinking about a move to New York. I'm pretty upset about it, being so close with my brother and sister." I shrug, sadness over the prospective move piling onto my frustration over Selima leaving this morning. My dad sides with Alana when he's talking with me. Selima sides with Marcus and Camille. My hands fist at my sides. A few splashes of Jack in my Coke sound really good right now.

Ella licks her lips, presents her best seductive grin. "Really? So," she takes a step closer, runs her finger down my chest, "does that mean you may move to New York? That would be amazing. We could have fun like we used to."

My skin tingles and not in an excited way. Instead, Ella's attempts to seduce me ignite my anger over Selima's departure all over again. Selima spent the night with me last night—something protectors are not supposed to do. She was upfront when we started dating, telling me how she had to spend all her nights under the moonlight. Since it was a rare event, I stayed awake as long as possible and held her while she slept. Her sweet, sleeping face and even, gentle breaths made her appear fragile.

"Why are you smiling?" Ella asks. She presses herself against me.

I suppress a shudder and take a step back, all while beaming my famous grin at her. "Easy tiger, I'm with Selima now. What's up with the séance you held on Saturday night? We didn't get a chance to talk about it. Since when are you into the supernatural?"

It's Ella's turn to pout. "You're no fun anymore." She turns away from me. "Let's get back to Lucy in the living room."

I snake my arm out, take hold of hers. Ella flinches in response to my grip. *Tamp it down, Dylan. Grab gently. She needs the use of her arm,* I remind myself. "Cut me some slack, okay? I'm struggling right now. I may lose Ethan and Brandi. It's been rough."

Selima's bailing on me to go help her conniving stepmother, too, but I don't want to go into that.

238

She touches my arm. "Poor Dylan," she says absently. She looks past me nervously.

Ella is definitely hiding something.

"I...I have missed you," I say, beating down the nauseating feeling of betrayal.

Ella's attention is back on me in a nanosecond. I swear I can hear her purr.

Her cloying perfume fills my nostrils. With the heat of the oven, the space in the kitchen suddenly feels too warm, too confined. I want to shake her hand from my arm. I override the urge to shove her away.

Aiden's words fill my head. *"Deep breaths. Will it down. Always remember that you are in control of your strength and your power."*

I am in control, I echo.

Her arms wrap around me.

What is taking Lucy so long?

I grab her waist gently with both hands. More than anything I want to shove her across the room. Instead, I pull her close and kiss her.

CHAPTER THIRTY-THREE

– Lucy Walker –

—

Ella cackles in the kitchen. Good. They're still occupied.

A quick search of Ella's dresser drawers turned up nothing. Same with the space underneath the behemoth piece of furniture. The closet took more time. How does Ella find anything in the jam-packed space? Anxiety nudges me to keep moving, keep searching, but faster.

How long can Dylan keep her occupied in the kitchen? *Work faster*, I remind myself. The area under Ella's bed is crammed full of stuff. Why does one girl need so much? I shove aside bins full of clothes, baskets full of nail polish, makeup, lotions, and body scrubs. Wait. As I scoot a purple plastic basket aside, the shine of my flashlight lands on a box tucked further back. I almost missed it. It's black and blends into the nothingness. I scoot beneath her bed, hoping like crazy I don't get stuck. Sometimes there is a benefit to being a shrimp. The box isn't large or heavy, but it takes both hands to grab it and slide it forward.

Did I hear voices just now? *Crap! Please Dylan, do whatever you need to do to keep her attention diverted a little longer.*

The box looks like the kind Sheldon and Bernard use to store their photos at home, except theirs are all blue, green, orange, and pink. Once the lid is off, I see the box is full. Inside are papers, handwritten notes, greeting cards, and photos of Ella by herself and with other people. Probably just a box of keepsake stuff, but I dig through it anyway.

My fingers touch a soft cloth. I lift the stack of papers, cards, and photos and set them aside on the lid beside me. I shine the phone flashlight into the box. Beneath the fabric is a photo of Ella, Caroline, Suzy, Cloe, Katie, and me from a day together at the beach last summer. As I unfold the cloth an oblong plastic object drops back into the box. Leaving that alone for a moment, I shine the light on a sheet of paper beside our group photo and stare dumbfounded at a copy of my class schedule. Why does Ella have this? Without looking at what I'm reaching for, I grab the credit card-sized item that was wrapped in the cloth and flip it over. My missing school ID. Anger burns inside of me. Since when did Ella turn into a thief?

Another burst of laughter from down the hall. This time it's Dylan. His laugh is a sign. I am out of time. I shove my school ID and schedule in the back pocket of my jeans. What about the photo of all of us girls? I probably should leave it since it rightfully belongs to Ella, but I don't trust what she plans to do with it. I fold it in half and take that, too. If I can make it to the living room undetected, I can transfer the items to my purse. If not, well, I better come up with a hell of a story to cover why I've been in her bedroom all this time.

As I exit her room, I consider the long hallway that leads to the living room. To my left is the bathroom. I dash inside, flush the toilet, wash my hands, then stroll to the living room and silently sit down on the plaid couch just as Dylan and Ella laugh obnoxiously.

"I'm sure Lucy's fine," Dylan says loudly.

"She's been alone for, like, *ever*," Ella says. "Who knows what she's getting into?"

There's no time to move the items from my pocket to my purse. Instead I take the most laidback pose I can manage on the couch, willing my heartbeat to slow down. I hope my cheeks aren't flushed.

CHAPTER THIRTY-FOUR

– Lucy Walker –

Dylan follows Ella into the living room. Ella's eyes sweep the room, then fall to me. Behind her, Dylan's expression is tight. He glances down the hall, then longingly at the front door.

Ella narrows her eyes. "You could've turned on the TV."

I pause noticing her smeared lipstick. Dylan's expression is hard, but there are traces of Ella's lipstick around his mouth. My heart sinks.

"And miss eavesdropping on you two? Forget it." The teasing tone I was aiming for falls flat.

An alarm starts to *beep...beep...beep* in the kitchen.

I smack my hands together and rub them. "Good timing. I'm starving."

"You're always starving. You should be a cow with how much you eat," Ella snaps as she returns to the kitchen.

"Glossy pink doesn't really suit you." I glare at him.

Dylan's expression darkens. He wipes his mouth without saying a word.

I dive for my purse and transfer the contents from my back pocket.

"Don't get off your duff to help me," Ella complains when she returns and plunks a plate loaded with eggrolls onto the coffee table along with a small bowl of yellowish dipping sauce. She dashes back to the kitchen and grabs two fresh Cokes and one Diet Coke. "Use a coaster," she says to me snottily.

"Did you find your earbuds?" Dylan asks, taking a seat next to me on the couch.

"Or were you too busy listening to us this whole time?" Ella asks. She grimaces at Dylan's proximity to me.

Can it be any more obvious that she doesn't want me here? She's been hoarding my stuff, so I know she at least wants *something* from me.

"Didn't find them, which is strange. I could swear the last time I saw them was on Saturday when I packed my bag for the sleepover."

Now that I found what I came for, I'm ready to leave. The smell of the eggrolls gets the best of me, though, and I help myself.

"I was planning to watch a movie tonight. Want to stay and watch it with me?" Ella asks, sitting down next to Dylan.

Feeling claustrophobic on the crowded couch, I take my plate and move to the coral-colored armchair.

"We're not going to watch a movie tonight," I say between tiny bites of the scalding hot eggrolls. How pissed will she be when we announce the real reason we came tonight.

Pouting, Ella turns to Dylan. "She's no fun. Please tell me you drove separately?"

Dylan swallows and wipes sauce from his lips with a napkin.

"Afraid not. Here's the thing, Ella. In addition to Lucy's missing earbuds," Dylan says, keeping up our cover story, "we also came to talk to you about Seamus McAllister." He meets her gaze before grabbing another eggroll, dipping it, then taking a big bite.

While I wonder how he's not burning his tongue and throat from the hot food, Ella leaps up from the couch. Her eyes fix on Dylan, her expression a mix of shock and hurt, edging on panic.

"What are you talking about?" Her cheeks burn red and I wonder if it's because we're onto whatever dark stuff she's playing with or that Dylan manipulated her. Maybe it's both.

"This is serious. Scary serious," I say.

"You are in way over your head," Dylan says, firm but calm. "He's dangerous."

Ella manically paces the living room. She shoots visual daggers at Dylan and me. She chokes out a sob. "You think I don't know that? He came to my house. Twice!" she shakes her head in fear and disbelief. Her eyes fill with tears.

"Did you invite Seamus McAllister to the séance? Was he the one who tried to kill me?" I ask. Ella's attention flickers to me as I touch my throat. Tears spill onto her cheeks.

"Do you know what he is?"

Ella is full out crying now.

She's scared, but I can't tell if she's afraid of him or that we're on to her, I say to Dylan.

We have to play along if we hope to get any information from her, Dylan says back.

"I don't know if his goal that night was solely to hurt me or all of us," I say. "He's a demon, Ella. Seamus McAllister is a *demon*."

Ella stops pacing, her eyes so wide, so shocked, I'm certain she didn't know that. "He told me he was a magician." The words come out of her as if she's having an asthma attack.

"He lied," I say.

"Have you been following the murders of high school kids around Chicago?" Dylan says. "He's behind them. Seamus killed those girls."

Ella crosses her arms over her chest, clutching her elbows. Her entire body trembles.

"We can help you, Ella. First, you need to tell us what Seamus wants from you," Dylan says.

She considers our request. She speaks only to Dylan.

"A *magician*. You must think I'm an idiot." With a heavy sigh, she returns to the couch beside Dylan. She pulls her legs onto the cushion, and wraps her arms around them. "He wants to know about Lucy."

"Is that why you and Katie came to my dad's house?" I ask.

Ella nods. She looks worn out all of a sudden. "He started out as this nice old man. Claimed to be a friend of your grandmother's. He told me he was worried about you. Then things changed. He stopped being nice."

"What will you tell him about me? About what you and Katie saw?" I ask.

Ella rests her chin on her knees. She trains her eyes on the wall across the room. "He really tried to strangle you. That's so messed up."

She sounds out of it. We're telling her the truth about a killer and she looks like she's ready for a nap. Maybe she's in shock? I don't care. My calm demeanor evaporates.

"It's more than messed up, Ella. He would've killed me first then probably moved on to the rest of you," I scold her. "You would risk Caroline's life? Katie's? The rest of us?" Heat throbs along my arms, settles into my hands. I shove my hands beneath my legs so that I'm sitting on them. I could lob a fireball at Ella, toast her in an instant. Show her what a demon is really capable of. "What were you thinking?"

For the first time tonight, Ella focuses on me. There's no malice in her expression. Does that mean she's listening?

"You have to stop helping him," Dylan says firmly.

Ella turns to him. She looks and moves as if she's sedated. "You don't get it. The old man is a lot scarier than either of you."

"What did he promise you in return?" I work hard to keep my voice even.

Ella scoots off of the couch. She crosses the room slowly and opens the door. "I need you both to leave," she says quietly, her eyes focused on the floor.

"Ella..." I try again.

Her eyes flash. "Go!"

Dylan and I leave. Once in his car, I consider the items I found beneath Ella's bed and our conversation with her. We drive in silence for a few minutes.

"Back when Persephone and I performed a protection spell on Jude to keep him—and me—safe, I had to provide her with something that was personal to him, that he touched. I had the business card he had given me the day I arrived in Chicago, with a handwritten note on the back. It worked for the spell." I pause, upset with myself for being so careless and furious at Ella's calculation. "Ella had my school ID, my class schedule, and a photo of me with the girls hidden in a box under her bed." I turn to him. "Why else would she have taken those items? What does Seamus want with my stuff?"

"There's no way it's for a protection spell," Dylan says tightly.

Ella was conspiring with Seamus to hurt me.

"I thought for just a moment she was going to tell us everything," Dylan says. "But it's like she said, he's a lot scarier than we are."

We fall back into silence for the rest of the drive home, lost in our thoughts and worries. Once Dylan pulls up to my house and I climb out of his car, he calls out to me.

"I had to kiss her. She was going to look for you," he says. "I hated every second of it."

His expression, clear in the glow of the dome light, is morose. I believe him.

"Are you going to tell Selima?"

He pauses for a long moment. "You think I should?"

I consider that. "When Marcus found out you and I had kissed, he was furious and very hurt. I think what upset him the most was that I hadn't come clean about it. He found out on his own."

Dylan nods thoughtfully but doesn't say anything.

I close the car door. He waits until I'm inside before he pulls away.

CHAPTER THIRTY-FIVE

– Lucy Walker –

"You think the demon who wants to kill you is the same person...I mean, demon...or thing..." Katie's eyes widen in alarm and she smacks her palm to her forehead. "I did not mean to call demons...*things*. Sorry."

We sit side by side on the roof of the three-flat on Tuesday night, our backs pressed against the short wall and a large bowl of popcorn between us. It feels strange to be up here without Marcus, but I needed to talk to Katie and with my uncles home, this is the most private place available.

"Relax, Katie," I say, bumping my shoulder against hers. Now that Katie knows the truth about me, I feel tons lighter. Like every other aspect of my life, I need to talk through stuff with her. I fill her in on my history with Seamus and the visit Dylan and I paid to Ella. "They didn't join teams out of concern for my well-being, like Ella told you. Seamus wants me dead. Ella hates me. I guess I didn't realize just how much."

I shiver as I share this last part. Katie moves closer to me. She scoops another handful of popcorn.

"This loser wants you dead. Why don't we go after him? Take him out? You aren't planning to wait for your dad to come home, are you?"

Katie makes it sound so simple.

"There is no *we*. You have no involvement in this," I say.

Katie looks at me like I'm an idiot.

"The guy—demon—has had it out for you since you arrived in Chicago. Then Jude kills his daughter. Jude is out of town, leaving you vulnerable. If I were this nut case, all jacked up on vengeance, I wouldn't leave you alone."

Has Katie always been this badass or did it kick in when she learned that monsters and magic are real?

"He strikes me as someone willing to die for his cause—his crusade of one."

"It's a crusade of two, now," I correct her. "Don't forget Ella's involvement."

We fall silent for a moment.

"I don't get it. All these supernatural people in your life and he keeps coming for you." Katie glowers.

"I'm still here because of all the supernaturals in my life. Thanks to my own powers, too. I'm sure it drives Seamus crazy that he hasn't taken out little Lucy Walker."

Katie's expression hardens. "If I had powers, I wouldn't sit by waiting for him to show up. Why sit on defense when we could go after him?"

Katie's words hang in the air between us. I have asked that question in my mind a dozen times. Hearing it said aloud, though, I'm forced to really consider it. After all Seamus has done to me, should I keep taking a defensive position? All the protection spells, safeguards, watching, and waiting. Is it fear? The demon has hurt me more—*worse*—than Garret and I killed *him*. Then there is the matter of the dead girls. Jude believes Seamus is behind those murders. Knowing that, I have a responsibility to stop him.

"Katie." A sense of resolve fills me. "Thank you for saying exactly what I needed to hear."

Katie cocks her head. "What are we going to do? What's the plan?"

"The first step is to end Ella's involvement with Seamus."

Katie considers this. "Makes sense, but how?"

"Ella teamed up with Seamus to hurt *me*. If Seamus could have broken into the séance, he would have hurt you and the others. There's a good chance he was planning to use dark magic—soul magic—against the group of us."

Katie shrinks against the wall. "Based on your tone of voice, I'm guessing that would've been bad."

"Deadly bad," I confirm.

She clasps her hands on her lap, but not before I notice that they're trembling. She tries to look brave.

"Time for offense," I say.

I climb to my feet and extend my hand to Katie. With a shaky exhale she accepts. I pull her to her feet.

"You aren't going to hurt Ella, are you?" she asks.

"We're trying to help Ella, not hurt her." I squeeze her hand reassuringly. "I need to end Seamus before he ends me—or anyone else. It's like you said, I can't sit around waiting for him to come for me again." *I will strangle Ella when all this is over,* I think to myself.

"How can I help?" Katie asks, her voice a little stronger.

"If Seamus needs personal items of mine for whatever he plans to do to me, that means Ella will try to steal from me again. You and I need to make sure she doesn't get her hands on any of my stuff. Don't allow her to take any photos—solo or group shots."

With the popcorn bowl in hand, I lead Katie to the stairs at the far end of the roof. I want to tell her I'm sorry, that I never wanted to frighten her with stories of demons, witches, dark magic, and death. Secrets almost destroyed our friendship. The truth is scary and horrible, but it's what Katie said she wanted. The question is: can she handle it?

"You okay?" I ask.

"Still processing all of this," she says, smiling weakly. "I really do want to help."

"You listening to me while I work through it all helps a lot," I say, although I hope I haven't put Katie's life in danger by revealing the truth to her.

CHAPTER THIRTY-SIX

– Lucy Walker –

"Hello, my pets," Ella says pleasantly as she reaches the lunch table on Wednesday.

She and Caroline are usually the first two at the table in order to mark their territory. Like anyone would be dumb enough to go up against Ella. When Katie and I arrived, we found Caroline, Cloe, and Suzy sitting there without Ella. My spidey senses leapt to attention worrying what horrible scenario her absence could mean. Is she off plotting my death with Seamus? Since I took my items back that were hidden beneath her bed which she presumably planned to give to Seamus, will he hurt her if she can't produce them?

We spotted her moving through the lunchroom, head held high, looking darkly regal like she was Darth Vader. My senses remained on high alert.

"It's early in the year and too many newbies don't understand the lunch table hierarchy yet. Three people tried to sit here. It was about to get savage," Caroline complains.

Ella's eyes glitter. "Savage? I love it."

"Not funny. Don't make a habit of it, or we're liable to lose our table."

"I doubt that," Ella says. The certainty in her voice sends a chill down my spine. "Besides, I had to take care of something."

"Someone's being secretive," Suzy teases, a hint of a smile playing on her lips. "Are you attending homecoming committee planning meetings and not telling us?"

"I already told you I'm not on the committee. It would preclude me from a nomination as queen," Ella says.

"Oh, right. I forgot," Suzy says. With dramatic flair, she flips her hair and smiles an exaggerated, plastic smile. She waves at each of us with beauty pageant perfection.

We all burst out laughing, except for Ella.

"Funny you should mention secrecy, Suzy." Ella winks at me.

The cafeteria fills with the normal swell of conversation, jangle of silverware, even the group chanting way in the back of the room as a crowd surrounds a girl and a guy who try to out-rap each other: all of it dies away with that wink. Katie eyes me nervously. She clutches my hand under the table.

"Ella..." Katie warns. She shakes her head.

Caroline looks at Ella in confusion. "I don't get it. Fill me in."

Ella laughs. "Don't worry, Katie. I don't believe in outing people." Her gaze shifts to me. "I'm more interested in negotiating."

Ella must know by now that I took my stuff back. What does she mean by negotiating? Did Seamus visit her again?

"I'm on the committee. Homecoming is going to be epic this year," Caroline chimes in, although no one is listening to her.

Ella grins. "I have big plans for Lucy and me. *That* will be epic."

"Hello???" Suzy snaps her fingers at Ella. "You're speaking like an alien. Explain what you're talking about or give it a rest already."

Cloe pulls her eyes away from the screen of her phone. "Your plan is stupid. Plain stupid."

Ella's eyes widen. "How would you know, Nerd Queen?"

Cloe smirks. "Because all of your plans are stupid."

She gives Ella a long look before returning to her game.

Ella throws her head back and laughs, a maniacal sound that bounces through the room. She clasps her hands together, that glittery look back in her eyes.

"I'll fill you *all* in soon. I think you will be surprised. Maybe even impressed."

Suzy and Caroline prod Ella for details of her scheme, but she refuses to share. Katie frowns, but doesn't say a word. She eats silently, aggressively attacking her food. It reminds me of Dylan. The bell rings and Suzy and Cloe file out of the lunchroom, waving goodbye to the rest of us. Suzy whispers to Cloe and they both laugh. The rest of us trail after them.

"Hey, Lucy," Ella grabs my arm.

Katie slows down her pace, her attention fixed on Ella's grip on my arm.

I yank free of her grasp.

Caroline pauses, waiting for her BFF, but Ella waves her on. "Let's meet at my locker after next period."

Caroline whirls around and exits the lunchroom in a huff.

Ella fixes her bright eyes on me with a conspiratorial smile. "You and I are going to spend a lot of time together, study buddy."

Her words set my spider senses tingling again. Ella jitters, unable to stand still. Is she mega dosing on Red Bull again? "Why is that, Ella?"

"You are going to become my private tutor. I want to learn everything you know about magic."

I stiffen. Leave it to Ella to be brazen. "I don't know what you're talking about."

Ella's smile grows wider. "You will teach me." She waits a beat. "If you don't, I'll tell everyone in school about you. Then I'll learn magic from Seamus McAllister. You and Dylan want me to end my conversations with him. This is my condition. Share your magic with me so I don't need to get it from him."

I am floored by her recklessness. Why is she so desperate to become magical? What does she think it will get her? Oh, right. *Power.* Problem is, she will wind up powerfully dead.

"Stay away from stuff you don't understand," I tell her.

Katie jumps in, the anger in her voice barely controlled. "I was such an idiot to trust you. You aren't worried about Lucy at all. You nearly got her killed."

Students file into the cafeteria for the next lunch period. Several people greet us as they pass by. I glance nervously at Katie. We should not be talking about this out in the open.

Ella takes a step closer to Katie "There's a whole other world you and I didn't know about. This is our chance." She gestures to me. "Why should Lucy get to have all the fun?"

Katie's eyeballs nearly pop out of their sockets. "Since when is nearly dying fun?"

"You lack vision, Katie. Always have," Ella says before turning back to me. "You'll do it, then? Teach me what you know—share your power? Who knows what kind of damage I'll do if I learn it from the wrong source?"

A bell sounds and I groan. Thanks to Ella, I may earn my first demerit.

"I'll see you later," I tell Katie.

Ella calls after me, not bothering to keep her voice down. "Your rich dad who lives in the mega mansion in Lake Forest— he's the powerful one? Has to be. Your mom was a drunk and she's dead, so she's not teaching you anything."

"Ella!" Katie cries.

I flinch as if slapped. After a moment, I square my shoulders and force myself to continue walking. I can't look back at Katie. Once again she betrayed me. Is there any part of my private life she hasn't shared with Ella?

CHAPTER THIRTY-SEVEN

– Dylan Douglas –

Thirty minutes of sprints and an hour of lifting in the weight room followed by a long shower. My car is one of the last vehicles left in the school parking lot by the time I exit the building. Katie Stevens sits on the expensively maintained lawn beneath a tree near my car. She pulls earbuds from her ears and waves as I approach.

"Did you miss Lucy?" I ask, confused by her presence.

"Nah, I told Lucy I had to stay late to work on a project in the library," Katie says, climbing to her feet. She brushes bits of grass from her black pants.

"That project is?" I ask, feigning indifference as I notice faint smudges along the side of my car. My baby needs a wash and another hand wax. I click the key fob to unlock the door.

"Talking you into giving me powers," Katie says evenly.

I whip around to face her. "Lower your voice!"

Katie shrinks away from me.

I scan the parking lot. There are only a couple of cars within close proximity to mine. All appear empty.

"Sorry. Didn't mean to snap," I say. "Just keep it down."

She gives a tight nod in response.

"Climb in. I'll give you a lift home," I say.

What the hell is she thinking? Powers? Has Ella rubbed off on her?

Once inside the car, Katie confronts me. "I'm serious, Dylan. Your dad was a normal person like me. Jude gave him what he wanted. I don't want success or fame or money. I want powers so I can help Lucy. That demon wants to kill her. With Marcus and her dad gone, she needs help. Between you, Lucy, and me, we can battle that lunatic. You have magical blood. Your dad drank a goblet of Jude's blood. Bleed into a cup. I will drink it. Give me power so I can help my best friend before that crazy creep kills her."

She lays all this on me in record time.

"You're nuts. Jude is a powerful demon. One of the biggest after Lucifer. I'm a peon by comparison, incapable of giving you anything," I say as I pull out of the parking lot.

"Let's try it. If it doesn't work, fine. If it does, we wipe this scumbag off the planet."

I'm impressed with Katie's guts, but if I allow her anywhere near Seamus, she will be toast. Then Lucy will kill me for allowing her fragile friend to get involved.

"Forget it," I tell her. "Don't go down the same path as Ella. She's crazy for getting involved with Seamus. You're smarter than that."

Katie crosses her arms over her chest and slumps against her seat, her face set in a stony grimace. "Her reasons are all wrong, but at least she's going after what she wants."

She makes a solid point about Jude and Marcus both being gone. That fact chews at me constantly.

"I have a lot to make up for. Because of me Ella knows Lucy is magical. I trusted the girl who hates Lucy to the core—all because of some stupid jealousy. I screwed up royally here, Dylan. Let me fix it. Share your powers with me so I can help save Lucy from whatever that demon is cooking up."

With a firm set of my jaw, I jerk my head from side to side.

Katie slinks low in her seat. "You're making the wrong decision. I want you to know that." Her eyes are saucer-large and worried. "If Seamus and Ella kill Lucy, it will mostly be my fault but partly yours, too."

If only Katie could see herself as I do. She's puny. I look at her and see Brandi in a few years. Seamus is a high-level son-of-a-buck and one swipe of his finger through the air as he mutters a basic spell and Katie would slam into a wall, all of her bones smashed. I can't let that happen.

"I will keep her safe," I say and flex my biceps. Katie needs to understand that I am better suited to protect Lucy. I'm strong—more so since Jude started juicing me up from the underworld.

"Yeah, how do you plan to do that?"

Damn, the girl is persistent. I rub my eyes and suck in a deep breath. *Keep your frustration in check, D-Man,* I remind myself.

Katie narrows her eyes at me. "Ella has two classes plus lunch with Lucy every day. That's opportunity. Then there's our non-academic hours. Are you watching Lucy when she's out of school?" she demands. "I may not be in the same classes as Lucy, but I see her at lunch every day. We commute to and from St. Aquinas. We study together. I live across the street from her. Opportunity and proximity are on my side, not yours."

"Give it a rest, Katie," I tell her. I hit play on my car stereo and turn the volume up loud.

CHAPTER THIRTY-EIGHT

– Lucy Walker –

It's Wednesday and according to Marcus's text, he will FaceTime me at five o'clock. I grab a glass of iced tea and a handful of Bernard's homemade oatmeal cookies with extra cinnamon from the kitchen then race to my bedroom.

"Tell Marcus we say hello," Sheldon calls out while he and Bernard start to make dinner. Neither of them remark about me snacking beforehand. There is never a risk of me ruining my appetite.

"Will do!" I tell him before closing my door, but not before I hear Sheldon mutter something about not hurrying back.

I log in to my laptop, eager to see Marcus's face on a screen larger than my phone. In less than thirty seconds the ring comes through.

"Marcus!" I say as soon as his face appears.

"Hey Lucy," he says.

I have missed his crooked smile, his big brown eyes, and the sound of his voice. All of these things, these parts of Marcus, trigger a deep ache inside of me. I trail my finger along the screen as I take an inventory of his face, the random wave of his hair, the inches of skin along his neck that show above his navy T-shirt. I look for any sign that he has changed since Monday morning. I study his expression. Is he happy? Excited? Resolved that he already prefers being with other protectors more than me? Actually, his expression reveals only one thing. That he is happy to see me. The dark circles under his eyes tell me he isn't getting enough rest.

"What's it like there? Tell me about Selima's mom. What are the other protectors like? Have you seen Camille? How is she?" I say in a rush before chomping on a cookie and turning the conversation over to him.

Marcus laughs. He runs a hand through his hair. "It's been a marathon since we arrived."

I swallow the bite of cookie, unable to remain silent. "Where are you? Are you allowed to say?" With one foot on the floor, I swivel my chair back and forth, eager for details.

"Minnesota, although I can't be more specific than that. It's beautiful here. I bugged Selima to tell me before we got here. She wouldn't. Honestly, I don't believe she was forbidden to tell me as much as she wanted to surprise me. I never would've guessed." Marcus leans closer to the phone. Or maybe he brings the phone closer to his face. "Lucy, you would love it. The trees. The open fields. The fresh air. It's...lush. Yeah, that's the word for it. Really, it's another world. But this isn't the only...place. Protectors live all over the world."

"Really? But the council members are all where you are? They all live there?" I ask, eager to know more.

Marcus shakes his head. "Only a few members live here. The rest traveled for the meetings and hearing."

While I've been sour about Marcus's trip, worrying that he'll prefer it there versus here with me, I have to admit that his excitement is contagious.

Feeling brave I ask the question that's been on my mind. "Would I be able to go with you...the next time you visit, after things with Camille have been resolved?" By resolved, I'm hoping that means she'll be alive when this wraps up.

Marcus smiles patiently. "Let me get through this first." His expression turns serious. "The protectors here are not like Garret. I didn't believe Selima when she told me that. Now that I'm here and I've met a lot of people, I see that she was telling the truth."

I exhale a huge sigh. "That's great to hear."

Marcus nods. His expression doesn't reflect the lightness I expect after that news.

"When was the last time you had your time under the moon?" I ask, addressing the dark circles beneath his eyes.

"I will tonight. Selima has been showing me her favorite places to fly," he says.

Marcus's eyes dance with pleasure. Selima was the one who taught him to fly properly. Before she came along, he only used his wings to descend from rooftops. Having watched the two of them in the night sky together—as best as I could using the flashlight of my phone—I witnessed their playful banter which quickly became competitive.

"What did you and Dylan find out about Ella? Your text didn't say much," he says, switching the subject.

I tell him about finding my stuff in a box hidden beneath Ella's bed and confronting her about teaming up with Seamus.

Marcus erupts. "She *wants* demon powers? Is she insane? Did you tell her about the other girls?"

"Of course I told her!" I snap, ticked off by his attack. It takes a moment to calm down and get my thoughts back in order. "She seemed afraid that night, but something changed since then. Instead of asking Dylan and me for our help getting away from Seamus, she demanded I give her powers. She said that's the only way she'll stop working with Seamus." I shake my head, rocked with disbelief all over again. "She really is insane."

Marcus's nostrils flare. "That girl is trouble. I warned you about her early on. Have you told Persephone about this? Have you met Mirabelle yet? With Henry out of town, you need to tell them both everything."

Does he think I'm a magical newbie? Our conversation is going downhill fast.

"I'm keeping Persephone informed," I say tersely.

"Good," Marcus says curtly. "Let me know what she says."

"Or you could ask her yourself."

More than anything I want to hang up on Marcus. It's clear that I can't do anything right in his eyes. It's tempting to tell him I need to go, that I have to get my homework done. It occurs to me then that if I don't get an update about his mother, he will hold that against me. I don't want all of our conversations to be like this one. After a lengthy pause, I try to sound calm. "How is your mother? Have you seen her?"

His gaze flickers away from the screen. "Not yet. Selima and I were hoping to see her today, but couldn't. Camille has specific visiting hours and already had committed to meeting with others—including Selima's mom. I'll see her in the morning."

That catches me off guard. "She's your mother. Why didn't Selima's mother make it happen?" I'm curious how Selima's mother would rank over Marcus. "Or does the council determine who gets to see Camille?"

Marcus's jaw clenches. "My mother decides."

That makes me pause. "I don't understand," I finally say.

"Camille is focused on strategy meetings. Now that a date has been set for the hearing, she's working to solidify her defense. I am low on the totem pole for strategy."

I sink in my chair. He and Selima rushed out of here to go fight for Camille. Now she can't take the time to meet with her son?

All excitement is gone from Marcus's face. The edges of his mouth turns down into a grimace. "There is evidence against her, that she was as involved as Garret. Camille claims it's manufactured, that people are trying to frame her." His eyes focus on mine, troubled. After a moment his gaze softens. "I wish you were here with me. I miss you—and I'm sorry for being so tough on you."

A lump forms in my throat and it takes a moment before I'm able to speak. "I miss you, too."

Marcus's gaze drops to my mouth. I read the longing in his eyes. As quick as I can, I take a long draw from my glass of iced tea. Marcus's fast changing moods and his sudden desire for me...it's all more than I can cope with at the moment. My top priority is to figure out what Seamus is up to, but there's nothing

Marcus can do to help me with that. My second priority is to help keep my boyfriend healthy in any way I can given the distance between us.

"Would you do me a favor?" I ask.

"Yes," he says, raising his eyes to meet mine.

"Get your time under the moon tonight. Promise me." My voice is firm.

Marcus looks deflated. "Not exactly the favor I was hoping for, but, yes, after I finish my homework and e-mail it to my teachers, I will go to the roof." With an exaggerated gesture, Marcus crosses his heart with his finger. "Let's talk tomorrow night?"

There will be no hug. No kiss. This virtual stuff sucks.

I nod. "I love you."

Marcus's dark eyes travel slowly across my face. He doesn't utter a word as he appears to take in my features, detail by detail. The scrutiny causes my cheeks to flush hot.

"Will you promise *me* something?" he asks. His voice is serious.

"Yes," I say.

"Find out what Ella's up to. Keep Persephone and Mirabelle in the loop. Henry, too, once he's back from LA. Don't try to handle this on your own." His voice isn't harsh like it was earlier in the conversation and I appreciate that.

"I will."

My frustration with his anger dissolves. Marcus always worries about me. I know it's not easy for him to be away right now.

"I love you, too," he says with a tired grin.

CHAPTER THIRTY-NINE

– Ella Rosenthal –

"Miss Walker was practicing magic, you say?" Old man McAllister says, watching me intently. "What exactly did you see?"

It's Friday evening. I was super freaked out when the lying *demon* called and suggested we meet in the woods. I had refused. How stupid and gullible did he think I was? He could hurt me and no one would be around to help me. What he did to Lucy at my party—his long-distance, invisible magic—scared me. If he finds out I talked with Lucy and Dylan, that they know he was behind the attack, will he try to strangle me next?

I refused his suggestion to meet even after he made several juicy promises. Not only would he give me powers, but he would help me turn my beauty and fashion blog into a huge success. I would finally become an *influencer* beyond the walls of St. Aquinas. He also said he could help to get my dad back home. Was it that last part that changed my mind? The details are fuzzy. He managed to convince me and my fear disappeared.

"Lucy throws fire with her hands, like a baseball," I say, using Katie's words.

I didn't believe Katie at first, but I made her repeat every detail multiple times. Katie is the worst liar I've ever met. I know she's telling the truth about what she saw. I should've gotten out of my car so I could've watched with her. A quick getaway was my focus that day. Throwing fire is not a skill that I'm interested in, so I'm hoping Seamus McAllister has more interesting powers to share with me. Mind control would be a good one. Dylan would dump Marcus's sister in a snap.

The old man doesn't seem surprised by Lucy's fire power. Did he know about that already? "Among the others who were present at Jude Morgan's home that day, you mentioned a boy, Dylan Douglas. What powers did he wield? Tell me who else was there," he says in his ancient raspy voice.

"I don't think Dylan has any powers," I say. Katie didn't mention him except to say he was there. Besides, his human attributes are impressive enough. "He didn't demonstrate anything."

"Who else present had powers? Was Jude Morgan home?" McAllister asks impatiently. He is dressed in a drab brown shirt and old blue jeans. Drab pretty much sums up his style. Once I have powers of my own, I intend to step up my wardrobe. Not only will I be named Best Dressed in the yearbook this year, and launch my fashion and beauty blog, but I will be crowned Homecoming Queen.

"Lucy's boyfriend, Marcus Turner, was there. He has wings, so he can fly," I say. His sister was there. She's *so* not worth mentioning. "Aiden, Marcus's older brother, was there, training Lucy. Maybe he can fly, too?" I tap my foot on the filthy ground.

My shoes are caked with mud because of the rain last night. Meeting in the woods was a stupid idea. I'm going to have to hit up my dad for new Nikes if I can't get them clean. "Lucy's dad is still out of the country as far as I know."

Lucy can hurl fireballs. Her boyfriend can fly. Dylan? He can bench press more than anyone else at school and every girl at school wants him. Meanwhile, I have nothing. Why does the old man stand there with the same stupid squinty-eyed look he always wears? Does he think he can pull some Jedi mind trick on me?

"I held the séance. It took a lot of work to get Lucy to come, but I did get her there. I reported to you what happened at her father's house." I tick these things off on my fingers all while keeping my voice light. "Are you going to share your powers with me?" I want what's rightfully mine. Then I would love to never see or hear from the lying demon creep for the rest of my life.

Old man McAllister turns away from me, leaving me access to his profile. "I can share some of my powers with you today, but just a little. I need to see if you can withstand the magic. Not everyone can." He trails off those last words as if to scare me. This guy has no idea who he's dealing with.

When he faces me again, he offers me a cigarette. It's not the normal kind from a pack purchased at the store. This one is hand-rolled. The kind my grandfather used to smoke. It grossed my dad out whenever we would visit and Grandpa would sit in his chair, old and worn, and roll cigarettes. That was long after my grandmother left him for her third husband, a respectable and wealthy man. Dad always offered to buy Grandpa proper cigarettes, but he preferred his own.

"Who smokes cigarettes anymore?" I ask, incredulous. My grandmother said the quickest way to a wrinkled face is to smoke cigarettes—that included vaping.

"If you want to acquire magic, you will. This is my very own blend, which includes cloves and powerful herbs. This is the first step you must take if you want to have the kind of magic we talked about."

"Once I smoke this, will I have powers immediately?" I ask, eyeing the wrinkle-producing, cancer stick with suspicion.

"It depends how much of the herbs you consume. If you are strong, you will finish it all."

I tap my foot again. To be honest, I don't want to smoke his wacky herbs. Drinking alcohol is fun. A little buzz is harmless. Weed never appealed to me. It smelled bad. "What kind of magic will I be able to perform, *specifically*?"

McAllister watches me intently. For the first time, I notice a mark on his right forearm. It's like a red ink splotch the size of a small orange. In the dim lighting of the shaded woods, I wonder if it's a birthmark or a scar.

"If you are not ready yet, we can wait for another day," he says.

I roll my eyes at him and pluck it from his palm. "Give it to me." *And stop being a creep.*

The old man presents a small box of matches, strikes one against a tree next to me, level with my face. I flinch. He touches the flame to the tip of the cigarette and I inhale. It stinks like moldy socks and rotten cabbage. I stifle a gag as a slight burning sensation fills my lungs. With that first inhale, everything goes very wrong. The burning turns to scorching. I clutch my chest in panic. Gripped in a coughing fit, I can't catch my breath. I grab for the old man who steps aside, out of my reach. Off balance, I fall to my knees, hacking. As I try to inhale again, my lungs seize. *Will I die?* Suddenly, through the burning pain, I am able to pull in air. My eyes burn from the toxic smoke and tears. I take another cautious tiny breath. I lie still, my lips pursed like a kiss, as I suck in teeny, wheezing inhales. I flinch from the pain, fearing that he will cut off my ability to breathe altogether again.

McAllister stands over me looking bored. "You are wasting your chance at magic. I believed you when you said you were strong."

My body convulses and I heave again.

McAllister eyes me with disdain. "You were supposed to bring me the items I asked for. There are consequences when you fail me, Miss Rosenthal."

The anger in his voice intensifies. His eyes blaze with rage. He towers over me with his sunken eyes, protruding cheekbones, and yellow teeth. His horrific face will star in my nightmares. I know that. *Demon.* From my position on the ground, I cower, afraid he will crush me. All it would take is an angry stomp of his heavy boot on my windpipe.

"Stolen." Tears stream from my eyes. It feels as if I swallowed a scalding metal chopstick wrapped in barbed wire. Lucy's school ID and class schedule were in a box under my bed. Now they're gone. So is our group photo. I know she stole them.

"What about the second séance?" McAllister asks. "Is it scheduled?"

"Soon," I grunt. There's no way the girls will show up. When he finds out, will he kill me?

McAllister crouches over me. I whimper.

"You failed me," he says quietly.

The demon grabs me by my upper arm and jerks so that I sit upright. His fingers stroke my neck, down the length of my windpipe. In an instant the fire and thorny pain are gone.

"Keep at it," he gestures to the cigarette lying on the ground.

I shake my head quickly.

"I needed to teach you a lesson. The blend has been perfected after some failed attempts. You will be fine now," he says. "You have earned the right to some of my power."

Again, I shake my head. For all I know he's trying to kill me.

"I could make you stronger than Miss Walker. Would that please you?"

I blink, afraid to turn him down again.

McAllister murmurs under his breath. Strange words.

"What?" I ask, amazed and relieved my throat is pain-free.

"If you finish both the first and second doses, you will have keen senses and tremendous strength. You could move a piece of furniture with the flick of your finger. Like a God, you could influence the elements—make it storm, send a tornado to destroy your rival prom queen's home."

All hesitation disappears.

Under his watchful eyes, I pluck the partially smoked cigarette from the ground and take a teeny-tiny drag. It doesn't hurt this time. Cautiously, I take another puff. The smoke doesn't burn my throat or my lungs.

"Finish as much as you can," the old man encourages.

I could wind up more powerful than Lucy. If I have the ability of persuasion, too, I could help Dylan get over Marcus's sister. He will come back to me. Next, I would convince my dad to move back home fulltime.

McAllister interrupts my thoughts. "Marcus is a protector. It is illogical that his brother, who would also be a protector, would train a demon-witch."

"What's a protector? Who's a demon-witch? You mean, *Lucy*?" The cigarette slips from my fingers and falls onto the muddy grass as a wave of dizziness fuzzes over my vision. A cramp strikes my belly like an angry fist.

"Are you...trying...to *kill me*?" I slump over and curl into a fetal position.

"I would have done something far more spectacular if my intention were to kill you," the wicked geezer says. "The herbs are working through your system. Nothing more. Now get up."

I whimper. Seconds later the real pain hits. I arch my body against the agony as something slices through my insides. I scream until my voice gives out.

Psycho McAllister grabs a fistful of my hair and yanks me off of the ground.

I claw at his hands. He yanks harder. I scramble to my feet, hunched over as the pain continues to rip through me.

"Find out why a protector is training Lucy Walker. You have twenty-four hours."

He releases me and I fall into a heap on the muddy ground. He flings tufts of my hair at me in disgust. I jerk my head back and release one more bloodcurdling scream.

The pain lessens. I curl into a tight ball on the ground.

"Get me the three items I asked for. Schedule another séance without delay. Make sure all of those same girls are present. Someone helped Lucy that first night. There was a power present that I did not recognize. I want to know who it was." He reaches into his pocket and tosses a small item at me. "Here is your second dose. If you are serious and truly ready for your powers, ingest the second dose."

I groan.

"If you fail me, I will enlist your friends to assist me."

McAllister turns and walks away. I gasp and squeeze my eyes closed.

One...two...three...four...five...

By the time I reach two hundred, it's nighttime. He doesn't come back. My legs don't work, so I begin to crawl.

CHAPTER FORTY

– Dylan Douglas –

"What the hell?" I mutter as I reach my car late Saturday morning. It is parked in the back of St. Aquinas. What is it with Katie Stevens intruding on my post-football practice high?

Katie sits cross-legged on the ground, leaning against my driver's side front tire. She jumps to her feet as I approach. She grabs a light blue duffel bag, which she had used as a seat cushion.

"Go home, Katie."

"I called you last night and this morning," she points out. "Why haven't you called me back?"

Katie slides to the left, blocking my access to the car.

"Stop calling me and stop showing up like this. The answer is still *no*. Turn your butt around and leave."

"I'm not leaving until you hear me out. Ten minutes, that's all I'm asking for," she says.

"Katie..." I won't listen to her insane requests.

"Five minutes," she counters, her voice pleading. "It's important, Dylan."

I drop my arms to my sides. "Fine. Five minutes—not that I will consider anything you have to say. You understand that," I hold up my cell phone where I have set the timer, "I will physically move you out of my way when my timer goes off."

Katie clears her throat. "Here's the thing. You claim that you are too weak a demon for your blood to have any effect on me."

"Shhhh!" I scan the parking lot. Since Jude's last audio visit, I make it a point to park as far away from everyone else as possible. "That's not what I said."

Katie's expression grows fierce. "It's pretty much what you said. You know it and I know it." She pauses for a beat. "I think we should test your theory."

I hold my hand up to stop her. "We're done here. Go home."

"No, you listen to me," Katie snaps. She pokes me in the chest with a sharp finger. "Ella texted me. Said she was finally getting powers from Seamus McAllister."

"What?" I ask stupidly. I never believed Seamus would carry out his end of whatever bargain he had negotiated with Ella. I assumed he would get her to do her part, then ghost her.

Katie pulls her cell from her pocket and shows me the text. The message is from yesterday, about an hour after school let out. The second part of Ella's message makes my skin turn cold.

The best part? My powers will be stronger than Lucy's.

Katie glares at me. "It's time for you to stop sitting on the sidelines, stop being a chicken, and think of how we're going to save Lucy. She can't fight both of them. She'll be toast. I've tried calling and texting Ella to find out when she's supposed to meet Seamus, but she's ignoring me. Maybe it's already happened.

That demon is creating a monster. We both know that. Now we have to increase the strength of Lucy's side, the good side."

Sweet Katie Stevens turned into a demon? I can't think of a worse person to gain powers, especially the dark kind. Except Ella.

"What you're suggesting...It's a terrible idea."

"What's your alternative?" Katie asks, exasperated. She pokes me in the chest again. Her angry expression—which is about as potent as a killer Chihuahua—would make me laugh except that this is Lucy's life we're talking about.

I flip off the timer on my phone. "I don't have one. Not yet anyway."

Katie raises her eyebrows. "How many times has Seamus tried to kill Lucy since she moved to Chicago? Now he's recruiting Ella to help him. If you give me powers, Lucy stands a chance."

"What if it doesn't work?" I ask, honestly doubting my ability to give Katie what she wants.

"We have to try," she says, her steady gaze meeting mine. "If it works, have Jude take my powers away later on. I don't care. We need to do something *now*."

"There are no take backs. Once you're in this, you're in it for life," I snap, annoyed that she would suggest something so stupid. How I would've loved to give up my demon powers, Sunday training sessions, Jude's control over my life. Would I give up my friendship with Lucy? It only takes a millisecond to reach an answer. *No.*

I study Katie for a long moment. What's the worst that could happen? She could drink some of my blood and puke? She could drink my blood, keep it down and—poof!—nothing happens? It will be one or the other. Katie's right about Seamus. He's a problem. He has the power to turn Ella into some demonic minion. In a flash, I make a decision. I will placate Katie with her stupid experiment, let her feel like she's helping. Then I will figure out how to contact Jude. We need to locate Seamus and destroy him.

"We can't do it here," I say finally. "Get in. We're going to Jude's house."

"Fine with me. My mom and Jerry are on a romantic getaway for the weekend. As far as they know, Lucy and I plan to spend the weekend together watching movies and binging on junk food. I have the whole weekend available for my transformation."

I shake my head in frustration. Katie has this all planned out.

"What else did Ella tell you?" I ask once we're on the highway.

Katie scrolls through messages on her phone. "You're not going to believe this. She's planning another séance."

"She's completely lost it," I snap. "Did Lucy fill you in on what happened at the last one?"

"I know all about Seamus and his jackhammers, if that's what you mean, and that he was the one who tried to strangle her."

"Clearly he wants another chance at her," I mutter in disbelief—not over Seamus's persistence, but over Ella's idiocy. Lucy and I told her how dangerous Seamus is, that her involvement will only get her hurt or killed. Why is she still helping him? Why is she so willing to put Lucy's neck on the line?

"Convince the other girls not to go." It's the best I can do right now.

"I doubt I can convince Caroline to go against Ella on anything, but Suzy and Cloe will side with me. Suzy totally thought the whole thing was lame last time. Cloe believed Ella was messing with stuff she shouldn't be," Katie says. She pulls her phone from her pocket.

I drive while Katie texts. My control and agility behind the wheel have improved big time. I used to drive fast. Since becoming a demon, I drive faster. Today is an exception. I glance at Katie while her thumbs go to work on her phone. I am in no rush to get to Jude's house.

For the next twenty minutes I replay every one of my drills—and those of my teammates—during today's practice. Normally I would think about Selima while driving. During our call last night, she hinted that she'll be in gargoyle land longer than two weeks. Many of the clan members want her to stick around. They trust her objectivity, rely on her judgment as someone who can work with the council to arrive at the truth. Problem is, according to Selima, everything takes longer than they expected it to. My view is simple: Camille is bad news. So was Garret. End of story. Thinking about it riles me up. Anger is not an emotion I want in my headspace when I'm about to take a knife to my own flesh. Has Marcus informed Lucy about the likely delay? She was freaking out before he left. I can't see her taking the news calmly.

Once we make it through Jude's gate, I pull into my normal parking spot. Katie climbs out of the car, shielding her eyes as she takes in the massive house, the manicured landscaping, and the humongous trees. At the rate she whips around, I worry she will wind up with whiplash.

"This isn't your first time here," I remind her as I stride toward the front door. "You didn't check out the house when you were here spying on Lucy?"

"I didn't have time to focus on anything last time," Katie says as she gawks. She ignores my dig.

Jude gave Lucy and me keys to his house during one of our last training sessions with him. He suggested we let ourselves in on training days while he was typically busy in the kitchen cooking for us.

Katie stops abruptly once we're in the foyer.

"Exactly how rich is Lucy's dad?" she asks, her eyes bugging at the grand staircase and chandelier.

"I never asked," I say dryly.

Katie shakes her head as if to get her wits about her. She holds up her light blue bag. "Where's the bathroom? I need to change into clothes I don't mind getting blood on."

I point down the hall. "Third door on your right."

While I wait in the hall, my mind races. Am I doing the right thing? Doesn't matter. It won't work. Then what? Lucy will need help. Am I enough with Jude and Marcus gone? Selima's gone, too. Persephone is on the injured list due to her hip problem. Henry's on a business trip. Mirabelle is in town, but I don't even know her. Would Aiden help if Lucy winds up in trouble?

Katie returns wearing a black T-shirt and black shorts. The color doesn't suit her, but she's right. If any blood spills, it's the right color to hide stains.

"You sure you want to do this?" I ask her.

She raises her chin. "Positive."

While her voice rings strong, the lines creasing her forehead and the thin set of her lips give her away. Katie is afraid.

I wave for her to follow me to the kitchen.

We sit across from each other at the modest-sized table. Katie oohs and ahhs over Jude's restaurant-quality appliances and the collection of copper pots that hang from the ceiling. She takes in the giant mural painted on the wall that looks like one of those vintage French posters. A fat guy with a big smile and rosy cheeks introducing the circus to an audience, his arms thrown wide. Katie looks enthralled. Lucy loves that painting, too. I leave her to her ogling.

I pull one of the many knives from the butcher block on the counter and place it on a navy towel between us. A voice in my head that sounds distinctly like my mother's reminds me to wash the knife. Just in case. I return to the sink and scrub it with soap. Next, I dig through the cabinets for a glass. A regular water glass won't do. Besides, it would take a heck of a lot of blood to fill it. No, the occasion—my very own bloodletting—calls for something fancy. I reach for an etched wineglass. It's heavy, probably crystal. I bring it to the table along with the knife.

"Last chance. We can stop now and I will drive you home," I say as I brandish the knife, hoping she will take me up on my offer. We could stop for burgers and curly fries.

Katie hesitates. Her eyes widen at the sight of the knife in my hand. Its blade gleams in the light, looking scary sharp and menacing. Her hands, one clasping the other, squeeze so tight her skin turns white beneath her fading tan.

Her gaze meets mine. The corner of her mouth twitches. "If you're asking if I'm sure I want to help to save Lucy, the answer is yes. The part where I drink your blood will be gross, though, so you need to do whatever you can to help me not barf afterward." Her eyes drift back to the knife as her voice drops to a whisper. "Asking you to cut yourself...I'm sorry about that. It's going to hurt."

Through all the years that I hung out with various girls—my ex-girlfriend, Rachel, Ella, Caroline, and others—how is it I never paid attention to little Katie Stevens? She is kinder than all of them. It took Lucy coming into my life for me to finally see good people versus the users and social climbers. It makes perfect sense to me that Katie and Lucy would be close.

"Don't worry about me," I say. For effect, I raise both arms and show off my bulging biceps.

Katie giggles.

"Lucy isn't the only one who's been training at Jude's house all this time. Pain is something I am used to. Besides...I heal fast. You'll see."

I slide the wineglass next to the knife. According to my father, he drank a goblet full of Jude's blood. I never learned what kind of powers my dad gained as a result of drinking the blood, only that Jude's magical genes passed to his firstborn. *Me.* I'm guessing Jude stifled any effect on my father. Just helped him to become über successful and to make a boatload of money. The blood from pureblood demons transformed the gargoyles. I saw it with my own eyes at the battle. There must be *some* effect my blood will have on Katie, even if I'm only part demon, right?

Katie reaches out and places her hand on mine as I grasp the knife. "We're doing the right thing," she says as her eyes meet mine.

She's tough. I will give her that.

"Look away if that's easier on you," I offer.

Katie pulls her knees up and wraps her arms around them. "Yeah, right. So you can slip something into my drink?"

I chuckle darkly at her joke.

I grasp the simple black handle and draw the blade down the length of my wrist—exerting what I hope is enough pressure, without slicing a tendon. *This is not the time for wussies,* Coach Skillman would say.

Katie watches intently as I turn my wrist over to bleed into the glass. I set the knife onto the navy towel and use my fingers to keep the wound open. Hopefully half a glass will be enough blood. At the rate I heal—even forcing the wound open—I can't imagine I'll get more than that.

Who knew Katie could be so cool in the presence of something so gruesome? I see the fear in her eyes. None of that matters, though. What she is about to do makes her tougher than just about anyone I know.

"Have you ever tried it?" Katie asks, nodding at the glass.

"Blood?" I ask. The flow is slowing and I force my wound open wider. "Not like this. I've had Marcus's though. Just a little bit."

"Why?" Katie asks. She pulls her mouth down in distaste.

"His blood has phenomenal healing properties," I tell her.

"You just said you heal fast. Why did you drink his?"

I shake my head. "Marcus can heal others. I can't do that." The stream of blood slows again. "After I had a particularly nasty fight with another supernatural, he healed me. The level of his magic is pretty miraculous."

Katie narrows her eyes at me. "I remember you showing up at school looking awful. Whoever did that to you was a psycho."

The ferocity in her tone makes me smile. She's like a protective kid sister. I pause for a beat taking it in. I like that someone feels that way about me.

Shifting slightly, I peer at the wineglass to gauge how much blood has accumulated. By this time, my blood flow has slowed to a trickle. "Half a glass. I wonder if it's enough."

"It's probably not a good idea to lose anymore," Katie says. "Hand it over."

I clutch the glass with my uncut limb and hand it to her. Katie grabs it with both hands, which is a good thing since she's shaking. I grab two bottles of juice from Jude's fridge, one apple and one grape. I loosen the cap on both and plunk them down in front of her.

"Chasers," I say. "Take your pick."

Katie nods. She closes her eyes as she brings the glass to her lips.

"What the *hell*, Dylan?" comes an angry voice from the doorway.

Neither of us heard Aiden come in.

CHAPTER FORTY-ONE

– Dylan Douglas –

Aiden wears a navy-blue suit with pale pinstripes. His blue and yellow patterned tie is undone and the top two buttons of his dress shirt are as well. This new version of him—Aiden 2.0 as Lucy and I refer to him—takes some getting used to. He's a total Jude wannabe in his expensive clothes, hairstyle, and power vibe, but differentiates himself with the white takeout bag he holds in one hand and the laptop tucked under his arm. According to Lucy who heard it from Marcus, Aiden is never without that laptop or his phone. He takes both to bed with him. Due to the time zones in Europe and Asia, sometimes Aiden has to get up at crazy hours to attend video or audio conferences.

Aiden's cursory gaze takes in Katie and me. He raises his nose an inch and sniffs. It strikes me as an animalistic gesture. Aiden studies Katie for a moment, assessing her.

"What are you two up to?" he asks. He sounds tired and pissed off.

Katie shrinks beside me. Her trembling hands tighten around the wineglass.

"Would you believe me if I told you we were studying?" I joke.

Aiden's pained expression is one I know well from our days training together.

"I would love to tell you both to take a hike, but I can tell you've indulged in things you shouldn't have," he says. His voice is not filled with its usual intensity. Today he seems deflated. "Seriously. What are you two playing at? Wait," he holds up his hand, "if I don't eat, I'm going to pass out."

Aiden tosses his bag of food onto the table and sets the computer beside it. As he stalks over to the cabinet and grabs a glass which he fills from the tap, Katie leans in close to me. "He's definitely the grumpy brother," she whispers.

"It's true, but today is a low caliber day for him," I say.

Katie's attention falls to her glass, which she studies uncertainly. "Should I chug this quick?"

I consider her question for a moment. "No, let's talk to him first."

Katie's posture sags.

Aiden drops into one of the kitchen chairs. He completely ignores us as he downs half his glass of water then goes to work on a sandwich piled high with deli meat. After half the sandwich is devoured, he wipes his face with a napkin.

My stomach grumbles.

"I smell the blood. Is it yours?" Aiden asks. He aims his dark eyes at me.

"Can you tell if it's mine?" I ask with genuine curiosity, leaning forward to rest my arms on the table. Bad idea. The smell of Aiden's sandwich fills my nostrils and I am suddenly ravenous.

Damn. I haven't eaten since breakfast. I should've eaten a second meal by now. A quick glance at my phone and I realize I would normally be on my third by now.

Aiden snaps his fingers at me. "Focus, Dylan."

I return my attention to him.

"What the hell were you thinking?" Aiden growls. His eyes flash with hostility.

Katie presses herself to my side. I pat her arm. "Don't worry. I can take him if he gets out of hand."

"Don't be a smartass," Aiden says. His temple throbs.

"I'm trying to comfort her. Maybe if you would back off, I wouldn't have to do that," I say, an edge creeping into my voice.

Aiden pauses. He attacks more of his sandwich and drinks more water. I feel Katie relax at my side once his burning expression is no longer aimed at the two of us.

"Tell me about the blood," Aiden says between bites, calmer now.

I remind him how my father drank a goblet of Jude's blood all those years ago.

"I know the history," Aiden says. He shoves the last bite of his sandwich into his mouth and proceeds to finish off his glass of water.

"Remember how Jude said Seamus has been trying to team up with someone to go after Lucy? That someone is Ella Rosenthal. A friend of hers," I point to Katie. "Ella has teamed up with Seamus."

"It's true," Katie says.

"Our team is down in numbers. Do you think Lucy and I stand a chance against Seamus and his protégé?"

Aiden blinks as he absorbs it all. "You're taking it upon yourself to create a supernatural?"

The icy calm of his voice causes me to swallow hard.

"I demanded it," Katie says. "I betrayed Lucy. This is my fault. Ella tricked me into revealing information about Lucy and her powers. Marcus too. I would do anything to make it right. Give me power so I can help Lucy. You can take it away once Seamus is dead. They're coming after Lucy. We need to help her. I—"

Aiden stares Katie down until her voice dies away. Her ferocity shrivels. "You breached Jude's security gate and spied on us during training last Sunday."

"Yes," Katie admits weakly. "I'm sorry about that. Ella told me Lucy was in danger and that her father was going to hurt her. She tricked me. Seamus is coming after Lucy. He's using Ella to get to her. Ella used me." Katie's gaze falls to the table as a blush creeps to her cheeks. "All I care about is helping Lucy. This crazy demon needs to be stopped. Lucy's been through enough."

I'm impressed that she said what she did, given that Aiden glared at her the entire time she spoke. Brave little Katie.

"I get that you're super ticked off. But you can't deny we need help," I say to Aiden. I gesture to Katie. "Blood drinker," then I point to myself, "demon blood donor." I point to Aiden. "What we need to know from you is what to do next? What kicks the magic into motion?"

"You are an idiot," Aiden says, his voice harsh. "Both of you. Didn't it occur to you to consult with someone *before* you went off on this half-cocked scheme?" He turns to Katie, his teeth clenched. "Humans have died drinking demon blood."

I didn't consider that possibility. "I'm such an idiot."

Katie blanches. "I...I didn't know," she whispers before aiming her harsh teddy bear glare at me.

Aiden reaches over and snatches the glass of blood. He storms over to the sink and pours it down the drain. He rinses the glass, then sets it upside down in the stainless-steel dish drainer.

I suspect Katie would love to launch several choice expletives my way right now.

"How would we explain that to her mother?" Aiden returns to his seat. He flashes his red-hot gaze back at me. "If this turns horribly wrong, we all risk exposure. Not Jude, of course, because he is not around." Aiden shakes his head. "We should've killed you when you were in a coma."

My entire body tingles icy-hot. My fists curl on my knees as I lean forward. "You were going to kill me?"

"You're still here, aren't you?" Aiden's tone is patronizing. "Which ritual did you perform to call the demon powers forth?"

My anger flatlines into confusion.

Katie peers up at me. "Ritual?" With a guttural moan, she drops her head into her hands. "Unbelievable."

Aiden shoves his trash into the white bag. He leaves Katie and me to throw his garbage away. "No ritual, no demon transformation. At least there's no risk Katie will die. Now go home and leave me alone," he says as he washes his hands at the sink.

I blink a few times. *Ritual?*

I turn to Katie. "Be right back."

I move to the counter next to Aiden where he scrolls through messages on his phone at rapid speed. Is that a demon thing? A gargoyle thing?

"I'm in Latin class. I can create my own rituals with some guidance," I tell him, crossing my arms over my chest, which I flex for effect.

"You won't get it right," Aiden says, his tone disinterested.

"Then I will talk to Jude and tell him how I'm trying to reinforce Team Lucy and you refused to help. You know he and I keep in contact."

Will he see through my bluff?

Aiden raises his eyes from his phone. "Nice threat. Tell him whatever you want. I am keeping his enterprise running smoothly. Jude and I are solid."

His words sound good. His left temple twitches again.

"Okay-dokey. I will share this with him and get his advice on how to beef up protection for his daughter. See you around." I beckon to Katie. "Let's go."

We are both at the front door when Aiden stops us.

"I can get someone to help you. Give me a couple of hours. I'll contact you," Aiden says. His voice is not hostile exactly, more steel-edged. Aiden is working hard to keep it even. In fact, his lips barely move as he speaks.

Shocked, I nod, my body partially blocking Katie. "Thank you."

"Last chance, kid," Aiden says to Katie. "You should back out. I can have Persephone erase your memory of this whole mess. You can go back to hanging out at the mall or playing with makeup or whatever."

Katie zips around me. "Don't treat me like a dumb girl. You'd be surprised how far I'd go to help Lucy."

The strength and clarity in her voice as she stands up to Aiden impress me.

Aiden studies Katie for a long moment. Finally, he nods. "Give me a couple of hours."

Aiden disappears down the hall into Jude's office. He returns a few minutes later with two accordion files of paperwork and grabs his laptop from the table. He maneuvers around Katie and me and exits the front door.

Chapter Forty-Two

– Lucy Walker –

"You can't be happy about this potential move," I say to Arnold once I am in the backseat of the black Lincoln Town Car, after my day taking care of the Douglas kids. Mrs. Douglas arrived home today at five o'clock. That's early for her. I wonder if her time with Ethan and Brandi during the New York trip rekindled some kind of desire to bond with them. What else would drive her to leave her club activities and society friends to come home? I shake my head, ashamed of myself for being suspicious and critical.

Arnold, who has worked as the Douglas family's driver for many years, turns in his seat. He looks smart in his black suit. His warm dark eyes meet mine. Today he doesn't wear his easy smile.

"Those kids don't belong in New York City." He punctuates each word.

"I agree. Have you spoken with Mr. Douglas? I'm only hearing Mrs. Douglas's side and it's clear this is what she wants."

Gone are the days when I would mind my manners and zip my lip over my true thoughts about what goes on at the Douglas household. Arnold and I often see eye-to-eye on things so we speak openly once we are in the car.

My cell phone chirps in my purse. A text from Marcus, I wonder hopefully? I retrieve it and check my messages. It's from Katie.

Need to cancel movie night tonight. Working on a project with Dylan. He will message you.

What project? The two of them aren't in any classes together. Did Katie take me up on my suggestion that she talk to Dylan if she had more supernatural questions? With my uncles at their Restoration Society fundraiser gala tonight and Katie's mom at a romantic weekend away with her boyfriend, Jerry, Katie and I had our choice of hanging out at her house or mine. I guess I'll have my very own movie night tonight. Feeling deflated, I turn my focus back to Arnold.

"...picked them up from the airport the day they arrived home. Mr. Douglas looked frazzled. It was a silent ride home. According to Charlene, he nearly ran to his office and locked the door, claiming urgent business matters needed his attention. No one was to disturb him for the remainder of the day. He's been spending long hours at the company every day since then."

"What do you think that means?" I ask. Is it too soon to feel optimistic? "Will he override Mrs. Douglas?"

Arnold mulls that over, his dark bushy brows pulled together. "Your guess is as good as mine," he says finally.

Arnold turns back to the wheel. "By the way, Dylan asked that I take you to your father's house in Lake Forest."

I pull my phone from my purse. Not a single message from Dylan. "Why didn't he run that by me first?" I ask, curious as I wait for Arnold's eyes to meet mine in his rearview mirror. They don't. First Katie cancels plans and now this? What are the two of them up to?

CHAPTER FORTY-THREE

– Dylan Douglas –

Katie and I pull up to Jude's gate for the second time today, the smell of Gonnella bread fills my car and my mouth waters. Since we had some time to kill and I had multiple meals to make up for, we made a quick food run.

"As soon as Lucy told me about her father, I wanted to check out his big, fancy house. When he left the country and she started coming here every weekend, I kept waiting for the invite. It never came," Katie says.

Katie's loyalty and fear for Lucy are obvious—so is her guilt for helping Ella. The resentment in her voice catches me off guard.

"You don't understand," she says, an edge creeping into her voice at my look of surprise. "Lucy and I told each other everything. At least that's what I thought. The night I witnessed Marcus carrying her to her bedroom window, saw that he had wings, I kept expecting her to tell me about it. We're super close and here she was dating a guy who was some sort of mythic creature. She kept that from me." Her eyes are full of hurt. "Then I find out she's spending time not just with Marcus, but with you and Selima and Aiden, too. It's like Lucy has two classes of friends and I'm not part of the cool group. I'm used to Ella treating me like a low-level friend, but not Lucy. It sucks to be excluded."

How am I supposed to respond to Katie's confession? Her spy mission now makes sense. I only wish she hadn't conspired with the girl who teamed up with Seamus McAllister to screw Lucy over. Katie knows she messed up. I figure the best thing I can do is to stay out of it.

As we exit my car, a blood-red 2019 Aston Martin glides into the parking spot normally occupied by Jude when his car is outside of the garage. No one is allowed to park in his spot.

That rule doesn't apply now as a woman with long glossy black hair climbs out of the sports car. Darcy. Lucy had admired her for her beauty, ability to speak multiple languages, and a wardrobe that runway models would kill for. That ended when Darcy threatened me the night Jude had his shape-shifting dog pack kidnap Marcus from the homecoming dance. That was the night I was introduced to the supernatural world and my grasp on the ordinary world splintered into a thousand pieces.

"Good. You are here," Darcy says in her thick Eastern European accent.

Katie gapes at our visitor who is wearing a knee-length sleeveless white dress decorated with splotches of color. The deep red color catches my attention. It's the exact color of my blood. The design of the dress reveals Darcy's pale shoulders, throat, and collarbone. If Darcy's nasty side comes out, I will go for her throat first.

Katie sucks in a breath. "Wow."

"Close your mouth. You're catching flies," I chastise Katie.

"Excuse me?" Katie asks, insulted.

I nod my head toward Darcy. "Foe, not friend," I tell her.

Katie readjusts her expression into an angry frown. "Chic villain. Got it."

"Why are you here, evil kitty?" I ask. I cross my arms over my chest as I block Katie with my body.

Darcy raises one perfectly shaped eyebrow as she takes me in. She inspects Katie, what she can see of her.

"You two are adorable. It's good to see you are finally over Lucy. That was a dead end," Darcy says. She hooks her finger at us and points to the house. "We should get started."

It hits me then. Aiden and Darcy work together at JM Industries.

"Don't tell me you're the one Aiden called to help us. Because if you are, we—*I*—decline. Just turn around and leave."

"You're so cute, Dylan. Aiden dumped the two of you in my lap. It's now my job to keep this girl alive as we turn her into a demon. I would prefer to keep my job—and my head—when Jude returns. Now, get inside."

Katie's eyes bob from me to Darcy, her eyes so large I fear they will pop out of their sockets.

"If there is even a small chance that I could die, and this woman can prevent it, I would rather you get over your issues with her," Katie says.

Katie has a point. I despised Jude in the beginning. Aiden too. Heck, I didn't even like Marcus much. Now they rank pretty high in my book. Funny how perspective changes when an enemy more horrific than the last one comes into play.

Darcy watches us with a smirk on her face. She blinks her impossibly long eyelashes. Everything about her oozes condescension. I really can't stand the cat lady.

"Fine. Let's go," I mutter.

We follow Darcy as she makes her way up the sidewalk to the front door, the heels of her stilettos clicking along the sidewalk. I focus on those four-inch designer daggers. Potential weapon, I note to myself.

Darcy unlocks the front door and holds it open for us. Her generous lips pull into a practiced, welcoming smile.

Soon Katie will become a part of this life. Different since she's choosing it while Lucy and I didn't. Regardless, when will all of this end?

"Never," I mutter under my breath.

"What?" Katie leans in close. "I didn't hear you."

I shake my head.

"Where should we do this?" I ask once Katie and I follow her into the foyer.

Darcy taps her foot on the marble tile as she mulls that over. "Not in the kitchen since Jude would be furious if we made a bed for her there. His sacred cooking space and all that." Darcy rolls her eyes.

"Forget the living room," she continues. "If you stain the carpet, he will lose his mind. It took forever to find exactly what he wanted."

Katie shivers. I pat her shoulder in an attempt to reassure her.

"The dining room should be okay, right? We used it the night we, uh, dealt with Lucy's medical situation," I suggest vaguely for Katie's sake while at the same time flinching from the memories of that night.

Katie looks at me quizzically, but I shake my head. No way I'm going to rehash that night with her right now.

Darcy inspects Katie thoughtfully. "Good choice." She turns to me. "Grab blankets from the closet at the top of the stairs. There is a twin mattress in the last bedroom on the right. Get that, too, if you want the girl to be comfortable while she recovers."

I bound up the stairs three at a time. No way I'm going to leave Katie alone with the cat lady for long. I retrieve the blankets, run down the stairs, and continue to the dining room in time to see Darcy bite her wrist—literally—before bleeding into a mug.

"Jesus, Darcy!" The smell of the blood is too much in addition to the fresh memories of Lucy on top of the dining room table, her head cracked open. My body collides with the frame of the doorway as I lose my balance.

Katie's big, round eyes focus on me. "Did you see that? She bit her wrist like an...*animal*." She wraps her arms around herself and I sense that it has nothing to do with the temperature in the room and all to do with shock.

"You don't have to do this. We can leave right now," I tell Katie. Every doubt that I've had about this comes screaming back at me. Why did I agree to this? Why did I force Aiden to get involved? Hysteria tries to edge its way in, but I punch it in the face to keep it at bay.

Katie shakes her head.

I knew that would be her answer, but I had to try. Once Katie crosses the line, there is no way back. The demon genes will blend with her blood and take over, giving her powers she's never dreamed of. She will be in this for life. Darcy—or Jude, I'm not really sure which—will own her. She will have to train with Aiden. Katie will become a supernatural.

Ridding the world of Seamus won't fix the problem. Once we kill Seamus there will be another baddie. Like Garret. No doubt Jude has enemies all over the world. Each of them will come eventually to exact some kind of revenge. How gleeful each of them will be to find Jude's beloved daughter lives nearby. Katie and I will always need to be on standby.

"Dylan?" Katie says, her tone urgent as she studies me. "Please don't flake out on me. Okay?"

I shake my head. "Just wish you weren't getting involved in this freak show." I drop two blankets onto a chair and hold the third out to her. "Wrap this around yourself. I'll be right back."

Katie takes the blanket from me. Back upstairs, I pull a mattress from the bed as Darcy suggested and return to the dining room where I drop it onto the floor in the corner.

"Help me lay these out," I say to Katie, whose eyes are fixed on the mug Darcy bleeds into. Giving her something to do might keep her sanity intact. Couldn't Darcy have pretended to be a civilized demon and cut her wrist with a knife?

We spread two blankets onto the mattress.

Darcy's mug is filled an inch from the rim. It appears to be about three times more blood than I donated to the drain in

Jude's kitchen. *How will Katie ever get all of that down?* My stomach convulses.

"Katie, is it?" Darcy says, rising from the table. She presses a washcloth to her wrist. "It's time to drink up."

My pulse throbs manically in my temples. "Now? Is there something we can do to, you know," I glance at the mug uneasily, "dull her senses or something?"

Katie straightens her posture. "Stop it, Dylan. Delaying it will just make it worse."

"Do you have the incantation or whatever it was Aiden referred to?" I ask nervously. "We have to get this right or she could..."

"I came prepared," Darcy says.

Katie gestures to Darcy to slide the cup of blood across the table. She squeezes her eyes closed as she clutches the mug with both hands.

"But..." I say, feeling helpless. Katie brings the cup to her lips. She chugs the contents, making loud, gulping sounds. I force myself to keep it together. To gag now could trigger Katie to barf. The visual nearly triggers another gag reflex.

Katie continues until the mug is upside down over her face. She returns the cup to the table with a thud. Her complexion is a pale shade of green. Above her mouth, a blood-red mustache stains her skin. She takes a series of slow breaths. I want to go to her, wipe her face, but worry that gesture will make me appear weak in Darcy's eyes. Instead, I remain in place, nausea churning in my gut at the sight of this sweet girl who is about to become a monster like me.

"Through your mouth, Katie. Breathe through your mouth," I

urge. My backpack rests against the doorway. Do I have time to grab her a chaser before we start the ritual?

Katie nods vaguely before laying her head on the table. "Just give me a minute." She groans softly.

"Katie? You okay?" I ask, inching over to my pack. Will the juice put her over the edge? Will it be too much on her stomach? Best to let her decide. I grab both bottles.

Darcy hisses. "Put them away. She will vomit if you try to introduce a beverage right now."

Decision made. No juice. I shove the bottles back in my pack.

"Room...is spinning," Katie murmurs softly.

Darcy moves to the other side of the table. "Dylan." She beckons me to come closer.

Darcy and I take a seat on each side of Katie.

"Sit up, Katie. The two of you need to take my hands," Darcy instructs. It's the gentlest tone she has used so far today. "Then each other's."

Katie lifts her head and blinks. She teeters as she attempts to sit upright.

"Katie?" I slide a little closer, ignoring the fact that I am now within splatter range if she hurls.

"S'fine. Just a...little..."

Her voice trails off. Just a little what? Before I can ask for clarification, Darcy tugs my arm. I take hold of Katie's small, clammy hand then Darcy's.

Our circle reminds me of the spell work I had performed with Persephone and Henry, drawing on power and help from each other. The familiarity comforts me a little.

"I will state the incantation in Latin, then in English. Focus on my words. Believe in the action, direct your energy into the desired action. I will repeat it three times. Now, close your eyes."

Without waiting for questions, Darcy dives in. Unlike the kids in my Latin class where all of us are novices, she speaks the words fluidly, as if this were her native tongue. The words send a chill down my spine.

Once she finishes with the Latin version, Darcy charges into the English version.

Allow this powerful blood to
Mingle with her own,
To regenerate, to grow powerful
So that she is reborn
As one of his children

Katie clutches my hand tightly. While I am tempted, I don't dare open my eyes. What would Darcy do if she caught me? Would we have to start over from the very beginning? I don't want to see her bite at her own flesh. After seeing Marcus bite his wrist the one time he helped to heal me—just a tiny tear compared to what Darcy did, I'm guessing—I don't want to see anything like that again. Most of all, I don't want Katie to have to drink another drop of blood. Ever.

We repeat the spell three times.

"Open your eyes," Darcy orders.

I turn to Katie who drops her head in her hands as if the effort to sit upright is too much.

"Now you must rest," Darcy says to Katie. "Dylan, help her to bed. She will be light-headed."

Katie is so groggy that she can barely walk. I carry her to the mattress. She doesn't say a word as I tuck her in. Did some part of the process go wrong?

CHAPTER FORTY-FOUR

– Lucy Walker –

Dread propels me from my car to the front door of the house I have visited so many times. My father's house. Something very wrong has happened here. *I feel it.* With my hand on the doorknob, I pause to allow my senses to reach into the house, to comb room by room, quickly. This is not a skill I use often, so I don't try to push it beyond the first floor. What happened to bring Katie here?

With my eyes closed, I reach with my mind, flex through the door with searching mental fingers. There is no activity in the foyer or the hallway. I stretch further. Jude's office sits quiet, empty. The dining room? Movement. Voices. Multiple people. Dylan. He is one of them. Is Aiden here? Is he punishing Katie for spying on us during training?

One voice is sharp. A female. It's not Katie. I cut off any attempt to further assess activity inside. I pull my mind back and take a moment to settle within my body. As I adjust to physical movement instead of mental exploration, I force my fingers to take the key from my purse, slide it into the lock, and I push my way inside. The lights are on in the foyer. Voices murmur down the hall, to my right and I walk that way. I coax my power and, instantly, heat races along my arms, settles into my hands. Whoever is here with Dylan and Katie, they are in for a shock. Yet, as I approach the dining room, the hushed voices hold no animosity or fear.

Shock stops me cold as I enter the dining room. The murmurs cease and two sets of eyes focus on me. The lighting is dim, but I identify the woman seated across the large table from Dylan. My fingers twitch. My arms ache from the heat rolling along my skin.

"What are you doing here?" I ask Darcy, my voice choked with anger.

My attention moves to the mattress on the floor. I would recognize the blond head poking out from beneath the blankets anywhere. "What is *Katie* doing here?"

Take down your anger, Lucy. I will explain everything. Dylan's voice fills my head. *You will only freak Katie out more than she is already.*

How dare you bring Darcy here! She wanted to tear you apart the last time we were together in this house.

Dylan narrows his eyes at me. *I didn't invite her. Aiden did. Pull yourself together. We don't need fireballs thrown around, hurting people, burning the house down.*

Dylan is right. I take a couple of deep breaths, exhaling slowly with each one. Once the heat fades from my limbs, I cross the room to the side of my best girlfriend and kneel beside her. Katie is cocooned beneath blankets while an extra one has been kicked to her feet. The overwhelming smell—thick and coppery—clobbers me. *This room. This table. Blood. Blankets.* Images of my broken body, *nearly dead*...all of them flicker like a horror film through my mind. I stumble backward. I land hard on my behind.

I can't believe you. Have you lost your mind? Katie and Darcy in the same room? And the blood...I'm going to be sick.

Katie is safe...from Darcy, anyway.

NONE OF THIS MAKES SENSE, DYLAN! I shout, my gaze blazing at him.

Dylan ducks his head, clutches both sides of his skull.

We need to focus on Katie, Dylan says slowly. *Can you calm down so we can talk openly?*

I make a face at Dylan. *Calm down?*

Darcy watches me silently. I make it a point to ignore her as I press my hand to Katie's cheek and yank it back, alarmed by the heat. Her beautiful blue eyes flutter open. A tear streaks down her cheek. She tries to smile, but the expression twists into something else. Sadness? Guilt? Pain?

"Want to tell me what's going on?" I ask her, brushing her hair from her sweaty, hot forehead.

"Lucy..." Dylan says.

"Not from you, Dylan," I keep my voice easy and calm. "I want to hear it from my best friend."

I sense Dylan's flinch. Like I care about his feelings. He has a lot to answer for.

I stroke Katie's hot cheek as I compose my expression into something less angry. "What happened to you?"

"I am going to help you," Katie says, her voice thick with fatigue. "The three of us, we're going to defeat Seamus McAllister."

My breath hitches and I blink at her in horror. My sweet, fragile friend wants to face off against Seamus?

Hold it together, Lucy. Don't scare her, Dylan warns.

Shut up and get out of my head, I tell him. *It's taking everything I've got not to incinerate you right now.*

I shift my attention back to Katie.

"Remember what happened when your mom forced you to take that exercise class with her before you went to Fort Myers?" I ask.

Katie smiles weakly. She blinks in slow motion. "A disaster." Her voice is thick with sleep. "Nearly broke my ankle. Strained my abs."

"Going up against a demon is worse. Much worse." I work hard to keep my voice gentle. I saw the scar on Dylan's wrist as I approached the table. The thick, metallic smell in the room makes my stomach churn. In what universe did he think it was okay to allow Katie to drink his blood? If he thought Jude's beating earlier this year was bad, just wait until I take my turn.

"Darcy will help. She did...ritual. By tomorrow night, I...demon like Dylan..." Her words trail off and her eyes close. The flush of her cheeks intensifies. I press the back of my hand to her forehead, then to each cheek. The heat has increased within the last two minutes.

"How do we reduce the fever? She's cooking," I snap at Darcy and Dylan.

Dylan comes to my side to retrieve the wet cloth next to

Katie's head before jogging out of the room. "Back in a minute." He pauses and turns before exiting through the doorway. "Lucy, don't be mad. I mean, you can be mad tomorrow or in a couple of days, just not tonight. Katie made her choice. She wanted this—fought for it. We need to help her through her transformation. I don't want it to be horrible for her like it was for me."

The quick padding of his feet echoes as he jogs to the kitchen. I climb to my feet to face Darcy, who remains seated across the giant wooden table. Porcelain skin, expertly applied makeup, sleek long hair, designer clothes. She sits there calmly. As hate radiates through my body, so does the heat. My limbs burn with the need for release, to hurl fire.

"I don't know how you fooled Dylan, but you don't fool me," I say, bitterly. "Was killing Katie your idea? Aiden's? Or do you work with Seamus now? Maybe you're like the red-eyed crows that Seamus commandeered from Jude? You're a traitor?" Forget fireballs, I indulge a fantasy where I rip her throat out.

Darcy meets my gaze dead on. "I came at the direction of Aiden. I didn't offer to help; I was instructed to. It seems Aiden is under orders from your father to do whatever is necessary to keep you safe. This idea," Darcy gestures to Katie, "was concocted by your idiodic friends. I am only here to help them execute their plan correctly, without one of them dying."

"I don't believe you," I growl.

Darcy blinks, her full lips twist into a sneer. "I don't care."

Dylan returns, eyeballing Darcy and me nervously. He applies the wet cloth to Katie's forehead. She moans softly as her eyes flutter briefly, then close again.

"After Katie drank Darcy's blood, Darcy performed the necessary ritual."

"Adding a supplemental spell, one that would act as a sedative. It will help as she transforms," Darcy says.

"Darcy's blood? You allowed Katie to...to...drink *her* blood?" I sputter. Heat blazes down my arms, hums powerfully beneath my skin like overactive power lines. I nearly cry out from the painful throbbing along my arms. With a groan I shove my hands under my armpits to keep from sending both Dylan and Darcy up in flames. "What have you done?"

Dylan confronts me, his expression tight with anger. "You think I wanted this? Katie demanded it. You should've seen her. So determined. Fierce. She would've found someone else to help her."

"Like who?" I untuck my arms and punch him hard with both fists. It was a useless attempt to hurt him. His pecs are as hard and unyielding as the ogre-like trees in Jude's yard. "In case you haven't noticed, there aren't many supernaturals around offering to help convert everyday people into demons."

Dylan grabs both of my hands in his. "That's the part you don't get," he leans close, locking his eyes with mine. His voice is urgent. "Seamus got to Ella. What if he goes after Katie next?"

The photo I found in the box beneath Ella's bed included Katie. It also included Cloe, Suzy, and Caroline. Would Seamus work his way through my friends?

My anger drops from a boil to a low simmer. I nearly slump against Dylan, overcome with worry and fear and in a weak moment, craving his comfort. I resist the urge.

"Katie demanded to help," Dylan repeats. "In case you haven't paid attention, we don't have much help the next time Seamus comes for you."

Dylan's words make sense, but I still reject them. "You should have turned her down," I say, watching my frail friend on the mattress.

"Dylan's right. Seamus would get to Katie like he's gotten to the other girl," Darcy says from behind us.

I had been ignoring the other person in the room. Grudgingly, I turn to Darcy.

"Maybe if Seamus gets you mad enough, you will go after him. If he kills you in self-defense, that would be different than if he set out to attack you unprovoked." Darcy shrugs. "At least that's what I would do if I were him."

"What is your problem? I thought you were part of Team Jude. If you don't want to help, why are you here?" I ask, coldly. My best friend is on the floor, her stomach full of demon blood. Her blond hair is caked to her skull in sweat. Her skin—despite her tan—looks sallow.

"Don't talk to me about Team Jude. The birth of this half-breed was not ordained by Jude. Yet, my blood now flows through her body, transforming her. I was ordered to help you, but I do not approve. There will be consequences, naïve girl." Darcy sneers, pointing to Katie with disgust. "An action of this magnitude doesn't get a free pass."

Consequences. I shiver at the word. Whenever supernatural favors are involved, there is always a price to be paid.

"Why did you do it then?" I ask.

"If Seamus kills you, Jude will hold Aiden responsible. Since I have been asked to help, he will hold me responsible as well."

I absorb her words as I return to Katie's side.

"What happens next?" I ask Darcy, my tone unfriendly.

"We keep her comfortable over the next twenty-four hours. Make sure she keeps all the blood down. By tomorrow night she should complete the transformation."

I brush Katie's hair from her face before I peer over at the demon.

Something doesn't seem right. *Twenty-four hours?*

"That can't be right. Dylan's transformation took a lot longer. He was hospitalized. Why would this be faster?"

"Dylan's transformation was different, but only because his demon genes lay dormant until Jude called them forth. The incubation period was still the same," Darcy says.

"French fries?" Katie murmurs thickly from her makeshift bed.

"You're awake." I return my hand to her scorching cheek.

"She can't eat," Darcy says. She leaves her chair for the first time since I arrived and peers down at Katie. She kneels on the floor by the mattress. Her long hair fans along Katie's side while thin fingers grasp Katie's wrist. Darcy stares blankly at the wall.

I don't like Darcy's proximity to my friend. I suppress the urge to shove her away.

After a long moment Darcy releases Katie's wrist, laying it across her stomach. She nods approvingly.

"How is she?" I ask.

"The transformation is progressing, but if she throws up, we have to start all over," she says, returning to her chair.

"Forget the fries," Katie says weakly. "Can I have water?"

"Ice chips," Darcy says crisply. "Nothing more."

"I'm on it," Dylan says.

Before he leaves the room, I toss the cloth back to him. It had already grown warm against Katie's skin.

Katie's eyes open. "Your hand feels nice." She tries to lick her lips, but her tongue sticks to her skin. Dylan needs to hurry with the ice.

The color of Katie's eyes has changed from their normal deep ocean blue to something muted. Is that normal during the transformation? I look around at the lighting in the room to see if there's another explanation.

"I'm struggling to wrap my head around your decision," I say patiently, sitting on the floor, my back against the wall.

"You need me," Katie says. Her voice sounds soft and scratchy, as if she's got a sore throat.

"What are you talking about?" I say.

Katie's brow crinkles. "I helped Ella. My fault." Her eyes fill with tears. "Everyone but Dylan's gone. You *need* me."

Seamus got to Ella. Would he really go after Katie next? A tingling sensation runs along my spine. I pull my hand from Katie's face.

"One order of ice chips," Dylan says with forced cheerfulness as he returns to the room. He drops to his knees. After handing me the filled cup, he applies the cold cloth to Katie's forehead.

"I'm running for food, but I'll be quick," Dylan says softly.

He doesn't jog this time. His shoulders slump as he walks away from Katie and me. While I am furious that he chose to help

314

Katie put her decision into motion, it couldn't have been an easy decision for him to make. Watching her turn into a demon has to be a painful reminder of his own nightmarish transformation. Dylan did not want this life.

"I keep hearing about this Ella person. Tell me who she is," Darcy says after the front door closes behind Dylan. Her voice is sharp, her expression lethal. "Why is she working with Seamus?"

Katie sobs softly. "Ella didn't mean anything by it. She was jealous. Don't let Darcy hurt her," Katie pleads. She struggles into a sitting position. She sways, almost collapsing back onto the makeshift bed. I hold out my arms to steady her. "Help me get up. I need to go."

Darcy stands, ready to spring. "You're planning to warn your friend? No way. You stay here." She glares at me. "Tell me how to find this girl who conspires with Seamus."

"Relax." I don't care that at any moment she could turn into her panther form and tear me to pieces. "No one is going anywhere." I turn back to Katie. "You aren't well enough to go home right now. If you don't want to go through with this—the transformation—fine. Better than fine, actually. I would prefer that. We can undo it. Then you can go home a lot sooner." How long has the blood been in Katie's system? If we made her vomit now, would we be in the clear? "Once Dylan gets back, we will come up with a plan to talk with Ella."

Darcy's eyes blaze. I am guessing she isn't used to being told what to do by anyone other than Jude and Aiden.

"Can we talk?" I ask Darcy, gesturing to the hallway. "Please?"

I touch Katie on the arm. "I'll be back in a minute."

Her glum expression turns pleading. "Don't let her do anything to Ella."

"I won't," I promise her before I climb to my feet and follow Darcy out of the room.

"I respect that you are Jude's daughter, but don't you dare think you share his authority," Darcy says once we stand in the hall outside of the dining room.

"Hurting Ella isn't going to help us. Let me question her," I say before lowering my voice. "If Katie vomits all the blood, will the transformation be stopped?"

Darcy grimaces. "You would waste magical blood? *My* blood?"

I close my eyes for a moment and work to wrangle my emotions. When I open my eyes, Darcy watches me expectantly.

"Have you ever had someone in your life who is precious? That you want to protect? For me that's Katie. I can't risk her getting involved with our fight against Seamus. I can't live with myself if anything happens to her."

"Katie made a choice. She feels the same way about you apparently. Besides, she is not your responsibility," Darcy says flatly.

My responsibility? The words ricochet around my skull like a bullet. Momma was my responsibility. I failed her. I will not fail Katie.

"As if you could understand," I mutter in frustration. How could she? She's just a demon.

I return to Katie and sit on the floor beside her. Her skin continues to burn. She sleeps, though her breathing is labored. Darcy mentioned consequences. For the moment, I am grateful

Marcus is out of town. The distance keeps him safe. Dylan is strong—getting stronger all the time. He can protect himself, can't he? What about Katie? She's small like me. By drinking Darcy's blood, what kind of powers will she inherit?

Will Katie pay the price for her choice? All she's trying to do is help me. *Oh, Katie.* I press my hand to her flushed cheek. She stirs a little, but doesn't wake up. A little knowledge about the supernatural and suddenly my best friend believes she can stand beside Dylan and me and go up against a vengeful demon. I can't risk her getting hurt. Not by Seamus and not by whoever is in charge of doling out consequences. If there will be a punishment, I have to make sure it is imposed upon me and not Katie.

Across the room Darcy scrolls through messages on her phone. What was Aiden thinking getting her involved? Just another issue to delegate? Why didn't he stop Dylan and Katie? He's certainly strong enough. What did Dylan say to convince him it was the right thing to do? Why would Dylan want Katie to become like him when he's always resented his supernatural existence? The questions just keep coming.

The next hour crawls by while Dylan, Darcy, and I eat burgers and fries. The fact that Darcy eats fast food comes as a shock. I had her pegged as a filet mignon or sushi kind of woman. She surprises us all when she jumps to her feet, her eyes fixed on her phone. "I will grab a round of Cokes from the kitchen," she says, rushing from the room.

Dylan watches her leave. "Do you think Cat Woman desperately needs to pee? Or a problem on the work front?"

"Don't know, but it's nice to have her out of the room," I murmur.

"So long as she's not taking off to go after Ella," Katie says weakly. "Can you sneak me a couple of fries?"

My fries are already gone, so Dylan pushes away from the table and delivers several fries to Katie from his plate.

"What happens next?" Katie asks. She slumps against the wall, taking birdlike bites of a fry. "With my transformation?"

Dylan returns to the table and we look at each other for a long moment.

I turn my chair to face her. "Dylan's situation was unique. I'm not sure yours will be similar."

My first inclination is to keep Dylan's horrific history a secret from Katie. I don't want to scare her. What if it will spook her enough that she may change her mind?

I nudge him with my foot. "Want to fill her in?"

Dylan swallows the last bite of his second burger then smacks his hands together. "Like Lucy said, our circumstances are different."

"I can take it. Just tell me the truth. What am I in for?" Katie asks, softly.

Dylan nods reluctantly then fills her in on his demon transformation, which included violent nightmares, paranoia, and hallucinations. Things reached such a drastic level that his father intervened, asking me if Dylan was on drugs and sending him to a neurologist.

"He wound up in a coma. We thought he was going to die," I add.

Katie shakes her head, stunned. "I'm so sorry, Dylan. It sounds horrible."

"It was," he says.

Darcy returns carrying three ice-cold Cokes. She passes them around.

"Aiden's going to stop by," she says casually.

The shift is subtle, but I watch as Dylan's posture stiffens and his hands curl into fists on the table.

"You planning to bail?" Dylan asks, his voice sharp.

"I am not going anywhere. Aiden wants to check in," Darcy says.

The careful tone of her voice causes the skin on the back of my neck to prickle. Do we have anything to fear from Aiden? Will he be the one to dole out consequences?

The room echoes with a loud crack as Dylan opens his Coke and proceeds to chug most of it in a series of quick gulps.

Katie eyeballs Darcy and me, then asks me in a carrying whisper. "Are we in trouble?"

Dylan is about to attack the last of his fries, but freezes, his fingers suspended over the greasy carton.

CHAPTER FORTY-FIVE

– Lucy Walker –

Dylan? What's going on? I ask.

Katie releases a small gasp. I whip around to check on her.

"Cold," she says urgently as she reaches for the blankets. "So cold."

Damn...Damn...Damn... Dylan mutters the words mentally as the front door opens.

Katie pulls the blankets up to her chin. Her teeth chatter. So strange that she went from burning up to freezing. Is it a fever? Has the transformation kicked in? Are we passed the point of no return?

Two sets of footsteps approach. My breath halts in my throat. Aiden did not come alone.

Darcy leaps up from her chair, but makes no move to our side of the table. Her eyes narrow. A sharp breath escapes her lips.

My entire body spasms with fear. *Katie!* I scream mentally.

In a flash Dylan scoops Katie from the floor and sets her in one of the large chairs, her blankets piled on top of her. He and I shield her.

Dylan slides his hand into mine. I understand the gesture. If I need to use my magic, I am twice as powerful when Dylan and I merge our powers. I have a strong suspicion I am going to need all the help I can get to protect Katie, Dylan, and myself.

"What's going on?" Katie asks through chattering teeth.

"How dare you!" Darcy growls as Aiden enters the room.

"We have a situation. He came to address it," Aiden says.

It's the tone of his voice. The strangled emotion is something I have heard once before, when he showed up after the battle at St. Aquinas and he saw the extent of Marcus's injuries. Pain. But...

Oh, my God, Dylan says in my head.

The white-haired man enters the room. His three-piece deep gray plaid suit, blood-red tie, and glossy tobacco-colored leather shoes scream power. His black eyes sweep the room.

My heart hammers in my chest.

Katie's teeth chatter so hard I worry they will break. Her breaths come out in a stutter.

Darcy stands straighter. She glares at Aiden.

The white-haired man hooks his finger toward Darcy and she goes to him. He cups her cheek.

"Darcy," he says the word more like a command.

"I have the situation under control," she replies, her voice full of deference.

"I trust you do. However, a law has been broken. Now I am here to uncover the facts."

Darcy bows her head. "As you wish. I am here to serve you." She backs away from the man, giving him access to the room, to us.

Aiden stands off to the side, his hands at his sides. His fingers twitch, but otherwise he is still.

The man's black gaze fixes on Dylan and me. His expression is not one of anger, more curiosity. He crosses the room, each step deliberate, purposeful. My stomach clenches painfully. He could kill us with the snap of a finger. I have seen him do it.

He stops in front of me, his eyes focus on my face.

"Lucy," he says warmly.

I gulp, inclining my head toward him like Darcy did moments ago. "Lucifer."

CHAPTER FORTY-SIX

– Lucy Walker –

"You don't seem pleased to see me," Lucifer says, the affection in his gaze plain.

Dylan clasps my hand tighter as we stand guard, hiding Katie behind us. The blankets piled on her do nothing to stop the chattering of her teeth. Is it the progression of her demon transformation that causes her to feel so cold all of a sudden? The room does feel chillier. Could Lucifer's arrival have anything to do with that?

Lucifer doesn't try to hug me or touch me. That's a relief. Jude's physical touch when we first met was shocking. Literally. Lucifer's gaze probes mine. I squirm under the weight of it. Can he read my thoughts? Tell if I lie?

"It's not that," I say. "I'm...I'm just surprised."

Lucifer doesn't respond. His gaze flickers to Dylan.

"Won't you introduce me to your friends?" Lucifer suggests finally.

"I...Of course," I say, gesturing to Dylan with my free hand. "I'm not sure if Jude told you about Dylan Douglas."

"Ah, yes, Pierce's boy. Your chosen mate," Lucifer says, appraising Dylan. He studies our intertwined hands.

"We're not mates," I clarify quickly, yanking my hand from Dylan's.

"It's not like I didn't try," Dylan says.

"My *boyfriend* is Marcus Turner. He is away right now," I say, forcefully.

Aiden flinches behind Lucifer. Did I say something wrong?

"The *gargoyle*?" His face contorts with anger. "The life that I spared after the gargoyle attack?"

"Yes." I stand tall, fighting the urge to cower in the face of his anger.

"What does your father think of this gargoyle?" Lucifer asks darkly.

The hard look on Aiden's face frightens me. If only I could read him, know his thoughts. It's as if he wants me to say something specific, but I have no idea what that is. All I can do is tell the truth.

"Marcus has proven to be loyal and protective during several dangerous situations. He saved me after Seamus's attack when all other magic wasn't enough, even Jude's," I say, the words filled with conviction. For some stupid reason, tears fill my eyes and my throat burns. "During the gargoyle attack, he fought on the side of the demons. For those reasons, my father tolerates him."

"I see," Lucifer says.

He relaxes a fraction just then. I hope that means he is satisfied with my explanation.

Past Lucifer's shoulder Aiden relaxes a little, too.

The room falls so quiet that Katie's stuttering breaths carry across the room.

Lucifer moves to inspect Katie and I stiffen.

"This is my friend, Katie." I place my hand on her shoulder, applying pressure so she will stay seated.

Lucifer leans in, takes a lock of Katie's shoulder-length hair between his fingers. My hand trembles against Katie's shoulder. I want to shove Lucifer away from her, yank Katie out of her chair and take her far away from him.

"So much like Fiona," Lucifer murmurs.

Look at Aiden! Dylan orders in my head.

I glance over and see Aiden sag against the wall. His eyes are closed.

Who is Fiona?

How would I know? Dylan says.

"It's nice to meet you," Katie says, openly gawking at Lucifer. "How do you know Lucy? Who is Fiona?"

I want to clasp my hand over her mouth. The sadness in his voice over the name scares me. A demon in pain can turn moody and dangerous in an instant. She shows no fear, though. This is the most powerful demon in existence. He could kill her in the time it takes to blink.

"Fiona was my daughter," Lucifer says. He releases Katie's hair with a sigh and steps back. "Lucy is my namesake."

Fiona? I've never heard of her. Was she Aiden's mother?

Katie cocks her head to the side. "What's a namesake?"

Lucifer nods at her confusion.

"Her father named her after me. It is my responsibility to

serve as a second father if anything should happen to Jude. Ultimately, I am her protector."

"But..." I interject. As far as I know, this is the hypothetical definition of the term, nothing more. Over my shoulder I look to Aiden.

Aiden glares at me and gives a tight shake of his head.

"What is it you all are doing here today?" Lucifer asks. He appears unable to tear his eyes from Katie. His entire demeanor changed once he saw her. He is no longer frightening.

"We—" Dylan begins.

"I would like to hear it from the girl with the white hair who looks so much like my Fiona," Lucifer says, flashing a look at Dylan that stops him cold. The white-haired demon slides a chair near Katie and sits down.

"Will you tell me?" Lucifer asks Katie, his voice gentle.

Katie's big blue eyes meet Lucifer's, unblinking. Maybe she is drunk on Darcy's blood. Maybe it's the transformation kicking in, but Katie looks at ease when speaking to the leader of the underworld.

"Seamus McAllister, the demon who has been trying to kill Lucy—do you know him?" she says softly. It's as if the two of them are having a private conversation. I tighten my grip on her shoulder. "With Mr. Morgan gone and Lucy's boyfriend gone, Lucy has very little protection left. I am going to become supernatural. Dylan and I will help Lucy fight Seamus McAllister and the others he gives his power to."

"All this blood drinking. It's a crime you know," Lucifer says. He mimics her, keeping his voice low as he leans close.

Back away...back away...back away... I chant the words in my head, willing Lucifer with my thoughts. I am ready to fling myself at him at the first sign of a threat toward Katie.

Katie sits back in her chair, surprise evident all over her face. "An actual crime?"

"Dylan and Katie came to me—" Aiden begins.

"I was ordered to help," Darcy chimes in.

"It's my fault. Mine alone," Dylan says at the same time.

Lucifer holds up his hand and they all fall silent.

"I don't know about any laws, so I'm sorry about that. I had to do this. I won't allow someone to kill Lucy. I love her like a sister." Katie settles her huge eyes on Lucifer. "Seamus McAllister is bad news."

Lucifer peels his attention away from Katie and looks at me.

I pull myself upright in the glow of his attention. Unlike Katie, meeting his probing gaze is difficult for me.

"An ongoing feud. I suppose this is my fault," he says.

His words register in my mind, but my attention is hyper-focused on his hands, his eyes, and his demeanor. There is a reason Lucifer came here. Will this be like his appearance at St. Aquinas? Is he here to take someone or several someones out? Is there cleanup that needs to be done since laws have been broken?

"Feud?" I ask, my cheeks burning. I did share with Dylan and Katie the dramatic love triangle gone wrong involving my grandmother, Jude, and Seamus so many years ago. Seamus lost out in the end and has held a lethal grudge ever since. There is also the matter of Jude killing Seamus's daughter, Daphne.

Lucifer leaves his chair. He moves to the center of the room. The tight feeling in my chest lightens a little. Lucifer's voice returns to full volume. "I am talking about two members of my team, climbing through the ranks, outshining all others, competing for the top spot. They were both superior demons." Lucifer stands still, his index finger pressed to his lips as he loses himself in thought. A flash of pride crosses his face. "Jude was the superior of the two," Seamus beams.

The longer he is silent, the more I want to scream.

Like my father, Lucifer can stand perfectly still for extended periods of time. Meanwhile it takes all of my effort to keep my own movements to a minimum, shifting just a little every few seconds, my body too fidgety to remain static.

Do you think he plans to kill me? Dylan asks.

I don't know, I admit. *I keep trying to figure out why he's here, what he plans to do.*

You have clout with him. You'd better be prepared to use it.

That's it. I can't stand waiting.

Not yet! he shouts in my head.

"Lucifer, with all due respect, how does this work?" I say, embarrassed that my voice trembles when Katie's was rock steady. Will he strike me dead for my insolence?

"So much like your father," Lucifer muses. "You have some tough decisions to make today, Lucy. A law has been broken. I understand the reason behind it. However, punishment must be doled out and I want you to be the one to do it."

CHAPTER FORTY-SEVEN

– Lucy Walker –

"Me?" My stomach spasms with fear. I press my hand to my mouth, willing the veggie burger and French fries not to reappear.

Keep it together, Dylan says. *Katie is the weakest one here. Make sure she stays out of the fray. The rest of us can handle torture.*

Torture? I shoot him a look of horror before remembering myself.

I look back at Lucifer. My legs tremble. I lock my knees to force them to hold me upright. Katie clasps the hand I have rested on her shoulder.

"How does this work?" I ask.

"It appears that everyone here except for you was involved in the blood drinking. Consider this an introduction to leadership training. You shall choose a punishment for everyone involved."

I take in Aiden's expression—a cold, blank mask, followed by Darcy's erect posture and bowed head. Upon closer inspection, I catch her sideways gaze, which is desperate and, what I find most

329

confusing of all, fixed on Aiden. Dylan stands stoically with his arms at his sides, his shoulders drawn back, and his eyes focused respectfully on Lucifer.

My gaze drops to Katie, my heart and stomach colliding painfully inside of me. "I would like to take Katie's punishment upon myself," I say, without hesitation.

"Instead, may I respectfully request that you double my punishment?" Dylan says loud and clear, stepping forward.

"You don't know what you're saying," Aiden protests.

"It's my decision," Dylan shoots back.

"You are a fool!" Aiden responds.

"Lucy, let us proceed," Lucifer interrupts smoothly. "Punishment options are as follows: physical discipline by my hand, relocation to the underworld for six months, or strip him or her of power for one year."

Dylan, what should I do?

Let's talk through it. What are your initial thoughts? Dylan asks.

I refuse to have anyone tortured and I don't want to strip anyone of his or her powers, I say.

Okay, so that leaves sending them to the underworld.

I can't send Aiden to hell because he has to run Jude's empire while Jude is already there.

Ask for a deferral, Dylan suggests.

Lucifer won't go for that!

No harm in asking.

I study Dylan for a long moment. *What about you? None of those options will work for you.*

330

Physical discipline.

No!

"I opt for physical discipline," Dylan says to Lucifer.

"A double portion? Yours and Katie's?" Aiden says through gritted teeth. "You would not survive."

"Am I allowed to suggest my own punishment?" Katie asks Lucifer. She looks so small as she peers at him from under her pile of blankets.

She no longer shivers.

Lucifer nods at Katie, his expression softening again. "What do you have in mind?"

"I believe you and I both want the same thing, sir, to keep Lucy safe. Make me strong. Give me a little bit of your power. I will protect your namesake. It will be my duty to serve as her guardian."

Lucifer studies Katie. Slowly he nods. "A fine idea, servitude, although to be fair, that is not exactly a punishment. I shall devise the remainder of your punishment. We will reconvene once I have decided."

"That's fair," Katie says. She settles back in her chair.

"You said I would decide." There is no way a punishment doled out by Lucifer could be anything but deadly, despite his gooey glances at my best friend.

Lucifer nods. "You are right, I did say that. You and I shall decide together."

Before I can utter another word, he directs his attention to Dylan.

"A single dose of physical discipline for you."

"I thought the choices had to be made by me," I protest, my voice rising an octave.

"An individual can certainly choose his or her own punishment," Lucifer says. On the surface his tone is calm, sounds reasonable. However, there is a firmness beneath his words that forbids any argument. "Now what do we do about my grandson and Darcy?"

I have seen the scars on Aiden's back. He has had enough torture. "I opt to send Aiden to the underworld—" I say.

"Have you lost your mind?" Aiden asks, his face flushed with anger and incredulity. "I have a business to run!"

"Please allow me to finish," I say, struggling to keep my emotions under control. "But only if we can get a delayed start. We have to wait for Jude's return before Aiden can leave. One of them has to be here to run JM Industries."

Lucifer nods thoughtfully as he walks toward Darcy. He cups her cheek again. She raises her eyes to meet his. Without looking at me, Lucifer asks, "What do you propose for Darcy?"

"Take away her powers," Dylan suggests. It takes a moment before I realize he said the words out loud. I can't tell if he is trying to spare her torture or if he wants to ensure she can't pose a threat like she did the night of homecoming.

"So much for doing you a favor," Darcy says icily.

"Payback, kitty kitty," Dylan responds sarcastically.

"What would you prefer?" I ask her. While I am furious that she shared her blood with Katie, I recognize she was trying to help my friends. She deserves at least a say in her own sentence.

Darcy pauses, caught off guard. "If I get to choose..." She glances at Aiden, catches his eye. He nods tightly. "I will join

Aiden in the underworld. Given that each day there is the equivalent of a month here, I can be helpful, go back to teaching finance and language classes."

"A fine contribution. Thank you," Lucifer says, releasing her cheek. He turns to Dylan. "Now, for your punishment."

"Can we find an alternative?" I plead.

"No," Lucifer says flatly.

"The other two options won't work," Dylan adds quickly, bowing his head in deference. "Take me out back or to the basement. Whichever you see fit."

"*No!*" I feel like this whole thing has spiraled dangerously out of control. "I don't want him beaten. I decide. You said so. *I decide.*"

Lucifer catches Aiden's attention. Aiden taps his watch, then nods toward the door.

"We have an obligation to attend to," Lucifer says. "Dylan, walk me to the door."

I take hold of Dylan's hand and try to tug him back to me.

Lucifer studies our intertwined hands, his lips twitching. "Darcy, find out who Seamus is giving his powers to. We will need to address that situation," he says. He pauses mid-step then turns, his eyes falling on Katie. "You really want to help Lucy? To serve as her guardian?"

"Yes, sir," Katie says, meeting his gaze.

"Come to me," Lucifer orders.

Katie obeys, her blankets fall to the floor as she stumbles to him.

Lucifer flicks his finger and blood starts to flow from the tip.

He holds up his finger, offering it to Katie, waiting for her to make her choice.

A wave of nausea sweeps through me.

Katie wraps her hands around Lucifer's, pulling at his finger like a hungry infant.

Lucifer caresses Katie's hair with his free hand. "It is like seeing a ghost or an angel."

I wrap my arms around Katie. "That's enough." I pull her away.

Blood and saliva drip down her chin. Her eyes are too bright as she turns on me. "Why did you do that?" her voice is sharp, feral.

"You've had enough," I repeat.

Lucifer touches my cheek. "I will see you again soon. Stay safe."

He hooks a finger toward Dylan, who follows him and Aiden toward the door.

BEG HIM TO RETURN MY FATHER! I say to Dylan mentally.

Dylan hunches, clutching his head.

Sorry, I add.

He aims a dark look my way before following Lucifer and Aiden out the door.

Katie circles the table, pacing like a caged animal. "We need to train. *I* need to train. Who will teach me to fight, to defend you?" Gone is my weak, unsteady friend. Katie vibrates with energy. It's as if she just pounded a six-pack of Mountain Dew. Her eyes dart around the room taking in every detail in warp speed.

"This will be fun," Darcy says, moving to my side as she watches Katie.

I tear my attention from Katie for just a second. "What do you mean?"

Darcy smiles with dark pleasure. "You no longer have to worry that Jude is gone and that your winged boyfriend is gone. With full power and proper training, Katie will crush this Ella person."

Katie crosses the room. She moves fast. Without any concept of her strength, she yanks open the door and tears it from its hinges. Alarmed, she flings the heavy wooden slab to the floor. She screams and jumps as it crashes to the floor with a loud BOOM. My friend turns to me, her face contorted into a look of horror and alarm.

I rush to her side, cramming down my own fear and panic at her strength, the noise, and the damage.

"I...did...whoa...I didn't mean to..." she gasps.

"I know." I pull her into a hug, inspecting the damage to the doorframe over her shoulder. "You got your wish. You are now a supernatural like Dylan and me."

Just a much stronger version.

CHAPTER FORTY-EIGHT

– Dylan Douglas –

Aiden leads the way out the front door, followed by Lucifer and me. It's dark out. I have lost track of the time, but I don't dare pull my phone from my pocket to check. Lucifer and I remain on the porch while Aiden walks over to a dark metallic gray Land Rover parked in front of Jude's house. He opens the back door of the vehicle and stands there obediently. Small plastic containers clatter onto the ground. Aiden picks them up and tucks them inside the vehicle. Chocolate wafts through the air. Compared to Darcy's car, Lucifer's is a disappointment.

Suddenly, I hear a loud boom inside of the house. I cringe but stay put. Unless Lucy sends me a mental SOS, I have to trust that she and Darcy can handle it.

Lucifer turns on me then, a gap of two feet between us. "A gargoyle?" he demands, his voice sharp as a knife. He punches the air at waist level.

A sharp pain bolts through my gut and knocks the air out of me. Gasping, I clutch my abdomen, trying to protect myself from another attack. Aiden's face twists into a grimace behind Lucifer.

"Look at me!" Lucifer demands.

I do as he commands, wheezing.

"She was supposed to fall in love with *you*." His eyes burn into mine.

Lucifer thrusts his head hard against the air between us. An invisible object, hard as crowbar strikes the lower half of my face. Pain blazes through my face as my jaw crunches. I am blinded by tears.

Suck it up, Dylan. No time for wussies!

"I...she..." I begin, but can't form words with a shattered face.

"The enigmatic Dylan Douglas. Stud of the school. Worshipped by his comrades. You *failed* me," Lucifer says, his words seething. Flames burst from his mouth with those last three words. Red and orange and absolutely terrifying. The heat touches my face and I flinch. Will he set me on fire? Melt my face?

I shake my head. *Big mistake.* Laser sharp pain beams through my jaw. The fire is gone. I close my eyes. Hallucination? Is Lucifer messing with my mind? As I open my eyes, I bite back a shriek. Lucifer stands so close our noses almost touch.

"No," I whisper, the word distorted into a groan because of my lame jaw.

"Yes." The leader of the underworld stares into my eyes, his own eyes fire-engine red.

Lucifer raises his hand. With a flick of his fingers and a jerk of his wrist, my shoulder is yanked from its socket. In the same moment, he punches me in the shattered lower half of my face.

I scream. My legs quiver, nearly giving out. Bending at the

waist, I stumble, and fight the urge to puke. I force my knees to lock. Using my good arm against my leg for leverage, I slowly stand.

"I thought you were tough, Dylan. Jude bragged about your strength. Your power. All the praise he showered upon you when he announced to me that he had found the perfect mate for our Lucy," Lucifer rages. "You are not so strong. If you were, you would have fought for her. Instead, you gave up. You allowed a gargoyle—the enemy of our kind—to have her. What can you say for yourself, Dylan? Are you as tough as Jude said you were? Show me your power. Show me your strength!"

Facing off against Lucifer, I wonder...Am I allowed to fight back? Is that what this is about? If I slug the leader of hell, will he snap his fingers and turn me to dust like he did to the mutant gargoyles? I draw upon the extra juice from Jude. It fills my muscles. It energizes me, gives me a kind of euphoria I have never felt before.

The fury that I've been stuffing down, all those football practice sessions, all the games, where I had to maintain control so I wouldn't hurt anyone. *Tamp it down, Dylan.* The mantra repeated over and over. Screw that.

The pain of Lucifer's attack dims a little as whatever enhancements Jude FedEx'd from hell are finally let loose.

With more force than a grizzly bear, I lunge at Lucifer. My fists pummel his torso. Not every swing lands. Lucifer is fast. He's able to dodge most of my punches. Doesn't matter. Many of his swings do land. This is blind rage. This is freedom. This is the most powerful release I've ever experienced. I reach for his arm; he pulls free before I take hold. I grab for his other arm. He slips away. With a flat hand, Lucifer aims a power punch at me. I twist so that he hits my shoulder, forcing it back into its socket.

Thank you very much!

With two functioning arms, I go to work on him.

Lucifer spins and lowers himself to the ground to sweep my feet out from under me. I leap and kick him in the shoulder. He growls. Lucifer wraps one hand onto his shoulder, presses hard, then leaps to his feet. Did he just heal himself that fast? Lucifer roars like a fierce rhino.

He moves to strike, two fingers aiming for my eyes. I jerk to the left. The head cheese of hell counters and clobbers the left side of my head, delivering a blow to my ear that renders me deaf on impact. Disoriented, I stumble. A strange low tone fills my head, further throwing me off. Lucifer's hands attack with speed so fast his movements appear blurry as he pummels my abdomen. His feet strike out and shatter my knees. I am on the ground. His expensive shoes approach my face.

This is where it ends, I realize. *He will drive my nose into my brain. Then it's lights out.*

"Lucifer, stop!" Aiden yells. "His punishment has been fulfilled. You will be late for the opera."

The assault suddenly ends. Out of one swollen eye, I see Lucifer straighten his jacket, adjust his tie. He blinks and the red is gone from his irises.

Aiden flinches as he scans my body, the damage. Probably imagined. Aiden cares about Aiden and no one else, except maybe Marcus.

"Lucy will resent you," Aiden says to his grandfather.

Lucifer's black eyes assess me. A frown creases between his eyes.

"If you want Dylan to help protect Lucy, you will need to restore him." Aiden turns away from me, faces his grandfather. "The blond girl is out of control, needs training. Dylan can be tasked with that when I am not available. Lucy will not be strong enough to discipline her friend."

"Very well. You will continue to train them. Dylan will assist. Include Darcy as needed until the two of you relocate upon Jude's return," Lucifer says before settling his gaze on me. "Before I fix you," he kneels until his face is inches from mine, "I want you to know that I will tear you apart over and over again, allowing a longer delay each time. You failed me, Dylan. Now you will suffer. A gargoyle killed my daughter. I swore a gargoyle would never again become part of my family. You have allowed another one in."

CHAPTER FORTY-NINE

– Dylan Douglas –

I land each step gingerly across Jude's foyer as I confirm my knees are back to normal ball and joint construction and not a mess of splintered bone. Lucifer restored me. He didn't erase the memory of the injuries or the agony. What I want to know is how the hell is it my fault that Lucy chose Marcus as her boyfriend? Lucifer's going to come after me again. He said so. There's no way I can take another round with the strongest demon in existence.

My cell vibrates in my pocket.

"Hello?" I say without looking at the screen, testing out my jaw to ensure it functions again. My hand trembles and I nearly drop my phone. The beating is still too fresh.

"Dylan? It's Caroline. Thank God you answered. I need your help. There's something wrong with Ella. Very wrong. I thought she was okay, but then...Oh, Dylan. We need your help. *Please.*"

Not trusting Lucifer's restoration, I keep running mental checks on my body. Even my bad ear works again.

Caroline's voice reaches screechy levels.

I tune in. "What about Ella?"

Caroline starts to cry. "She's so sick." Her sob is muffled and it takes a moment before she continues. "She refuses to go to a hospital, Dylan. Can you please come and help me? Help us?"

I'm paying attention now. Mostly. "What happened?"

Caroline fills me in on Ella as I walk carefully to the dining room. Now that Lucifer has it out for me, could he re-break my knees all the way from the opera?

Now Ella's sick? Things keep getting worse and weirder.

"*Drugs.* Who knew? Does that seem like Ella?" Caroline says.

Ella has never experimented with drugs as far as I know. She's a fan of the bottle and boys. Not much else. How is it my knees and my face don't hurt at all? Will Lucifer come back for me later tonight? Maybe Aiden won't be around next time to stop him.

Caroline starts crying again. At the same time, a shouting match erupts in Jude's dining room.

"Caroline, I need to get off the phone if you want me to come over."

"Okay. Please hurry," she sniffles.

In the dining room Lucy lectures Katie—hollers, really—her face flushed with aggravation as she waves her arms toward broken chairs and the door ripped from the frame.

"See what you've done? So, the answer is no! You can't touch anything!"

"You're the worst demon mentor ever!" Katie cries.

Darcy laughs from where she sits in the corner of the room. "You are going to have a fun time with your new little demon."

"Dylan," Lucy says, relief flooding her voice. "We need to go. I want to take Katie back to my house."

342

I take in the damage in the room. Jude's furniture is much sturdier than Lucy's uncles' furniture. "Is that such a good idea?"

Lucy pulls her hair back from her flushed face. She looks exhausted. "My uncles are out," she says. *I need to talk to Persephone when she gets home from the event with my uncles. Maybe she can help me develop a potion to slow down Katie's abilities, tone down her strength,* she adds.

Great idea, I tell her. I raise my eyebrows at her. "Can you handle Katie? Caroline just called, pretty hysterical. Ella is sick," I say aloud.

Lucy cocks her head. "Sick...how?"

"Caroline suspects Ella did drugs with a guy in the woods last night. She's been super sick all day."

"Ella doesn't do drugs," Katie says. "Caroline's an idiot if she thinks so." She rests her arms on her knees as she sits on the mattress. Her irritation over whatever she and Lucy were arguing about has vanished.

Lucy's expression darkens. "Seamus likes to use his magic out in nature."

"Ella texted Katie yesterday and told her Seamus was giving her powers, so that's a good guess," I say. I gesture to the doorway. "I'm out of here."

Darcy interrupts. "Seamus may be a powerful demon, but unless he has learned some new skills, he has no idea how to share his powers with a human. This girl will not survive his magic."

Katie leaps from the mattress. "We need to help her, Lucy!"

She moves so fast. I stare dumbly from Katie to Lucy to the broken chairs. Way too much is happening. I can't get a grip on it all.

"You can't go," Lucy says sharply to Katie, pointing to the mattress. She turns back to me. "Go help Caroline with Ella. I'll take the Tasmanian devil home with me. Can you call me once you know something?"

"What about her?" I ask nodding at Darcy. "She could help."

"Are you insane?" Lucy snaps. "She wants to get close to Ella so she can kill her."

I leave them then and hope like hell we can figure out a way to save Ella and to keep Lucifer from coming after me again.

CHAPTER FIFTY

– Lucy Walker –

"How long before I can use my arms again," Katie complains as I pull up to the curb in front of the three-flat. It's the fifth time she has asked the question during our drive from Jude's house. There was no way I would allow her inside my Lexus without restraints and even less of a chance inside my uncles' apartment.

"Darcy said your urges will calm down within a few days. Your mind-body connection to your powers will adjust and you will have a better sense, better comprehension of your strength."

Katie looks alarmed. "A few days? I need the use of my arms *tonight*. What am I supposed to do for school tomorrow?"

I open her car door and unbuckle her seatbelt. "The binding spell will wear off in a little while, I promise, and you're not going to school tomorrow."

My uncles will be at their fundraiser party until late. As I get Katie settled on the couch in the living room, Dylan calls.

"Caroline wasn't kidding. Ella's house is a mess. Vomit everywhere. Bloody vomit. Who can survive this?" he says grimly.

"Ella's gone. She's not answering her phone or responding to messages—not even mine."

I close my eyes. Panic creeps up my throat like a high-speed escalator. I open my eyes, realizing that I need to keep an eye on my newly demonized BFF. Dylan continues with the bad news.

"Caroline showed me Ella's clothes from yesterday. They're filthy—covered in dried vomit and mud," Dylan says.

"Mud on her clothes would confirm she was in the woods," I say. "Going by the text Ella sent to Katie, I don't think Ella met some random guy."

"I agree," Dylan says. "The bloody vomit worries me. So do the muddy clothes. How does a clean freak like Ella wind up covered in mud?"

Neither of us say it, but we both read the newspaper articles online. All those girls who died had one thing in common. Vomit—lots of it, some of it bloody—near their bodies. Half of them were found in wooded locations, poisoned according to Henry.

"If he shared his magic with her, we have another club member in addition to Katie on our hands," Dylan says grimly.

"You think Seamus successfully transferred power to her? You're basing that on vomit and muddy clothes?" I ask, stuck on the mental image of Ella's corpse. Ella surviving and becoming a demon hadn't occurred to me.

"I'm basing it on the fact that Ella ripped a steel handle from the shower wall today with her bare hands. Caroline showed me the damage," Dylan says.

Anger surges through me and a feeling of helplessness is not far behind. "Now she's missing." I say. First, Katie transforms into a demon who breaks everything she touches. Now, Ella's gotten her wish and is armed with dark magic. I don't know how much more I can take. On top of that, the sound of Dylan's screams still echoes through my brain. I haven't let on to Dylan that I know just how badly Lucifer hurt him. At the moment I would like nothing more than to turn in my supernatural card.

Katie nudges me again. "I need something to eat."

"Let me know if you find her," I say finally, pulling Katie from the couch.

"Actually, I'm on my way to your place. I suggested to Caroline that she call Cloe to sit with her at Ella's house while they wait for Ella to return. Caroline said Ella has been trying to contact Katie since all of this happened. I think we should have Katie try to call her. That might be our best bet to finding her. Otherwise, we're going to have to look for her." Dylan says before ending our call.

Why has Ella been so eager to talk to Katie?

"Ella's missing," I tell Katie once I have her seated at the kitchen table with some cookies. "Any idea where she would go?"

"The mall," Katie says promptly. She eats the cookies so fast it appears as if she doesn't bother to chew them. "The only place Ella ever wants to go is the mall or the beach."

"But she's very sick," I remind her.

"Seamus got to her?" Katie asks, her face scrunched with worry.

There's no point in lying to her. I nod.

Katie's eyes fill with tears. "She'd probably call her dad, but he's in New York. What can he do from there?"

My doorbell rings.

For once I'm grateful that Dylan drives so fast. It'll be a relief to have him here to help me keep Katie under control, especially once her magical restraints wear off.

After I open the apartment door, I cross the foyer and peek through the peephole of the building's front security door.

I gasp and duck. I slide my phone from my pocket and dial Dylan's number. "You're not going to believe this," I whisper. "Ella just showed up here."

"I'll be there in a few. Lucy, whatever you do, do not let her in," Dylan says.

CHAPTER FIFTY-ONE

– Lucy Walker –

"Open up, Lucy," Ella says, her voice muffled through the door. "I know you're there. I can here you breathing."

Am I suddenly panting like a marathon runner or does Ella have supersonic hearing? "Caroline called. She's worried about you," I tell her.

"Let me in and we can call her."

"Caroline said you went to the woods last night. Did you meet with Seamus McAllister again?"

"Confess that you stole my stuff and I'll tell you," Ella snarls.

I raise to my tippy toes and with one eye squished against the little peephole, I can see her face. She looks like a mess, but she also looks mad—even distorted by the fish-eye effect of the eyehole.

"I confess that I took items that belonged to me—that you stole from me in the first place," I snap back. I pull my eye from the door with a huff. Katie is sitting in my kitchen. Will she follow instructions to remain there until I return? How long will it take for Dylan to show up?

"He made me do it. You get that, right? Seamus McAllister—he has a temper. He hurt me." Ella's voice is thick. I can't tell if she's crying or tired or crazy from demon magic.

"He shared his powers with you?" I ask.

Duh, Lucy. How else could Ella tear metal apart with her bare hands.

"Please let me in," she says. She rattles the doorknob and pushes against the door.

I glance back at my apartment hoping Katie isn't trashing the furniture like she did at Jude's house. My uncles don't have the money to replace it all.

"He liked hurting me," Ella says. "I bet he liked choking you the night of my party."

Her voice is off. It's deeper, monotone, almost a tired moan. A noise from the kitchen catches my ear. Have Katie's restraints worn off? Mentally, I race through the spell to replace them with new ones. Suddenly, something hits the door from the outside with such force, I bounce off of it. I scramble to the eyehole again in time to watch Ella gear up and kick the door again. The force of it sounds like she's going to tear it from its hinges. How would I explain that to Sheldon and Bernard?

"Fine, I'll let you in." I quickly open the door.

While I know the girl standing before me is Ella, she doesn't look much like her tonight. Her red hair has corkscrew curls on the left side of her head while the right side is thin and matted. She wears no makeup. It's her eyes that make me cringe. The reptilian green contact in her right eye appears to have partially melted. Her left eye has no contact at all. It's the first time I have seen her natural eye color—pale blue. Her eyes shift between narrow and angry, to bulging and panicked. Her mouth twists and wiggles as if trying to hold a wild salamander inside.

"Let me in," Ella demands, through gritted teeth. She attempts to shove past me toward the apartment.

I press my hands against her shoulders to block her entry. "Let's talk first."

Ella growls. She smells strange. I pick up the scent of soap, but there's something else, too. Something rotten. Ella's clothes appear clean. Where is the nasty odor coming from?

"Think hard about this, Ella. If you force your way in, if you've come here to hurt me, then I'll hurt you back."

It's not just me at risk if Ella gets inside. While Katie is certainly strong enough to protect herself—and her magical restraints are due to fall off any time now—I don't want her to accidentally break Ella. How is it that I'm stuck in a house with two newly created supernaturals? Where is Dylan?

A quick check behind Ella and I spot a couple of neighbors out walking their dogs. There's no way I can send Ella off, not in the state she's in. I consider the time. How long before my uncles return home?

A spell. That's what I need right now. Should I restrain her like I did Katie? Or cast something to defuse her anger? There's no time to put together any rhymes. I have to trust that the spell will be just as effective if my intent is strong. With my eyes locked on Ella's, I cobble together words that I believe will accomplish what I need. I whisper soundlessly while focusing on my intent.

Take away her anger, take away her pain
Calm her better than a sedative
Take away her anger, take aw—

A twitchy smile tugs at Ella's mouth. "Time's up," she says. With a grunt she shoves me hard. I stumble backward and fall. My head slams into the bottom wooden stair that leads to the second floor. Pain stabs the back of my head. Ella darts past me into my apartment.

Katie!

I scramble to my feet while clutching the back of my head. It throbs painfully. Nothing wet, so I know I'm not bleeding. Inside the apartment, Ella paces. Her breathing is ragged and sharp like a caged wild animal. She whirls to face me.

Focus, Lucy, I remind myself.

Take away her anger, take away her pain
Calm her better than a sedative

It's super difficult to focus when Ella looks ready to spring on me. What is Katie doing? Please, please, please let her stay in the kitchen.

"Did you really think you could get away with turning my friends against me?" she yells. She wipes sweat from her brow. Strange since the central air is running and the living room is cool. "Taking Dylan from me?"

I shuffle backward as Ella approaches. The backs of my legs butt up against the couch. If I blast her or throw her across the room, I will destroy all of the knick-knacks and family photos my uncles hold dear. Instead, I try to reason with her. "Whoa, Ella. Dylan is just my friend—like a brother. Marcus is my boyfriend, remember?"

"Why did you turn him against me?"

That *smell*. As she stalks closer, it grows stronger. I struggle not to make a face. *What is wrong with her?*

"I didn't. I swear. All he talks about these days is Selima."

Ella clenches her hands at her sides and stomps her feet. "You stole Katie from me, too. McAllister may be a psycho, but he was right about you. You *use* people, manipulate them to get what you want. I know you had it out for me from the beginning, saw me as a threat. I am beautiful and popular, so you set out to take things from me, to hurt me."

The apartment door bursts open. Dylan rushes into the room. He is out of breath. He eyeballs Ella.

"Back away from her, Ella," he orders.

"Lucy's Boyfriend Number Two," she sneers.

"No, Ella. Selima is my girlfriend," Dylan says, his voice surprisingly calm.

Can you go check on Katie in the kitchen? I say to Dylan. *Not sure how long before the spell wears off and she can use her arms again. I don't want her going after Ella.*

I'm not leaving you alone with her, Dylan says, glaring at me.

I've got this. Please go to the kitchen. We need to keep them apart. Two new demons, one who's pissed off and the other who's breaking everything...It's a bad combination.

Fine, Dylan says.

353

"Be back in a minute," Dylan says to us.

Ella watches Dylan's departing figure for a moment before she turns back to me.

"All I've ever wanted is to be your friend," I tell her.

What do you want me to do with Katie? Dylan asks from the kitchen. *Her hands are still bound, but she's been eating like a sumo wrestler in training. The kitchen's a wreck.*

Hide her. I think we can manage this if we keep them separated, I tell him.

Ella scowls at me. "Nice try. McAllister was right. You and your father are evil. You take whatever you want."

I don't know how long I can listen to her crazy talk. I decide to try to reason with her. Nothing else is working and my focus to cast a spell sucks. "Seamus McAllister lied to you. He's got a major grudge against my father for lots of reasons. Seamus is the selfish one. Are you really going to listen to an old, crazy demon who is out for revenge? He's only using you and he will keep hurting you."

Ella blinks. Is she listening?

"Please let us help you, Ella. Caroline's worried about you. She said you were sick at home—very sick," I say. "In order for us to help you, I need to know what Seamus gave you. We need to make sure whatever it was is not going to make you sicker."

Katie is hidden. But...we have another problem, Dylan says.

Can you handle it?

"Where is Katie?" Ella asks suddenly, scanning the room.

"You know Katie. She can't get enough time with Trevor. The two of them are attached at the hip," I say, with a crazy grin on my face.

A slow smile spreads across Ella's face. That's when I notice that one of her teeth is missing. Her pointy left canine.

"I smell her. One of my skills now that I'm a *demon*, too," she says in a hushed voice. She winks at me and the rest of her reptilian contact melts away. "No one can hide from me now."

Ella walks through the living room giving me wide berth. "Katie Stevens, come out come out wherever you are," she says in a singsong voice. Goose bumps break out along my arms.

This is going to be bad.

"You don't want to do this," I warn Ella, far more worried for her than I am for Katie. "Let me take you home."

Ella confronts me. "The only way this ends is for you to die. I want my friends back. I want Dylan back. I want my life to go back to the way it was before you showed up."

At the casual mention of my death, red-hot anger floods my body. My arms zing with power and heat. I'm tired of Ella's drama. The poor little rich girl who's been spoiled her entire life. Suddenly, she decides she wants magic and she thumbs her nose at caution, fear, and the rules.

"Don't push me, Ella," I tell her, my voice cold, hard, and totally fed up.

Ella has never been my friend, but the absolute hatred in her eyes makes me recoil.

Ella takes off down the hall. I race after her as she enters my bedroom. She sniffs the air, turns, and exits the room.

There's no way I'm letting her near Katie. As I reach out to grab her arm, she shakes me off and continues on. I hurry after her and tackle her, my arms around her waist. Both of us fall to the hall floor.

Ella rolls over. She grasps my face with both hands and slams my head into the wall. I cry out and my eyes flood with tears at the pain. Her strength is alarming.

Ella jumps to her feet and stalks off down the hallway. I climb to my feet and stare daggers after her, gasping as heat pulsates along my arms to my hands. The last thing I need to do right now is hurl a fireball at Ella and wind up setting my uncles' house on fire. I will the heat to subside. The effort to stifle my magic is painful. I need an outlet soon. I shuffle after Ella.

"Hey, Ella. You looking for me?" Katie calls out. She stands at the top of the basement stairs.

"Katie! You were supposed to stay hidden." The sound of my own shout causes a laser beam of pain to stab into my brain.

"While Ella hurts you? Not a chance. I promise I won't hurt her, though," Katie says.

"Like you could." Ella laughs.

Katie gets a good look at Ella. "Wow. You look terrible!"

"Shut up, Katie," Ella snaps.

"Seriously, did Dylan see you looking like this?" Katie taunts. "Maybe I should take a photo. Or we could send it to your dad. Let him know what you've been up to." Katie narrows her eyes at Ella and I stare on stupidly, never having seen this side of Katie before. "Better yet, we could submit it to the yearbook committee."

Is Katie crazy? Ella's trembling with rage. I'm trying to keep the peace so no one gets hurt and my uncles' home doesn't get trashed.

"Maybe we shouldn't have this conversation right now," I suggest, inching toward Ella. My head continues to pound, but I concentrate as hard as I can on my spell.

Take away her anger, take away her pain
Calm her better than a sedative
Take away her anger, take away her pain
Calm her better than a sedative

"I've got my phone here somewhere," Katie says, padding her pockets with her bound hands. "I think your dad would find it interesting that you've been hanging out with a demon, plotting to kill your friends."

Ella bares her teeth, showcasing her new gap, and growls.

Katie persists. "Lucy was able to stop Seamus from joining the first séance. Your demon buddy didn't like that, did he? So, you agreed to plan a second one. Smart idea, right? Give him another chance to kill Lucy and the rest of us?" Katie asks. She stands still as a statue. No, as still as my father or Lucifer.

"Stop it, Katie." Everything she says is true, but I need her to back down.

She ignores me and charges on. "If your dad knew the crap you were into, Ella, I think he would hustle his butt home. It's time we clue him in." She pulls her cell phone from her pocket, aims it at Ella. Bursts of light from the camera's flash brighten the hallway as Katie snaps a series of photos.

Ella shrieks like an animal under attack.

I murmur my spell under my breath fast and desperate.

Lucy, come down to the basement. We have a problem. Dylan interrupts.

Not now, I tell him. *Got a demon girl fight on my hands.*

I grab hold of Ella before she lunges for Katie. I spin her around. Ella clutches a handful of my hair and yanks *hard.* I bend one of her fingers backward until she screams and releases my hair. Using her other hand, Ella slaps me across the face. Clutching my cheek, I consider several maneuvers I could perform that would cause her the most pain. Unfortunately, every one of them would also annihilate the apartment.

Dylan's voice booms in my head. *Why are you letting a newbie demon kick your ass? You're better than this! I have seen you fight and it's not this weak crap! Take her out!*

Ella's been hurt enough, don't you think? And if I destroy the apartment?

She's a demon, Lucy. Fight!

Butt out. I'll handle this my way, I tell him.

Ella goes after Katie, shoves her against the wall, lifting her off her feet. Ella wraps her fingers around Katie's throat. Katie gurgles as her eyes bulge.

"Give me your camera," Ella roars.

Katie tries to speak, but nothing comes out.

So far, Katie sticks with her promise not to hurt Ella.

"Want to see fire up close, Ella?" I ask.

Ella whips her head around. Her eyes grow wide as she spots the fireball balanced in my hand. She releases Katie, who drops to the floor.

"Pretty isn't it?" I ask, bouncing it from one hand to the other.

"Katie told me you make fire," Ella says, looking dazzled, her eyes glued to the glowing ball. She approaches me cautiously.

The look on her face is not the death stare she gave me when she slapped me. She looks sort of normal—a bedraggled and smelly version of normal—and a little awestruck.

"Can you teach me to make fire?" she asks, her voice almost a whisper.

"I could teach you things if we were on the same side, if you weren't trying to hurt Katie and me."

Ella frowns, confusion flashing across her face.

I cup my hands together and the fireball is extinguished with a hiss.

"Do you want to be on our side?" Katie asks, still on the floor behind Ella. "Or with Seamus? Make a choice."

Ella's eyes flash. Her attention flickers from Katie to me. "Now you're both manipulating me!"

"Oh, please, Ella." Katie rolls her eyes. "Lucy and I don't manipulate people. Why can't you just try to be nice for a change?"

Did my spell work at all? I thought it had, but Ella's temper keeps flaring.

Ella closes her eyes and rolls her head from side to side. Bones crack. She opens her eyes. "I nearly died," she says. I don't know if I can trust her, though. She keeps wavering between regular Ella and demonized Ella. Her eyes fill with tears as she slumps against the wall. "Maybe he still plans to kill me."

"I can protect you, but only if you stop working with him," I tell her.

"You don't get it," Ella says. "He keeps showing up. Keeps demanding things. Keeps hurting me."

"I have a bunch of supernaturals in my life. We can make sure he doesn't hurt you anymore, but only if you promise to stop helping him. Can you promise me that?"

"You can hide with me while Lucy, Dylan, and the others figure it out," Katie says. She grabs Ella's arm. Ella gasps at Katie's grip.

Uh, oh. *Katie's got the use of her hands back.*

"You're hurting me!" Ella yells. She slams Katie into the wall, leaving an imprint of her body caved in the drywall.

"Stop attacking me!" Katie yells back. She sweeps her hand through the air, sending Ella crashing to the floor.

How did she learn to do that? Some kind of demon instinct?

Ella leaps to her feet, her eyes blazing. "Lucy shared her powers with you?" Ella whirls around to confront me, her eyes blazing. "You lied! You told me you couldn't share them with anyone!"

"Ella, if you want my help against Seamus, you need to stop!" I want to tell her that I didn't give Katie any powers, but then I would have to reveal who did. That would make things worse.

Ella returns her attention to Katie. She presses her lips together in concentration. She attempts several gestures with her hands, trying to mimic Katie's magic. With a jerk of her wrist and a twist of her hand, Katie's head slams into the wall. Before Katie can retaliate, Ella does it again.

I grab Ella from behind, holding her arms to her sides. "Leave her alone."

Katie glares at Ella as she raises her hand to strike.

"Katie—no!" I yell.

Enough, Lucy. Get your butt down here, Dylan orders. *Pronto!*

"I need to go to the basement," I tell Katie.

Katie grins. "Great. Leave Ella with me."

"Psycho suits you," Ella sneers.

"Nice try, but you've already earned that crown!" Katie grins. She flicks the air in Ella's direction and Ella shrieks as a red welt appears on her cheek.

With a heavy exhale I realize I can't leave these two nut jobs alone.

As I work to formulate a spell, I focus on Ella.

I need to bind her arms. That's my primary goal. Her friendship with Katie. That can be fixed, too, right? Maybe add some loyalty to me. Deep breaths as I work through it in my head. The rhyming comes easier this time. It helps that the violence between these two is calming down.

Press her arms to her sides—they are bound
Her friendship with Katie—reborn and newfound
Transform her allegiance to Katie, Dylan, and me, make it profound
Her belief in Seamus McAllister, change to dumbfound
Ella's loyalty to Seamus—unwound

I focus all of my energy on this spell, then repeat it. As I sink deeper into an absolute calm, into that place in my mind where anger and violence don't exist, I silently chant the spell for a third time. It's peaceful here, in the deepest part of myself. I breathe deeply and enjoy the respite. Slowly, grudgingly, I climb out of my tranquil place.

"Meek little Katie. Give her some magic and she thinks she can be me. *As if*," Ella jeers, rubbing her cheek.

Katie rolls her eyes. "I have never wanted to be you."

Ella glares at Katie.

My best friend is on a power trip and Ella's lost her mind. I need to leave them to find out what Dylan has found in the basement.

Suddenly, Ella droops in my arms.

"I'm sorry, Katie," Ella mutters, her body slack while her arms remain tight to her body. "You, too, Lucy."

Katie raises her eyebrows at me, questioning.

I nod at her. "It looks like we've got Ella back. Maybe even a humbler version."

"If your apology is genuine and not some kind of trick, then I'm sorry, too," Katie says to Ella. The ferocity is gone from her eyes.

I set Ella on her feet and turn her around to face me.

"Can I trust you two alone up here?" I ask, taking in Ella's tear-stained face before looking at Katie.

Katie tilts her head to study Ella's arms, which are pressed to her sides. She glances at me and I nod again. Katie pulls a tissue from her pocket and reaches for Ella's face.

"Gentle," I urge Katie firmly. "With your strength, you need to think of her face as a flower petal. *Everything* is a flower petal."

Katie gently dabs at Ella's tears. "Flower petal."

That's progress.

"If we're going to continue to be friends, we have a lot to talk about," Katie says as she leads Ella to the couch. "You won't get to boss everyone around anymore. We're going to start being really honest with each other."

Ella sits down awkwardly next to Katie on the couch. "Um... Katie? What's wrong with my arms?"

Katie glances my way. "It's leftover magic. It will wear off."

I give Katie a thumbs up before disappearing to the basement to meet Dylan.

CHAPTER FIFTY-TWO

– Lucy Walker –

"Dylan?" I call out as I reach the bottom of the stairs.

Off to my right are two washers and two dryers which are available to everyone in the building. To my left are floor-to-ceiling shelves filled with bins. No sign of Dylan. I file past the shelves and the TV room my uncles set up for me and my friends.

In the back, Dylan says, sticking with telepathic communication.

As I pass the room where Aiden, Selima, and I, together with Max and his kinder demon partner, Warrick, held our ceremony to summon Lucifer earlier this year, I shiver.

"What's so urgent? I could've used your help upstairs," I complain as I enter the second storage room. This is where Gram—and now my uncles—store my Uncle Zack's stuff.

"You're going to want to see this," Dylan says. He is on his knees sliding a small plastic thermal container from beneath a low shelf. "We weren't supposed to find them. Whoever they belong to hid them pretty well. It took me a while to find them all."

As I study the shelves filled with mostly Uncle Zack's humongous record collection, a bitter metallic odor hits me. It's faint, but I pick up on it.

I grimace. "Blood?"

"Yup. That's what drew me here when I was trying to hide Katie," Dylan says, finally talking out loud.

"You did a terrible job, by the way," I say, dryly.

He peeks up at me. "You try restraining Lucifer's spawn."

He's got a point.

Dylan pulls one more of the containers out for a total of four. "I think this is the last one."

That's when I notice that each container has a power cord extending from its back panel.

"Why do they need electricity?" I ask. A major case of the creeps oozes over me. "Please tell me those containers aren't filled with organs."

"Nope. Not organs." Dylan shifts from a kneeling position to sit on the floor. He lifts the lid on one container. "Take a look."

On my knees beside Dylan, I lift chilled storage packs like the ones Sheldon and Bernard receive each month tucked inside their shipment of vitamins. I pull a test tube from a small rack filled with a bunch more of the glass vials, all with seafoam green plastic tops. I pull another tube from the refrigerated box. I hold them up high so I can inspect the contents against the light. Dark liquid. Thicker than water based on how it swirls against the glass. The light quality isn't so great in the storage room, but I would bet the liquid is red. I grab another and inspect it. Then another. The glass containers clink against each other.

A sickening feeling settles in my stomach.

"The blood I smelled. Is it human, protector, or demon?" Again, I swirl the blood around the cylindrical tube as if it would somehow reveal a clue.

"I know an easy way to check one of the three," Dylan says. He pulls a knife from his pocket and unfolds the blade. I almost stop him, about to claim there is no need to shed his own blood, but we need an answer. Instead, I watch as Dylan draws the blade across his palm. He wipes the shiny metal on his pants, folds it, then tucks it into his pocket. I unstop one of the test tubes of blood.

Dylan nods. "Pour a little on my cut."

I dribble the red liquid onto his palm. We wait five seconds. Nothing happens.

"Give it a little longer," I suggest, watching and waiting. His cut shows no sign of healing.

Ten seconds later there's still no improvement on the cut.

"We can rule one of them out," Dylan says. "Gargoyle blood would have healed me already."

"Protector blood," I correct him. "Go wash your hand in the bathroom. It's around the corner from the washers and dryers."

He leaps to his feet. "Back in a sec."

While I wait for him to return I consider everyone who has access to the basement. Of all the people who live here, I can think of only one person who would know about the blood being stored down here.

Dylan returns moments later. His hand is clean and he smells of soap.

"We can assume this isn't human, can't we?" I ask, peering up at Dylan from where I sit on the floor.

"Yeah. Human blood doesn't do anything for anyone. It's not like we're dealing with vampires." Dylan chuckles.

The sound of his laugh rocks me. Nothing is as it should be. Today I babysat Dylan's brother and sister, who are petrified that their mother will move them to New York, far away from their friends, their brother, and me—all in an attempt to allegedly get away from Jude. Dylan and Katie conspired behind my back to turn Katie into a demon. Lucifer showed up acting tender and paternalistic to me and even more so to Katie before he tortured Dylan. Ella is a crazed demon as a result of her alliance with Seamus. Now Dylan finds a stash of blood in my basement. All of this on top of Marcus's mother's problems. I'm tired of all the supernatural plots going on around me. It's all too much, way too much.

Dylan freezes. "You have a look on your face that makes me nervous."

"Feeling overwhelmed." I rub my eyes, willing them not to tear up. "Plus, Ella and Katie damaged the house. My uncles are going to flip out. This passed the point of manageable three catastrophes ago."

Dylan sinks to his knees and rubs my back. "Persephone could always erase Bernard and Sheldon's memories to get you off the hook," he suggests.

"Maybe," I say, knowing I would never do that. Persephone and Henry have already tinkered with Sheldon and Bernard's brains a couple of times. I can't risk scrambling their minds merely to get out of a punishment.

Dylan squeezes my shoulder enough to comfort me.

I heave a deep breath. "This is probably demon blood. Who does it belong to and why is it here?" I ask, getting back on track.

"What's it intended for? Dosing should have ended when Garret died. Even if Camille carried on with it, shouldn't the blood drinking have stopped once she was in custody? All the morphed-out freaks were incinerated by Lucifer. Is someone planning to have another go at forming an army?" Dylan says, frowning at the containers.

The squeak of a door hinge makes us jump. Our eyes meet. What if the blood thief is back to pick up his stash? Or could it just be Katie? Dylan shuts the container. We slide all four of the coolers beneath the shelves quickly and move random boxes in front of them. Dylan shoves me behind him as we make our way through the basement, nearly colliding with Aiden. He carries Marcus's guitar over his shoulder and a box under his other arm.

"What are you doing down here?" Aiden grumbles. He moves past us to the area we just left.

I glance around him to see if Lucifer is with him. "Where's your grandfather?"

"Not here," Aiden says. "Where's the baby demon?"

Dylan and I glance at each other. Technically, we have two baby demons.

"Katie is upstairs," Dylan says carefully.

"What are you doing with Marcus's guitar?" I ask, noting that the box he carries under his arm is not insulated and does not have a power cord. "What's in the box?"

Aiden aims an annoyed glance over his shoulder at me. "Not

that it's any of your business, but Max is on his way over here. I'm hiding Marcus's stuff. If Max sees anything interesting, he'll come back while I'm gone and steal it. No doubt he knows all the pawn shops in Chicago by now."

Max is the demon my father recommended I reach out to if I am ever in a jam. Max owes Jude a lot of favors. Aiden and Max used to be friends a long time ago, I think. Aiden doesn't like him anymore.

Before I can spew off a few choice words about an ex-friend who would steal my boyfriend's belongings, especially his beloved guitar, Dylan interrupts me.

Max! Of course! Dylan says in my head. *Maybe the blood is his.*

Do you think he's selling it? I ask.

We stand in the doorway to the storage room. Aiden moves to the corner of the room, relocating boxes so he can carefully lay Marcus's guitar over several plastic crates. Dylan and I glance at each other.

"I don't think that stuff will be safe in here," Dylan says.

"Max can pick any lock he meets, true, but I don't think he'll think to look down here," Aiden says dropping to his hands and knees. He shoves a box aside and slides Marcus's belongings underneath and back against the wall.

"Someone else has been spending time down here," I say. "Someone who isn't a friend...unless..." I turn to Dylan, pointing a finger at Aiden, a question on my face.

Dylan shakes his head. "Too much of a Boy Scout."

"What are you two mumbling about?" Aiden asks, irritated, as he crosses the room to a shelf full of bags of out-of-season clothing and linens.

Dylan and I face Aiden. I could swear Dylan's biceps twitch and grow larger. *What the heck?*

"I don't want Max to see me leaving the basement, so make it snappy." Aiden stuffs bags in front of the guitar and turns to us. "What's up?"

"Are you draining demons of their blood?" Dylan asks.

So much for being delicate.

"Maybe you have a deal with a few demons, you know, for blood donations in exchange for cash or favors," I suggest.

Aiden makes a face. "Last time I checked I'm half-demon. Other than a few dirtbags—one of whom happens to be on his way to my apartment—I don't have an issue with them. What do you mean by blood donations?"

"Someone's using the basement as their personal blood bank," I say.

Aiden turns to me, his expression icy. "You have one minute. Tell me what's going on."

I cross the room and kneel next to the shelves. Dylan follows and helps to reveal the hidden coolers. Aiden crosses the small space as Dylan opens one of them.

"Damn it. When did you find these?" Aiden asks, squatting to get a closer look.

"Just a little while ago," Dylan says. "While Lucy was upstairs dealing with Seamus's recruit."

"The girl you mentioned back at Jude's? She's here?" Aiden asks.

"She showed up full of rage and power—compliments of a donation from Seamus—and ready to cause trouble. The apartment took a bit of a beating. So did my skull," I say, reflexively touching the back of my head. I wince. "I cast a spell on her to calm her down."

Aiden's gaze burns into me as if he doesn't really see me. Dylan and I wait, barely breathing, unsure what to do. Finally, Aiden climbs to his feet, gesturing to the test tubes. "You sure it's demon blood?"

"We tested it. It's not protector blood," Dylan says.

"Give me one of those tubes. Move the rest. Take them to Persephone's apartment or to the attic, somewhere you can plug them in. After I meet with Max, I will come to your apartment." Aiden is about to leave when he turns back. "Any idea what time your uncles will get home from their fundraiser?"

"They said it would be late," I say.

It hits me then, with all the fear and adrenaline no longer coursing through me. My uncles really are going to come unglued when they see the apartment.

"Ella and Katie had a fight. I have no idea how I will explain the damage to the apartment. Any suggestions?"

Aiden pulls his brows low. "Tell them you had a party, that it got out of hand."

I push to my feet. "That's the dumbest idea ever. I'm not a party girl."

"No kidding, Miss Prim. Tell them some other kids brought alcohol. You are missing Marcus something terrible. Cry to them about that. Get back upstairs to those girls. Their problems are much bigger than yours right now." Aiden leaves the basement with a glass tube of blood in his hand.

All this time I've been focusing on how hard the day has been on me.

Dylan touches my arm. "Aiden's a jerk. Don't let him get to you."

"No, he's right," I say, my eyes landing on Marcus's guitar. I shift my focus to Katie and Ella.

"We've been down here too long. I need to check on them, make sure they aren't trying to kill each other," I say.

"I'll move the blood," Dylan says. "Remember whose blood is coursing through your blond hellion's veins. I put my money on her over Ella."

"Good point," I say, remembering how Katie broke several of the solid, heavy chairs in Jude's dining room. Suddenly, I am extremely worried about Ella.

It occurs to me that I am going to need Aiden's help. I don't know what to do with Ella. Once my spell wears off, what then? Will she be back to her mission to help Seamus kill me? Will a spell work if I renew it several times a day?

"Hold the door," Dylan says.

I hold the basement door as he jogs past me carrying all four refrigerated containers. I trot through the living room past Katie and Ella to the apartment's front door and open it for him. He runs past me and up the stairs.

Hopefully Max isn't here yet. If I could smell the blood while I was near it in the basement, no doubt he—a full demon—will smell it's trail up the stairs, I say to Dylan.

Imagine how pissed off he'll be that it's missing, Dylan says.

I leave the door open an inch so Dylan can come back in without using the hidden key. On the couch, Ella sleeps curled up on Katie's lap with a pillow under her head. Katie watches me, absently stroking Ella's hair. There is a bald spot on the side of Ella's head. It's caked with blood.

"You were downstairs a long time. What's going on?" Katie asks.

I collapse onto the chair next to them and try not to look at Ella's head. With a heavy sigh I consider my options. How much do I want to tell Katie? Is there a reason to keep this from her? Who am I kidding? Katie drank Lucifer's blood. Ella's asleep, based on her deep, rhythmic breathing. So, I tell Katie about the blood Dylan found in the basement. I fill her in on the battle at St. Aquinas and how Garret doped protectors to build an army so she understands the significance behind demon blood.

"All in order to kill Jude. And you," Katie says, referring to Garret's grand scheme. A frown creases her forehead briefly, then disappears. Her eyes don't register panic or fear. Either Katie is wearing a brave mask or she is adapting quickly, faster than I did, to the world of demons, witches, and protectors.

"What happens next?" Katie asks.

I glance at Ella's sleeping figure. "I don't know what to do about her yet."

"Let's focus on—" Katie begins.

"Taken care of," Dylan says as he closes the apartment door behind him. "Persephone's going to need a new door knob."

I raise my eyebrows at him. "What about the key beneath her mat?"

Dylan grins sheepishly. "Didn't know about that." He waves at Katie; gives Ella a cursory look then exits the room. "Grabbing grub. I'm starving."

I pull my cell phone from my pocket and send a quick message to Persephone.

"How did you know Dylan found the blood in the basement?" Katie asks.

"What?" I ask, pulling my attention from my phone. "He showed me when I got down there."

"Yes, but how did you know to go down there in the first place?" she asks, confused.

"Oh, that. He and I can communicate," I point to my head, "telepathically."

Katie grins, raising her eyebrows in surprise. "Will I be able to do that?"

"I don't know. Remember when I told you that we share Jude's blood? That's our connection."

My phone vibrates in my hand.

Come upstairs. Mention the blood stash. Keep Katie's blood donor between us.

I show Aiden's text to Katie.

A few minutes later Dylan returns to the living room with a plate piled with four peanut butter and jelly sandwiches and a bag of corn chips. He hands a sandwich to Katie and one to me, keeping two for himself.

"Someone's gotta clean the kitchen. It's a mess," Dylan says through a mouthful.

It's Katie's turn to look sheepish. "I was starving and my hands were bound. I'll clean it when we're done at Aiden's," she says.

I relay Aiden's message to Dylan.

"Should we wake her?" Katie gestures to Ella.

"She's sleeping pretty hard. Maybe we leave her here?" I suggest to Dylan.

Dylan shrugs as he finishes his first sandwich, dropping the bag of chips onto the coffee table. We file out of the apartment and head upstairs. "What's the worst that can happen?"

CHAPTER FIFTY-THREE

– Lucy Walker –

As Dylan, Katie, and I enter the apartment on the second floor, I feel Marcus's absence everywhere. No guitar propped in the corner of the living room. The Neil Gaiman graphic novels are missing from the coffee table. The stacks of CDs and albums are tucked away somewhere. Maybe in the box Aiden hid in the basement? Even the pile of college applications Marcus mentioned is gone from the kitchen counter.

"Jude's offspring? Missing lover boy so much you come to visit?" Max says, cocky as ever. He leans back in one of the dining room chairs.

This scumbag would steal my boyfriend's guitar and albums to sell them? I take a step toward him ready to produce a fireball.

Dylan's voice pulls me from my momentary descent into Crazy Town. *Remember why we're here.*

I decide to ignore Max.

"We did as you asked, Aiden," Dylan chimes in. He jabs an elbow into my side.

Aiden blinks, but keeps his expression bland. "Took you long enough."

I stay silent, not sure what angle we're going for here.

The blood. We dropped it off at Jude's since he's due back in a couple of days, Dylan says in my head.

Nice! I say back.

Katie stares at Max without saying a word.

"We took all those vials of blood we found in the basement. Dropped them at my father's house like you asked. He'll be back in two days, so maybe he can figure out who they belong to," I say.

Aiden doesn't miss a beat; he just nods. "You plugged the boxes in somewhere, right? Otherwise they will spoil." He turns to Max. "Can you believe it? These two found four containers full of blood hidden in the basement."

"No kidding!" Max says, the pitch of his voice higher than it was a moment ago. He shifts his body in his chair and his beady eyes dart to the door.

Aiden retrieves a test tube from the kitchen fridge and shows it to Max. "You wouldn't know anything about this, would you?"

If Max paid attention, he would notice the hard set of Aiden's mouth, the darkening of his gaze, but Max's twitchy eyes are solely focused on the door. His fingers drum against the table.

"Nope," he says. "What's bringing Jude back so soon? I thought he was going to be overseas for a while."

"Once we called him and told him about what we found, he decided to pause the trip and come home. He wants to figure out who's behind this," Dylan says. "He's pissed. Can't blame him. Someone's dealing in demon blood. Demons are dying."

"Who says they're dying?" Max asks. He chuckles. Twitches. "I mean, I'm no expert, but maybe some are merely donating. You know, demons will do all kinds of things when compensation is involved. Hypothetically speaking, of course."

Katie chuckles. Quickly she smacks her hand over her mouth.

Confusion clouds Max's face. He shrugs dismissively, pushing his chair away from the table. "I should get going."

The tension in the room is thick. Is Max so oblivious that he doesn't read Aiden's body language?

"I thought you had some favor to ask," Aiden says.

Max waves him away. "No biggie. I'll figure something out."

"Sit down, Max," Aiden orders.

"Dude. I have to go—"

In one swift motion, Aiden grabs hold of Max by the hair and slams his face into the kitchen table. Several bones in Max's face crack. He shrieks. Aiden lifts Max's head, still holding him by the hair. Max's nose—which is now flat—gushes blood.

"I don't think so," Aiden says, his lips pressed thin against his teeth.

Subtly, I lean into Katie. "You okay?" I whisper.

"It's disgusting, but I want to hear why he did it." She cranes forward inquisitively.

Max pulls his shirt up to catch the blood pouring from his nose. "You bastard!"

"You heard the girl, Max. Let's hear why you did it," Aiden says.

Max squeezes his nose. "Can you get me some ice? A towel?"

I move toward the kitchen.

Aiden jabs a finger in my direction, fixing me with a blistering glare. I slide back several steps to my spot between Katie and Dylan.

"Man, I didn't—" Max says.

"Wrong answer," Aiden says. He jabs two fingers into Max's nostrils and yanks.

Max yowls in pain. I flinch. My stomach convulses nauseously. I wish Aiden would stop. As much as I believe Max is a criminal, is it really necessary to hurt him?

"You don't understand," Max pants, the sound of his words blunted by his smooshed nose. "She will *kill* me."

Aiden's expression, from the profile I can see anyway, remains hard as stone in a super creepy, soulless kind of way.

"The world would be a better place for it. Tell me or I slice off your ears next."

I press my hands to my stomach, willing myself not to vomit onto the floor of my boyfriend's apartment.

Max sputters, sending bloody saliva in a shower on his lap and on Aiden's shirt. "This is how it's going to be? Aiden the street thug is back?"

"Who's paying you to bleed out demons? Last time I'm asking," Aiden says. He leans forward, his body ready to spring.

It takes a long time for Max to answer. "You already know who it is," he says softly, his words barely intelligible as he continues to clutch his shirt to his nose.

Aiden reaches down and slides his pant leg up. He unsheathes a knife braced to his lower leg. It's not the same one he aimed at Dylan during training. The substantial chestnut brown handle fills Aiden's grasp. The blade is thick and runs five inches long. It's smaller but still looks lethal.

Max shrinks from Aiden. "Aiden, dude, this isn't you. Not anymore."

Aiden leans toward Max.

Max nearly tips his chair over backward as he tries to get away from Aiden and his knife.

"Aiden, come on..." I say.

Hold it together, Lucy, Dylan says in my head.

I suck in a deep breath and will the nausea down.

"You're certifiable! Get the hell off me! It's Camille. She pays me for the blood." With every shriek, he sprays Aiden with bloody spit.

"You always make things harder than they need to be," Aiden says. He grabs Max's hair and hacks off a fistful. He presents it to Max, shoving it in his face. "A warning. If I find out you lied..."

A thought tries to grab at me, but I can't think straight with all of the beating and blood splatter.

Max pushes out of his chair, knocking it over. One look from Aiden and he immediately sets it right. "My hair? You're back into the dark arts? I thought you championed the new laws to crucify anyone who dabbled?" Max sneers as his gaze sweeps over Katie, Dylan, and me. "They all think you're a good guy, right? Do any of them know your violent history? That you were an expert in straight up torture? You haven't changed so much after all." He shakes his head on his way to the bathroom.

I knew Aiden went through a bad spell. But torture? Did Gram know this about him? How much does Marcus know about his brother's violent past?

Aiden shoves Max's hair into a sandwich bag he grabs from the kitchen. He sheaths his knife.

That's when the nagging thought crystalizes in my mind. I gasp.

The blood in those tubes is not frozen, I say to Dylan.

Yeah, so what? he says back.

I take my time to pull the thought forward, think through the illogical part...the timing.

"You're out of the blood dealing business. All of it: demon, protector, human, animal. Are we clear on that?" Aiden calls after Max.

Max returns to the kitchen a few minutes later, keeping his distance from Aiden. He is clearly in a hurry. He scrubbed his face clean. No one will notice blood on his black clothes. His nose has doubled in size and purple bruises stand out beneath his eyes. He made no attempt to fix his red hair, which is missing a hunk on the left side.

"Can I leave now?" Max asks.

"Get out of here," Aiden says, disgusted.

"Wait a minute." I move to the door.

Max glares at me. "What?"

"When was Camille supposed to pick up the blood?" I ask.

"She's occupied at the moment. I'm guessing you already know that," Max says.

Looking at his face makes me queasy, but there's more to this. I know it. For Marcus's sake, I need to figure out what it is. "When my father and I spoke recently, he mentioned you. He said if I needed anything, I should go to you. He assured me you would be helpful. Yet, here I am asking you a question and you won't give me a straight answer."

"How nice it must be to have a powerful daddy," Max says, glaring at me.

His stubby, sarcastic tone sounded as mean as a cartoon character. His face is hideous.

"Answer her. When is Camille supposed to pick up the blood?" Aiden demands.

Max hesitates. I hold my breath waiting for his answer. "In two days," he says with a heavy sigh, glancing at Aiden nervously.

Aiden swears under his breath.

Camille is dealing blood while a team of people are fighting on her behalf, defending her innocence to the protector clan's council. How long had she and Garret been scheming—a scheme that she continues? What's the point of building an army of monsters? Garret communicated that their whole goal was to take out Jude who he and the clan believed was killing demons and draining them. That turned out to be a big fat lie. What was the true goal? I feel sick at her betrayal.

"What time?" Aiden asks. "What time is she picking up the blood? And where?"

Max looks nervous. Is he upset over the money he will lose on the sale? Or is he afraid of Camille, a human? Or is he afraid of Aiden who has a violent history?

"Tomorrow at midnight around the corner," he says.

Aiden joins me by the door. "Did you alert Camille or anyone else while you were in the bathroom that we found the blood?"

Max shakes his head.

I'll bet you a hundred dollars Max still plans to get his hands on the blood, Dylan says.

Major scumbag, I say back. *So is Camille.*

"Don't tell her. Keep the appointment," Aiden instructs Max. "I will let Jude know you cooperated."

"But..." Max begins to protest.

"Expect to hear from me tomorrow," Aiden says. He opens the door and shoves Max out.

Under Aiden's orders, we all help to clean up the disgusting mess.

"We've been up here too long. Let's check on Ella," Dylan says to me and Katie after handing a trash bag to Aiden.

Aiden stops me at the door. "You should be the one to break the news to Marcus about Camille. When he's ready, have him call me."

"Okay." I am grateful for his offer, but how am I supposed to tell Marcus the truth about his mother? The baffling part is that she's under house arrest with security guards stationed at her home. How will she be able to leave her house and travel to Chicago? Max appeared to be afraid of her. It makes no sense to me that a demon is afraid of a human. Camille must have some serious muscle behind her—supernatural muscle.

"Will Max go to Jude's house to look for the blood?" Dylan asks.

Aiden smiles darkly. "Darcy will be waiting for him and not in her human form." The smile disappears, but his ruthless expression remains when he says, "Find out what magic Seamus used with Ella. Get back to me as soon as you know. That will determine whether we can fix her or if we need to...find another solution."

Katie whirls around to face him, alarmed.

Dylan pulls Katie and me out of the apartment. Katie lets him.

"Another solution?" Katie gasps once we pull the door closed behind us.

"Don't worry about that right now," Dylan says.

Halfway down the stairs, I stop. "No..." I groan at the sight of my uncles' apartment door standing wide open.

I rush down the remaining stairs. Dylan and Katie follow me inside where we find the couch empty. We split up and perform a quick search of the apartment, including the basement. Ella is gone. Katie is positive because, like Ella, she has an extra keen sense of smell.

Katie pulls out her phone to call Ella, her movements strangely exaggerated as she tries not to smash her cell to bits. "Straight to voice mail," she says, sliding her phone back into her pocket using two fingers.

Dylan shakes his head. "Ella probably woke up and wondered where we took off to."

I need to call Marcus to tell him about his mother, but Dylan, Katie, and I have to find Ella first. I don't know how long my spell will last. Once it wears of, she will be dangerous.

"Let's go find her," I mutter, ticked off and fed up. Maybe it was the blood and the violence. Maybe it was the discovery about Camille. Or both of them on top of everything else. Today has been a marathon session of bad stuff heaped onto more bad stuff.

Where is my protector boyfriend with his calming powers when I need him the most?

"I'll drive," Dylan says, leading us out the door. He and Katie scan the street.

"Ella's car is gone," Katie says.

"Call Caroline, see if she saw or heard from her," Dylan says to me as he slides behind the wheel.

I close the back door behind Katie before I climb in the front passenger seat.

"We should call Cloe and Suzy, too," Katie says from the backseat.

The instructions push me over the edge.

"Give me a minute, okay?" I say, my voice way too loud in the enclosed space.

Dylan and Katie fall silent. As if watching a film on fast forward, the events of the day replay in my head. Bloodshed, magical transformations, violence, and deceit. I can't allow myself to think about it all. If I do, I will burst out of the car, run inside and climb into bed, and never get up again. Instead, I focus on one thing. Camille. How am I supposed to tell Marcus about his mother?

"You okay?" Katie asks after a moment. She doesn't touch my shoulder and that's a relief.

"No. It's been a really bad day." I whisper, my eyes filling with tears. If I told Katie that I felt emotionally and energetically mowed down, would she get it? Or is the demon blood giving her extraordinary staying power? Aiden was right. I need to focus on the girls right now, which means finding Ella.

I clear my throat and wipe away the tears from my cheeks. It's time to get moving. "Let's assume my spell wore off and Ella drove herself somewhere." Although the very idea of Ella behind the wheel scares me to death. "We'll go to Ella's house first to see if she's there. Could you call Caroline? Find out if Cloe is with her?" I ask Dylan before I twist in my seat to face Katie. "Call Suzy. See if she's heard from Ella. Think of your phone like an uncooked egg and handle with care."

Katie beams. "I'm on it."

"Keep supernatural references out of the conversation," I tell Katie. I can fill her in on Cloe and her connection later.

All the while Katie manipulates her phone, she mutters under her breath, "Uncooked egg, uncooked egg."

What are we going to do once we find Ella? My goals are to keep her from hurting anyone and to save her life. What kind of concoction did Seamus give her? She looked like he'd put her through hell. Was Seamus trying to share his magic with her and poach her soul to fuel his own powers? Jude had said it was a two-step process. Has her demon transformation already occurred? Is the Ella who came to my house soulless?

"We need help," I say to Dylan. "Ella's sick. We have no idea what we're dealing with and there's no way we can take her to an emergency room."

Dylan glances at me, looking as worn as I feel. "You thinking of Persephone?"

I nod and text my witch mentor a cryptic summary of what has happened and that we're going to need her help once we find Ella. She messages me back simply to tell me that Henry is back in town and at the charitable gala with her and Mirabelle. That's good. I have a feeling we are going to need all of them to save Ella.

I text Marcus next.

Update. Katie is now part of Team D. Seamus has turned Ella, so she is, too (and missing). Max has been dealing in the red stuff, taken from Team D members. I pause, my thumbs suspended over my phone. Is now the right time? I think of everything going on here and how much I need him. I think of Camille and what I learned tonight. How much she betrayed him. *I love you. Vera always loved you.*

Will he remember our code?

CHAPTER FIFTY-FOUR

– Dylan Douglas –

While on the drive over to Ella's house, I touch a button on my steering wheel and call out, "Dial Caroline Appleberg on her cell."

"Hey Dylan," Caroline says, out of breath, her voice coming through the car's speakerphone. "I'm headed to my bedroom."

"We had Ella, then we lost her. Have you heard from her?"

"Not a word and I'm totally freaking out. Ella had left me a couple of messages last night. I listened to them again a little while ago. She kept calling me Katie. The messages were really weird. I don't know how long she's been drugging, but it's bad, Dylan. She kept crying and was in so much pain. She repeated that someone was trying to kill her. I don't know if that was a trip or if the guy she met up with hurt her." Caroline's voice breaks off in a sob.

I work to keep myself under control. Light grip on the steering wheel so I don't rip it from the dashboard. What the hell did McAllister do to Ella? Was the suffering a side effect from sharing his powers? Or did he actually torture her? I flashback to my discipline session with Lucifer and shudder. She was an idiot to get involved with him. Should I have paid more attention to her? Maybe then she wouldn't have gotten so jealous and partnered with the psycho. I think back to the night at her house when I tried to keep her occupied while Lucy searched her bedroom. The kiss. My gut twists sickeningly. No way. Ella's in charge of her own choices.

"Caroline, I'm with Lucy and Katie headed over to Ella's house. We're going to look for her," I tell her.

As we pull to a stoplight and Caroline repeats her observations about Ella from earlier, I can't stop thinking that Seamus McAllister—an old and experienced demon—set out to hurt Ella, a measly human. He knew what he was doing, even if Ella didn't. He hurt all those other girls, too. Were his experiments long-term goals or something he devised to hurt Jude and Lucy? Was his vendetta that strong? If so, this guy's a major sicko. With a tight smile I realize how much I look forward to coming face-to-face with this demonic dirt bag.

Katie pokes her head over the seat. "Caroline, it's Katie. What about Ella's grandmother? They were super close. Have you checked with her?"

"Grandma Z moved last year. Her step-grandpa didn't want to deal with winters here anymore. They sold the Lake Forest house and live at their place outside of San Francisco fulltime now."

"Lake Forest?" Lucy mouths to me, surprise on her face.

"You spoke with Ella's dad, didn't you? When is he coming home?" I ask.

"He's trying to book a flight for tomorrow. He has to wrap up a couple of things in New York before he can leave. Worst case, it will be Monday."

Lucy and I exchange a worried look.

Hopefully, we find Ella and have her under control by then, I say to Lucy.

If she's still alive by then, Lucy says.

I grip the steering wheel and take a breath.

"Thanks Caroline. We'll call you if we find her."

"Please, please, please find her," Caroline whispers urgently.

"We'll do our best," I say before hanging up.

"You don't think she would go to my dad's house, do you?" Lucy asks. "In her wacky state of mind and with the Lake Forest connection?"

"I hope not. When I was with Caroline earlier, she told me Ella's car was pretty banged up from her drive home from the woods. The long drive to Lake Forest would be a disaster for every other person on the road if her temper flares up," I say.

"I don't remember her telling us that Grandma Z moved," Katie says sadly. "Ella worships that woman. The move had to crush her."

"With her dad traveling to New York all the time, does she have any adult relatives around here?" Lucy asks.

"No," Katie says. "It's no wonder she became such a pain when you moved here. She lost Grandma Z and her dad took that promotion and was never around. I know it bugged her, hearing about your uncles and your dad who were so good to you."

Lucy glares out the windshield. "She was a perfect mark for Seamus."

Katie taps me on the shoulder. The movement is slow and careful. It makes me smile. "Cloe and Suzy both texted me back. Cloe said Caroline never asked her to come over. Maybe Caroline is trying to keep this from her parents? Suzy said Ella's voicemail is full. They will let us know if they hear from her."

CHAPTER FIFTY-FIVE

– Lucy Walker –

A low rumble erupts from the backseat. I turn in time to see Katie shrug sadly as she points to her stomach. "I'm very hungry, but it's okay. I don't want to stop until we find Ella."

"Check in there," Dylan says, pointing to the glove box.

I pop it open and find half a dozen sticks of beef jerky and two Snickers bars. I hand one of the individually-wrapped sticks and a candy bar to Katie.

"I was always hungry as a regular person," she says, tearing the candy bar open. "I guess that hasn't changed now that I'm a demon."

"We need to find Ella before Seamus gets to her again, although I can't figure out what his next step would be," I say. "Will he give her more magic? Suck out her soul?"

"She's not doing so hot now. There's no way she can take more," Dylan says darkly.

I take a shaky breath and continue, glancing from Dylan to Katie. "If Ella refuses to help him anymore, he's going to hurt her more than he already has. We need to talk to Persephone and

Henry, find out how we can hide her until we deal with Seamus."

"Let's kill him ASAP. Problem solved," Katie says as she chomps on the candy bar.

In what universe could I ever imagine a night where Katie nonchalantly talks about killing someone? My sweet friend who cried last fall after her cat escaped the house and killed a squirrel.

She raises her eyebrows. "We should make a plan, right? Should Dylan protect Ella while you and I go after Seamus? I don't have to treat *him* like an uncooked egg, right?"

Dylan barks out a laugh. "No, Katie, you don't."

Is violence the only answer? With a lunatic like Seamus, it is. There's no way we can convince him to leave Ella and me alone. Is it possible that killing Seamus won't have the same aftereffects that killing Garret had on me?

I turn to Katie, "Chill out, little demon. We haven't determined your role in this yet."

It's a bad sign when we pull up to Ella's house and her car is not parked in the driveway. The aluminum garage door looks like she rammed it repeatedly. If she's not here, where else would she go?

"Maybe she couldn't get the remote to work?" Katie suggests as we exit Dylan's car.

Maybe she went nuts is more like it, I want to tell Katie.

Would demonized Ella take the time to park in her garage?

Dylan jogs around the garage then back to us. "No windows, so I can't see if she managed to park inside," he says.

The house is dark. Katie rings the bell twice. After several minutes, there's no movement inside.

"Do you know the code for that?" I point to the keypad mounted to the doorframe just inside the screen door. "Let's make sure she isn't sleeping or..."

"Being tortured by Seamus?" Katie finishes.

I'm not so sure I like this blunt version of Katie.

"They've used the same code forever," she says. She stands on tiptoe and with exaggerated caution, she types in a four-digit code. Out pops a house key.

Before we enter the house, I stop Dylan and Katie. "We go in and look for her. If there's no sign of her, then we leave. Okay?" I touch Katie's arm. "Let's stay together, but if we do separate and you run into trouble, call me or Dylan immediately."

"Got it," she agrees.

"Katie," Dylan says, his voice full of warning, "uncooked eggs, remember?"

She nods.

I don't know what to make of the scene once we're inside.

The TV is playing a rerun of a detective show with the volume turned off. All three of us are knocked back by the smell. I quickly cover my nose and mouth with my hands as I take in the large stains on the carpet. There is a blue bucket half full of filthy water and a floating rag on the foyer floor. Someone tried to clean the vomit from the carpet. It's that rancid smell that was coming off of Ella earlier at my house, but more potent.

"So gross." Katie chokes back a gag as she, too, covers her face.

"Let's check the garage," I say, my voice muffled.

We enter the kitchen and find the freezer door standing wide open. Bags of frozen vegetables litter the floor in puddles of water. A jar of pickles lies shattered beside them. A quick check of the pantry reveals no Ella or Seamus hiding among the shelves of food. Other than closing the freezer door with my elbow, I leave the kitchen exactly as we found it.

We file through the mudroom.

Dylan clutches my arm on our way to the garage, pulling me back.

"Let me go in first," he says.

"If Seamus is in there, I'm going to flame broil him," I tell him, pushing my way around him.

"Don't argue with me—just this once," he says sharply. His expression is so stern. Just then the sounds of Dylan's cries and grunts as Lucifer beat him on Jude's front porch echo in my head. I step back and allow him to lead.

Dylan holds me behind him with one arm while marching stealthily past the washer and dryer. Katie follows both of us. Dylan opens the door to the garage and flips on the light. Ella's car is there, what's left of it. The front end is mashed up, the side panel on the passenger side is dented beyond repair, and the rear passenger window is smashed out. As we walk around the car, we see the rear bumper has been torn off.

Katie yanks open the passenger side door. In her determination, she forgets the uncooked egg rule. With a deafening groan followed by metal grinding against metal, the car door comes off in her grasp. She drops it to the concrete floor with a thunderous boom.

"Katie!" I jump back from the deafening sound. "Keep the noise level down. We don't want the police to show up."

Dylan's expression is sour as he watches Katie crawl inside the car. "Like we could explain any of this in a rational way."

We both shield our faces from the rotting smell coming from inside the car.

Katie turns the interior light off and scrambles back out of the car. "Vomit inside. It's bloody." She grimaces at her gunk-coated knees before turning to Dylan. "Were you sick during your transformation? Puking? Is this going to happen to me?"

Dylan shakes his head. "The magic that turned Ella is dark stuff, nothing like ours."

Katie nods, reassured. "I found this in her cup holder," she extends her palm, showing us the end of a home-rolled cigarette. "Ella likes her alcohol, but she doesn't smoke cigarettes or weed. So, why does she have this?" She raises it to her nose.

"Don't!" I snatch it from her hand. Under the garage ceiling light, I inspect it.

Dylan leans close. "Seamus's concoction?"

"Based on the odor, probably." I hold it away from me. "Do either of you have gum? I need a stick. Just the wrapper, actually."

"Hold on," Katie says. She returns to Ella's car digging in the center console. She returns with a stick of gum. "Vomit free," she announces.

I unwrap the stick and put the gum into my mouth. Next, I wrap the butt of the cigarette inside the non-minty side of the wrapper. I shove it into the pocket of Dylan's pants. "You're in charge of guarding that so we can turn it over to Persephone later."

Dylan nods. "Let's go find Ella." He leads us back to the house, his troubled gaze flickering back to the mangled car.

Once inside, we make our way to the second floor. There are four bedrooms upstairs: Ella's, her dad's, a spare room, and one which was turned into an office. All the bedroom doors are closed.

"Let's split up. You two stay together and go that way and I'll go—" Dylan says.

"Katie and I will take Ella's bedroom," I tell him.

Dylan frowns. I turn away before he can argue.

With each step into the hall, the smell grows stronger. My eyes water and I gag.

I reach for Katie's hand then decide against it. If we get a surprise, I don't want her crushing my fingers. Instead I press my lips close to her ear.

"If Seamus is here, knock him off his feet or hurl him against a wall. Simple gestures, not that different than what you did earlier with Ella." I demonstrate a couple of new moves with my hands. "With each move, you have to focus on the outcome you're after. I will torch him."

The idea of setting anyone on fire hasn't gotten any easier for me. Even now I recall the overpowering smell of burning flesh the night of the fight in Jude's backyard, then later, at the battle in my school gymnasium. This is Seamus, I remind myself. The only way I can have a life and save Ella is if he dies.

I throw open the door to Ella's bedroom. Katie and I spring over the threshold. I produce a fireball in each hand. Katie squats, her hands lifted and ready to strike. Well, sort of. She looks more prepared to karate chop Seamus than knock him off his feet.

That same smell nearly sends me running from the room.

No one attacks us with magic or fists. The light from the hall allows us to see that Seamus and Ella aren't here. Katie flips the light switch on the wall. The comforter and sheets are crumpled into a tangled mess at the end of Ella's bed. The fitted sheet covering the mattress is dark and splotchy. The mirror mounted on the wall above the dresser is shattered into a spiderweb-like design. Dresser drawers lie open with their contents spilled onto the floor. The boxes from beneath the bed have been pulled out and dumped.

"The cleaning service definitely should be fired," Dylan says from behind us.

Katie and I both scream in surprise at the same time I lob a fireball at Dylan. He dodges it and stomps the flames out on the carpet.

"Don't sneak up on us, you idiot!" I chastise him. I press my hands together and extinguish the second fireball.

"Do you think she trashed her own room?" Katie asks.

"Maybe she just went crazy," I say.

"Or someone else was looking for something," Dylan suggests.

I nod, meeting his eyes. "Maybe the stuff Ella stole from me? Do you think Seamus came looking for it?"

"Maybe, I dunno. He told her to steal it for a reason," Dylan says. He pulls his shirt up to his face, covering his nose and mouth. "Sorry to state the obvious, but there's something horribly wrong with Ella."

I approach the bed. The awful stench is so strong that I am forced to hold my breath.

I grunt with disgust and fear as I spot the gunky mess hidden beneath a pillow.

"How does a person live though this?" Katie wonders aloud.

"Dylan, did you check the other two bedrooms for Ella?" I ask, unwilling to acknowledge Katie's question.

"No. I followed you in here to make sure there wasn't a demon waiting for you," he says.

I am tempted to remind him that Katie is here, that she is much stronger than either of us, but I see the worry in his eyes and say nothing.

CHAPTER FIFTY-SIX

– Lucy Walker –

Once I open Mr. Rosenthal's bedroom door, the now familiar putrid smell hits me. It's not as bad as it was in the living room, Ella's car, or her bedroom. The arctic temperature in the room might have something to do with that.

I flip on the light switch and gasp. Ella's red hair, matted and dingy, is visible on the blue and brown pillowcase while the rest of her is tucked beneath the matching comforter. Dylan and Katie, equally startled, gape at the sleeping figure in the bed.

"Ella." I cautiously approach the bed with Katie right behind me. "It's me, Lucy. I'm here with Katie and Dylan. We're here to help you."

Ella groans. Her body shudders beneath the blankets.

Dylan swears under his breath. He stands by a small panel of buttons on the wall. "It's fifty-eight degrees in here," he says, quickly adjusting it.

Tears trickle down Katie's cheeks. She reaches for Ella, but Dylan heads her off. "You can't touch her. She's too fragile."

"Ella?" I touch her cheek, her forehead, and gasp. Katie's fever back at Jude's house was bad, but Ella's is worse. "She's burning up."

"What can we do to help her? Ice bath?" Dylan asks.

I pull my phone from my pocket and dial Persephone.

"Lucy? Did you find Ella?"

"She's at her house. It's really bad." I describe Ella's condition and the state of the house. "How do we help her?"

Katie pulls herself free from Dylan. She climbs onto the bed and gently strokes Ella's covered body. Dylan hovers, reminding her to be extremely careful.

"Do you have any idea what magic Seamus used?" Persephone asks. "We need to know that before we can work on a potion and a spell."

"Let me have the gum wrapper," I say to Dylan. "We found the butt of a homemade cigarette in her car."

Ella groans. Her shaky hand slides from beneath the comforter.

"Ella?" I lean in close to her and wince. He breath smells like decay. "What is it?"

"Smoked...two of them..." Ella holds two fingers weakly against the pillow. She cries out before curling into a ball.

"We need to find this creep," Katie cries.

The pain must pass because Ella's expression clears and her body relaxes. "Said smoke second one...to...gain...magic," she says.

I reiterate Ella's words to Persephone.

"Any idea what was in them?" Persephone asks.

401

I push the speakerphone button on my phone.

"Ella, do you know what was in the cigarettes? Did Seamus tell you?" I jostle her.

"No," she mumbles. She burrows further under the blankets.

"Persephone, she's burning up with fever."

"You need to bring her to my apartment. Quickly," she says. "Mirabelle, Henry, and I are on our way home from the fundraiser."

"We're leaving now," I tell her.

Dylan scoots me aside and picks Ella up. Once the comforter falls away, I am overcome. Her body is needle thin. Her cheekbones stand out against her sunken face. My brain replays images of Momma the night she died. I swallow against the hysteria rising in my throat.

We are not going to lose Ella, I vow to myself.

"Give her to me," Katie demands, blocking Dylan's exit from the room.

"Katie, you and I need to watch for Seamus, keep Ella and Dylan safe," I say. "Let's focus on getting her to the three-flat, to people who can try to save her."

Katie grimaces and steps aside.

After I snatch a clean comforter from the bed in the spare room, I lead the way down the stairs. Katie takes the rear. Kudos to Dylan, who carries Ella quickly without hurting her frail body and without complaining about the smell.

Once at the car, Katie climbs into the backseat with Ella.

Alarmed, I try to pull Katie from the car. "Let me sit with her," I say.

Katie shakes her head, her hands clasped together in her lap. "I promise I won't hurt her. Uncooked eggs and petals of a flower. Just let me sit with her, reassure her that we're here with her."

"We need to go," Dylan calls from the front seat.

"Fine," I mutter as I shove the comforter next to Ella. "In case she gets cold again."

The drive is rough. No matter how careful Dylan is to avoid bumps, potholes, and aggressive turns, Ella whimpers. Dylan flinches with every one of her cries. I text Caroline to let her know we found Ella and that we're getting medical attention. At Persephone's recommendation, I tell Caroline she has to stay away until Ella is stable. I send the same message to Suzy.

Next, I text Cloe. *We found Ella at her house. P, H, and M are on standby at the three-flat to help. It's bad.*

Automatically, I send an update to Aiden. The night Seamus threw me from the roof at Jude's house, breaking all sorts of my bones, including my skull, a whole team of people worked to keep me alive. Aiden was one of those people. Tonight we need all the supernaturals we can get.

CHAPTER FIFTY-SEVEN

– Lucy Walker –

Dylan turns onto my street. It startles me to see house after house looking dark and peaceful. Families have gone to bed although some are still up watching late night TV or reading. Doing normal things. A sense of disconnection washes over me and I push it away. Now isn't the time to start feeling sorry for myself.

I place a quick call to Persephone to confirm she's home.

"Let me carry Ella inside," Katie says. She slides her arms under Ella and lifts her easily.

"Not a good idea. I know it's late, but if any of the neighbors see you carrying her, they will freak out over your strength. Let Dylan carry her," I say.

My stomach sinks as I spot Katie's house across the street. How can I ever let Katie go home? She'll do something to blow her mother's mind within two minutes of walking in her front door. Actually, the front door wouldn't survive this new version of Katie.

"I've got her," Dylan says, carefully taking Ella from Katie. "You did a great job taking care of her during the ride."

Katie nods solemnly.

I walk ahead of Dylan and hold the doors while Katie follows behind him holding Ella's comforter and chanting her mantras about eggs and flowers.

CHAPTER FIFTY-EIGHT

– Lucy Walker –

As we enter the vestibule, I gesture for Dylan and Katie to proceed upstairs to Persephone's apartment. "She's waiting for you. I'll be up in a few minutes. Dylan, be sure to give Persephone the homemade cigarette."

"Got it," Dylan says. He climbs the stairs with Katie right behind him.

Once inside my apartment, I see that the living room looks exactly as I left it. I follow the sound of my uncles murmuring in the kitchen. The dent in the drywall looks worse somehow. There are hairline cracks around it and chunks of plaster have fallen to the floor.

"Hi, Sheldon, Bernard," I say, exhausted and afraid as I lean against the doorjamb.

I imagined this confrontation several times, and the disappointment my uncles wear causes my throat to tighten. Tears fill my eyes.

"What happened here tonight?" Bernard asks, his hands sweeping around the mess of dishes and food.

I forgot about Katie's hungry rampage.

"I'm sorry about the mess and the damage. Jude's got a guy he hires for repairs. I'll pay for it out of my own money." My words come out sounding strangled. The emotions...the overwhelm that I've worked so hard to contain all night is threatening to erupt.

"You're a witch?" The words burst from Sheldon's lips like a sob. His bushy eyebrows pull together in hurt and disbelief. "How long have you known? When did you come into your powers? Why...why didn't you tell us?"

Bernard wipes his eyes. He covers his mouth and turns away from me.

How do they know? I worked so hard to hide it from them, made sure to keep the herb and spell books in my desk drawers. Big on trust, my uncles never believed in snooping.

"No. No, I'm not," I stammer. Persephone and Henry's orders: keep the secret. "That's crazy."

Sheldon narrows his eyes at me, daring me to keep lying to him.

I sigh, confused but relieved. My eyes fill with more tears. All of a sudden, the adrenaline, fear, and anger that have been fueling me on and off all night evaporate. My knees tremble and I don't fight it. Instead, I slide to the floor. I tuck my trembling hands between my knees.

"How could I tell you?" I choke out the words. "I was under orders from Persephone and Henry not to. They said you didn't know about Gram." I peer up at Sheldon, his eyes full of hurt and betrayal. "But you did...you do."

Sheldon presses the heels of his hands to his eyes as he exhales a roar of a sigh. "Damn them. Damn Persephone and Henry! They behave like gods, determining who is allowed to know what!" He pulls his hands from his face, which flushes with anger. "Vera was my sister! After I witnessed her practicing magic, I approached her about it, expressed curiosity. She showed me the attic, the sacred space she, Persephone, and Henry shared. She allowed me to see her altar. It was an *honor*. She took after our mother, a woman we both adored as our matriarch but also for her talents." Sheldon pulls out a chair and lowers himself onto it. He taps Bernard's leg and gestures for him to sit.

Instead, Bernard circles the table and tugs my arms until I stand. He pulls me against him. "You look exhausted. Have you eaten?"

Without warning I let loose everything I had stored up since finding out Dylan and Katie conspired behind my back to make Katie magical, since finding out that St. Aquinas's resident Mean Girl was given magic so she could hurt me—maybe kill me, magic that will likely kill her. I cling to Bernard. All this time I needed my uncles, to confide in them, reason through all of the magic, my fears, but that wasn't allowed. Bernard holds me tighter.

"Playing God seems to be a trend," I say through my tears.

"Come and sit. Both of you," Sheldon says, gesturing to the chairs beside him.

Bernard presses a kiss to my forehead. He leads me to the chair next to Sheldon then sits on my other side.

"I can't believe you knew," I say, wiping my eyes.

Sheldon pauses, his expression still angry. "We had to hide what we knew," he says. "Persephone and Henry ordered Mirabelle and Vera to erase our memories. We weren't allowed to know about the magic. Vera and Mirabelle refused to do that."

Bernard takes my hand. "We've both been great actors all these years," he says with a shaky laugh.

"When we returned from the fundraiser, Mirabelle stayed to talk with us while Henry helped Persephone upstairs. She told us about Seamus McAllister. She told us what Henry and Persephone shared with her, some of what you've been through." Sheldon's face crumples. He attempts to rub away the tears as soon as they escape his eyes. "You're just a girl, so young."

Bernard's lips tremble. "You should never have had to go through all that. All those times I was angry about the damage to your clothes."

I laugh as I wipe away my own tears. "Yeah, sorry about that." I need to get back to Dylan, Katie, and especially Ella. "I promise to tell you whatever you don't already know. Right now, one of my friends is sick. Seamus McAllister hurt her to get to me." It's a stretch to call Ella my friend, but it's the word that comes out of my mouth.

Sheldon's expression darkens. Bernard gasps.

"She's upstairs with Dylan and Katie. Persephone, Henry, and Mirabelle are going to try to save her. They need to figure out what kind of magic he used on her." My eyes fill with tears again, as if I'm a faucet with a bad leak. She probably isn't going to make it, but I can't stand to say it out loud.

"Shouldn't she go to the ER where doctors can treat her?" Bernard asks.

I shake my head. "They wouldn't know how to treat her sickness."

Sheldon rises from his chair. "I guess I can't stop you. This is going to be an adjustment."

"If there is anything we can do, please let us know," Bernard says. He pulls his hankie from his pocket and blows his nose. "It was good to see that Marcus is back."

I freeze. "Marcus is back?"

Sheldon and Bernard look at each other before turning back to me.

"You didn't know?" Sheldon asks.

"I have to go. We'll talk more later," I say before I run from the room.

CHAPTER FIFTY-NINE

– Lucy Walker –

Outside of the apartment, I jog up the stairs to the third floor. I let myself in since Persephone's doorknob lays in a heap on the hallway floor. Persephone meets me in the living room still wearing her fancy dress. Her expression is severe.

"We figured out one of the ingredients Seamus used on Ella," she says.

"What is it?" I ask, breathless and, I couldn't help myself, a little bit hopeful. If she and the other witches were able to identify one ingredient, they could save her, right? They could create a potion or a counter-spell and reverse Seamus's destructive grip on Ella?

"Yew. It's a powerful poison, both the tree itself and the hard seed inside the berry."

Marcus comes into view behind Persephone. I feel a flood of relief at the sight of him.

Persephone glances over her shoulder and sees Marcus. "I need to get back in there to help Mirabelle and Henry. You two catch up, but don't be long," she says, limping her way to the second bedroom.

"Marcus," I say as I rush into his arms. "My uncles told me you were here. I can't believe it."

He wraps his arms around me and immediately a sense of calm seeps into my body. He feels steady, solid. I cling to him. Tonight he is my anchor. My rock.

Marcus strokes my hair. "You used our code. Of course I came."

"I didn't think you would," I say, my face pressed to his throat. "With your mother..."

"We'll talk about her later," he says, anger edging into his voice. "I spoke with Aiden who was able to arrange my last-minute flight. He filled me in on what you and Dylan found, Max's involvement, and my mother's."

I pull myself out of his embrace just enough so I can see his face. "I'm so sorry."

His expression hardens. "I'm grateful to know the truth."

I wish I had the power to calm him.

"Is Selima here?"

"No, but I called her and filled her in. Selima, her mother, and several others are guarding her, making sure she doesn't sneak out for a blood run over the next several days." Marcus's tone is sarcastic. His eyes meet mine. "Who else do you know is conniving enough to manipulate her way out of house arrest? She played me—played all of us."

I gesture to the hallway. "Have you seen Ella? How is she?"

Marcus checks over his shoulder. "It doesn't look good for her, but I've seen them work miracles before."

"Speaking of miracles," I say, working up the courage to ask a favor for the girl with the flaming red hair who has never been my friend, who Marcus doesn't like or trust, but who needs as much supernatural help as we could possibly give her. "The subject of blood is not one I want to bring up right now, but I have to." I meet his eyes. "Yours could help her. I am asking you to put aside all of your feelings about Ella, to help her. I know that I'm asking for a lot, but I don't want her to die. I can't stand the idea of allowing Seamus to take another life."

Marcus doesn't look happy.

"Please..." I say. "He did this to get to me."

Marcus meets my eyes for a long moment. His tight expression finally eases and he nods.

"Before we go in there, I need just one thing," Marcus says. He dips his head and his lips press against mine.

His mouth is warm, his kiss tender. The emotions behind our kiss leave me feeling raw, near tears. My arms circle Marcus's neck and I hold tight. Finally, I pull away.

"Thank you," he says, his voice deeper than it was moments ago. Marcus is battling his own mess of emotions. It's all over his face.

"No, thank you," I whisper back. "Let's go." I tug his hand toward Persephone's second bedroom and Ella.

As we approach the bedroom, my skin prickles. Is this strange surge of energy in the air caused by Mirabelle? Or the combination of three powerful witches under the same roof?

Once we enter the room, I notice Ella's complexion has turned yellow, waxy. Dark circles have formed under her eyes. A woman with the blackest skin I've ever seen sits beside the bed to Ella's left. Her hair is cropped short and speckled with gray.

She nods at me. "You must be Lucy. I'm Mirabelle. I wish the circumstances were different, but I am glad to finally meet you." Her voice is deep and she has a slight accent.

"I'm glad to finally meet you, too," I say with as much of a smile as I can manage.

I can't stop staring at her. Gram's third close friend, the fourth witch. Cloe's grandmother. There's something about her energy that makes my entire body tingle. She is electric.

"Ella's not responding anymore," Katie says, sniffling. She sits cross-legged on the bed beside Ella, her hands tucked beneath her legs.

The photos and books that normally fill the top of the dresser are gone. Instead there are a variety of labeled Ziploc bags that contain herbs and powders and glass jars filled with liquids of various colors.

"Marcus is willing to give her blood," I tell the witches and Katie.

Henry nods, his grave expression flickering over to Marcus briefly. "Thank you, Marcus. That's generous of you."

The three witches surround the bed, equal distance apart. Mirabelle on the left, Henry at the foot, and Persephone on the right. Persephone retrieves a large Mason jar from a TV tray beside her. The jar contains crushed herbs. Mirabelle and Henry hold identical jars. All three of them chant under their breath. They each set their container down, light a match, and toss it inside. Flames spark inside the jars then a cloud of smoke poofs from the top. The three witches wave the smoke over Ella. After a couple of minutes, Persephone slides a large book from the bed. She speaks in a rush, her voice a quiet murmur as Henry and Mirabelle continue to treat Ella with the magical smoke.

"Where's Dylan?" I whisper to Marcus.

"Downstairs with Aiden, asking him to initiate contact with Jude. We need to find Seamus."

My cell vibrates in my pocket. The interruption surprises me. Dylan? He could come up one flight of stairs if he needs me. I don't dare answer my phone. Instead I watch as my witch mentors and Mirabelle work their magic in an attempt to heal Ella. Minutes later my phone vibrates again. Now the three witches form a circle around Ella, chanting in unison. Maybe Caroline is calling for an update? She can wait. When it pulsates for the third time, I can no longer ignore the persistent caller. With an annoyed huff, I retrieve my phone. *Ella Rosenthal* appears on the screen. Heat courses down my arms with such intensity, I nearly buckle under its power. Marcus catches my eye.

My uncles, I mouth and point to my phone. Before he can read my expression and detect a problem, I leave the room. Marcus must stay to help Ella.

"Hello?" I say once in the hallway outside of Persephone's apartment.

"Miss Walker. It has been too long."

The sound of his dry raspy voice fills me with so much hatred, I produce a fireball on reflex. I fling it in surprise and nearly set a wall on fire. I stomp it out immediately. I'll need to explain the scorch mark on the wall later.

"Seamus McAllister, you monster! What have you done to Ella?"

"I gave her what she wanted. You see, Miss Walker, she wanted to be like you."

"You poisoned her. She's going to die. This is *not* what she wanted."

"She lasted longer than the others. Besides, she didn't fulfill her end of our transaction."

"As if her outcome would've been any different. You are a coward, using a young human girl to accomplish what you're not able to. Ella's out of commission, so if you want me, you better come and get me yourself."

"I have done exactly that, Miss Walker. Leave your friends and join me on the roof of Vera's beloved home."

The image of Ella's rail-thin body comes back to me. Those high school girls—victims of Seamus's sick experiments. *Katie.* It is because of Seamus and his attempts to kill me, his continued pursuit of me, Katie felt the need to throw away her precious normal life to help me. The despicable demon has destroyed so many lives.

"I am on my way, coward."

I disconnect and leave the phone on the floor beside Persephone's wrecked doorknob. Fueled with a surge of emotion, I sprint down the hall and up the stairs to the attic. Persephone and Henry are the only two people who have keys to this sacred space. I press my hands to the door and blast through. Wood splinters shower the floor.

"I'm sorry, Persephone," I whisper. "I promise to replace it later."

Across the attic are windows that will give me access to the rooftop.

"This is for you, Ella and Katie," I say aloud, before I climb out the window.

416

CHAPTER SIXTY

– Lucy Walker –

Seamus McAllister looks more human than the last times I'd seen him. He wears blue jeans and a White Sox T-shirt. He is learning to blend in. It's the context that's wrong. What had Ella said about Seamus coming to her home? Even in her messed up condition, I understood the shock and offense mixed in with her fear. He violated her boundaries. Tonight, Seamus chose the rooftop of my home, Gram's home, to confront me. It's not the first time he's been here, but the three-flat is where my uncles live. It's my safe haven. It's super messed up and insulting to Gram's memory that he would come here to kill me.

"Miss Walker."

The sound of his voice causes my anger to swell. Quickly, I reign it in, maintain control. I need to think clearly.

"How dare you come after my friends," I demand. Heat races along my limbs as my power ramps up. It vibrates through my body.

"Miss Rosenthal is not your friend. Not really," he muses.

"That was your point, wasn't it? To go after someone like Ella, someone you could manipulate into hurting me?"

Seamus watches me before his eyes scan the rooftop. He looks for others, not believing that I came alone.

"She joined me quite willingly," he says in his phony-frail voice.

"Bargaining with magical powers, offering them as some sort of precious gift," I say, disgusted. "Did you happen to reveal the danger, how much she would suffer? That she'd die once you attempted to transfer your power?"

The demon responds with cold silence. Seamus isn't going to explain himself to me. Across the roof, he stands poised and ready to fight me.

What will he do first? Knock me off my feet? Cast spells? Or, will he try to kill me quickly? Tonight, I am on offense, no longer defense. It's time to plan my first move.

Bind his hands together as if in prayer
Allow nothing to pass between not even air

"It could be different with you and me," Seamus says. "You could join me."

With a shock, my spell slips out of focus. "Change my alliance from my father to you? Why would I do that?" It takes effort to keep the incredulity from my voice. Teaming up with Seamus—the very demon who's been trying to kill me since I moved to Chicago—is the craziest idea I've ever heard.

"We would be powerful. I could prove to Lucifer that I am a strong and capable leader. He would put me in charge."

"In charge of what?" I ask. *Is this a tactic to distract me?*

"The underworld," Seamus says, reverently. "You see, Miss Walker, I want to go home."

"What's stopping you?" If only he had gone months ago, he would've spared those girls and Ella. Katie wouldn't pose a threat to the entire City of Chicago.

"I am aware that your father is currently serving as the interim ruler." Seamus pauses, allows his words to sink in.

I swallow hard. He knew Jude was gone all this time.

"Lucifer gave the role I have been working toward my entire existence to your father, albeit temporarily," he says bitterly.

Great. Just great. As if Seamus didn't already have a list of reasons to hate my father. Now he confesses his desire to rule hell, but his nemesis already got the job—never mind that Jude didn't want the position in the first place.

"There was no way for me to know that Lucifer would come *here* when he did," Seamus continues as if to himself.

Lucifer came *here* because I summoned him. I had begged my godfather of sorts to help save my father and me, but I'm going to keep that bit of information to myself.

"I don't understand. How could I have helped you?" I ask.

Seamus smiles. "I have mastered a form of magic that will allow us to partner together, to tether our magic." He clutches his hands together, looking positively euphoric.

Tether our magic? Partner together? This is not the first time I've heard the words *tether* and *magic* used together. The sicko is referring to soul magic. My father was right all along about what Seamus has been up to and now this masochist wants to perform his special brand of killer magic on me? He clearly has no idea that I know what it is. There's one more thing that I need to know before I kill him. "What about all those other girls, the ones who died?" I ask through gritted teeth, trying mightily hard to control my temper. I need to hear him admit what he did to them.

"You figured out that was me." He nods approvingly. "Victims of my process. I needed to learn the precise blend in order to develop my magic. Miss Rosenthal has survived longer than any of the others. I am very close." He beams with pride.

I take a steadying breath, trying to gain control over my wide range of emotions, but the one that stands out the most is fear. If I'm unsuccessful tonight in my quest to kill him, he will continue his murderous journey.

"I'm not interested in partnering with you," I say contemptuously.

Seamus watches me, his ink-black eyes void of expression. "Dear girl, you misunderstand me. I am not asking for your permission. I am informing you."

"I would rather die," I tell him.

The demon appears stunned which quickly turns to anger. "You disappoint me, Miss Walker. Let us see who will get their way."

CHAPTER SIXTY-ONE

– Lucy Walker –

Since this will be my last chance to talk with the demon my grandmother worked so hard to hide me from and my father took the fall as the bad guy all these years, I can't help but get in one dig on my father's behalf.

"It must drive you crazy that you can't beat my father," I say. A frown pulls at his expression. *Good.* "Lucifer told me how you and Jude competed for top spot, how Jude won out over you every time."

Seamus's anger flares. "You are such an arrogant child. So much like your father. All of his hard work to build a life here and Lucifer sends him back home. Not at all part of Jude Morgan's grand plan. Big business came easy to him. So many things came easy to him. He desperately wanted a child—his twisted need for a family and to enjoy a *human* existence." No missing the distaste in his voice at the mention of humans. He and Marcus's mother could start a hating-on-the-humans club together. "I had a daughter. Do you remember Daphne? Jude killed her."

After Jude found out about Daphne's role in my uncle's death, I want to say, but there's no point. "You know what your problem is, Seamus?" I ask, irritated. I'm tired and worried about Katie and Ella and myself. I really want Seamus to die already. He grimaces at my informal address. "That you've never learned to heal and move on. That's something valuable you could learn from *humans*," I say. All the while I keep track of his hands, his eyes.

"Unlike your father, I have no interest in being anything like humans," Seamus replies, distastefully.

The demon shifts his body slightly, getting ready to strike. Before he can make his first move, I sweep my hand through the air, knocking his legs out from beneath him. His body barely touches the ground before he rights himself. Seamus focuses on me with indignant rage.

Instantly, I have a fireball in each hand which I hurl, one at a time, at my enemy. Seamus veers to the right to avoid the first one. He whacks the second fireball back at me with the flat of his hand. I leap to the side to avoid being hit. Immediately, I hurl another. With a pinch of his fingers to his thumb, Seamus extinguishes the flames. I produce two more and launch them. One slams into his shoulder, singeing his shirt. The smell of burned flesh reaches me. I ignore it.

"Beheading and fire," Henry had said when I asked him and Persephone how to destroy a demon.

Tonight, that's my plan.

Seamus flicks a finger in my direction and I drop to the ground, out of the way of whatever spell he sent my way. Sharp pain blasts through my knees upon contact with the ground and I gasp. Without losing my focus on the demon, I whisper my spell.

Bind his hands together as if in prayer
Allow nothing to pass between not even air
Keep his fingers stiff
So they cannot shift
Seal his lips tight
So he cannot smite

Seamus's eyes trail my every move. Suddenly, he thrusts his hands above his head. He moves his long arms through the air in a circular motion which causes his entire body to sway. Wind sweeps around us. Slowly at first but gradually it picks up speed. The demon's body undulates back and forth, back and forth. The leaves on the trees around us rustle in response, branches creak and bend. My hair flies into my face, stinging my cheeks and my eyes, making it difficult to see.

From my grounded position, I repeat my spell. The wind begins to howl. The wind and the noise and general fear distract me. I can't sink deep enough to power the spell. In the instant it takes to pull my hair back from my face, Seamus disappears. I whirl around to find him standing behind me. He jams his hands at the air between us. The pressure of his magic hurts as I go flying across the roof. *Can't breathe.* The sense of weightlessness is over quickly and I crash sidelong onto the three-flat roof. Pain throbs along my left hip, arm, and shoulder.

What was I thinking, coming up here alone? Marcus and

Dylan are both downstairs. I could really use their help. Scratch that. Marcus needs to stay with Ella, to give her protector blood. That, together with the witches' magic, are our only hope to keep her alive. If Dylan joined me, maybe he could get close to Seamus, debilitate him just enough so I could set the demon on fire and destroy him.

You're on your own, I remind myself. *Think of Ella. Remember what he's done to her and those other girls. It's time to end him.*

I climb to my feet, struggling against the pain, and focus on Seamus. The wind has died down. He's done tinkering with the weather. Seamus's eyes are trained on me and his lips are moving. Despite my pain, I refuse to stand still as I repeat my spell.

Sinking deeper into my focus while I dodge his attention, I imagine Seamus as petrified wood, his hands pressed together. His fingers unable to move. His lips closed tight.

Several things happen at once. Seamus grunts in protest and his eyes widen in surprise as his hands close together and his mouth presses into a thin line against his will. With a murderous glare, he drops into a squat and stabs violently with his joined hands in the direction of my legs. Before I can register his goal, I am knocked off of my feet and face plant against the hard ground.

The pain in my nose nearly blinds me. I choke on blood and mucus and in a panic to open my airway, I gather as much as I can in my mouth and spit it out.

Don't you dare lie there or he will kill you! The nagging voice in my head screams.

Dazed, I attempt to rise to my knees, but fail. I blink against the tears, fight to overcome the sharp pain. Blood drips from my throbbing nose, oozes from my chin.

This is what my father trained me for. Aiden, too. It all led to this, I remind myself with as much of a pep talk as I can manage. *Be brave. Be ruthless.*

I force myself to crawl, each movement jarring my face, my nose, making me want to cry out. I keep my mouth shut and my eyes locked on him as I move.

Seamus touches his bound hands to his mouth and mumbles behind his closed lips. He flaunts his freed hands for me to see before he jumps to his feet and begins to head my way.

Something crashes behind me and I jump. Is it a ploy by Seamus to distract me? I don't dare turn to look and I don't stop crawling.

"Ouch. Crap!" Katie mutters.

Katie? My heart sinks. What is she doing here? I don't care what powers she has, the last thing I want is for my best friend to face the revenge-crazed demon. I keep my attention fixed on Seamus who appears confused by Katie's appearance.

Another crash. "Maybe you should've stayed inside," Dylan mutters.

"Shut up. I'm her guardian. *He* said so," Katie grumbles.

Dylan! Get Katie out of here! I call out through our mental connection.

Pretty stupid of you to take off solo when we have a house full of reinforcements, Dylan says.

"Whoa, this is Seamus McAllister?" Katie says.

I flinch at her stealthy arrival behind me then wince in pain.

"The one and only," I say, keeping my eyes on the demon. "He's got mean moves. Watch his fingers, hands, legs, and lips. Stay out of his line of sight and the point of his fingers, hands, and toes. This is sort of like dodgeball, but with magic."

"Why are you talking so funny?" Katie asks. She moves to my side and her expression turns ferocious as she takes in my face. "He did this to you?"

Katie turns to Seamus. "You like to beat up girls? Wait until you see what we're going to do to you!"

She pulls me to my feet, nearly yanking my arm from its socket. Dylan's jaw tightens when he sees my face. He looks from Katie to me before turning to Seamus.

Seamus's expression darkens as he assesses the three of us, figuring out his next move.

"Let's keep moving so he doesn't kill us first," I say, although it comes out sounding unintelligible because of my damaged—probably broken—nose.

"Lucifer's a lot more impressive," Katie whispers.

Seamus whispers another spell, his attention following me as I move. Good. I don't want his eyeballs on anyone else.

Seamus's gaze flickers to Dylan and his expression registers vague recognition. Seamus saw Dylan on Jude's roof the night of the homecoming dance. Does he remember him? His eyes quickly inspect Katie. Just then he sniffs the air. His expression transforms rapidly from confusion to surprise to disbelief. Is it possible he can detect the identity of her blood donor?

"Remember your moves earlier when you confronted Ella?" I ask Katie, although my words come out blunted. I hope she understands me. "Use your imagination. Go wild. Now," I encourage.

In a series of swift motions, Katie kneels beside me and curls her hand through the air with one hand while shoving hard with her other. Her movements are so quick, I have to stop myself from gawking. Seamus preemptively drops to the ground out of the way of her magic.

I lunge to the left as his fingers flick toward me from his low position. A violent burst of air whooshes past me. Seamus missed me. Quickly, he twists slightly and shoves his hands against the air toward our newest demon.

"Katie!" I yelp too late as she goes flying.

My best friend grunts as she hits the ground. Almost immediately she is back on her feet, muttering all sorts of nasty things about our opponent.

With a rush of anger, I punch the air at face level, followed by a side kick, waist-high. Seamus presses his hands to his face as he stumbles backward. Dylan sidles up to me and grasps my waist with both hands. The unexpected touch makes me jump.

"Roast him," Dylan says.

While I'm used to his hand clasped in mine as our usual form of connection so he can fuel my powers, Dylan is right. I need both of my hands right now. The surge of energy causes my brain to sharpen.

I take aim at Seamus, eager to pull his focus from Katie. I also want to burn him to a crisp.

It's time for a fireball marathon, I announce to Dylan. Dylan works hard to keep in step with me. It really is like playing dodgeball, I think grimly.

I hurl fireballs one after another after another. Two hit their mark. Seamus mutters something under his breath about heathens.

"Keep moving, Katie," I huff as I jog to the left. Thanks to Dylan's magical supplement, the pain in my face lessens. He and I move awkwardly—it's not like we've rehearsed our moves—but even one of Dylan's hands on my skin will amplify my powers. "If Seamus can't fix his attention on you," I remind my BFF as I continue to aim and fire, "then he can't attack you with his magic." I jog to the right and hurl another fireball at Seamus. "Think target practice."

Seamus cocks his head, his eyes brightening. He smiles at me.

Uh-oh. I don't like the look on his face, Dylan says.

"You think you are powerful with your fire," Seamus bellows.

I don't waste my breath responding. The truth is, I've never been equipped with this much firepower. It's thanks to Dylan who has been supercharged by Jude long distance. A good thing, because my dark gift is how I plan to finally end Seamus.

I weave and dip as I lob a succession of fireballs at Seamus.

Eighteen, nineteen, twenty...

Katie moves like a modern dancer. She mimics my actions as well as Seamus's. Her limbs twist, wave, thrust, and shove as she attempts magical gestures and absorbs the results. Katie is a quick study. She delivers two major blows to Seamus. All the while she heeds my advice to continue to move and stay out of the demon's line of sight.

After several more rounds of fire throwing, I realize Seamus has changed tactics. He keeps moving his lips, but his eyes no longer focus on me, Dylan, or Katie. I inspect the rooftop, never taking my eyes from Seamus for longer than a couple of seconds at a time. Dylan continues to move with me.

Dylan, I don't understand. He's executing a spell, but I don't see or feel anything. If he's not directing his magic at us, who is his target?

Dylan taps my waist. *I've got a bad feeling about this. I'm going to let you go. We need to go at him separately, get his attention back to us so he can't target anyone inside.*

I nod and pull from his grasp. Immediately I feel unplugged. Fatigue hits me hard.

Dylan kneels, unsheathes two knives strapped to his calves beneath his pants. He springs to his feet wielding the weapons.

Compliments of Aiden, he says.

I continue to hurl fireballs at Seamus, although at a much slower rate.

Seamus no longer bobs and dives. Instead he whacks my fireballs over his shoulder as if batting away an annoying insect. I continue to launch one after another. Now that he stands still, some hit him on his chest, his shoulders, his arms. He bounces the rest over the edge of the roof, some to the left, others to the right. The look on his face is intent focus. I frown in confusion.

"Katie, I need you to get creative. Destroy his focus," I tell her.

Katie grins and nods eagerly. She punches the air. Seamus's head jerks back sharply. She crouches and sweeps one hand through the air, knocking the demon's legs out from under him.

He crashes to the ground. Still, the demon seems to be focused inward. It's like he's in some meditative zone.

Dylan expertly throws one knife and sinks it into Seamus's left leg. The demon howls in pain, momentarily distracted from whatever spell he was casting. Dylan throws the second knife. It plunges into Seamus's abdomen.

Seamus closes his eyes. He wraps both hands around the knife protruding from his stomach and yanks it out. He shifts to a squat. Wincing, he removes the blade from his leg. I take advantage of his injured state and hurl three more fireballs at him. Every one hits their mark. Seamus ignores my assault and staggers to his feet. I had watched as Jude incinerated Seamus's daughter, Daphne. Why won't my fireballs ignite and consume Seamus? Is it solely a matter of power level?

He homes in on Dylan, one hand pressing against the wound in his gut. He points to the knives on the ground with his free hand and sends both knives whizzing through the air at Dylan.

Katie and I both scream.

Dylan catches a knife in each hand and flashes a grim smile at Seamus. I breathe a sigh of relief.

With grim determination, Seamus turns his attention to me, his gaze murderous.

I attack the demon with more fireballs. With Dylan's high-octane powers no longer feeding me, the pain is back in full force. Sweat drips down my face, my neck, my back. Every breath I take burns as if my throat is lined with shards of glass and sandpaper. If the fire doesn't catch soon, I have to come up with a Plan B.

Seamus bats the fire over the edge of the roof, wearing that far-off look on his face again.

I freeze.

"Why'd you stop?" Katie asks, crouched and ready to attack. She glances from me to Seamus in confusion.

Lucy? Dylan asks.

The demon sent a whole bunch of my fireballs over the edge of the roof, his focus intent on something.

Dylan, is it possible he's directing the fireballs?

Dylan considers my question.

Just then we hear Persephone's scream from inside the apartment building.

Chapter Sixty-Two

– Lucy Walker –

I am seized by cold terror.

"Katie, bring Seamus to me," I shout.

From her predatory crouch, Katie narrows her eyes at Seamus. She pulls the air as if tugging an invisible rope, hand over hand.

"How dare you!" Seamus bellows as he struggles against her hold, his heels scraping along the roof floor. The front of his shirt is stained with blood and covered with burn holes. His pant leg is caked with blood. Demons heal fast.

Katie's face flushes with effort. Her body arches backward as she struggles against Seamus's resistance.

The smell of burning things fills the air. My grandmother's home is on fire. My uncles, the witches—especially Persephone with her bad hip, Ella, the ravens. They need help.

"Dylan, go inside. We'll be there soon," I yell.

"I'm not..." Dylan protests. He rises to his full height and puffs out his chest, as if to remind me of his strength. Or maybe he's just trying to intimidate me into letting him stay.

"My uncles need you. *Please!*" No way I'll mention that Ella and the witches are inside.

Dylan lets loose a long stream of profanities as he races away from us to return inside.

"You can still join me," Seamus urges in his raspy voice, struggling against the invisible rope as Katie tugs and pulls. "We can impress Lucifer together."

"Tethered magic? You mean, soul magic?" I ask.

Seamus looks surprised that I know something about his special brand of dark magic.

"I would die, right? You conveniently left that part out," I say. "Instead, why don't you tell me how we can save Ella from the herbs you gave her?"

Seamus looks at me smugly. "My magic is irrevocable. You cannot undue what I have done."

"Ella's going to die?" Katie gasps.

Another scream from inside.

Smoke surrounds us. It won't be safe up here for much longer.

"Once you are dead, your father will come to me. I will finally end him." As if to punctuate that statement, Seamus karate chops the invisible rope and frees himself.

The demon shifts his hands and suddenly thrusts his fist in my direction at waist level. I double over and clutch my stomach against the pain, all wind knocked out of me. My legs give way. So quickly that the movement is nothing more than a blur, Seamus is beside me. He clutches the back of my head and slams me onto the roof floor with crushing force. Pain blasts through my nose, forehead, and cheeks on contact. Bursts of light flash behind my closed lids. He touched me. The filthy demon actually touched me.

"Lucy, watch out!" Katie cries out.

I open my eyes in time to see Seamus clench his fists together and move to bring them down upon me like a hammer. I roll out of the way and scream at the pain in my face. If my nose wasn't broken before, it definitely is now. Better than him crushing my skull.

"No, you don't!" Katie punches the air in Seamus's direction and his face jerks to the left. She punches again and he stumbles backward. She thrusts both hands at Seamus. He drops to his knees to avoid her magic. With blinding speed, Seamus's lips begin to move as he raises his hands into the air. Katie didn't move in time. He sends her flying.

"No...No...No..." I moan, my blunted voice a mix of desperation and fear.

"Let me go, you creep!" Katie yells, struggling against invisible binds.

Can't allow him to hurt Katie.

Slowly, I climb to my feet, gritting my teeth the whole way. The smell of smoke surrounds us. Sirens blare in the distance. I can't help but imagine the damage as the fire travels through the building. Family photos gone forever. Marcus's guitar. Persephone's beloved plants. Fierce indignation burns inside of me.

Through swollen eyes I see Seamus dangle and spin my best friend in mid-air. This monster is to blame for her choice to become a demon, but I won't allow him to kill her.

"Seamus McAllister!" My feeble attempt to shout sounds distorted and croaky.

He glances my way but only for a second before he returns his attention to Katie. He whispers a spell. He spins her faster. Is he going to throw her over the edge of the roof? Against a tree?

I look to the towering trees that surround the three-flat building. If Henry and Persephone are right and I have a connection with nature, I need their help right now. Quickly, I cobble words together, infusing my intent with love and respect. I also keep an eye on Katie. I have to work fast.

Oaks, maples, and ash trees
Grant me the gift of your power
Of yourselves
To disable an enemy
Shed your leaves
Lend your acorns
Give your fronds
Pummel the gray-haired demon
Who only does harm

I slip into focus as I repeat the words, all while keeping my eyes trained on Katie. Reiterating the spell quickly, fueled by an energy I hope comes from nature, I raise my arms. During my lessons with my mentors, I learned to fuel my spells with emotion. Tonight, I charge my objective with determination.

A breeze lifts my hair, caresses my neck. Through my intention, I bid the wind to grow. I repeat my spell. Swiftly, the wind turns to gusts. The power swirls around us. Seamus looks to the sky, confused. He glances over his shoulder at me, his expression indignant.

"How dare you!" he bellows.

As I recite my spell, I invite all of the surrounding natural elements to join me in eliminating Seamus, a being who takes life.

Abruptly, a swarm blasts Seamus like killer bees. Instead of buzzing insects and stingers, leaves and twigs slap, tear, pummel his skin. The maple's helicopter-like seeds rain on him, blinding him, while acorns pelt him like bullets.

Seamus roars with rage. He covers his face with one arm and with his other, he is about to hurl Katie at a tree.

Aiming at the side of his neck, I strike the air hard with my fist. My face and abdomen scream in protest from the effort. Seamus rocks backward. He stumbles as he clutches his neck while also covering his face from the continuing onslaught. Katie drops to the ground. She cries out upon impact, more an expression of frustration than pain.

With Katie out from under Seamus's control, I release my spell and the assault dies down. The three-flat roof looks like a forest floor.

Seamus leaps to his feet with a guttural cry of frustration. He is on me in an instant. He grasps my neck with both hands and squeezes. "You will not live past this night," he grunts. He whispers a spell as his furious gaze burns into me.

Should I attempt a reflection spell, send whatever spell he is creating back at him?

No time. His hands tighten. Panicked, I grab for his eyes, try to plunge my fingers into the sockets, but he jerks his face back and forth. I kick my legs at his back, at his head. My feeble strikes are useless. Black spots bloom across my vision. I shouldn't have ended my spell so quickly, I realize.

"Leave...her...alone!" Katie screams.

Seamus topples over beside me. I heave in a lungful of air and the fiery pain is unbearable.

The demon leaps to his feet and rushes for Katie. *Why can't he stay down?*

"Katie!" My voice comes out raspy and weak. Uttering that one word sets my throat on fire. Clumsily, I roll to my side. I struggle against the pain in my throat which is about equal to the pain in my face. I spot Katie who is going berserk on Seamus McAllister. With unbelievable speed, she boxes and kicks the air, pummeling Seamus. Her face is red with the effort. Sweat drips from her skin and plasters her hair to her scalp. Her determined gaze never leaves the gray-haired demon.

Seamus's body jerks and convulses from Katie's blows.

I blink to clear my vision and pull air into my lungs in tiny puffs. Seamus's face, neck, and exposed torso are covered with bruises and cuts from the bombardment from the trees. The demon's fingers twitch at his side. In a flash he raises his hands in a gesture, a kill move that I have watched my father execute. A move I had forgotten about until just now.

Reflexively, I wrench my hands in a violent, wringing gesture like I'd seen Jude exact upon two morphed gargoyles, the same move Seamus was about to execute on Katie. My intention is powered by the need to save Ella, to make up for Katie's loss of a beautiful human life, and to honor the lives of those girls that

Seamus murdered. Seamus drops to the ground, his head twisted at a sickening angle.

Katie scrambles over to me. She throws her arms around me. I half-wheeze, half-cry out from the impact of her body against me, her face presses to mine.

"Please tell me he's dead!" she cries, staring at Seamus's still body.

Tears stream down my face. I wrap one arm around Katie while wiping my eyes, needing to keep my vision clear. Seamus may not be dead. He could jump to his feet again and come for me or for Katie.

"Lucy!" Marcus shouts from behind us.

Katie and I turn. I immediately regret the movement. *Pain, pain, and more pain.*

Marcus lands on the three-flat roof, coming from the back yard. He is shirtless. His face and body are covered with soot and sweat and burns. All of that is eclipsed by the beauty of his fully-extended wings. He spots Seamus on the ground.

"Everyone is out of the building and safe. They are looking for you. My God…" Marcus says, alarmed as he takes in my face, his voice ragged from the smoke.

Katie gawks at Marcus's wings, her mouth falling open. "Up close and personal…you look like an angel," she breathes, absently wiping tears from her cheeks.

Marcus cautiously approaches Seamus. He kneels beside the demon and inspects his neck with both hands. "Broken," he confirms before raising his eyes to meet mine. "You know what we need to do?"

I nod. Cut off his head and burn it separate from the rest of his body.

Katie frowns at the gusts of smoke surrounding the house. "Whatever we need to do, let's get it done."

Persephone and Henry's instructions come back to me.

"If a demon is burned to ash, he or she can regenerate. It's only if the ashes are separated and kept apart that a demon is truly destroyed," Persephone had said.

"This is the only way to end Seamus. If you and whomever else is helping you don't dispose of his ashes properly, he will come back," Henry had said.

I spot Dylan's knives near the broken window and retrieve them. They are covered with blood. I limp toward Seamus's body.

"What're you going to do?" Katie asks.

"We need to cut off his head," Marcus says so I don't have to.

"Can I do it?" Katie asks, a thrill in her voice. "Really, I *want* to do it. That monster was going to smash me into a tree!"

I consider her request. Why not let her? I am tired, have zero strength, and hurt worse than I have ever hurt in my life. I am about to hand her the bigger of the two knives when I survey Seamus McAllister one last time. This monster, fueled by hate and an obsessive need for revenge, tried to kill me *again*. He tried to kill Katie. He tortured Ella. He set the three-flat—my grandmother's and my uncles' home—on fire.

I give a tight shake of my head and grimace.

Carefully, I lower my body onto the ground next to Seamus. I grit my teeth and steel my resolve, then get to work.

CHAPTER SIXTY-THREE

– Lucy Walker –

Two fire trucks and a ladder truck line up in a row in front of the three-flat. The deafening rumble of their massive diesel engines causes my head to throb. The violent blasts as their air brakes release their pressure cause my hypersensitive brain and nerve endings to surge with panic as if I'm still under attack. The swirling emergency lights stab at my brain like an ice pick.

Two squad cars and ambulances add to the already overcrowded street. Additional cruisers block access to the street on both ends. Fire hoses trail through the yard, through the flowerbeds, and crush the delicate plants in their path as violent gushes of water extinguish the flames licking and thrashing the three-flat, destroying our home.

Bernard and Sheldon run to Katie and me.

"Thank God you're—" Bernard stops short. With a choked sob, he takes in my face which must appear gruesome to him. Never mind the purple bruises circling my neck. "Lucy!"

Sheldon gingerly takes my face in his hands, his own a dirty smear of smoke, ash, and tears. "Who did this to you?" he demands thickly, looking from me to the house to the crowd around us. "Who? Tell me!"

"I..." I cough from the effort, from breathing in the smoke. Tears sting my eyes. I shake my head and point to my throat.

Katie tugs on Sheldon's arm. He jerks back in surprise against her strength, then allows her to pull him close. "He's dead. Team Lucy wins," Katie announces excitedly. The reflection of the flames dance in her eyes, making her look truly demonic.

"Did you say *dead*?" Bernard wheezes out the words.

Quickly, I press a finger to my lips. Bernard's eyes widen at the same time he nods. No one else heard the exchange above all the noise.

My uncles study Katie and me for an excruciatingly long moment. "We will talk about this later," Sheldon says.

I nod.

Bernard grimaces again as he takes in my swollen, purple, and bloody features. "You need to go to the hospital!" He frowns, glancing over his shoulder at Persephone and Henry. "We're supposed to tell the doctors—and everyone else—that you jumped from the roof and landed on your face."

"Let's take you over to the paramedics, let them look at you. Your nose..." Sheldon pleads, gesturing to the ambulance.

I'm not sure how that excuse will account for my neck, but at the moment I'm grateful that my mentors figured out a cover story so I don't have to. Thanks to Marcus giving me a small dose of protector blood—all he could spare after treating Ella—my pain has ratcheted down from excruciating to semi-moderate. More than anything, I want to get away from the lights and the noise, to climb into a bed—any bed—and sleep.

I resist his gentle tug. "Tomorrow," I squeeze out the word. The last thing I want is to have people poking and prodding me. Even with Persephone and Henry's cover story, they would ask a lot of questions. I give Sheldon a meaningful look. He nods and lets me go.

"Kathryn Stevens!" Ms. Stevens calls out from the crowd of people. "Come here! Come here, right now!"

When did she get home? Did my uncles call her away from her romantic weekend with Jerry? Quickly, I snake my arm toward my best friend as she trudges toward her mother, but I am too slow. Katie tucks herself into her mother's embrace, her arms pressed tight to her own chest. Ms. Stevens stumbles backward. She peers down at her daughter, curiously, for just a moment before shrugging and wrapping her arms tightly around her.

"I'm so glad you're safe," Ms. Stevens sobs as she kisses Katie's head and cheeks.

Sandwiched between my uncles, the three of us watch the men and women in uniform fight to put out the fire that is doing its best to destroy our home. After severing Seamus's head, I set his body on fire with a dozen fireballs. His corpse burned fast, surprising given how hard it was to kill him in the first place.

Marcus took off to deliver the detached head to Aiden, who was parked two blocks over. Aiden will burn it in Jude's back yard then bury the ashes. Katie washed Seamus's blood from my hands and arms with the garden hose. She also did her best to help me clean some of the blood from my face. I stare at my house, envision the loss of everything inside, evidence of memories, of love. Seamus and I are both responsible for its destruction. The realization is too much and I slump against my uncles.

"What do we do now?" I ask, surprised that I can squeeze out more than two syllables. Marcus offered to give me a second dose of blood tomorrow. I might take him up on it, because I know that later, after I have slept, this will hurt so much worse.

"We rebuild," Sheldon says. He looks at me, at my wounds, and appears outraged all over again. He starts to ask a question, but I give him a look that stops him.

Bernard strokes my hair, his touch ginger as he and Sheldon exchange a worried glance. "Since the structure is made of brick, I bet a lot of it can it be saved." He tries to sound optimistic.

Marcus and Dylan approach us.

Sheldon pats my arm. "We need to speak with the Fire captain, kiddo. Can we turn you over to the boys? Will you be okay?"

I nod.

Bernard presses a careful kiss to my forehead before the two of them join Persephone and Henry who are talking with firefighters at the edge of the yard.

Dylan takes in my face. "You look terrible."

He is nearly asleep on his feet. His normally perfect hair is a mess. His T-shirt is dirty and torn and there is blood on his knees.

Right back at you, I say, unwilling to speak aloud.

I turn back to the house. Marcus takes hold of my hand. It occurs to me just then that his feather, the one I tuck under my pillow most nights, is probably burned to bits by now. Would he give me a new one?

Katie joins us while her mother speaks with my uncles, Persephone, and Henry.

"The paramedics took Ella to the hospital," Dylan says.

I struggle to get out my next question. I can't stand the idea of more bad news. "Will...she..."

Katie looks at Dylan, bright-eyed.

My best friend is full of hope and optimism and still has plenty of energy. I have none of those things. Not tonight.

"Persephone spoke with the EMTs. She said she'll fill us in later," Dylan says, his arms crossed over his chest as he glances at Marcus. The four of us stand close together so we can hear each other. "Ella looked better after her...treatments. Thank you."

"Yes, thank you for that," Katie says to Marcus.

I interpret Dylan's response to mean that Ella no longer looked like she was going to die in the next half hour, but beyond that no one knew.

The four of us stand mute, watching the water put out the fire while at the same time causing its own damage to the house. I sway on my feet, barely able to keep my eyes open. Marcus leads us to the edge of the lawn where we sit on the grass by the curb. I lean against him and despite the noise, the pain, worrying if Ella will survive, the looming conversations to be had with my uncles, I grasp onto a single thought. Seamus is dead. With that tunnel focus, I close my eyes.

"Your uncles are coming," Marcus says, gently patting my leg.

I jolt awake, not sure how long I was out. Every inch of my

body aches as I straighten. Marcus carefully pulls me to my feet. Dylan and Katie cease a murmured conversation they were having.

"Aiden has generously offered us the use of Jude's home. Persephone has the ravens in their cages in the car," Sheldon says, placing his phone in his pocket.

I hope Aiden was thorough in his cleanup after he disposed of Seamus's head. The smell of burning flesh and hair is something I know too well. It's disgusting and impossible to explain away.

"We will need to go shopping tomorrow for food, clothes, wine..." Bernard says, his voice catching. I rub his back.

"In a few hours, I will call St. Aquinas to let them know you won't make it to school today or tomorrow," Sheldon says, eying my face with a squinty expression. He cocks his head. "My eyes must be playing tricks on me. I could swear your face looks better already."

I shrug. There's no way I'm telling my uncles about the healing properties of protector blood.

"Can Katie come with us?" I ask, standing close to my uncles.

Sheldon begins to protest.

"Please," I say.

Sheldon and Bernard exchange one of their silent looks. They may not be supernatural, but as a couple they have their own method of private communication.

They understand by the damage to my face and throat that I suffered a trauma tonight. They want to get me alone so they can find out what happened to me, but I won't be ready to tell them anything until I get more of my voice back. They realize that, too.

"If her mother will allow her to take off from school, Katie can spend a couple of days with you," Sheldon says.

I need to babysit the new demon. Once my throat heals enough, I will tell Sheldon and Bernard about Katie, that she is a danger to her mother, the family cat, and the student body at St Aquinas. Persephone and Henry will need to help me convince Ms. Stevens that Katie needs some time off from school. Surely there is some kind of illness they can make up.

CHAPTER SIXTY-FOUR

– Lucy Walker –

The transformation of Jude's football field-sized backyard is astonishing. A mammoth white tent has been erected. Chandeliers hang from elaborate beams constructed within the tent ceiling. Strings of white lights and vines of ivy wind around every post. Each table is covered with a slate-gray tablecloth. The centerpieces, an elevated oak bowl, overflows with sprays of pink and cream ranunculus, roses, and peonies mixed with greenery. Portable heaters have been erected at regular intervals to keep everyone toasty warm. As a result of the fire and all of its devastation, Bernard and Sheldon (mostly Bernard, I think) opted to move up the date of the wedding. The June ceremony became a late October event. Bernard had to rethink his entire color scheme—not that he minded so long as the centerpieces included ranunculus, one of his favorite flowers. The gray skies were not enough to dampen anyone's spirits. After the "rough patch," as my uncles delicately refer to that time in September, everyone is ready for a celebration.

Jude offered his yard for my uncles' wedding. Marcus told me it was really Aiden's idea. Aiden genuinely felt bad about the damage to my Gram's building. Darcy was in charge of hiring a team of wedding planners and the event was put together in record time.

Henry officiated the ceremony after going online to obtain his certification. I walked my uncles down the aisle where tulle and organza draped along row after row of white wooden folding chairs. Bernard had cried while reciting his vows. Once he started, so did I. Persephone too.

"You look beautiful," Marcus says once the wedding concludes and he and I make our way to the back of the tent for beverages. It's open bar, so we get to drink as many of them as we want. I order sodas for both of us. Marcus runs his hand down the length of my back, his fingers gliding along the silky pink fabric of my dress. Goose bumps break out along my skin.

"Thanks," I say.

In six-weeks' time, my healing is complete. Marcus provided a second blood donation after my hospital visit. The blood helped to accelerate the speed of my recuperation, especially my nose after it was set by the doctor.

Marcus removes his suit jacket and drapes it over a nearby chair. He wears a white dress shirt together with a blue and white tie in a pattern that reminds me of a honeycomb. If I stare at it too long it makes me dizzy.

"I say this each time I see you in a suit, but you look super handsome," I say, appraising him with a big smile. Honestly, the moment he descended Jude's staircase in his formal clothes,

Marcus took my breath away. His response to my compliments is always the same. He gives me that lopsided grin that I love so much.

"Lucy!" Katie jogs over to me, carrying a plate of appetizers. She is barefoot and her knee-length lavender dress ripples behind her. She pretends to be a little winded and I smile. She has really gotten it down, this whole pretending to be a normal human thing. "Isn't the music great?" Katie's boyfriend, Trevor, and Suzy were hired as DJs for the reception.

"How are you feeling?" I ask as she orders a Sprite from the bartender. No more caffeine for my BFF, Aiden's orders. I take a brie and phyllo dough appetizer from her plate and pop it in my mouth.

Katie rolls her eyes. "I haven't broken anything in three days if that's what you mean—and that was an accident. I swear."

Katie's mom shared with my uncles the story of their refrigerator door falling off while Katie was getting something to eat. Persephone helped to convince Ms. Stevens the door was loose to begin with. In the end, Ms. Stevens was relieved the detached door didn't crush Katie's feet.

Dylan and Selima join us, both carrying plates loaded with food.

"I think we should have a big celebration every time we knock off a bad guy," Dylan says, pausing to eat a bacon wrapped water chestnut. "No disrespect to Sheldon and Bernard, but I'm celebrating both events today."

Dylan and Katie talk about their weight lifting schedule for next week—Aiden's recommendation so that Dylan can keep tabs on our baby demon and to provide a cover story for her impressive strength. The story goes that Katie always wanted to work out, but never had anyone to teach her. Enter Dylan, a willing trainer.

Selima and Marcus murmur in low voices, their heads pressed close together. I catch mention of Camille, but leave them to their private conversation. Marcus will fill me in when he's ready to.

As I watch my friends, I am overcome with love and gratitude for them. We accomplished what I had believed deep down to be impossible. Seamus is dead. With my father's departure, followed by Marcus's, I thought I had to solve the problem of Seamus by myself. That belief—that decision—nearly got me killed. What would I do without my muscle-bound best friend, Dylan? I rely on him to be my voice of reason and to fuel my powers. I do best when he and I confront the bad guys together. There is no one I rely on more to stand beside me when facing life-threatening danger.

Now I have Katie, too, as a part of my supernatural tribe. She has adapted so fast. Initially, I was petrified that her change into a demon would alter who she is at her core. It didn't. Katie's strong sense of right and wrong, fairness, and compassion remain intact. She has proven to be a cunning and intuitive fighter, too. Lucifer continues to be fascinated with my friend who looks so much like his late daughter. That scares me to death, but I will deal with it after the wedding and once my uncles and I move back into our own house.

"I couldn't have done it without the two of you," I say to Dylan and Katie.

"I know," Dylan says with a grin, "but it sure will be great to move on with our lives." He gazes at Selima and I see love in his eyes.

Which I interrupt. They can make googly eyes at each other later.

"Speaking of moving on, let's hear it. Of your three acceptance letters, which school have you chosen?" I ask Dylan.

Selima smiles at her boyfriend. Her emerald-green dress is made of satin. Her pale skin glows in contrast to the rich color. "Yes, handsome, please share with the group."

Dylan's smile is so big, so infectious that I can't help but mirror it even though I have no clue about his decision. I hold my breath in anticipation of his answer. Will he stay in Chicago?

"Tell us already!" Katie says. She playfully punches Dylan in the arm and he flinches. Her smile falters as Dylan gives her a pointed look.

"Sorry," she murmurs.

"Enthusiasm is good, just keep your hands to yourself. I can take the impact, but others can't. Always remember that," Dylan chides her in a low voice.

Katie nods, meeting his eyes. "I will. Promise."

Dylan sets his plate on the table next to us. He wipes his mouth with a fancy paper napkin. "My father confirmed that he and Alana plan to stay in Chicago. Turns out Alana couldn't line up satisfactory household help or a nanny in New York City. Thanks to Cloe helping me clean up errors on my school records," Dylan scans the crowd briefly. "Where is our computer-hacking genius? Anyway, Northwestern had no problem accepting me into their business program. After graduation from St. Aquinas, I start football camp with the *other* Wildcats."

Ethan and Brandi are staying in Chicago and Dylan's college dreams are coming true. My face flushes at the same time my eyes fill with tears. His eyes meet mine.

"They're really going to stay?" I ask. "My little pipsqueaks?"

"*Our* little pipsqueaks," Dylan corrects. He looks away as he clears his throat.

"Speaking of Cloe," Katie says nodding past me.

"The tangy meatballs are amazing," Cloe says, forking another one into her mouth and smiling with delight. She surprised us all by straying from her typical black, white, and gray clothing to wear a long-sleeved, scoop neck yellow dress made of lace. She hugs me and Katie. Katie keeps her arms to herself as she presses her cheek to Cloe's.

Once at my side, Cloe lowers her voice. "I checked on Ella earlier today. She had a follow up appointment. The doctors are amazed at her recovery. Of course, they don't know about the special supplements she's received." She flashes a thumbs-up to Selima and Marcus.

"What about her dad?" I ask.

"He plans to stay put in Chicago. Turns out he has a girlfriend in Manhattan who works for a cosmetics company. Mr. Rosenthal told Ella about the woman—Rose is her name. Ella and Rose have talked over the phone a few times. Rose is coming for a visit and plans to take Ella shopping. Apparently, Rose also offered to help Ella and Caroline with their blog. But..."

I frown. "But what?" Everything Cloe tells me is great news and will make Ella happy.

Katie moves closer to Cloe and me. Marcus, Dylan, and Selima listen in.

Cloe takes a deep breath. "Mr. Rosenthal believes that Ella was using drugs and he's signed her up for an intense rehab program."

While those suspicions are not correct, no one will set the record straight. Not even Ella. "Sounds like her dad and his girlfriend are both trying to be there for her. I hope Ella finds a good therapist while she's in rehab," I say.

"I'll call her tomorrow. Hopefully, I can see her before she starts her program," Katie says, eagerly.

The group falls quiet just then. Dylan looks over at me. So far Katie's visits with Ella have been video chats. We all thought it would be best for Ella to fully heal and for Katie to gain further control over her own power before the two got together.

"Maybe you should keep up the video chats for a while longer," I suggest.

"Why does Cloe get to visit her?" Katie complains.

Cloe rolls her eyes. "They're not social calls, Katie. Ella's a newbie demon like you," she whispers. "So far my Nonna and I have been able to use magic to keep Ella's capabilities shackled. You're very strong and no one's binding your powers. Lucy's right. The two of you shouldn't get together just yet."

Katie sticks her tongue out at Cloe and we all laugh.

"Does your grandmother really have to head home on Monday? I thought she might like being here, close to Persephone and Henry," Marcus says to Cloe. His hand brushes my waist while his eyes track the location of my uncles. It seems whenever they aren't paying attention, his hands find their way to me. I don't mind a bit.

Cloe rolls her eyes with a huff. "Honestly, I'm ready for her to go back to New Orleans. Now that I'm showing a small interest in her *hobby*, she's determined to cram a lifetime's worth of lessons into my head. She refuses to accept that I have other interests. Do you have any idea how far behind I am on my YouTube posts?"

"I understand why she's pushing you. You're good at it," I point out.

"You're good with your demon powers. Do you want to devote all your time to it?" Cloe whispers, eyebrows raised.

I hold my hands up in surrender. "I get it."

"Sorry to break up the party, but I'm stealing my boyfriend," Selima says, pulling Dylan by the arm toward the dance floor.

Dylan beams and allows himself to be led away.

"I like that idea," Marcus says. His fingertips caress their way down my arm to take hold of my hand.

"Interested in joining me to get more food?" Katie says to Cloe. Cloe points to her plate still half full then shrugs. They link arms.

"Don't even think about muscling me around, demon. I've learned a thing or two from my Nonna," Cloe says sternly. "You know the main buffet is going to open soon. Don't overstuff yourself on the appetizers."

"Not even possible," Katie says.

I smile after them.

"You have no idea how hard it is, how hard it's *been,* day after day, not to take you in my arms and kiss you," Marcus says once we reach the large wooden floor. His lips press close to my ear, his voice low. It sends a delicious shiver down my spine. "I feel like Sheldon is constantly watching me. Now that I have you, I never want to let you go."

"So, don't," I say. I turn my head and our lips meet briefly, neither of us caring if my uncles see the quick kiss.

He gently massages my back while we dance. Every press of his fingers works like magic to soothe my muscles, my anxiety over Ella, Katie, and Lucifer.

I sigh happily.

"I opened my stack of mail this morning," Marcus says finally. His cheek brushes against mine.

How many times had I approached the subject of college with Marcus? Even Persephone expressed frustration at his refusal to tell her where he submitted applications, if he needed her to review his essays, or if he wanted references from her and Henry. He promised to fill her in by November first.

"And?" I ask, my voice catching. We continue to sway to the music. We move slowly, out of time with everyone else on the dance floor. My thoughts which were fuzzy from our kiss and his touch are now uneasy.

Will Marcus stay in Chicago? Or does he plan to move closer to his mother? He's had several weeks for his anger to calm down. Despite her bad behavior, her crimes, Camille is his mother. Deep down I know that means something to him.

The DJ changes to another song with an upbeat tempo, but neither of us acknowledge it. Unable to separate from him, I watch him expectantly while my arms remain circled around his neck.

He grins mischievously. "I received acceptance letters from University of Wisconsin—Madison, St. Olaf, and DePaul," he says. "Those are the ones that matter to me anyway."

St. Olaf? The one school on his list located in Minnesota. He could live near the clan, fly with protectors on the weekends, and continue to heal his relationship with his mother...which *I would support,* I remind myself.

"Have you decided on one?" I ask. My clasped hands at the back of his neck suddenly feel clammy.

Marcus runs his fingertips along my cheek. Once again, without bothering to search for my uncles, he kisses me right there in the middle of the dance floor.

A sense of worry clouds my thoughts and I break our kiss. If he's going to leave, I want to know now. "Please tell me," I say.

"I chose DePaul," Marcus says, a slow grin spreading across his face.

"DePaul? Henry's alma mater?" Does my face show the shock I feel?

It's as if fifty pounds of worry have been lifted from my shoulders. On my puny frame, that's a lot. Seamus is dead. Marcus is staying in Chicago. Ethan and Brandi are too. Could I really be that lucky? Quickly, I tap the wooden planks of the temporary dance floor with my sandal so that I don't jinx myself.

A new song begins to play and Marcus and I continue to dance. I catch glimpses of Dylan and Selima, two of the best dancers on the floor, showing off for the crowd. Cloe keeps Katie fed and as far away from people as she can. We've all taken turns babysitting Katie today. It will be Selima's turn soon.

After dinner and a whole bunch of toasts, I dance with Sheldon and Bernard. Just one spin apiece. As the main attraction, they are in high demand.

Chapter Sixty-Five

– Lucy Walker –

It's Sunday afternoon. Marcus and I travel through our favorite woods on foot instead of by air. The ground is covered with fallen leaves and acorns that crunch beneath our feet. The air smells of autumn.

"Sheldon and Bernard left at lunchtime," I tell Marcus, tucking my free hand in the pocket of my favorite purple sweatshirt. I pull the hood up to protect my neck and ears against the chill. "They were blown away by the gift of a honeymoon in Tuscany."

"Jude has been very generous," Marcus says. He laces his fingers through mine as we walk down a worn path.

"It was nice of Jude to include all of our names on the card," I say. "Without some persuasion from Henry and Persephone, I don't think Sheldon and Bernard would've accepted the gift."

"I think you're right," Marcus says, peering over at me. "It wasn't just their pride over the expense. You get that don't you? Seeing how badly Seamus hurt you, they didn't want to leave you. It's going to take them time to get over that and to digest all that you've told them."

I squeeze his hand. "You didn't tell Persephone and Henry that Sheldon and Bernard know about me, did you?"

"No. Didn't tell Aiden, either. I promised you," Marcus says. "I'm glad they know the truth about you."

We fall silent for a while as we continue along the path. Birds call out to one another, coast above our heads, bobbing from branch to branch in the dense cluster of trees. The occasional scatter of critters under the bushes makes me smile. My light mood doesn't last long. Something is off. I can feel it. Marcus is tense, distracted.

I tug his hand. "Come back to me, Marcus. Tell me what's wrong."

He takes a moment as if he's still working through something. "It's about my mother," he says. His hand tightens its grip on mine. "The council made their decision. She was found guilty for dealing in demon blood and continuing to dose protectors as part of her and Garret's psychotic experiments." Marcus shakes his head in disbelief. "She was also found guilty of abusing protector blood. She's an addict—been using for years, apparently."

The fact that Camille continued to dose protectors blows her prior claim of innocence. Did she feel a twisted need to finish the plan that she and Garret started? Were they working on their own or, as Selima had suspected, collaborating with others high up in the protector clan?

Marcus presses his lips into a thin, tight line. "Her punishment is death," he says finally. His grasp on my hand is so tight it begins to hurt.

I pull him to a stop and remove my hand from his so the blood can resume circulating. "There's no other option?"

Camille stood by Garret's side as he conspired to kill my father—which would've killed me, too. She lied about her reason for coming to Chicago. Her addiction? Well, my own mother battled alcohol and drugs, so I can't say much about that except...how did she get the blood? If she paid for it or it was given voluntarily, then it's a matter where rehab can hopefully help. If she obtained it by killing, that's a whole other story. Does she deserve to die? After a rapid inner debate, I come to the conclusion that while she absolutely deserves to be punished for her crimes, she doesn't deserve to die.

Marcus looks past me into the trees. "Aiden has been speaking with his connections in the clan and suggested an alternative, an idea he and Darcy came up with together."

"What is it?"

"That he and Darcy take Camille with them."

"To hell?" I raise my eyebrows as I digest this news. "For how long?"

"Permanently. It was the only alternative the council would consider."

"Permanently," I echo.

Marcus kicks at the ground, sending several stones skittering along the trail. "The council won't let me say goodbye to her, not that I want to see her. She would just feed me more lies." His voice sounds grim at that last part. His eyes focus on the trail.

I'm guessing there's a lot of sadness beneath the anger, but he won't show that to me. Not now. Marcus has had to cope with the fact that the memories of his mother stored in his brain from the time he was a little boy are very different than the version of the woman in his life today. Now Marcus is about to lose her again and it will be forever this time. There's nothing I can say to help him. Or is there? If I were in his shoes, what would I need to hear more than anything else right now?

"Marcus," I say, rushing to catch up as he resumes his way along the path.

He doesn't respond and I sense the snarl of emotions pulsating off of him.

"Marcus!"

He stops. With his back to me, he points his face to the sky. He is breathing hard and it has nothing to do with physical exertion.

I press my hands to his back and slide them until they rest on either side of his waist. "I love you," I say.

Marcus does not turn around.

"I'm here and will never leave you."

"You can't make that promise," he says, his voice tight.

"I just did and I mean it."

Marcus turns to face me. "You still have a year of high school left. You don't know where you'll go to college. Even if you go to a university in Chicago, you could land a job in another city. Don't make promises you can't keep."

With my hands on my hips, I narrow my eyes at him. "Do you know me at all?" My voice is way too loud, but I don't care. "For fifteen years I wished, no *begged* my grandmother to let me move to Chicago. Unlike other kids my age, my daydreams never featured rock stars or famous actors or the latest video games. I fantasized about waking up in my bedroom in *her* house, the smell of food cooking in her kitchen, playing with the ravens in the yard, taking the train downtown, walking along the lake front, eating the best Asian takeout and pizza on the planet. My biggest dream came true the day my plane touched down at O'Hare Airport. Sure, Gram's gone and I live with my uncles instead, but that's the second-best thing I could've wished for."

"I look forward to visiting other cities. Heck, I plan to explore the world when I'm older and can afford to, but my home is right here. My home and my *heart*. That's never going to change."

"The people I love don't typically stick around," he says, his voice full of caution.

His words strike a familiar chord deep inside of me. It's my turn to come clean with Marcus.

I take his hand in both of mine. "From the day I met you, I knew you were special, so special that I was sure I'd lose you. When your mother showed up, I prepared myself for it. At the battle, I was sure you were going to die." My voice comes out too fast and my accent is causing my words to tangle all over each other, but I can't help it. My insides are so hopped up with emotion that I can't slow myself down. My eyes burn with tears. "When you left to go to the clan to help your mother, I thought the time had finally come and you were leaving me for good." I swallow hard. "Why did I feel that way? Because the people I love don't tend to stick around, either."

Marcus watches me, a slow smile sneaking across his face.

"I'm not going anywhere. You're pretty much stuck with me," he says softly. He takes hold of my hand, weaving his fingers through mine. I sigh at his touch. Marcus's eyes burn into mine, holding me captive, as if my protector boyfriend has suddenly gained the ability to hypnotize me. I tear my gaze away, my cheeks flushing.

He clears his throat dramatically. "Aiden made me promise to tell you something. Now seems like a good time to do that." He leads me over to a fallen log. We both sit down.

My defenses rise up immediately. After our emotional revelations, is he going to ruin it all now?

"If it's coming from Aiden, it can't be good," I say, ruefully.

Marcus suppresses a smile. "I think you'll be surprised," he says.

I roll my eyes and give him a gentle elbow to his side. "Let's hear it." I wanted him to treat it like a bandage on a wound. Rip it off quick.

"He wanted me to tell you that as your trainer, he's proud of you."

I pull back from Marcus. "Are you making that up?"

Marcus grins. "Ask him yourself when we get back to the house, but you can trust me. Protectors don't lie." He takes hold of my hand, his expression serious. "You handled a lot more than anyone expected you to. You showed real strength and courage. More than you should have, in my opinion." He frowns at me to make his point. "Henry and Persephone can't stop talking about you. Aiden thinks you expressed admirable maturity and problem solving for such a young supernatural. Loyalty, too."

Based on the grumpy edge to his voice at that last part, I can tell he's referring to Ella.

I scoot closer to Marcus on the log until our bodies touch. Smiling, I rest my head on his shoulder. We sit together like that for a while. Aiden is proud of me. If he saw me fighting Seamus, he may think differently. I remind myself that Seamus is dead. My lessons will continue with Persephone and Henry and with Aiden until my father returns home. I will become a stronger witch and a stronger demon. Next time, I'll be a more skilled fighter and I won't try to battle alone. There will be a next time. As Jude's daughter, I know Seamus and Garret aren't the last of his enemies.

Marcus kisses the top of my head. "You, me, and Chicago," he says with a satisfied sigh.

I raise my head from his shoulder and grin at him. "Don't forget my bodyguards."

Marcus throws his head back and laughs. "Just what this city needs. More demons." With a finger under my chin, he raises my head until our eyes meet. "You, me, Chicago, and your bodyguards. Sure, why not. All that matters is that I have you," he says before dipping his head to kiss my lips.

"And that I have you," I add before our lips meet for a gentle kiss.

– THE END –

To All My Reader Friends

I hope you enjoyed reading The Girl and the Demon, the third installment in The Girl and the Raven series. Thank you to all the fans of the series who have shared their love for the characters and the books through their communications with me, on social media, and with friends. It took a while for this book to come into the world. I'm so proud of it and hope you love it as much as I do.

Do you want to share the book love? Please consider leaving your feedback on Goodreads and the book retailer site where you purchased the book.

I love to hear from fans. You can contact me at Pauline@ paulinegruber.com or visit my website: paulinegruber.com, where you can connect with me through Facebook or Instagram.

Thank you for reading The Girl and the Demon.

Want to know the latest?

About book releases and special announcements? Sign up for my author newsletter here: https://bit.ly/3njIqXt

ACKNOWLEDGMENTS

My sincere gratitude to the following:

My sister, Dale—For your unwavering support. Always.

To the people who helped me get this book together: Spencer Borup for editing, Martha Trachtenberg for copy editing, Kayle Allen for critiquing.

My incredible beta readers: Royelle Kashiwahara and Tracy Lyerly. Thank you for your hard work. You went above and beyond. I am so grateful!!

My nephews and nieces (related and not) for the use of your names in this series.

ABOUT THE AUTHOR

Pauline Gruber is a self-professed music junkie, cat wrangler, and travel nut. She went to Paris in the 90's where she discovered a love of three things: croissants, old cathedrals, and gargoyles. Deciding that the paranormal world could use a new kind of hero, Pauline translated her fascination with the protective gargoyle into a suspenseful love story. She is the author of the series: *The Girl and the Raven*, *The Girl and the Gargoyle*, and *The Girl and the Demon*. By day, Pauline is a legal assistant for a Chicago law firm where she steals identities and incorporates them into her books. If you tell anyone, she'll deny, deny, deny.

Pauline lives outside of Chicago with her precocious black cats.

Made in United States
Orlando, FL
27 February 2022

15174487R10283